SOMEONE ELSE'S BUCKET LIST

SOMEONE ELSE'S BUCKET LIST

AMY T. MATTHEWS

KENSINGTON
PUBLISHING CORP.

www.kensingtonbooks.com

KENSINGTON BOOKS are published by
Kensington Publishing Corp.
119 West 40th Street
New York, NY 10018

ISBN: 978-1-4967-4209-4 (ebook)

ISBN: 978-1-4967-4208-7

First Kensington Trade Paperback Printing: June 2023

10 9 8 7 6 5 4 3

Printed in the United States of America

For Tully,
my friend

And I didn't know whether to laugh or cry
And I said to myself, What next big sky?

—Laurie Anderson

In the midst of winter, I found there was,
within me, an invincible summer.

—Albert Camus

Chapter 1
Thanksgiving
Bree

The last months of Bree's life were, absurdly, full of hope. Hope like a burst of yellow; the vivid dash of goldenrod, daffodils, yarrow; a sudden splash of spring color in the monochrome of the wintery cancer ward. It came when she needed it most—when the world had narrowed to stark black and white. When she had all but given up.

It was a thickly snowy season in Delaware, many months into her internment in the ward. Tethered to the bed, she'd seen spring and summer froth and flourish through panes of glass that were perfumed only with Lysol, and she watched the tree-of-heaven outside her window turn bright as hot coals as September fell into October, its fiery orange leaves fluttering like Himalayan prayer flags. She'd arrived in May with a cough and was still here in November, sicker than ever. She'd thought watching summer flitter by had been difficult, but winter was looking to be infinitely worse. It was like being buried alive.

The hospital was muffled from late October on, with great drifts of constant snowfall. The gusting winds blew the last leaves from the trees well before Halloween, and November spat with ice storms and arctic temperatures. The windows fogged up and she lost her meager view. As Thanksgiving neared, Bree watched the perky newsreader on channel three sweeping her hand from North Carolina to Vermont, tracing the projection of yet another storm. The holiday was going to be bleak. Bree wasn't sure which was worse: the weather outside, or the conditions in here, where the ice-white fluorescent lights hummed, everything had a chemical smell, and the food was so soft that it turned to paste when you tried to cut it.

And then there was *chemo* . . .

Just the thought of chemo made her want to curl into a ball. She still had mouth ulcers from her last course.

"At least you'll be free and clear of it for the holiday," her oncology nurse had told her with brisk optimism. "You'll be able to eat some turkey."

Bree could only imagine what the hospital kitchen could do to turkey. She pictured dry white shingles of meat in commercial-grade tinned gravy. Wrinkly peas. A couple of stubby carrots leached of color. If she was lucky . . .

The nurses had hung desultory paper decorations around her room to lift her spirits. There were hand-stapled chains made from craft paper in the shade of overcooked pumpkin—which seemed apt. Wanda, one of the orderlies, had taped a cardboard turkey to Bree's door. It had a slightly startled look and a weird tissue-paper tail that was the exact same shade as Clorox Bleach and Blue toilet water. Bree didn't like the Bleach and Blue–tailed turkey on her door, but she didn't have the heart to ask Wanda to take it down. Wanda had been so proud of herself for "cheering the place up"; how could Bree possibly tell her that all the cheer made her feel infinitely worse? At night Bree listened to the orange paper chains making limp rustling sounds. Like old leaves. It was the sound of seasons past, of the end of things. It made her think of the tree-of-heaven leaves, snatched from their moorings by the wind and sent tumbling into the night.

Bree wasn't a person naturally given to despair. When she'd first come into the hospital with pneumonia last May, she'd been the kind of person who posted motivational memes on her Instagram, the kind of person who took a selfie featuring the stupid hospital gown, amused by the oddly stylish wraparound print of the garment. *This gown is snatched, you guys!* She'd put a warm filter over the photo so she didn't look quite so frightful. She hadn't felt despair when she was sent for round after round of X-rays, or when the awkward young doctor had told her she had pneumonia (she'd suspected *that*, it was why she'd come to the hospital in the first place). And when the same awkward young doctor lingered, cleared his throat, and then asked her how long she'd had leukemia . . . and could he have the number of her oncologist so he could consult about treatment options for the pneumonia . . .

She'd thought he'd made a mistake. He'd mixed up the tests. She didn't have leukemia. She had *pneumonia*.

That was about when his expression had curdled to one of horror and he'd just about melted at her feet. Like his bones had turned to liquid and there was nothing left to hold him up. *"Oh God, you didn't know . . ."*

"Know *what*?"

Even then, in that airless endless moment of realization, her first response hadn't been despair. It hadn't even been shock. It had *maybe* been denial. But it had definitely been *screw that*.

Because she was Bree Boyd. She was twenty-six years old; she had her whole life ahead of her. She had more than a million followers on Instagram; she'd had her photo posted with three (almost four) of the Kardashians; and she hadn't finished her bucket list yet. Hell, she hadn't even finished *composing* her bucket list. She couldn't *die*.

It wasn't even a remote possibility.

This was just one of those inspiring survival stories, and she was the heroine. Like a Hallmark movie, where the heroine is brave, and all her hair falls out, and there's a lot of weeping, but in the end, she gets the guy and finishes the film with her hair grown back in a cute pixie cut. Bree could carry off a pixie cut. "Right," she'd said to the boneless young doctor, way back in May when despair wasn't even an option. "What do we do about it?"

Because Bree was going to war. And at least she was doing it in a decent hospital gown, one with a faux designer-print. She'd be the first influencer to have hospital gowns trending, just wait and see. Hell, she'd have Adidas offering to sponsor her with athleisure wear before the week was out, just watch her! She'd be a goddamn beacon of positivity and light. She'd take her green-juicing, hot-yoga, world-traveler spirit—the same spirit that had taken her trekking through the Himalayas or vertical caving in the Cave of Swallows in Mexico; the same spirit that had seen her be the first person in her entire extended family to go to college; the same spirit that had made her an inspiration to hundreds of thousands of people—and she'd apply that spirit to kicking cancer's ass.

It never occurred to her that she wouldn't win.

Not until the second course of chemo.

It was around then that Bree ran out of memes to post. She was *so sick*. Nothing in her life had prepared her for chemotherapy. She'd given a lot of thought to losing her hair. She hadn't wanted to look like she had mange as it fell out, so she shaved it off before her first chemo cycle. She'd staged it as part of a fundraiser. Her younger sister, Jodie, had wielded the clippers. And one by one each of Bree's friends had sat smiling (some a little wobblier than others, it had to be said) as their hair fell to Jodie's enthusiastic clipping. Even Bree's oldest and bestest friend, Claudia, had surrendered to Jodie, and she never surrendered to Jodie on anything.

Bree had gone last, after Claudia had cheerfully shaved Jodie's head. Bree had filmed her hair falling, while her friends had belted "Don't Stop Believin'" at the top of their voices. The video had gone viral, and Bree had watched it proudly, over and over again. Then she'd worn a tiara on her bare head all through her first cycle of chemo. Her followers had increased tenfold. She was a warrior princess and she was kicking ass.

What an idiot. She'd honestly thought losing her hair would be the worst of it. She'd had no idea. By the time she finished the cycles of her first course, she felt like a soldier crawling back from the front.

They warned you—they gave you leaflets and links to websites—and in all the literature there were cartoons of people looking green. But green didn't do it justice. Nothing could prepare you for chemo vomiting. It was like turning yourself inside out. No, like drinking a bottle of sulfuric acid and *then* turning yourself inside out. Fifty times in a row.

At first, they'd given her injections to stop the vomiting, but nothing worked for long. And then after a while they'd given up, because Bree vomited no matter how many times they jabbed her with needles. Forget being a warrior princess, she was the Queen of Vomit. It got so that she'd vomit in *anticipation* of the chemo. They called it *refractory vomiting*. Refractory made her think of light, of Tiffany windows and carnival glass. Of chandeliers. It wasn't right to pair such a beautiful word with a word as repellant as *vomiting*. This wasn't *refractory* vomiting, this was odious, noxious, *vile vomiting*. This was the opposite of chandeliers and light. This was the darkness of a sewer, where carnival glass came to die.

This last chemo round, she'd spent the entire time with her head in a bucket. Just the smell of the boiled hospital food creeping through the corridors set her off. Actually eating something was out of the question. Resigned, the nurses fed her through an IV.

God, think of all the years she'd wasted dieting, she thought as she lay exhausted, inhaling the disinfectant lining her fresh vomit basin. How many times had she skipped breakfast in her life? How many slices of toast had gone unbuttered? How many pancakes un-syruped? How many tubs of yogurt had sat in the fridge, their foil seals never torn free? And don't even get her started on the years of un-tasted ice cream, or bags of Lay's, or, oh my goodness, the Cracker Jacks at baseball games. She'd loved Cracker Jacks when she was a kid. And what about all the times she'd had soda water instead of tonic with her gin? What a waste.

Look at her now. It was no effort at all to skip breakfast, and she was at her lightest weight since she'd been in grade school. And it was all so colossally awful. Who cared about being thin? She'd give anything to go back in time, to before the cancer, to sit at a ball game with her dad and Jodie and eat bag after bag of Cracker Jacks. She'd probably throw in a hot dog or two, a great big salty pretzel, and a few beers while she was at it.

She'd even post a picture of herself as she ate it all. And if she had a muffin top, or a love handle or two, she'd damn well post pictures of those too. #healthy #FoodJoy #FuckYouCancer

It was such a relief when the chemo ended and she could simply sink limply onto the rustling plastic-covered mattress and let go of the vomit basin.

Her mother came in every morning. She'd changed jobs so she could be with Bree through the hell of chemo. She came so early she beat the sun (which wasn't hard in the depths of a Delaware winter), carrying stacks of fresh magazines, fists full of hothouse flowers that she couldn't really afford, and treats to tempt Bree to eat. Grapes. Apples. Milk Duds. Once, a mango. Where had she found a mango at this time of year?

But the thing about chemo was, even if it was over and you weren't vomiting anymore, you couldn't taste anything. They didn't tell you *that* in the pamphlets. There wasn't a cartoon of some poor chemo-victim with no working taste buds. It was entirely possible that she'd never taste anything ever again. Ice cream tasted no better or worse than a handful of snow. The mango was just a slimy sensation in her mouth.

She'd tried to smile as she ate it, just to get the pinched look off her mother's face. But her mom wasn't fooled. She never was.

"Give it time," Mom said, trying to sound bright. She sounded about as bright as a flickering fluorescent tube in a subway car. Poor Mom. It broke Bree's heart to see what her illness did to her family. It had worn Mom thin, like a surface coat of paint had chipped away, revealing the primer underneath. But she was strong, Mom. She kept going. Day after day after day. And no one was keeping her from Bree's side. She'd changed jobs, to night shifts, so she could be with Bree during the day, and she came to the hospital, rain or shine, relentlessly optimistic, even if the primer shone through her flaking paint.

And Dad came by too, after he finished his shift at the warehouse. He always brought Bree a soda, from one of the pallets he spent all day moving. She couldn't taste that either. It was just a weirdly frenetic jumping of bubbles of her tongue. But she drank it and smiled. Dad always looked beat—the job was a rough gig for a man his age, and his body was already hurting from years of work on the line at GM, before the factory had closed. When Dad arrived, Mom vacated her seat for him, gave him a quick kiss, said her farewells and went off to her new job, cleaning schools at night. They worked hard, her parents, and always had. Retirement wasn't an option now, not with the medical debts Bree had racked up. Even working as hard as they did, they were barely able to make the minimum payments . . .

"Don't think about money," her dad said gruffly, whenever she tried to broach the subject. "Money will wait. You get well, that's your job. Money . . . that's mine."

He'd turn the television on and put his feet up on the bed and they'd settle in together through the long nights. Bree was glad of the company, even if he did tend to fall asleep ten minutes into whatever sitcom they were watching. Once he was snoring gently, she'd switch the channel and turn the volume down, but she often found her gaze drifting to her dad's face. Sleeping, he lost his cragginess; his thin lips softened, and his cheeks seemed fuller; she could see how he must have looked as a boy. In photos of his boyhood he always looked quizzical, head tilted, as though about to ask the photographer a question. There was something painfully vulnerable about him—as though he knew he was in for a hard life, as though he was preparing to savor the small joys, because the big ones were going to be hard-won. Asleep at the hospital, by her bedside, he still seemed so vulnerable, so easily hurt. Although he'd lost the quizzical look; now he looked as though he'd stifled all questions, because he knew he wouldn't like the answers. She loved him so much. Him and Mom and Jodie and Grandma Gloria and Aunt Pat. She'd had no idea how *much* she loved them until these last horrid months. There was something about the shadows cast by the cancer that made her love shimmer brightly, hotly, as pure as a gas flame. It was a jet. And the words *I love you* didn't do the feeling justice. Nothing in the world could tell them how she felt. All she could do was ask the nurse to throw a blanket over her father as he slept, and to drink the soda he brought her, even though it had lost all flavor and was just a mouthful of empty bubbles.

On her rare days off, Jodie brought Grandma and Great Aunt Pat in for a visit. If Mom looked flaked back to the primer, Jodie looked stripped bare. Like all of them, she performed, keeping a smile up for Bree's sake. But Bree could see she was sleep-deprived and worn out. Sometimes she'd nod off in the chair, even when Grandma and Aunt Pat were bickering at full bore. You had to be pretty tired to sleep through Grandma Gloria and Pat when they got going.

The two old women were night and day, just like Bree and Jodie were night and day. Grandma and Aunt Pat had lived in the same neighborhood their whole lives; in fact, their houses shared a back fence. They'd fashioned a gate decades ago and they popped in and out of each other's houses, harping at each other over endless cups of tea. When she was a kid, Bree had assumed that that's what she and Jodie would be doing when they got old. She assumed it was what all old women did. Had sisters who plonked themselves at your kitchen table and annoyed you, from the cradle to the grave. It had never occurred to her that cancer might get in the way.

The thought made her feel like one of those autumn leaves, brittle and trembling on the bough, at risk of being blown away.

What would she do without Jodie? Her angular, unsure, prickly younger sister. The person who brought her ski socks and leg warmers to keep her feet warm (in the most ridiculous colors and patterns); the person who'd thought to go get Bree's old stuffed cat, Ginger (who was black and white and not ginger at all) to keep her company in the hospital; the person who never once sugarcoated the horror of things, and who even when Bree was throwing up called her names and stole her pillow.

And what would Jodie do without *her*?

Jodie had always been awkward and anxious; moody; a loner. She had a sharp tongue and had never bothered to smile when she didn't feel like smiling (except here in the hospital, and how Bree hated to see that forced smile—it made the horror of it all too real). She'd never been the kind of girl to dress up, or color her hair, or wear makeup, or self-tan, or swoon over boys. She never brought her boyfriends to meet the family. Bree had only ever guessed *one* of Jodie's crushes, and that was because he was the only person (other than Bree) that Jodie followed on Instagram. But Bree had never dared ask Jodie about him. God forbid. Jodie would bite her head off.

How had they grown so far apart? When they were little, Jodie had been her shadow. When Bree wore red, Jodie had to wear red; when Bree had bangs cut, Jodie had to have bangs cut; when Bree got rollerblades, Jodie screamed blue murder until she got a pair too. But at some point, they'd gone in different directions. Jodie had eyed Bree's venture into "an international career in posing" (as she called it) with distaste. The only thing they still had in common these days was baseball—but Bree didn't even go to games anymore. Here in the hospital they'd got through Bree's vomitous summer by watching the Phillies; Jodie had lent Bree her precious vintage cap, the lucky one. Even after a cripplingly busy shift at the airport, where she worked in car rentals, Jodie came by, stuck the cap on Bree's bare head, and put the game on. Bree would lie there feeling ill, listening to the commentary, and trying not to hurl. From the corner of her eye, she could see Jodie flinch at every retch. Jodie's hand would reach out and curl around Bree's ankle, above the bunched-up ski sock, her thumb stroking Bree soothingly. She never said a word, but her presence meant the world to Bree. It calmed her. And when the vomiting was over and she couldn't stop crying, Jodie climbed into bed with her, uncaring of the stink and mess, and wrapped Bree in her arms. Now and then she'd ask Bree to vomit quieter, when she was interrupting the game, but she never let go.

But by the time the World Series rolled around, Jodie couldn't get into bed with her anymore; Bree was too sick and too frail. "I feel like I'd break you." Jodie sighed. But she kept a hand on Bree, cool on the back of her neck, or on her arm, or curled above the ski sock, tethering her to the room, and to the sound of the game, when Bree felt it would be easier to just shrivel away. The sound of the crowd, the crack of the bat, the low rise and fall of the commentary was like a beacon. When the season ended, Bree missed it terribly.

What if it's the last season I ever see?

Don't. Don't let any of those thoughts in. Keep the airlock closed and the pressure of the void out.

But as the vomitous cycles bled her dry and the leaves blew from the trees, as the baseballers packed away their mitts and bats, and the golden tones of October faded to the grays of November, the thoughts crept in, with more and more frequency. She grew used to the lung-emptying shock of them. It was like opening the door to the midwinter air: slappingly, painfully cold. Relentless.

By Thanksgiving, baseball seemed a long distant memory. And when Jodie came, she brought the damp smell of snow-melt with her; the smell of wet wool and . . . Lysol. Everything smelled of Lysol.

All of November the sky was low and distended, the color of dirty water. The streetlights were orange lozenges above the salted road. In advance of the holiday, there was traffic beginning to flow—people off to their Thanksgivings, their headlights cutting through the murky dawn. Bree would give anything to be in one of those cars, instead of up here, listening to the rubber squeak of the nurses' soles in the hospital corridor, and to the electronic chiming of the buzzers calling those nurses to patients' bedsides.

Bree was lucky to have a room with a view—or so the nurses told her. Even though it wasn't much of a view. She could see the back end of the east wing and the parking lot, and off to the right a small park and the road. The few trees that broke the monotony outside were leafless black slashes, like pencil drawings on an empty page. The whole season of her chemo had been surreal and suffocating. Like being trapped inside a snow globe.

But then, unexpectedly, the evening before Thanksgiving, that was when hope came with a burst of yellow.

Dr. Mehta brought the change, standing there in his silk tie and white coat, clicking his pen energetically. The conversation certainly didn't start out a hopeful yellow. If anything, it was pretty black. "There's no change in the cancer marker," he said. *Click*, went his pen. He was a stout man, with a round face that made him seem younger than he was. His eyes were large and luminous behind his wire spectacles.

"That's good? That's good, isn't it?" Mom's fingers had curled around the metal arms of her chair. She was sitting ramrod straight in front of the window, which was fogged up from the radiator. Bree's mother was gaunt and there were deep lines bracketing her mouth and grooving her forehead between her eyebrows. Her clothes hung loosely and she hadn't taken the time to go to the hairdresser; her roots were severely gray. She looked old. And not in a cuddly, grandmotherly way. "You're telling us it's *good*." Mom wasn't asking a question.

It wasn't good. Bree knew it wasn't good. *Mom* knew it wasn't good. She was just clutching at whatever straws she could. There was supposed to be a *reduction* in the marker; or, if miracles spangled into existence, it would have disappeared.

No change meant . . .

"It's not *worse*." Mom was flailing now and there was an edge of panic in her voice that hurt Bree worse than she knew she could be hurt. "If it's not worse, that means you did some *good*, right?"

"Mom," Bree said, reaching for her mother's wrist. "Don't."

"There's an option," Dr. Mehta said, in his usual slow way, proceeding as though Bree's mother hadn't spoken.

"Option?" Mom prodded the doc sharply. She didn't like him much. Not him, not the nurses, not the hospital. Mom blamed them all for how sick Bree was, for how hopeless the season had become. Being angry was probably better than being afraid. Bree knew that all too well herself. Fear tended to come late at night, when the corridors were quiet and the wind shuddered at the windows. A fear so airless and cold that it was like deep space.

Chemo had taught Bree that fear was an emotional black hole. It had gravity so dense it not only pulled you in, it pulled you inside out. It was best to avoid it. To deny it. To chart a course in the opposite direction.

"We could try a bone marrow transplant," Dr. Mehta said. He was staring straight at Bree. He tended to ignore her family in these meetings. She was an adult; it was her illness. She was the one who had to make the decisions. Because it was *her* cancer.

Lucky her.

But now . . . *bone marrow transplant.* The words were a spell, cast into the antiseptic air. Dr. Mehta clicked his pen three times, in quick succession. A staccato punctuation. *Bone-marrow.* Two more clicks. *Trans-plant.*

Bree felt a savage hope so bright it was dangerous.

She was going to live. *Of course she was.* Hope: yellow as sunshine, hot as summer.

She leaned forward. Dr. Mehta's dark eyes were very serious, but *he* didn't look scared. "Tell me," she said. She was still holding her mother's wrist; she could feel her mom's pulse hard against her fingers.

Click. Bone. *Click-click.* Mar-row.

"The cancer isn't responding to treatment," Dr. Mehta told her, his voice as bland as if he was ordering a coffee. "The latest round shows no change."

"Which is *not* good," Bree added, giving her mother's wrist a gentle squeeze. She heard her mom's breath catch and then Mom grabbed her hand. Bree couldn't look at her. She didn't want to see the expression on her face. It would be too awful.

"No," Dr. Mehta agreed. "It's not." He gave her a sympathetic look. It wasn't like him and it scared the daylights out of Bree. She didn't want sympathy. She wanted *fury.* She wanted him to go to war with the tenacious black threads of cancer curling through her blood.

"There are many reasons for a bone marrow transplant," he said mildly. "For acute myeloid leukemia, such as yours, we'd be looking to replace your cancerous stem cells with the donor's healthy ones."

As he outlined the procedure, Bree felt the day get brighter. She had sunshine in her veins. *Yellow.* Sunflowers of hope. "Who?" she asked, sitting straighter. "Who would the donor be?"

"You have a biological sister?"

Chapter 2

Jodie

Not without risks. That was the phrase the doctor had used over and over again. Jodie thought she'd understood most of what he'd said. But she'd had to work pretty hard at it. The medical talk was bad enough when you were feeling sharp, but Jodie was slow-witted after a twelve-hour shift at the airport. The holidays were brutal at Philly International; people came tumbling off their flights, dragging tantrum-y toddlers and insane amounts of luggage, their moods as filthy as the weather outside, and Jodie had been snapped at, cursed out, patronized and under-tipped since well before dawn. She was hungry and her feet were sore. But when Mom had left a message, urging her to come to the hospital, Jodie had got Nena to cover the end of her shift and come running.

Mom had already gone by the time Jodie got to the hospital. She'd had to get to work. Jodie had skidded in just as the doctor had been preparing to leave. He hadn't looked too thrilled at having to stay back to explain the "procedure" to Jodie. He kept checking his watch. Jodie wondered if he had a booking somewhere for dinner. She bet it was somewhere nice—it was a pretty fancy watch.

Not without risks. He kept saying it. Jodie looked at the pamphlets he'd given her. They had brightly colored cartoons on them. She wasn't sure if the risks were to her or to Bree, and she was too tired to work up the courage to ask. Jodie was more than a little intimidated by Dr. Mehta. He gave long-winded sterile descriptions of procedures that sounded like something out of a textbook. People like him made her feel stupid. There was a bunch of Latin words in there, and there was something about chemo . . .

"She doesn't need to know about that," Bree interrupted from the bed.

Jodie glanced at her sister. It felt weird to be having this conversation *in front* of Bree. But no one was in any doubt that Jodie would say yes to the bone marrow transplant. She'd do *anything* to save her sister. Even the horrible-looking things featured in these oddly cheery cartoons. If there was no chance Jodie was going to turn around at the end of Dr. Mehta's speech and say *no*, then there was no real reason for Bree not to be here. Although maybe it would have spared her having to hear about the "pre-transplant preparation" again, a preparation which seemed to include a lot more chemo.

"You don't need to know about that," Bree reiterated firmly, this time in Jodie's direction. Jodie knew how much she hated chemo. And from what Jodie understood from the doctor's long, confusing speech, this chemo was *not without risks*.

But what risk was greater than dying of cancer?

It seemed to Jodie they were past the point of risk assessment, and well and truly into the realms of desperation. "I'll do it," she said abruptly, cutting the doctor off. She thought of Bree vomiting endlessly into that shiny plastic basin . . . if Bree could do that, then Jodie could suffer through a needle or two. A spinal needle or two . . .

Oh God. Just the thought of spinal needles made her stomach go weak and wobbly and a cold wave run from her scalp to her toes.

"Bend over," Bree told her sharply. "Put your head between your knees and take even breaths."

"Is she sick?" The doctor sounded like he was speaking from a great distance, down a tunnel. That wasn't a good sign.

Jodie bent over. She kept her gaze fixed on the tips of her ugly but sensible work shoes and concentrated on breathing. Don't think about needles.

As if. *All* she could think about was needles. Long ones with horrible sharp points.

"No, she's fine," Bree said. "She does this all the time. She doesn't like needles."

"Not *all* the time," Jodie protested between breaths. That made her sound pathetic, and she wasn't pathetic. She was just anxious. A lot of people had anxiety, and a *lot* of people hated needles. Look at the cartoon woman in the pamphlet with her bugged-out eyes. *She* clearly didn't like needles either.

"To be a donor, she can't be sick." Dr. Mehta sounded very worried.

"She's *not* sick. She's just a dweeb."

Jodie put up with that, but only because it was good to hear some liveliness back in Bree's voice.

"Breezy-Breeze, have I got a treat for you tonight!" A staccato knock sounded at the door and an orderly sailed in with the dinner trolley.

Dr. Mehta looked relieved to see the orderly arrive. He gave his watch another glance; Jodie could see it out of the corner of her eye, even bent over her shoes. "I'll get out of your way," he said in a hasty retreat. "I'll forward the paperwork for the procedure."

The paperwork. Which would include the cost. A very underestimated cost, which would mount and mount as they did the "procedure," adding onto their already crippling debt. Jodie closed her eyes. Hell. She was going to be working at the rental stand at that airport every minute of every day, for the rest of her life. Jodie had packed up her apartment and moved home, and she'd switched her college degree from full-time to part-time, so she could help pay the bills. Not that she begrudged it. She'd do it all happily if this worked. She wouldn't even complain. Not if she could come home to a healthy Bree. Although if Bree was bouncing around again, she'd be off on one of her adventures, and not home at all. Jodie imagined Bree traveling again. Off in Madrid, or Santiago, or even in New Jersey. A blazing smile, a cascade of hashtags, full of joy.

Anything was worth that. Needles. Working at the airport. *Anything.*

Jodie sat up.

"Oh heavens, you scared me." The orderly put a hand to her heart in shock. "Where'd you come from?" It was Wanda. Jodie liked Wanda. She'd gone out of her way to brighten the place up for Thanksgiving. She didn't have to do that, but she did.

"She was feeling a bit woozy," Bree told her, eyeing the approaching dinner tray with distaste.

"The doc does have that effect on people. I tell him to just speak in plain English, but he doesn't listen."

"Maybe you should tell him in Latin, so he understands," Jodie muttered. She opened the pamphlet. Even the *cartoon* needles looked horrifying. She closed the pamphlet again.

"Thanksgiving's come early," Wanda told Bree, whipping the plastic lid off the smallest container. "Ta da! Pumpkin pie!"

"Is that what that is?" Bree gave it a dubious look.

Jodie wrinkled her nose. It looked like a wedge of brown Jell-O.

"So they tell me," Wanda said cheerfully. "No turkey—they're saving that for tomorrow—but there is cornbread."

"What's *that*, if it's not turkey?" Jodie asked, when Bree lifted the lid on her main plate, revealing a lump of white meat.

Bree prodded the white shingle of meat with her fork, as Wanda peered over her shoulder.

"Might be chicken."

"Might be?"

"You can cancel her turkey order for tomorrow," Jodie said, glad she wasn't the one who had to eat the chicken shingle. "We're going to bring in food; she won't be needing the turkey from a can, or whatever it is."

"Can?" Wanda looked appalled. "What do you think this is? We only have the finest around here. Our turkey comes in boxes, not cans." She winked at Bree on her way out.

"I'm going to get something out of the vending machines." Jodie sighed, ramming the pamphlets into her bag as she stood up. "I might call Dad and ask him to bring in a pizza or something on his way. You want anything?"

Bree shook her head. "I'll eat this. It all tastes the same anyway."

Jodie winced. Imagine. "I'll be back in a minute."

"I'm not going anywhere."

The thing about cancer, Jodie thought as she scuffed her way to the vending machine in the lounge, was that it was horrible in more ways than you could count. There was the big obvious horribleness, but then there were all these little awful moments. Like not even being able to just get your sister a candy bar. Because she couldn't *taste* it.

As Jodie stared at her dinner options (Fritos, Chex Mix or Doritos?) her phone buzzed. Cooper. Again. She didn't respond. She was sick of him and his random hookups. She wanted someone who cared that she was here in the hospital with her sister; a guy who'd feed her when she got home, exhausted and heartsore; a guy who'd wrap her up in a solid hug. It wasn't too much to ask, surely? For something more than a self-serving hookup. She punched the numbers into the vending machine and waved her card past the sensor, and then she collected her balanced meal of Fritos, M&M's, and a can of some revolting energy drink and headed back to her sister. At least it would keep her awake enough to perform for Bree and then drive home.

"I never thought I'd say this," Bree said dryly as she saw Jodie's haul, "but I think my dinner might be better."

"They clearly pumped you full of too many drugs today." Jodie popped the can and tore open the Fritos. "Sure you don't want one?"

Bree shook her head.

"Your loss."

"Did you call Dad to get pizza?" Bree asked, as she pushed the chicken shingle around her tray. She'd mastered the art of mashing her food up but not actually eating it. She thought Jodie hadn't noticed, but she had.

"Nah. He'll be too tired. I can eat properly when I get home."
Jodie sighed. Although she wouldn't. She never did. By the time
she got home, she'd be too beat to face even microwaving soup.
She'd kick her shoes off and collapse on the couch, where she'd
fall asleep before she even turned the television on. Then a couple of hours later, she'd wake up grumpy and have to get herself
to bed, so she could get a few hours of proper sleep before she
got up and did it all over again. You know. Just the usual fun life
of a twenty-something.

Luckily Jodie finished her junky dinner before Claudia arrived. She would have died of mortification if Claudia caught
her eating M&M's for dinner. Again. She already felt like a
clumsy slob whenever Claude was around. She didn't need to
confirm Claude's suspicions that she ate garbage every night.
Even though she *did* eat garbage every night.

Claudia swept into the room in her usual cloud of Coco Mademoiselle, chic as ever, her still-short hair covered by a raspberry beret. Only Claude could carry off an actual raspberry
beret. How did women like Claudia do it? Jodie's anxiety rose
in its usual sweaty, skittery way, with its perpetual sense there
was something deeply wrong with her. That everyone else knew
some secret she didn't.

Claude was weighed down by packages and parcels but still
somehow managed to get a hand free enough to snatch the limp
cardboard turkey off the door on her way through. It made a
rasping ripping sound as it tore.

"Claude! Wanda put that there!" Bree tried to sound appalled, but Jodie could hear that she was secretly thrilled. That
was the thing about Claudia. She made things like ripping down
a cardboard turkey seem wickedly mischievous and fun. If Jodie
had done it, it would have just seemed mean.

But that was probably because Jodie wouldn't have replaced
it with anything, whereas Claude pulled a wreath from one of
her packages with a flourish, looking for all the world like a magician pulling a rabbit from a hat. And of course it wasn't any
old wreath; it was the *perfect* wreath. Handmade. Enormous.
Glorious.

The circle of entwined branches was decorated with autumn leaves in shades of amber, gold and pale yellow; there were grapelike clusters of berries, the soft greenish yellow of citrons; and spotted throughout were puffs of cotton pods and tightly furled pinecones in shades of unripe limes.

"*Yellow.*" Bree breathed. Her eyes had gone all sparkly in their deep shadowy sockets and Jodie felt a stupid bolt of jealousy. Hell. Why hadn't she thought to bring a wreath?

"Did you make that?" Jodie asked, unable to keep the sourness from her voice. Who made a wreath like that? Who had the *time*?

"I did," Claude said, tossing aside the poor ripped-up cardboard turkey. "I also made *these.*" From one of the magic packages came yards of bunting.

"Are those real leaves?"

They were. They were real leaves. The madwoman had gone and strung fall leaves onto yards and yards of string. Where did she even get them all? The long strands of leaves were heartstoppingly pretty. Strung on simple brown string, the leaves (tangerine, apricot, saffron, ruby, claret) glowed like embers. Bree was glowing too, as she watched Claude shove an armful of the crackly things in Jodie's lap. There were long golden serrated oak leaves; blazing tri-pointed crimson maples; fanshaped, green-edged sycamores; and curling wheat-brown ash leaves; and here and there were finger-slender coal-bright tree-of-heaven leaves, brought in from the cold.

"Do you know tree-of-heaven is a pest?" Jodie said, running her finger down one of the leaves.

"Careful," Claude scolded, "they're fragile."

Even though she was exhausted, Jodie obediently hung the bunting where she was told. How could she not, when Bree looked so happy? More than happy. *Transported.* As Jodie and Claude decked the horrid little room in arboreal splendor, the hospital fell away and instead they were in a secluded autumnal glen. Far from all their cares.

Claude really was a magician.

When Wanda came back for Bree's dinner tray, she stood frozen in the doorway, her mouth open. She was so enchanted that she didn't even notice her destroyed cardboard turkey slumped on the floor. Surreptitiously, Jodie kicked it under the bed. She'd hate to hurt Wanda's feelings.

"Good lord," Wanda breathed. "Where did all this come from?"

"My fairy godmother." Bree laughed. Surrounded by jewel-bright leaves, she looked beautiful. The long pointy spinal-needles would be worth it, if this bone marrow transplant worked, and Bree could look this happy every day. Just like she used to. Hell, Jodie would put the needle in herself if she had to.

"You want to come decorate my place sometime?" Wanda asked. "They don't sell anything like this at my local dime store."

"I'm booked up, I'm afraid. But you can help yourself to the leftovers." Claude handed over the bag with the last strands of bunting.

"It's still a third full," Wanda protested.

"You must have been stringing leaves for months." Bree laughed. She'd sunk back into her bed, looking more like a Kewpie doll and less like a rag doll. Her eyes were all big and sparkly and her smile beatific as she watched the strings of leaves drift in the air conditioning.

Until Bree got sick, Jodie hadn't realized how painful love was. It stung. Like lemon juice poured on an open wound. But worse. It wasn't pink and pleasant; it was bloodred and visceral. Fearful.

"I might hang these in Mrs. Vincent's room. She's had a hard time with chemo this week . . ." Wanda took the enchanted-forest-in-a-bag with her, entirely forgetting about Bree's dinner tray. Which wasn't at all empty.

"Don't sit down." Claude blocked Jodie from the chair. "There's more."

Jodie groaned. "Don't you ever sleep?"

Out of the bag came a cheerful burst of color. It was a buttery soft, fat knitted blanket. It was wide knit, as though made on giant needles, and had a meticulous ribbed pattern.

"*Yellow!*" Bree just about squealed with joy.

"This is your lucky Thanksgiving blanket." Claude unfurled the blanket gently over Bree's legs.

Claude had made Bree a lucky blanket for summer too, Jodie remembered. It had been celestial blue and had been so abused by vomit over the season of chemo that it had been beyond saving. Here's hoping the yellow blanket would be luckier than the blue . . .

"Are you getting *any* sleep?" Bree asked Claude, running her hands over the soft wool. Jodie reached out and rubbed a corner between her fingers. It was divinely soft. Jodie wondered if Claude would make her one. Jodie had never had a nice blanket; or a nice anything. She was still using her baseball quilt from when she was ten. She could offer to pay Claude for a soft woolen blanket . . . only all her money went to medical bills.

"You know me. I don't ever sleep much." Claude absently handed Jodie another bag and sat on the edge of the bed by Bree's feet.

"What am I supposed to do with this?" Jodie asked. All she wanted to do was sit back down. Her feet hurt. "Where do I put these things?"

"Wherever. I'll fix it later."

Jodie rolled her eyes. Fix it later. Like she couldn't scatter a decoration or two without screwing it up. Claude treated her like she was still Bree's annoying little sister. Which she wasn't. She was Bree's annoying adult sister.

Jodie peered into the bag and inhaled a hefty dose of nutmeg and cinnamon. There were a bunch of candles in there. Overly scented ones.

"You know she can't light these in here?" Jodie told Claude, pulling a cinnamon candle as big as a dumbbell from the bag.

"They're decorative." Claude sighed. "Just put them out on the sill."

What was the point in candles you couldn't light? And Bree couldn't even really smell them anyway. Jodie shrugged. What did she care if no one was ever going to light them? The quicker she got them on the sill, the quicker she could sit down and put her feet up.

As she plonked the heavy candles along the sill, she listened to Claude and Bree talk softly. Everyone except Grandma Gloria and Aunt Pat spoke softly in the hospital. It was that kind of place. Like a library or a funeral home, it had a weighty hush to it. People spoke so low you could barely hear them over the toneless river of air pushing through the ducts. The place was pressurized with air sucked dry of life.

"You should sleep, Claude," Bree was saying in a papery murmur.

"I do. Just not much."

When Jodie couldn't sleep, she lay in the dark staring at the rind of orange streetlight around her blind. She roiled with thoughts, like gusts of blizzard ice that pelted her out of the darkness, stinging as they hit. She worried about money, about the future, about Bree, about her parents, about the way days ticked by and nothing ever changed or got better. She lay in the no-time between days and felt her feet throb, memories of endless days at the car-rental place flicking through her head. The voice over the tinny PA announcing flights to places Jodie would never go; the rubbish computer she worked on that crashed at least three times a day; the sick feeling in her stomach when customers got that tone in their voice that meant they were about to chew her out. Maybe she should follow Claude's example and get up and string leaves on brown string, or knit lucky blankets, or bake until the sun came up.

"How's your mother?" Bree asked Claude carefully.

"I don't know." Claude's voice was flat.

Jodie kept her back to them. She didn't want to look like she was eavesdropping. Even though she was. Claude's mother was a touchy subject; Jodie would never have dared ask about her, even though it was obvious when Claude was crafting like a loon that her mother had gone off the rails again.

Tactfully responding to Claudia's flat response, Bree changed the subject. Jodie didn't need to look to know that she was squeezing Claude's hand. "Let's get a picture with your leaves," Bree suggested brightly.

Jodie rolled her eyes, setting the last monolithic candle down with a *plonk*, but she felt her eyes prick. It was good to see Bree posing again. She had more of her old spark back now that the chemo was over . . . for now anyway. The bone marrow transplant would mean she'd soon be banning photos again, not wanting anyone to capture the gaunt pallor of the Vomit Queen.

Jodie slumped into the chair to watch the two of them pose against the backdrop of leaves. She'd never dare tell either of them, because she gave them hell about what posers they were, but she envied them this. They were the undisputed champions of turning a bruised moment into its opposite: glamorous, aglow, caught in a frame that cut out the worst of the world. They edited their stories down to the moments of gratitude. And they looked great while they did it. Bree's Instagram story tonight would be a carnival of leaves, with none of the lingering smell of Lysol, or loss of taste, or the perpetual pumping of tepid air through the vents.

Jodie caught her reflection in the mirror over the sink and pulled a face. Her honey-brown hair had never been anything special, but without it she looked angular and pinched. The fluorescent lights made her grayish eyes seem colorless. Thank God no one wanted a photo of her. She was an oatmeal-colored, drab, tired-looking wren. Instagram was for the birds of paradise of the world. For women like Bree and Claudia, who were luminescent. They looked so good together too. Before they'd lost their hair, they'd looked like bright scoops of expensive ice cream on a sunny day—Claude's natural blonde cool, Bree's pricey golden streaks creamy.

Jodie was just pale brown in comparison. Tan. Taupe. *Beige.*

She turned away from the mirror. Her whole involvement with selfies and posing was best limited to liking Bree's posts. Not everyone could be ice cream. Some people were just the cones.

"I can't stay too long," Claude told Bree regretfully once they'd posted their pictures. "I have to get back to finish off the pumpkin pie."

Jodie's mouth watered. She would give anything for a slice of Claudia's pumpkin pie right now. For anything other than Fritos and chocolate bars really.

"But before I go, one last surprise." Bree pulled a quilted purse from her handbag. "We're going to paint your nails!"

Jodie took her cue and groaned. "What do you mean, *we?*" She knew how this went. They'd done this a lot as kids. Claudia made Jodie paint Bree's toes, while she did her fingers, and she'd do nothing but bitch about how messy Jodie was. *Color in the lines, you dweeb!*

"Can't we do something less girlie?" she complained. But her complaints were halfhearted because Bree was wriggling with happiness.

Claudia was immaculate at nails, of course. She gave Bree the most fastidious French manicure. To spite her, Jodie alternated fluorescent green and orange on Bree's toes. Bree didn't mind. In fact, she loved it.

"Look at you two, getting along," Bree said blissfully, laughing when Jodie got smears of orange on the sheets. Jodie swore like a soldier as she spilled the green polish as she tried to mop up the orange.

Claudia didn't look up, but a muscle twitched in her jaw. Jodie could tell she was keeping herself calm by *not* looking at Jodie and the botch job she'd done on Bree's toenails.

"I love you *soooooo* much." Bree sighed.

"We love you too." Claudia kept her gaze lowered but her voice was choked up.

"Don't talk for me," Jodie said, horrified that everyone might start crying. "I merely tolerate her." She could feel her nose getting stuffy and hot like it did before tears came. They were supposed to be making Bree *happy*, not weeping all over the place.

"I dare you to tell Claudia that you love her," Bree teased. "We all know you always take a dare."

Jodie scowled. "Not anymore. Only when I didn't know how sadistic you two could be." She'd gotten herself into so much trouble as a kid, because of the dares Bree and Claudia had issued.

"Remember the time she stuck a swizzle stick up her nose and had to go to the hospital to get it removed?" Claudia said serenely.

Bree giggled.

Well, at least no one was threatening to cry anymore.

"That was child abuse," Jodie muttered.

"Or the time we dared her to roll through poison oak?"

"You two are sick." Jodie tried to wipe a blob of green polish off Bree's pinky toe. Her sister's feet looked like a Jackson Pollock painting. Jodie glanced up in time to catch Claudia's absolute disbelief.

"What?"

Claudia held out a baggie of cotton balls and the bottle of remover. "Do it again."

And she did. Because deep down she was still in awe of Claudia, a perpetual little sister tagging along after the big girls.

Chapter 3

Bree

Jodie had fallen asleep in the chair. She had her arms crossed and her chin burrowed down into them; she was frowning in her sleep, not pleased by whatever dreams were visiting her. Bree managed to reach far enough to put the yellow blanket around her. She almost fell out of bed doing it, but she managed it. How pathetic was that? Barely able to find the strength to put a blanket over someone, at the age of twenty-six. Once she'd hiked Machu Picchu.

Happy Thanksgiving, Jodie, she thought as she tucked the blanket in. And it *was* going to be a happy Thanksgiving, because now there was hope. And this wasn't the only Thanksgiving there would ever be—it certainly wasn't going to be her last. Next year there would be dinner at Mom's table, with that orange and cranberry stuffing Dad made, the one that was always too dry. She could practically see next year as she ran her hand over the yellow blanket tucked over Jodie's shoulders. There would be candied sweet potato, and pumpkin pie, and that sickly-sweet marshmallow casserole that Aunt Pat insisted on bringing every year, even though no one really liked it. And there would be new things too, things she'd always wanted, like a proper turkey from the butcher, a big free-range one, instead of the frozen thing from the supermarket. Bree knew just how they were going to cook it. Bree was going to rub it with garlic herb butter until it crisped up golden brown on the outside and was juicy and rich on the inside. There would be rye, sage and apple stuffing, and homemade cranberry sauce. Bree had a stack of magazines on the floor next to her bed; food porn for someone who couldn't enjoy food anymore. She'd dog-eared the pages with recipes and decorations and all the things she wanted for next year. She'd started doing the same thing for Christmas too. Next year was going to be the best Thanksgiving ever, followed by the best Christmas, the best New Year's, the best everything.

She dozed off imagining the candlelit table and the rich golden smell of roasting turkey. Her dreams were full of chatter and lazy music, of hot pumpkin-spiced lattes and laughter. She saw the narrow little dining room at her parents' house crammed full, extra chairs pulled in from the kitchen, and there was none of the pinched misery she saw when they visited her at the hospital. Mom's hair was freshly colored and Dad was ruddy-cheeked and bright-eyed; and even Jodie was rested and smiling. Claudia was there too, of course, and she was relaxed enough that she didn't even rearrange the table decorations when Mom moved them aside to put out the mashed potatoes. The dreams were suffused by Bree's love for them all; it flooded in like late-afternoon sunshine.

When her father woke her from her dreams of Thanksgiving-future, coming in to swap out with Jodie, Bree maintained the golden feeling of contentment from her dream.

"Sorry, honey, I didn't mean to wake you." He was like a big sheepish bear, hulking in the doorway. His coat was covered in spangles from the melted snow and sleet.

She just smiled at him. She didn't want to sleep. There was enough sleep once you were . . . not sick anymore.

"Would you look at this place!" Dad gazed up at the leaves, which were shivering and twirling on their strings. "I guess Claude's been here then?"

Bree grinned. "I don't think she can top this one!"

Dad snorted. "We'll see about that when Christmas comes. That girl could decorate the North Pole."

"Mom tell you about the bone marrow transplant?" Bree asked, as she watched him wriggle a Pepsi can from his pocket. He put in on her bedside table and dropped a kiss on her forehead. His lips were icy cold from the world outside.

"She sure did. That's some great news for the holidays." He was valiantly trying to sound cheerful, but Bree could hear the relentless caution in his voice. "The doctor thinks it'll work, huh?"

Bree hated the tremble in his voice and the way he wouldn't meet her eye. It sent an icy shaft through her. No. She wouldn't let the ice into her sunny day. The bone marrow transplant was going to work. Because it *had* to. She gave him her sunniest smile and cracked her soda can. "You bet."

He couldn't help but smile back at that. "Couldn't have happened at a better time. Gives us something to be thankful for."

They had a lot to be thankful for, even with leukemia, she thought as she watched him pull his sodden hat off and drop it in the sink. He ran his big hand, swollen from years of work, through his tousled, gray-flecked hair. There was *everything* to be thankful for. She took a sip of the flavorless soda and watched affectionately as he shook Jodie awake. The two of them looked so much alike, even though one was big and grizzly and the other was slight and fine featured. They had the same way of squinting grumpily when they were tired.

"When did Claude leave?" Jodie asked, yawning as she took the Pepsi can from her dad. *What's the point of working for PepsiCo if you can't treat your girls to a soda?* Dad would say with a wink when he came home from work and handed over their treats. It was one of the few perks of his factory job. Only he didn't say it anymore. And he didn't wink anymore. He just passed Jodie the can as she hauled herself out of the chair. She looked at the blanket by her feet in confusion, then gave Bree a rueful glance and put it back on the bed.

"Claude left ages ago," Bree told her, pulling the sumptuous blanket up over herself. "Pie crusts were calling."

Jodie gave a jaw-cracking yawn. "I'd best get on too. I promised Mom I'd do some sweet potato thing. I'll pick Gloria and Pat up on my way in tomorrow."

Bree felt a wild urge to beg Jodie to take her home. She wanted to sit in the kitchen, in the warmth, watching Jodie and Mom cooking sweet potatoes and making coffee. She wanted to go up to her old bedroom, and sleep in her childhood bed. She wanted to watch the witchy branches of the ash tree scratching at the window in the wind, just like she had as a kid. She wanted to go *home*.

"Drive safe," Dad grunted as he took over Jodie's chair. He dwarfed it. "It's icy out there. Looking to be a nasty night."

Jodie pulled a face. "Of course it is." She pulled her jacket off the hook on the back of the door. "Thanks for the soda, Dad."

"Anytime, peanut."

Jodie caught a whiff of Bree's desperation and met her gaze. "I'll be back tomorrow," she said huskily. "I'll bring Thanksgiving with me."

Tears rushed hot and itchy to Bree's eyes. "I know."

Jodie crept to the bed and bent down to give Bree a hug. She just about pulled her up off the bed. "I love you, Vanity Smurf."

"Don't call me that," Bree said by rote, but she didn't mind. She closed her eyes and buried her face in Jodie's neck. Her skin was warm. "I love you too."

"Look after the old man."

"Who you calling old?" Dad had the remote and was turning the television on. "What do you want to watch, honey?" he asked, as Jodie shuffled out for the night.

Thank God for family. Bree pulled the yellow blanket higher. And friends. As Dad tried to find something decent to watch, Bree reached for her phone. She wasn't alone. She had a million people out there—she just needed to reach out and they'd be there for her. It didn't matter what time of day or night; there would always be someone to talk to.

She snapped a picture of her dad, who had propped his feet out in front of him and was engrossed in some sports show. *This is what love looks like.* She turned her phone to the sky outside her window. The moon rode low and swollen in the winter sky. It made her feel small. She snapped a photo of it. In the frozen image, the moon hung suspended over the eastern wing of the hospital, smaller and whiter than it appeared in life. In real life it was a shimmering orange ball, speckled with rust. In the photo the rust was a faint stain, cream on white. *Sea of Serenity*, she captioned the image on Instagram. Although for all she knew, the speckles could have been the Ocean of Storms. But she didn't tell her followers that; she just watched as the comments unfurled beneath the no-longer-rusty moon. Each one made her feel a little less lonely, and a little less afraid.

Stay strong, Bree!

You've got this!

Happy Thanksgiving!

There were other comments too, from the trolls, but she was practiced at not reading them. Her gaze flicked across them as though they weren't even there. But even if you didn't read them, they were a shadow on things, like the rust on the moon. Sighing, she put her phone away.

Bree held Claudia's blanket close and let the excited blaring of Dad's sports channel wash over her. *I believe in yellow,* she told herself. *I choose yellow. And next year, I won't be here in this room. Next year I'll be sprawled on Mom and Dad's couch, looking forward to Thanksgiving at home, watching the fire dance.*

And when the moon rose over the snowdrifts it wouldn't be rusty orange. It would be golden yellow. The color of hope fulfilled.

Chapter 4
Thanksgiving
Jodie

One year later

Jodie hadn't had a day off in almost a month. She was pulling every shift she could, double and triple shifts, begging for every last paid hour she could get her hands on. But it was never enough. As far as she could see, there was no way out of the debt they were in. She could work this stupid job for the rest of her life and never even pay off the interest on Bree's medical bills.

The past year had made Jodie feel like she'd fallen down a chasm. She was deep down in the dark, looking up at the daunting distance between her and the world above. Up there, people were having Thanksgiving, streaming off planes and through the terminal, chattering as they waited at the bag carousels, fretting about stupid stuff like why she didn't have the hatchback they'd booked and could only provide them with a sedan.

Who cares? she wanted to snap at them. *It's a car. You ordered a car, you're getting a car. What more do you want?*

A hatchback.

Be glad you're here to want anything at all. Because my sister sure as hell isn't.

But it didn't do to think about Bree, not while she was at

work. That way lay disaster. Jodie knew from past experience. The last thing anyone wanted was the girl behind the rental counter weeping as she printed out insurance forms and handed over keys to the sedan-and-not-the-hatchback they'd ordered.

Tomorrow was Thanksgiving, so Jodie was fighting tears more than usual. What did she have to be thankful for? She was dreading the long night of cooking ahead, and the lunch tomorrow, where she'd have to force cheerfulness and pretend her parents weren't crying.

The airport was pumped full of pumpkin-spice fragrance, which only just covered up the smell of body odor and greasy food. It turned Jodie's stomach.

When her shift was over, she was out the doors within a heartbeat, sucking in the cold air, glad there wasn't so much as a hint of pumpkin spice. Claude was late to pick her up, but it gave her some time to cement her composure. Jodie fished her phone out of her jacket pocket and found the to-do list. Bree had been very specific. Thank goodness Claude was helping. The thought of forcing Thanksgiving cheer was horrid, but at least she wasn't doing it alone. And Claude could make anything sparkle, couldn't she? Even a holiday as heartbroken as this one was.

It was spitting rain out of a dirty sky by the time Claude pulled up. "I'm sorry," she said, "I got stuck on the window display at the department store. You wouldn't believe the tacky thing they wanted me to do."

"Did you do what they wanted?"

"Of course not." Claude's perfect nose wrinkled. "They don't pay me to be tacky. I did the superior version."

"And they loved it."

"They haven't seen it yet. But when they see it tomorrow, they'll love it."

Jodie didn't doubt it.

"How was your day?" Claude asked, darting a sideways glance.

Jodie tried not to roll her eyes. Claude clucked over her like a mother hen these days. And pecked at her like a vicious older sister. All her anxiety and grief seemed to focus on Jodie. It was exhausting. But also kind of nice.

"About what you'd expect. I got yelled at a lot. No one tipped. You know. The holidays."

"Did you get your assignment in before Thanksgiving break?"

Jodie managed a nod. She wasn't proud of herself and doubted she'd pass. She still had a year to go in her associate's degree in Exercise Science at Delaware Tech, but at the moment she wasn't sure she could get through the semester. Her grades were abysmal since Bree died; despair mixed with long working hours was a recipe for academic disaster.

"I printed out the list," Claude said. "It's in my bag."

Of course she had. Jodie dug it out. "I have it on my phone. You didn't need to print it."

"I made notes."

Now Jodie did roll her eyes. Claude's list was completely annotated. "Where to first?"

"The butcher. The turkey's the most important thing."

Jodie didn't know the first thing about cooking a turkey. Neither did Claude. But they were determined to make it the Thanksgiving of Bree's dreams, even though she wouldn't be here to enjoy it. And the first thing on Bree's list was a turkey. A real turkey. Not hospital-grade turkey shingles, but a great big horrifyingly expensive free-range bird.

Jodie had ordered the biggest one the butcher had, even though she would have to sell a kidney to afford it. She couldn't help but tally up which bills would have to be left overdue so they could afford the holiday Bree wanted. It was a waste of money. But who could say no to Bree? Even when she was dead.

"At least she won't have to eat my cooking," Jodie said glumly, as she contemplated the bird when the butcher hauled it up onto the counter.

"That's not a turkey, it's an elephant," Claude said in shock. "What on earth did you *spend*?"

That was rich, given Claude had been the one to recommend this obscenely expensive boutique butcher. If it hadn't been for Claude, Jodie may have just gone to Costco.

"I spent too much. I don't even eat turkey." Jodie sighed, sliding the big ball of meat off the counter. "I'm a vegetarian, remember?"

"As if I could forget? You're like one of those door-knocking evangelicals. I half expect you to hand me a newsletter every time I open the door." Claude watched Jodie wrestle with the turkey. She didn't offer to help. "It's just me and your family eating *that*?"

"For the next month or so," Jodie commiserated. "Think of all the turkey sandwiches, and turkey hash, and turkey noodle soup you can enjoy up until Christmas."

Christmas. Ugh. If Thanksgiving felt bleak, imagine how bad Christmas was going to be. Jodie didn't know if she could face it.

"Aunt Pat will have recipes for you, I'm sure," she reassured Claudia.

"Aunt Pat can *have* the damn turkey."

"I'm sure she wouldn't mind. She'd probably make a turkey marshmallow casserole with it."

"Oh, imagine."

"I don't have to. I've seen it with my own eyes."

Claudia looked appalled. She pulled on her woolen gloves and zipped up her coat as she opened the door for Jodie. They stepped out into the bitter November wind. The streets were icy from the rain and everything was gray. Claude yanked up the hood of her quilted black parka. As always, she looked like she belonged in an issue of *Vogue*. How she kept her mascara from running in this weather was a mystery. If Jodie had been wearing it, she would have had panda eyes by now. Even if she'd worn waterproof.

Claudia reached over and tugged Jodie's hood up too. It made Jodie feel like a little kid. But in a good way. She felt an absurd rush of tears. She didn't know why; it just seemed to happen whenever anyone was nice to her these days. She turned her face into the wind, hoping that Claudia would think its vicious snap was the reason her eyes were tearing.

They stored the turkey in the car. It was forty degrees; the trunk was colder than a fridge.

"Hurry up." Claudia stomped her feet to keep warm. "Before it starts raining again."

Jodie was glad Claude was helping her. The thought of shopping alone made her feel panicky. Hell. *Everything* made her feel panicky lately. Sometimes she woke in the night and just couldn't breathe.

But with Claude along it didn't feel so bad. For one thing, they argued a lot, and arguing was a great distraction. And it was easy to argue with Claude because she was *ridiculous*.

"This isn't a grocer," Jodie protested, when Claude led her into a bar.

"Yes, it is."

Jodie took in the tables and the long bar along the wall. There was a guy behind the counter pulling beers. "I hate to break it to you, but this is definitely a bar."

Claude rolled her eyes. "It's a grocery store *with* a bar. How can you not have heard of this place?"

"Easily. I don't even know what place we're in."

"This is Hopper's."

"How can you tell? There's no sign."

"Because I shop here every week." Claude led Jodie through the bar toward the open door on the back wall. The bar was full, even though it was only early afternoon, and they had to wind between the crowded tables. The people were like Claude: glossy. And the bar . . .

The era of blazing white walls and exposed air conditioning ducts seemed to be over; in their place were luscious wood paneling and forest-green paint. The chairs had deep velvet padding and there were oil paintings on the walls. These glossy people still liked their potted plants, though. How they kept them alive, Jodie didn't know. The only plant she'd ever managed to keep was a fake one, and it was so dusty it looked sick.

"This is some fancy grocery store," she observed as they stepped through into the store itself. They could still hear the civilized chatter and lazy jazz of the bar behind them; it made everything feel stupidly glamorous. The whole place smelled like spiced apples and nutmeg and pastry crust. And it was too pretty, like something from a magazine.

Of course this was where Claude shopped. No Trader Joe's or even a Whole Foods for Claudia. Not when there was a fancy store like this to swan through.

"It's great, isn't it?" Claudia snagged a wicker basket and headed straight for the fresh produce. "They have the best fruit in Wilmington."

"My local has the best day-old bread," Jodie said dryly. "And sometimes they even have milk *before* its use-by date."

"We'll need pumpkin, obviously." Claude could ignore Jodie better than anyone Jodie knew. It was like a superpower. "Where's your basket?"

"I took care of the turkey. I'm done for the day."

"You can still help me carry things."

"Like you helped me with the turkey?"

"Get a basket."

Jodie did. Because deep down she was still a little scared of Claude. She remembered when Bree first brought her home after grade school one day. "This is the new girl," Bree had announced, and it was evident to everyone that Bree was keeping her. Or maybe it was that she was being kept. Because even in her ragged jeans and dollar store T-shirt, Claude had been imperious. And too good-looking. As good-looking as Jodie's sister. Only where Bree was tanned and sandy-skinned, her hair streaked with butterscotch and caramel, Claude was an ice queen, pale as new frost, her eyes glacier green. Where Bree had a girl-next-door wholesomeness, Claude was like a movie star. The two of them together were ludicrously pretty. People walked into lampposts staring at them.

No one had ever walked into a lamppost because of Jodie.

Which was probably for the best. She'd hate that kind of attention. She hated *all* attention.

"Are we doing a green-bean casserole?" Claude asked, looking poleaxed as she reached the green beans in the produce section. "I forgot about green beans! And they weren't on Bree's list." *Poleaxed* became *stricken*.

"Sure, why not. Throw some in." Jodie shrugged. She couldn't care less about green beans.

"But they weren't on the list!"

"So, if they weren't on the list, don't cook them."

"But it's *Thanksgiving*. You need a green-bean casserole at Thanksgiving!"

Oh no. Claude was going to lose it. Right here in the fanciest grocery store in the world. Were you even *allowed* to lose it in here? Or did they haul you out for crushing the vibe?

"You want me to look up a recipe for green-bean casserole on my phone?" Jodie suggested. Since Bree's death, sometimes Claude glitched like this. Jodie knew how she felt. This Thanksgiving was a hellish idea. Who cared about turkeys and green-bean casseroles with Bree gone?

Bree, that's who.

Jodie's sister had left detailed instructions for Thanksgiving this year; it was going to be perfect, and they were all going to enjoy it. Even if they were worn brittle with grief and in danger of cracking.

"I don't know," Claudia wailed. "Do we even have time to cook it? My oven isn't that big, and it will be full of turkey . . ."

"Forget the casserole." Jodie grabbed Claude by the elbow and steered her away from the beans. "Who feels like eating anyway."

"You're vegetarian." Claude's panic was palpable. It was like being smothered in wet wool. "What if we don't have enough vegetables without it?"

"I'll eat the sweet potatoes, it'll be fine."

"You can't have just sweet potatoes for Thanksgiving!"

"Claude!" Jodie snapped, turning her sister's friend to face her. "Stop. We'll have enough to feed an army. *Stop*."

Claudia's gaze was treacherously shiny. Oh God, she was going to cry. And if she cried, then Jodie would cry, and Jodie couldn't take any more tears. It was bad enough with Mom and Dad . . .

"No." Jodie used the same voice she used on Aunt Pat's dog, a hyper little Jack Russell that liked to eat her shoes. While she was wearing them. "No. None of that. Not on Thanksgiving."

"It's Thanksgiving *eve*. I never promised I wouldn't cry on Thanksgiving eve." But the tears were less shiny now. She managed to blink them back.

"What's next on the list?" Jodie prompted her.

"Cranberries."

"Cross it off. I got a can at Whole Foods yesterday."

"A can?" Claudia looked horrified. She did horrified exceptionally well. And still managed to look pretty. "We're not having cranberry sauce out of a can. We're making it." She barreled ahead, leaving the momentary lapse behind.

"Oh God," Jodie moaned, following in her wake, "we're going to be up all night!"

"Probably," Claudia agreed. "We haven't even started the decorations yet."

"Decorations? Wait. *We?*" That sounded bad. Jodie watched as Claude loaded their baskets with silly things. Chestnuts and currants and all kinds of expensive foods that no one was going to feel like eating.

"Get that look off your face," Claudia warned, when Jodie examined the label of a tub of cream.

"*Bourbon* cream?"

"I know. I should make it myself." Claude rubbed her forehead and looked stressed. "You're right, I should." She reached for the tub, but Jodie snatched it away.

"No, you shouldn't." She waved the tub in Claudia's face. "Why does this even exist?"

"It goes really well with my candied pecan pumpkin pie."

"Just get regular cream," Jodie said, appalled.

Claude looked at her like she'd suggested serving the pie with kitty litter sprinkled on top.

Jodie sighed. "Well, if you have to have it, you're getting the premade. I'm not making bourbon cream at three in the morning. Not when you need me to paint pinecones, or whatever it is I'll be doing."

Truth be told, Jodie thought as she watched Claudia pile an insane number of pumpkins onto the checkout counter, she didn't mind painting pinecones all night. She couldn't sleep these days anyway. And sitting at Claude's kitchen table, painting pinecones and watching Claude do extreme holiday cookery, was better than the howling loneliness of Jodie's empty bedroom.

Once they got through the checkout, they had to brave the bar again.

"Hey, if it isn't my favorite type A," the bartender called out, leaning on the bar as they passed. "Not stopping for your usual today?"

Claudia broke stride. And no wonder, Jodie thought. The guy looked like a Hemsworth. The one who played Thor.

"I can't," Claudia said stiffly, "it's Thanksgiving."

Thor smiled at her. "Seems like the perfect time to stop for a drink, then." His gaze flicked to Jodie. "And who's this, your sister?"

Jodie snorted. She looked about as much like Claudia's sister as a giraffe looked like a racehorse.

"No, she's my . . ." Claudia turned to Jodie, at a loss as to how to explain their relationship without mentioning Bree. She sighed. "This is Jodie."

"Heya, Jodie. So, Type A, what do you fancy?"

That seemed a loaded question. And if Jodie wasn't mistaken, Claudia was looking flustered. Well, this could be fun. God knew they could use some fun in this season of misery.

"She'll have a cocktail," Jodie said, climbing onto a stool at the bar.

"No, she won't," Claudia snapped. "She's *driving*."

Jodie shrugged, unsurprised. Claudia wasn't one for drinking, even when she wasn't driving. "I'll have a beer," she told Thor. "And she'll have her usual." She paused. "What *is* her usual?"

"A double espresso," he said, rolling his eyes.

"You drink coffee in a *bar*?" Jodie turned on Claudia, who was still standing in the middle of the place, clutching her paper sacks of shopping. Those pumpkins weighed far more than the stupid turkey. Looked like her Pilates muscles worked just fine now.

"It's a coffee shop as well as a bar," Claude said defensively.

"I can make it an espresso martini for the holidays," Thor suggested.

"Yes." Abruptly, Jodie decided an espresso martini was exactly what was needed. Today had been *grim*, starting with her red-eye shift, and now she was staring down the barrel of the first Thanksgiving without her sister. She had the rest of today and all of tomorrow off from work, for the first time in ages. And look at these glossy people nursing their magazine-worthy cocktails . . . *that's* what a holiday should look like. That's what Bree would have made it look like. Insta-worthy.

"Two espresso martinis," Jodie said firmly.

"One," Claudia corrected. "I'm driving."

"Two," Jodie told Thor. "Just make hers half-strength." Jodie yanked a stool out for Claudia.

"You're so irritating," Claudia said under her breath as Thor moved away to make their drinks.

"What are you ladies doing for Thanksgiving?" Thor asked as he languidly worked the coffee machine.

"Painting pinecones."

"Painting *pinecones*?" Thor looked caught between amusement and despair.

"No one is painting pinecones," Claudia said stiffly. "She's just being a pain in the ass."

"Stringing leaves, then." The thought was almost her undoing. Jodie closed her eyes.

"There are no leaves."

Thor grinned. "I've got one of those cardboard turkeys from the dollar store at home. Does that count as a decoration?"

Jodie felt like she'd been winded. Memories flashed: kicking the torn cardboard turkey under the bed so Wanda the orderly wouldn't be offended; stringing the leaves up; Bree glowing, happy. The yellow blanket.

The one she'd been buried in.

Oh, screw this. Grief sucked so much harder than Jodie had ever expected.

"There you go, two espresso martinis: one full strength, one half-strength booze but double-strength espresso."

Claudia looked as winded as Jodie felt. She knocked back her half-strength espresso martini in one gulp. "Are you ready?"

"No." Jodie didn't think she could stand yet. She could barely breathe. Why couldn't you banish memories? The cardboard turkey with its blue tissue tail. The yellow blanket. The daffodils on the coffin. She took a deep draught of her martini. It was good. And it was strong.

"Yes, you are," Claudia insisted. "You have a turkey to cook."

Thor lazily polished glasses, leaning against the counter. "You're hosting Thanksgiving, huh?"

"No, my parents are hosting," Jodie told him, glad of the distraction. "We're just doing all the work. Well, Claudia will probably do all the *actual* work. She's a control freak," she confided.

"Yeah, I guessed."

"Oh *please*," Claudia interrupted. "How could you possibly guess that I'm a control freak? You see me for twenty minutes a week."

"I pay attention." He grinned.

He had Hemsworth-level charm to go with his Hemsworth-level looks. Claudia clearly thought so too, as she was all flushed.

"What was *that*?" Jodie asked later, as she dumped groceries in the trunk of the car.

"What was what?"

"*That*." Jodie waved in the direction of the bar/grocery store. "*Thor.*"

"Thor?" Claudia wrinkled her nose.

"Yes, you halfwit. Thor! The god behind the bar."

"He's not a god, he's a *bartender*."

Jodie was pleasantly full of espresso martini and far more relaxed than she'd been when they'd entered the grocery store, and *far* more relaxed than during the green-bean casserole scene. The aging hipsters might be on to something. All grocery stores should have bars, she decided as she climbed into the passenger seat of Claude's car. Maybe this Thanksgiving wouldn't be so grim after all.

Chapter 5

"So, tell me about Thor," she said later, as she watched Claudia try to stuff the turkey with apples and lemons and herbs. The ridiculous woman was wearing elbow-length rubber gloves and standing at arm's length from the bird, which didn't make any of it look easier.

Jodie poked around Claude's open-plan kitchen/living/dining room as Claude worked. Claude's apartment was a revelation. Jodie had picked Bree up from here a couple of times over the years but had never been invited in before. Now she could see why. It was a *pigsty*. Claude looked so immaculate; Jodie had assumed her house would be immaculate too. But the place was covered with discarded clothing and magazines and littered with dirty dishes. It looked like it hadn't been tidied in, oh, roughly a decade. The apartment underneath the mess was just as gorgeous as Jodie had imagined, though. It was on the third floor of an historic building on Orange Street, not too far from Jodie's college, and had hardwood floors and fancy cornices on the high ceilings. The huge windows looked into the bare branches of a sycamore, which had fairy lights strung up like glittery cobwebs. If Claude cleaned up once in a while, it could be incredible.

And if she bothered to do her dishes, Claude's kitchen would look like something out of a cooking show. All of the appliances were in glossy pastels and there were gadgets Jodie didn't recognize. She guessed you'd need a kitchen like this to make a pie fancy enough to deserve a dollop of bourbon cream.

"Don't hide yourself in the turkey," Jodie scolded, "I want to know about Thor."

"Thor?" Claude rammed an apple into the turkey. "There's nothing to tell."

"Sure, there isn't." Jodie opened Claude's fridge. "You got any beer?"

"No."

"Wine?"

Claudia sighed and brushed a stray lock of hair off her forehead with her forearm. Her hair had grown back perfectly after the head-shaving affair, Jodie noted. Typical. Her own had grown back in weird corkscrew curls. What was with *that*? She hadn't had curls before she shaved her head. Thank God for baseball caps, that's all she could say. "You must have wine. I'm going to need *something* to get through these festivities."

"The wine is for tomorrow."

"You think my folks drink wine? You have *met* them, right?" Jodie found the bottles behind the milk and cream. "Chardonnay?"

"It pairs well with turkey."

"How do you know? You barely drink." Jodie picked one out.

"Don't you dare open it. It's for lunch tomorrow."

"Look . . . what did Thor call you? Type A? Look, Type A, we are never going to survive twelve hours of turkey, pie, and pinecone painting without a drink."

"There are no pinecones." Claudia took a breath. Then came the sound of muttering. Counting to ten. "Make us a coffee instead," she suggested, after she got to ten.

"No more coffee. You've had so much coffee you're vibrating, and probably at such a high frequency that you're existing in multiple dimensions at once." Jodie put the chardonnay back. "Hey, there's champagne in here."

"That's for tomorrow too."

"How much are you expecting us to drink? You know Dad

will have a few Coors and then fall asleep. And Mom's a whiskey sour kinda girl."

"It's for . . . something. It's just important, that's all."

Jodie sighed and closed the fridge. This was going to be a long night.

"Fine," Claude said, surrendering. "There's some vodka in the freezer. Bree left it here the last time"—Claudia took a shaky breath—"the last time she came over." Then Jodie heard the turkey take a pummeling.

Knowing what she'd find, Jodie opened the freezer. But even knowing . . . the sight of the blue vodka bottles knocked the wind out of her. *Bree.* Damn it. The grief came out at you like a cheap scare. She was never going to get used to it. Not ever.

Jodie drew a beautifully rich blue bottle out of the freezer.

Bree had been sponsored by this vodka company for a while. That's what happened when you were a professional poser— people paid you to pose. The vodka people had paid for Bree's trip to the Himalayas. All Bree's snow gear had been in this same distinctive royal blue, with the logo in blazing white across her beanie, and every time she posted about her hike to the base camp of Mt. Everest, she'd included the brand's hashtag.

As well as giving Bree the all-expenses-paid trip (in exchange for product placement and hashtags), the company had sent five whole cases of vodka to Mom and Dad's, which had always been Bree's postal address. She traveled too much to bother getting her own place.

Hell. She *had* traveled . . .

Jodie hated this so much. She *had* traveled.

It was still hard to remember to use past tense.

Seeing the row of blue vodka bottles in Claudia's freezer was like seeing a ghost. Jodie turned the icy-cold bottle in her hands. It seemed surreal that it should still exist, when Bree didn't.

"You want one?" Jodie asked. She had to clear her throat, as her voice had gone all choked up and weird.

"Yes."

Jodie looked up to find Claudia crying over the stupid elephant of a turkey.

"Please." Claudia snapped her gloves off. "I don't know what I have to mix it with."

"Ha." Jodie closed the freezer and opened the fridge to fish out the designer cranberry juice they'd bought at the fancy grocery store.

"I need that for cooking."

"Nah. You need it for the vodka more." Jodie stuffed two wineglasses with ice and made them some very heavy-handed cocktails. "To Bree," she said, clinking glasses with Claude. "If she wasn't already dead, I'd kill her for making us do this Thanksgiving."

"To Bree," Claude agreed. "But I think this Thanksgiving is a good idea." She knocked back a third of her cocktail in one gulp.

"That's because it was probably *your* idea."

"Oh no you don't. I'm not taking the blame for this one." Claudia yanked a sheaf of papers off her fridge. A magnet went clattering to the floor. She waved the papers at Jodie.

It was a printout of Bree's email. The long one, with all her crazy plans for the holidays. Bree's email had covered Thanksgiving, Christmas, New Year's, Valentine's Day, Easter, Mother's Day, Father's Day, Fourth of July, Halloween, and right back to a second Thanksgiving. *The first year is going to be hard*, she'd written. *But I want you to celebrate the good times.* And she'd given detailed instructions for how each holiday was to be celebrated. Right down to the stupid turkey. *I'll be with you in spirit.*

Well, she was here in one kind of spirit, Jodie acknowledged, topping up their glasses with more vodka. "You know, Bree put you to shame in the control-freak game," she told Claude.

"You have no idea." Claude was looking a bit more relaxed now. Vodka would do that to a nondrinker. Especially after an espresso martini. Claude wasn't even stressing as she eyed her oven. "Do you think the turkey will even fit in there?"

"We'll make it fit."

"It'll have to go in first thing in the morning." She looked at her watch. Claude must surely be the only person under fifty to still wear a watch. At least one that wasn't a smart one. "This thing's so big, it may have to go in before sunrise."

"That's OK, we won't be sleeping anyway." Jodie looked around the kitchen. "What do you want me to do? I can start the decorations?"

"No, according to the schedule the pie is first." Claude put her rubber gloves back on and started rubbing herb butter all over the turkey.

"Fine, what can I do for the pie?"

"You can chop the pumpkin. We need to boil it."

Jodie groaned. "Why didn't you just buy pumpkin puree, you madwoman?" She topped up her vodka-cranberry and sat on a stool at Claude's counter.

"I want the pumpkin in evenly sized cubes."

"Why? You're going to mash it all up anyway." But Jodie did as she was told and chopped pumpkin into *mostly* even cubes. Mostly. Claude didn't trust her with the pie crust or the bread dough and relegated her to vegetables for most of the afternoon.

When Jodie ran out of vegetables, she left Claude to her doughs and put some music on. Claude had a turntable; she also had a pretty decent music collection. Once Jodie drowned out the horrible silence with some '90s-era Radiohead, she started cleaning Claudia's house for her. "You know you can buy perfectly good dinner rolls from the store," she said as she heard Claude start thumping dough about. "I bet that Hopper's place makes them out of organic flour and everything." She took the opportunity to snoop as she cleared mugs off Claude's bookshelf. The "serious" books were in the living room, but Jodie thought it was a safe bet that she kept an impressive collection of romance novels next to her bed. Claude had always been a sucker for romance; she'd brought bags full of her old books into the hospital for Bree. And when Bree got really sick, Claude used to sit next to the bed and read to her. Even after Bree couldn't hear her anymore.

"You keep dodging my question about Thor," Jodie reminded

Claude as she filled the sink to wash the mugs. She sniffed the detergent bottle. Where did she even buy designer detergent? Stupid question. *Hopper's.*

It had always staggered Jodie that Claude was single. Hell, if *Claude* was single, what hope was there for Jodie?

"I'm not dodging anything," Claude said, dodging the question again.

Jodie had to scrub hard to get the dried coffee out of the mugs. It had been there so long it had become a patina, like a pottery glaze. "What's his name?"

There was silence.

"You *must* know his name."

"His name is Hopper."

Jodie laughed. "*He's* Hopper? Like *the* Hopper, the one who owns the store? You said he was just a bartender."

"I didn't say *just.*"

"You might as well have." Jodie shook her head. "I wish some hot guy who ran his own business liked me. I'd still be in there, ordering drinks. Or double espressos."

"He doesn't *like* me." There was an irritable clatter as she threw her pie crust into the oven to bake. "And would you? I've never seen you hang around a guy in your life."

Jodie scowled at the suds.

"You never even *talk* about them."

"You mean during all those times we hang out? Like every time we go for drinks? Or have pajama parties and paint each other's nails? My bad."

Claude's silence dragged out. "Point taken," she said eventually. Jodie heard the ice clink as Claude picked up her nearly empty drink. "I don't think we *have* ever hung out," Claude admitted, "except . . ." She trailed off into one of those godawful silences.

"In the hospital," Jodie finished. She was sick of the way everyone trailed off all the time. She loved her sister as much as any of them, but she hated these potholes of emotion. If she had her way, they'd just drive right over them, even if their teeth rattled out of their heads and they broke an axle.

"Yes." Claude drained her vodka. "Another one?"

"Seriously?" This was unprecedented.

"I want to get drunk." Claude said it flatly, like she was suggesting they do their taxes.

"Sure. Why not? It'll make the pinecones easier to bear."

Only there weren't any pinecones. There were gourds. Lots and lots of gourds.

"What the hell even *is* this?" Jodie asked, picking up a yellow-and-green-striped gourdy-squashy thing.

"It's a delicata."

"A what?" She didn't bother to listen to Claude repeat herself. "How come it's all weird like that? This one's not." Jodie picked up another yellow-and-green-striped gourd thing, this one shaped like a regular pumpkin.

"Because that one's a carnival." Claude was pulling glass vases out of a cupboard. Lots and lots of vases. Who even had that many vases? Maybe men sent her flowers a lot. That would make sense.

"How do you even know all this?" Jodie asked curiously. Squashes seemed a pretty weird thing to be an expert on.

"I don't know." Claude sighed as she delicately stepped off the chair. She lined the vases up along the counter. They were all different heights. "I'll set one up, so you can see what to do, and then you can do the rest," she told Jodie.

Jodie poured another drink and watched as Claude filled a vase with gourds, arranging them so there was a mix of colors and shapes. She didn't stuff it full; it had a weirdly airy look. When she was finished stuffing the vase, she threaded a string of battery-powered fairy lights though the gourds. She flicked the lights on. "Ta da!"

It was very pretty, Jodie admitted. "Nice work, Martha Stewart!"

"Your turn."

Right. At least it wasn't painting pinecones. And as she overcame the first couple of disasters (too many green gourds in one; too many gourds altogether in another) Jodie found she quite enjoyed stuffing pumpkins into vases. Outside the wind slapped at the windows and the lights swung on their cobwebby wires in the sycamore, throwing spangles onto the steamed-up panes. It was all very cozy. Maybe Jodie should have taken up holiday crafting years ago. Or drinking vodka. One or the other. It was quite soothing.

Or at least it was until Claude exploded from the other end of the kitchen. "Oh my *God*!"

Jodie stopped cold, her arm stuck elbow-deep in a vase. "What? What have I done?" For a second, she honestly thought that her (mis)arrangements of gourds were the reason for Jodie's outburst.

"Oh my *God*." Claude turned around, holding her phone out in front of her. She looked like she'd seen a ghost.

Which she kind of had. Because there on the screen was *Bree*.

"Oh my *God*." Jodie struggled to yank her arm out of the vase. "What is that?"

It was a *video*. Of Bree. In the hospital. She was waving at them and grinning.

For a moment the world swam. Time went wobbly. For that moment Jodie felt *certain* that that Bree was alive again. She was *here*.

"Turn the volume on!" Jodie snapped at Claudia. She tried to grab the phone, but Claude held it away.

"It's *my* phone!" Claude bent over it like an addict over a fix. She swiped the video back to the beginning.

"What is that? Is that on Instagram?" Jodie was bent over Bree, like a second addict sick with jealousy. "How? Is it an old video? How does that work? Why has it popped up again?" The frozen image of Bree showed her wrapped in the yellow knitted blanket, which she'd worn even when the weather had warmed up. She'd always been cold at the end; nothing they did could warm her up.

"It's a new video," Claude breathed. "She *scheduled* it."

Even though Jodie knew Bree wasn't here, making new videos and uploading them on Instagram, and that she *couldn't* be here, and wouldn't ever be again, she hadn't been able to resist the impossible hope. And, as usual, when hope cracked like ice underfoot, grief came stabbing in, as painful as ever. A rusty nail right through her soul.

"Oh *God*." Claude was shivering. "Can you pour us another drink before we watch this?"

Grief was like weather: it had seasons and moods, and it could always take a turn for the worse. Today had started with lowering clouds of gloom and the rainy smell of despair; there had been razor-sharp, heart-hurting cold; then a bitter wind had blown in, churning the flat gray sky into a stormy sea of misery; and now there was driving, sheeting, pelleting sleet. The kind that flayed the skin off your bones. Jodie felt hyperaware of everything around her, but also at a great distance from it. Numb, like she'd been too long in the cold. She barely registered pouring the vodkas, but she must have done, because as they sat on the couch and Claude pressed play on the video, they each had a vodka cranberry in hand.

"Hey!" Bree waved cheerily at the camera. She was so *thin*. And her face had that awful look; haunted, shadowy. This was late in the game. When she was stretched so thin that she was near transparent. Like she was half in another dimension already, and it was taking every ounce of willpower she had to remain in this one at all. "If you're watching this, it's Thanksgiving eve," phantom Bree told them chirpily. Too chirpily, given the circumstances. "And my family will be preparing dinner. I'm imagining them all in Mom's kitchen."

Guiltily, Jodie and Claude looked over at the catastrophe that was Claude's kitchen, mid-preparations. Bree wasn't an omniscient ghost, then. And they clearly weren't following her script well enough. She hadn't said anything about Mom's kitchen in the instructions . . .

"I'm imagining Mom hovering, while Claude takes over."

"Well, you *did* take over, at least," Jodie mumbled, shuffling closer to Claude on the couch. But Mom wasn't here hovering. Mom wasn't capable of hovering anymore. She existed in a watery half-life of grief, where hovering was beyond her powers. She was probably already in bed.

"And, if my family are watching, I hope you got the biggest

turkey you could find," Bree said teasingly. Her breath was short and labored, and she was the color of damp chalk, but she was valiantly cheerful.

Claude and Jodie were transfixed. They were so fixated on the face in front of them that they barely listened to the words; time collapsed around them, erasing the months of hell they'd just lived through.

It was *Bree*. Breathing, talking, trying to laugh. The video ended, and then started again, on an endless loop. This time they tried to pay attention. Jodie could feel Claude's shivering worsen. It was shock, she supposed. She yanked the fluffy white throw rug from the couch and pulled it around Claude's shoulders.

"I know tomorrow is going to be just awful for my family," video-Bree told them. Or rather, her followers. Jodie glanced at the icons and comments. There were likes, by the look of it. And comments. Oh my *God* . . .

"Does that say three hundred comments?" she blurted. "Three *hundred*? When did she post this?"

"Shhhh." Claudia flapped a hand at her.

"We can watch it again," Jodie said defensively. "We already missed it once."

"*Shhhhh.*" Claude elbowed her.

At least she'd stopped shivering. Maybe it was worth an elbow or two, just for that.

"Claude, I know *you'll* be watching this," video-Bree continued.

"I am," Claude breathed.

"It's probably late, and you've just got home from my mom's. I bet that turkey is all trussed up, and the pie is ready to go. You probably color-coded her refrigerator before you left. I figure you're sitting down now to weave straw decorations or something, even though it's the wee dark hours." Bree smiled into the camera. "I know you're busy, but I need you to do me a favor."

"Anything." Claudia sounded shaky.

"Why is she asking you? I'm here too." Jodie scowled. Even

though Bree knew she hated Instagram and was as likely to check it on Thanksgiving Eve as she was to pull her toenails out one by one, Jodie was offended. *She* was Bree's sister.

"*Another* favor," video-Bree amended. "You've done so much for me already, Claude, more than I can ever repay."

Claudia sniffled. She was starting to cry now. It made Jodie's throat hurt and her nose felt like someone had shoved a woolen blanket up there. Screw this. Whoever invented grief needed to be shot.

"Tomorrow is going to be hard," Bree said, her shadowed gaze full of empathy. "I need you to be there for them."

"I'm here," Claude said, her voice hoarse.

"So am *I*," Jodie reminded them, even though one couldn't hear her and the other kept elbowing her.

"I can't even imagine what Mom and Dad are going through. And Jodie . . ."

Jodie's heart twisted. Oh, damn this all to hell. The sound of Bree's voice saying her name . . .

"I want you to help them enjoy tomorrow," video-Bree begged.

"That's a tall order," Jodie said gruffly. She wasn't going to cry. She *wasn't*.

"Eat that turkey, drink all the wine you can stomach, have second helpings of pie. And then at five o'clock, I need you to have a look at Instagram again, OK? I need you to get everyone to watch. Make them, even if they don't want to. Promise me?"

"I promise."

Bree smiled beatifically, as though she'd heard. "And to the rest of you, have a *wonderful* Thanksgiving." She was caught for one moment in a sun flare, as she bent forward slightly to stop the recording. She looked angelic. Then the video started again, and she was cheerily greeting them.

"She did this in spring," Claude said, her fingertip brushing the screen. "Look, there are the forsythia branches I brought her." The yellow flowers blazed in the background.

The horridness of it sank it. Because Bree had *known*. She'd known she was dying. The rest of them hadn't accepted it until after it had happened—maybe not even then. They'd certainly not spoken of it with Bree.

"What happens at five o'clock tomorrow?" Jodie asked numbly.

"Another message, presumably." Claude turned the volume down but let the video keep looping, so they could see Bree sunlit and alive. Smiling.

"How long has this thing been on Instagram?" Jodie suddenly remembered that she had her own phone and dug it out of her pocket.

"Looks like an hour or so."

Jodie opened the Instagram app, which she hadn't done since Bree died. "But there are *three hundred* comments!"

"Three hundred and seventy-five."

Judging by the comments, Bree's followers were as gob smacked as Jodie was.

OMG! Is it really her?

It is! It is her!

There were a lot of broken-heart emojis and crying kittens and all kinds of cutesy expressions of grief.

Has anyone in her family seen it yet?

Has CLAUDIA seen it?

None of them have liked it yet. . . .

"Like it," Jodie told Claudia, "so they know you've seen it."

"You like it."

Jodie snorted. "I don't Instagram."

"Feel free to start." But Claudia liked the post. Which set off another avalanche of comments.

She's seen it!

Sending hugs, Claudia!

This must be so hard. Much love!

More hearts and kittens and weepy faces.

"Who *are* all these people?" Jodie asked.

"People who loved your sister."

"Who loved the freak show, you mean." Jodie gave a sudden yelp. "Oh my God!"

"What?"

"*Mom* just liked it!"

"Oh my God!" Claude and Jodie shared a panicked look. "You need to get home, Jodie."

"How? You can't drive me, you've had a zillion vodkas!"

"We'll get a cab. Quick! Help me pack the turkey."

"Pack the turkey! In what? A suitcase?"

"We have to get to your mom's. Oh my God. Bree never meant for her to see that."

"Yes, she did—she said, 'if my family are watching.'"

"But not like this! Not *alone*."

"Dad's there."

But they both knew Jodie's dad would be asleep on the couch.

"Now *this* feels more like last Thanksgiving." Jodie sighed as she prepared to crowd into a car with a complete Thanksgiving feast.

Chapter 6

Jodie's father was the only one who slept through the night. He was still on the couch come morning, snoring like a freight train. He hadn't woken when the bitter wind blew in with Jodie and Claudia, or when she and Claude took multiple trips past him with arms full of turkey and pie, and vases stuffed with gourds. He hadn't woken when Jodie had dropped one of the vases with an explosive *smash*, or when they sat up with Jodie's mom, drinking tea at the kitchen table while Mom played Bree's video at full volume. Or when they tried to force Mom to bed. Or when they admitted failure, stopped pretending anyone but Jodie's dad was going to sleep, and got back up to clatter around the kitchen. No matter how much noise they made, Dad just lay there like a beached whale. One with a bad case of sleep apnea.

"Do you think she just wants to say Happy Thanksgiving?" Jodie's mom asked for the thousandth time. She was still in her robe at the table, bent over her phone, watching Bree's video. Jodie was heartily sick of video-Bree's cheery "Hey!" which just kept playing on loop, over and over and over again.

Claudia was off blow-drying her hair and airbrushing her face or something. Jodie wished she'd hurry up, because she didn't have a clue what she was doing with this stupid turkey. Besides, she was vegetarian—it was unethical to make her handle the meat.

"But why have two messages just to say Happy Thanksgiving?" Jodie's mom asked. She was treating the video like the Rosetta stone—as though it would unlock mysteries if only she could decode it. "Why not just say it *now*?"

"I don't know, Mom," Jodie said impatiently, wondering if she was supposed to do anything to the turkey. Was she supposed to baste it or something? Wasn't that a thing? "Can you get Dad up and get him to take a shower?"

"Let him sleep. It's better if he's out of the way."

"Is it? Because he could get going on his horrible stuffing."

"He's not making it this year."

That stopped Jodie in her tracks. "What do you mean he's not making it this year? He *always* makes it. It's on Bree's list."

Mom didn't look up from her phone. "He doesn't want to."

"But *I* want him to." Jodie realized, to her horror, that it was true. Thanksgiving wasn't Thanksgiving without his pan of dried-out stuffing. Without him turning the kitchen upside down to make it and putting it down on the table with a ludicrous amount of pride. Stupidly, she felt tears pricking. Bree might not be here, but *she* still was. Wasn't she worth making stuffing for?

You're being ridiculous, she told herself. *He's just lost his daughter; he has every right to take one Thanksgiving off . . .*

But she couldn't shake the hurt. Not that anyone noticed. One parent was still snoring, and the other was glued to her phone.

"Hey!" video-Bree chirped.

Oh my God, make it stop.

"Claude, help me!" she yelled up the stairs. Her parents' narrow two-story clapboard house was small enough that every noise traveled. She didn't need to go upstairs for Claude to hear her.

"I'm on the phone!" Claude called down irritably.

Oh. Jodie knew by her tone who she was on the phone with. Poor Claude. "Sorry. Say hi to your mom for me," she yelled back.

Dad snored.

"Hey!" video-Bree chirped.

"Mom!" Jodie snapped, pressing the heels of her palms into her eyes. She was getting a migraine. "You need to go take a shower."

"Eat that turkey, drink all the wine you can stomach, have second helpings of pie," video-Bree insisted for the gazillionth time.

Jodie reached over her mom's shoulder and punched the app closed. Then she took the phone away.

"Jodie! I'm watching that."

"You can watch it after your shower."

"Claudia's in the shower."

"No, she's not. She's in my room, on the phone." Jodie stuffed her mom's phone in the pocket of her jeans. "You're not getting it back until you've showered. *And* done your hair and put your face on." She propelled her mother to the stairs. "Up. I don't want to see you again until you're decent."

Dad snored.

Oh God, there was still him to deal with.

One step at a time. Was it too early to drink? She glanced at the clock. Yes. Yes, it was.

The smell of turkey roasting turned her stomach.

She wanted to scream when she heard the doorbell ring. What *now*?

She opened the door to a nasty gray day, complete with whipping rain and gusting winds. Grandma Gloria and Aunt Pat were standing stolidly against the buffeting gusts, each buttoned to the chin in their raincoats (Pat's a practical mustard yellow, Gloria's a shiny hot pink) and bearing baskets of food. Pat had her little dog, Russel Sprout, tucked under her arm. He wriggled and barked. Jodie had no idea why Pat insisted on bringing him. He'd probably much rather have stayed home in the warmth.

"I thought I was picking you up," Jodie yelped, jumping out of the way before Pat bulldozed her with a massive glass dish of marshmallow casserole. Russel snapped at her on the way past. Jodie wished she hadn't worn her new sneakers. He was bound to chew on them.

"We wanted to come early," Gloria told her. "And we've got

Lyft now. Put the coffee on, would you? I didn't sleep a wink, so you'll need to keep the pot going all day."

"Lyft?" As usual her family made her feel like she was caught in a mudslide. They just swept you along. She wrestled the door closed against the wind, which was punching at the entrance like it wanted to smash the door clean off its hinges.

"It's an app, dear. It sends a car." Gloria gave Jodie's father a disapproving look as she passed him on the way to the kitchen.

"I know what Lyft is."

"We have Uber too, but Pat won't let me use it." Gloria dropped her basket on the kitchen table and planted a lipsticky kiss on Jodie's cheek.

"I don't approve of their nonsense," Pat agreed.

"What nonsense?"

"Don't get her started," Gloria warned. Pat opened her mouth, but Gloria held out a red-taloned hand. "Pat! Don't start. It's Thanksgiving."

"I don't see what Thanksgiving has to do with anything." Pat pushed Gloria and her acrylic talons out of the way and kissed Jodie on the other cheek. Then she took a good look at her. "You look terrible."

"Thanks." Jodie pulled a face at her.

"It's to be expected," Pat said stoutly.

"You already have coffee on!" Gloria was delighted when she spied the full pot. "Good. It looks like we'll need it to get your father up." She busied herself pouring them mugs.

"I don't take sugar," Jodie protested, when she saw Gloria heaping a spoonful into each mug.

"Today you do. It helps."

"With what?"

"Shock."

"I'm not in shock."

Gloria fixed her with a sympathetic look.

"She has Instagram," Pat reminded Jodie.

"Oh." Jodie didn't resist when they forced her into a chair and pressed a mug of sweet milky coffee on her. "I think I'm supposed to be doing something with the turkey," she said weakly.

"Screw the turkey." Pat slurped her coffee. "You don't even eat turkey."

Jodie couldn't argue with that. She slumped back in the chair. "Today is going to suck." She sighed. She rubbed her face.

"I brought doughnuts." Without getting up from the table, Gloria contorted herself to get the box from her basket, which was on the counter behind her. "There's glazed and cinnamon. Don't let the dog eat any, they make him sick and I don't want to be cleaning up dog vomit today."

Jodie felt the hateful lump swelling in her throat again. Gloria always brought doughnuts Thanksgiving morning. Always glazed and always cinnamon.

A vertiginous surge of memory rose up. All the holidays spent in this house, flickering, one after another . . . they were overlaid like negatives . . . over this room and this moment. Jodie had spent every Thanksgiving morning at this table—even last year, which had been horrible. She and Mom and Dad had wrapped the Thanksgiving lunch in foil, to take to the hospital, while Gloria and Pat had sat right here, eating doughnuts and drinking coffee and telling them they were doing everything wrong.

And the year before that Bree had been here . . . picking at the corner of a glazed doughnut and putting each crumb in her mouth by hand, one by one, as though eating it crumb by minuscule crumb would somehow negate the calories. Jodie could see her so clearly, in her oversized dusty-pink hoodie, with the hood pulled up over her long hair. Bree always sat with her legs pulled up before her on the chair, her yoga body capable of pretzeling into positions that somehow, on her, looked completely natural. Even comfortable. If Jodie had sat like that she would have popped a hipbone out of its socket. And fallen off the chair.

"Hey!"

The sound of Bree's voice startled Jodie so violently she spilled her coffee. Her heart felt like someone had sent a thousand volts through it.

"If you're watching this, it's Thanksgiving eve. And my family will be preparing dinner. I'm imagining them all in Mom's kitchen."

Hell. She'd never get used to it. It was *fucked up.*

"Mom!" At the sound of Bree's voice Jodie felt grief so strong it made her jackknife out of her chair. "Turn the goddamn computer off and get in the shower!" Russel Sprout barked along with her.

The sound of the video vanished instantly but Jodie knew she was still up there watching it. She'd just muted it. And she was probably plugging in a set of headphones.

"Wait!" Grandma Gloria snagged Jodie's arm. "I'll go. She's my child."

"She's a grown-ass adult," Jodie snapped.

"Let's just remind her of that then, hmmm?" Gloria patted her and got up from the table. "You stay, Pat wants to talk to you."

Pat snorted. "We haven't even had a drink yet. Let's wait till later."

"What later? We've got a date with Bree after lunch," Grandma Gloria said wryly as she disappeared upstairs. "Oh hello, Claudia, darling," they heard her call, as her voice moved further away. "Are you on the phone to your mother? Say hello, won't you?"

Pat let Russel down from her lap. He made a beeline for Jodie's sneakers. Pat mopped up Jodie's spilled coffee and poured her another one. This time how she liked it, without sugar. Then she passed her a cinnamon doughnut. "Eat up, girlie."

"I'm not really hungry." She pushed Russel away from her sneakers, but that only made him more excitable. He rolled over her feet, his muscular body holding her sneakers down while his jaws gummed her laces. Every time. She couldn't be bothered fighting him off anymore. And the weight of him was weirdly comforting.

"No. None of us are hungry anymore. But eat."

Jodie ate. Cinnamon had always been her favorite. When she was little her dad would buy her hot cinnamon doughnuts after her baseball games. Grandma Gloria's doughnut tasted like happiness. But cold.

"What did you want to talk about?" Jodie asked, licking the cinnamon sugar off her fingers.

Pat cleared her throat. "Let's set the table while we talk, huh? I assume these ridiculous things are for the table?" She peered into the gourd-stuffed vases.

Jodie felt a stab of suspicion. Aunt Pat was as blunt as a hammer. If she was being cagey, something serious was up.

From the couch, there was a loud sawing snore. Russel snapped to attention and then trotted off to investigate.

Pat swore. "I forgot he was there."

"Mom said he's not making his stuffing this year," Jodie said flatly. For some reason, that was like a burr. She couldn't shake it; it was rubbing her raw.

"Well, he's depressed," Pat said in her practical way.

"*I'm* making things and I'm not feeling great either."

"You're not him." Pat stared into the dark living room, which was lit only by the flickering blue light from the television and the watery gray daylight filtering though the filmy curtains. She sighed gustily.

"I lost her too." Jodie didn't know why she couldn't drop it. What good was snapping at Pat? *She* hadn't done anything.

"I know, love. But losing a child is a whole other order of misery."

Jodie *did* bite her tongue this time. Pat had lost her son to suicide. If anyone knew about a parent's grief, it was her.

"Your dad has a lot on his plate right now." Pat sighed. "More than just Bree's death."

Jodie flinched. Yes.

She felt like a worm. A selfish, petty little worm. Of course he did. And so did Mom. They hadn't just lost a daughter; they'd gained a mountain of debt. Debt and extra shifts and a complete lack of hope for the future.

"I'll get him up and then we'll have a chat."

"I can do it," Jodie said hurriedly.

"No, no, no. You set the table. I'll do it." Pat rolled up her sleeves. "Right, Joseph, we can do this the easy way or the hard way," she brayed, diving into the living room and flicking on the overhead light. Jodie heard her father groan. "Hello, Claudia, love," Pat said as she dragged her nephew-in-law up the stairs. "I think Jodie needs help with the turkey."

Jodie kept her back to the kitchen as Claude entered, to hide the fact she was crumpling up like a used tissue. She hated thinking of the stress her parents were under. And, no matter how many extra shifts she took at the airport, her help was a useless drop in an enormous bucket. An enormous bucket with a hole in it. Goddamn it. No crying on Thanksgiving. She'd promised. They'd *all* promised.

"How was your mother?" she asked Claudia. No tears. She turned around.

Claude was looking worse for wear, as she always did after speaking to her mother. "Fine," she said shortly. "She's fifteen days clean." There was no pride or hope in the flat way Claude spoke. It was just a concrete statement of fact. She'd been here too many times to bother with hope. "Bitching about the quality of the food in rehab." Claude peered in at the turkey.

"Did I wreck it?" Jodie asked fearfully.

"Why? What did you do to it? You didn't baste it, did you?"

"I didn't do anything."

"Perfect. You did great."

"Nothing is what I do best." Jodie fished out the good silverware and headed for the poky dining room. She turned on the lights and swore.

"What?" Claude poked her head in and swore too.

The table wasn't even set up. It was covered with piles of bills and old newspapers. The place was a total mess.

"Guess we're cleaning up," Claude said.

"Not *we*," Jodie corrected her. "You need to cook, or we won't have lunch. I'll clean, you cook." She dropped the silverware back on the kitchen table with a clatter. "We need music for this."

"Nothing too aggressive." Claude was poking through the doughnuts. She didn't take one.

"It's Thanksgiving," Jodie snapped. "Eat a damn doughnut. You can diet tomorrow. Hell, have two."

"Put on that CD your grandma always plays."

Jodie groaned. "No."

"Do it and I'll eat a doughnut."

"I don't see how you eating a doughnut benefits *me*." But Jodie was feeling better now that Claude was here to snipe at. More in control. Thank God for Claude. In a fit of goodwill, Jodie caved and put her grandma's favorite on. Even if it was stupid Michael Bublé.

"Ohhhhh!" Gloria's voice came curling down the stairs. "I love this album!"

"We know," Jodie yelled up at her. "You play it every year!"

And every year, as Thanksgiving drew to a close, Gloria would put on his even stupider Christmas album. "To get us in the mood! Christmas is just around the corner."

"They haven't got any decorations up," Claude observed, standing in the kitchen doorway with her head cocked. "Where are all the decorations?"

"Is this you being passive-aggressive because I haven't put your gourds out?"

"*Our* gourds."

"Technically mine, because I assembled them all."

"I meant your mom's usual decorations. She usually has those colored lights up." Claude made a thoughtful noise and disappeared back into the kitchen.

Jodie looked around. Claude was right. Mom usually had the Christmas lights up by Thanksgiving, even though she left the tree until December. Jodie sat back on her heels and took in the shabby living room. They hadn't had much money since Dad lost his job at GM and had to take a lesser position at the Pepsi factory, but usually Mom kept it looking nice. And Thanksgiving was usually all twinkly and colorful. But this year they hadn't even put out the handcrafted decorations that Bree and Jodie had made in grade school.

Jodie's gaze drifted to the shrine her mother had put together on the mantelpiece. It consisted of a cluster of framed photos of Bree; in the largest one she was standing on a cliff's edge, her arms thrown out, her smile as wide as the heavens behind her. That was the photo that had always had pride of place on the mantel, even before she'd left them. Bree had been about to leap off the cliff edge into the glittering ocean below. Jodie remembered when that picture had arrived on her phone. Bree had been off on one of her adventures; Jodie had been finishing up a twelve-hour shift at the airport counter, ahead of an all-nighter working on her Functional Kinesiology homework. She'd been slogging to the parking lot through the slush of melting oily snow, braced against the rapier winds, when she'd swiped open her phone to find Bree's message. There on her screen was the blazing summer sun and the glittering ocean and that *smile*. That smile that Bree had always worn so well: a smile of pure unadulterated joy.

Bree had always been thrilled to be alive. She had a talent for it. Not like Jodie, who had a talent for . . . what? She hadn't quite worked it out yet.

In the mix of the framed photos of Bree, Mom had placed a fresh bunch of flowers in her good crystal vase. Nothing fancy. Just stalks of baby's breath, bought cheap. And there were saucers of guttered candles on either side. It was quite a depressing little shrine, really. It could have done with some twinkly Christmas lights.

Jodie should have thought of decorating the place for the holidays. *Claude* had thought of it. How hard was it to remember? Mom and Dad clearly weren't up to it, so it should have been Jodie's job to put the lights up. It's what Bree would have wanted.

If the dining room hadn't been such a mess, she might have dashed to the garage to dig out the box of lights, and the hand-crafted decorations. But she'd be hard-pressed to even get the table cleared, she thought with a grimace.

Best get on with it.

As Michael Bublé crooned his way through love songs, Jodie attacked the dining table. Dear God, look at all the *bills*. There was the usual run-of-the-mill sorts of bills (gas, water, electricity) and then there were the truly horrific ones. Oncology, hospital, CAT scan, blood tests, bone marrow transplant . . .

Jodie held the bill for the bone marrow transplant in her shaking hand. Less than a year ago . . . That bone marrow transplant had been horrific; it had hurt Jodie like hell and had put Bree through the worst round of chemo yet. And it hadn't even worked.

Not only that, they'd also be paying it off for years to come. Even though it hadn't saved her. None of this garbage had.

Jodie scooped it all into shopping bags: one for the normal bills and one for the medical horrors. Then she found a sheaf of papers that made her shriek.

"What the hell?"

"Jodie?" Claude was by her side before she'd finished shrieking. "Are you okay? Are you hurt?" Claude was giving her a once-over, checking for injuries.

"Yes," Jodie insisted, waving the papers at her.

Claude frowned, taking them off her.

"They're selling the house?" Claude gasped.

"They can't!" Jodie snatched the papers out of Claude's hands and dashed for the stairs, feeling shocked to her core. "Mom! Dad!" She took the stairs two at a time.

At least she did until she ran smack bang into Grandma Gloria. Who promptly turned her around and hustled her straight back down the stairs again.

"Hey," Jodie protested. "I need to talk to them."

"Later you can talk to them. Let them have some peace to get ready."

"They're selling the house!" Jodie hissed.

"So I heard."

"You know? *You* know?" *Betrayed* didn't even begin to cover how Jodie felt.

"I know everything, dear. I'm old."

"They can't sell the house!" Not the house too.

"They need the money, Jodie," Gloria told her sternly.

"I'm earning money!" Even as she said it, Jodie knew she

was being unrealistic. Her little car-rental-stand job was hardly making a dent. Those medical bills were murderous. Who could make those payments?

"Don't fret," Gloria clucked, pouring Jodie another mug of coffee and spooning an obscene amount of sugar into it. "Pat and I have a plan. Didn't she tell you?"

"No. She got distracted by Dad."

Gloria forced the mug into Jodie's hands.

"What's the plan?" Jodie demanded. "Are we moving in with you?"

"Heaven forbid!" Grandma Gloria rolled her eyes. "I'm not a *saint*. And if they sell this place, *you* won't be moving in with anyone. You should be back out on your own, like a proper woman your age. They should never have let you move back home in the first place. You shouldn't be looking after your parents; you should be off kicking up your heels." She glanced down at Jodie's feet. "Or your sneakers."

"I don't want to kick up my sneakers. I want to help."

"Well, you're not to. Do you hear? Denise is my daughter—it's my job to take care of her, not yours." Grandma Gloria poured herself a coffee too. She considered the sugar bowl. Then she shook her head, opened a cupboard and pulled out the whiskey. She poured a stiff shot into her coffee. "Bottoms up."

"Can I have one of those too?"

"No, you may not. You have a Thanksgiving to prepare."

Jodie glared at her.

"Stop your sourness, my girl. No one is selling this house."

Jodie held up the papers, which were balled up in a creased mess in her fist. "This says they are."

"No. It says they got a *quote*. And a rather paltry one, by the looks of it. But Pat and I shan't let this happen."

"Good." Jodie smoothed out the dumb quote.

"We'll sell my house instead."

"*What?*"

Grandma Gloria shrugged. "What do I need with a whole house, at my age? It's far too big for me."

"But where will *you* go?" Jodie felt like she was going mad.

Grandma couldn't sell her house. It was her *home*. She'd lived there forever.

"I'll go to Pat's, of course. She doesn't need a whole house to herself either." Grandma Gloria checked her lipstick in the microwave glass. She smoothed out the edges of her lips with a fingernail.

"You can't sell your house," Jodie said miserably.

"Of course I can. It's just a house."

But it *wasn't* just a house. It was the house Jodie had spent afternoons and weekends in through her whole childhood. It was where her first and last memories of Grandad were. It was where Grandma Gloria had made them buttermilk biscuits and cups of hot chocolate with giant marshmallows. It was where she and Bree had carved their initials into the porch posts, down near the bottom, where Grandma had never noticed. To say it was just a house was just *wrong*.

"It seems like a good solution," Claude said calmly, from where she was polishing the cutlery Jodie had dumped on the table. Who polished cutlery? "Would it pay off all the debts?"

"Some of them." Grandma Gloria sighed.

To her horror and embarrassment, Jodie started to cry. She felt like an abandoned toddler. This Thanksgiving was the *worst*.

Chapter 7

It didn't get much better. They were more than an hour late to sit down to dinner, as they had to set up the table before they even began to decorate it, and the turkey took longer to cook than expected. Claude wasn't used to the oven (whatever that meant) and Jodie's parents seemed supremely disinterested in helping. Jodie's dad put the television back on while they waited for the food, and absently watched a replay of the Macy's Thanksgiving Day Parade, accompanied by Russel Sprout, who had draped himself over Jodie's dad's knees. Jodie's mom was still obsessed with Bree's video. At least Gloria had forced her to put her headphones on, so she wouldn't ruin poor Michael Bublé's warbling. Grandma Gloria also confiscated the television remote and kept the TV on mute. Dad didn't seem to care; he just sat like a lump and watched the balloons drift silently down Sixth Avenue in New York.

By the time Jodie had set the table and Pat had a fire going in the living room, the rain was coming down hard. It lashed at the windows and rattled the panes in their frames. The watery light had become a pulsing deep gray.

"Hope the river doesn't flood," Pat said, as she went around turning on lamps. The grim day pressed at the windows, trying to get in.

"A flood would be all we'd need," Gloria agreed, although

she sounded more cheerful about it. She always liked a bit of drama. "We need candles, Jodie. In case the lights go out."

"The lights won't go out," Jodie's mother said sharply, tearing her gaze away from her phone. "They can't. We have to see Bree at five."

Bree's video was getting on Jodie's nerves.

"You'll still see the video, Mom," she snapped. "Your phone will still work, even if the power is out."

"Candles," Gloria reminded Jodie, clicking her fingers at her. "Even if the lights don't go out, we need them to cheer this place up."

"Not on the table," Claudia warned, hovering as Jodie found the candles and went to dump them on the dining table. "The fairy lights in the vases will light the table."

"Cluster them on the sideboard," Gloria instructed. "Clump them, don't spread them out like that."

"Do you two want to do this?"

They did. Jodie stepped back and left them to the Candle Wars. Michael Bublé was singing about feeling good. He clearly didn't know how bad things could get at this time of year.

Through the arch to the living room, Jodie had a clear view of the fire, which was struggling to cut through the gray day. Her parents were at opposite ends of the couch, sitting like zombies in front of their screens. The clatter against the windows signaled the rain was becoming sleet. God, it was grim. Only the scent of the turkey roasting in the oven made it feel like a holiday.

Well, screw that. Thanksgiving dinner was already late—it could wait a bit longer.

At that point Jodie had gone to the garage and dug out the boxes of decorations. She didn't think she could survive without them. As usual, the Christmas lights were in a tangle. Damn it. Couldn't *something* be easy today? She had a go at untangling them, but it was too cold in the garage to mess around. Her fingers were frozen stiff, and the lights were hopelessly knotted. And she couldn't even complain, because it was her fault. She'd been the one to rip all the decorations down last year. Sometime after New Year's she'd torn down all the lights and thrown them into the box. She cursed herself for her laziness now. She couldn't have taken ten minutes to wind them up properly, to spare herself future pain?

It was only as she was putting the box back on the shelf in abject surrender that she remembered the *other* decorations. The ones Bree made them use when she was trying to renew her sponsorship with the coffee company. She'd themed their entire Christmas in the company colors and had banned Mom's colored lights. Instead she had plain white lights—which Mom hated. She said they were too cheerless.

But they were cheerier than nothing. And they'd match Claude's fairy lights, which were also plain white.

Jodie rummaged around till she found the box. It had Bree's loopy writing on it, in thick black marker. *Coffee Lights*, it said. The coffee company *had* renewed sponsorship after all that light-filled online seduction, but only for a couple of months. Enough to pay for Bree's trip to San Francisco, which was all Bree had really wanted. Jodie smiled at the memory, at Bree's bouncy glee. There'd been a fair few carefully placed cups of coffee in her selfies on that trip. #DoubleFrothSkinnyMocha

Poser, Jodie thought affectionately. It should have been annoying, having a sister like Bree. But it never had been. Because Bree had been . . . well, *Bree*. Alight with joy. Her pleasure had been contagious, even when it was over something as simple as holding up a cup of coffee, as the bay sparkled behind her.

Jodie yanked the *Coffee Lights* out and, hallelujah, Bree's lights weren't tangled. They were neatly balled, with the power cords easy to access. Jodie tested them and they all worked. Thank you, Bree.

Claude looked momentarily horrified when Jodie came in from the garage carrying the box, but then her expression smoothed, and she gave an approving nod. "Yes," she said. "Good idea." She poured Jodie yet another cup of coffee and followed her into the living room. Mom and Dad already had mugs on the go. Good. That should kick some life into them.

By the time Jodie had strung lights up, the fire had relaxed into a merry snapping and the day seemed a little less dreary. She flicked the switch and the golden-white lights twinkled on, casting starry reflections in the fogged-up windowpanes. The lights immediately made the room seem cozier.

"Very nice," Gloria said approvingly. She'd set a plate of her traditional cheesy cornbread out, along with Claude's spinach dip, and Pat's bowl of supermarket pretzels. She and Pat had taken the chairs next to the fire and were looking Thanksgiving-ready. Which was more than Jodie could say for her parents.

Gloria had clearly chosen Mom's outfit. She looked like a younger, more rumpled version of Gloria, in colored jeans and a bright sweater. Gloria had whacked some pinkish-purple lipstick on her too. While they were Mom's own clothes, she'd never worn the sweater with the jeans, and Jodie couldn't believe she ever would have done so willingly.

"You look nice, Mom," she lied, as she offered her the plate of cornbread.

"I look like a parrot."

"A nice parrot."

"A parrot let loose in the makeup aisle at Target."

Jodie laughed. That was more like Mom. And at least she'd put the phone down.

"Be grateful you're not in your tracksuit anymore," Gloria observed, crossing her legs primly.

"Joseph's still in his," Jodie's mom said tightly.

"I'm not a miracle worker," Pat snapped. "Be glad that he's clean."

"I can hear you," Jodie's dad rumbled, not looking away from the parade as he reached for a handful of pretzels. "I was clean before."

"Good lord, it speaks," Pat remarked.

"It speaks and it wants a beer." He held his empty mug out to Jodie. "It thought the coffee was too sweet."

"Sweet was what you needed." Pat sniffed.

"Well, they're bickering, so that's a clear improvement," Jodie told Claude, as she got her dad's beer from the fridge.

They kept bickering through the appetizers and all the way to the table and, as Michael Bublé gave way to Jodie's dad's choice, the Eagles (classic Thanksgiving music if she'd ever heard it, Jodie thought with an amused eyeroll), things almost felt like normal. Until they realized that Jodie had accidentally set the table with one extra place setting.

Then silence fell like sudden darkness.

Hell. Bree. She'd set a place for Bree. Jodie went hot and cold with shame. How could she have?

"I'll move it," she mumbled, scooping up the cutlery.

"No," her mom said, "leave it. Please leave it." She sounded a bit desperate. "Don't take her away. It's nice if she's here with us."

But it wasn't nice. Not in the least. Maybe in another year it might have been a bittersweet gesture; it might have led to memories and laughter and some gentle tears. But this year it was like a gaping artery, pumping hot blood.

They tried to get through it. They oohed and aahed over the turkey, which Jodie had paid for and Claudia had cooked to perfection. They tried to eat it—well, everyone except Jodie tried to eat it. She stuck to the sweet potatoes and the mash and to Claudia's ridiculously fancy side dishes: Brussels sprouts with pistachios and lime; squash and radicchio salad with roast chestnuts; shaved carrots with charred dates; parsnips with pickled currants. It should have been a vegetarian's wonderland. Jodie wasn't hungry but she made herself eat. So did everyone else. Soon there was just the sound of cutlery scraping, to the background music of *Eagles Essentials*.

Claudia tried to pour the chardonnay, but no one really took to it. Jodie's dad just got himself another beer and Pat whipped up a round of whiskey sours, which Gloria and Jodie's mom hooked into. Jodie drank the chardonnay, just to get the disappointed look off Claude's face.

"You should open a restaurant, Claude," Jodie said, to break the silence. Although it was also true. Her cooking was out of this world. Who thought to put currants with parsnips? And who knew it would make parsnips taste so *good*?

"Do you know how many restaurants go under?" Claudia replied, shaking her head. "It's too high-risk."

"You can just say 'Thank you for the compliment.'"

"You can just say 'You're a good cook' and then I'd know it was supposed to be a compliment. I thought you were being serious."

"Oh my God, you're difficult. 'You're a good cook.' Happy?"

"Thank you."

They struggled through the rest of the meal, with Gloria and Pat trying to help Jodie keep a fairly lame conversation going. Thankfully they got onto baseball, which Jodie could always find a way to talk about. Even if everyone else's eyes glazed over.

"What time is it?" Jodie's mom asked roughly every twenty minutes. Half the time they ignored her, but it made for a tense meal. It was like there was a doomsday clock ticking. They all knew they were waiting for five o'clock, but couldn't they at least *pretend* otherwise?

"If you want to know the time, look at your phone," Jodie snapped eventually.

"I can't. You took it away. Again."

Jodie gave it back to her. "But if you open that video," she warned, "I'm throwing sweet potato at you."

"I'll use the headphones."

"I'll still throw sweet potato at you."

"Don't waste the sweet potatoes," Gloria scolded. "They're too good. Throw the marshmallow casserole instead." She paused. "No offence, Pat."

"None taken. It's a horrid casserole."

"Then why do you always make it?" Jodie asked, curious.

"Tradition."

"It's four thirty," Jodie's mom interrupted, pushing back from the table.

"Where are you going?"

"I'm getting Bree's old iPad. It's bigger. We'll all be able to see better."

Jodie swore. "This is miserable." She drained her wineglass and held it out to Claudia for a refill.

"It really is," Claudia agreed, pouring liberally.

"You should have one too, you'll need it."

"I'm waiting for the champagne."

Jodie had forgotten the champagne. "What the hell is that for anyway?"

"I'm assuming for the message." Claudia was looking quite wilted. "It was on the shopping list she made, with a note: *You'll know when to open it on the day.* I'm assuming the message is when we're supposed to open it."

Now Jodie really swore.

"Jodie Ann!" Gloria smacked the back of her head. "Ladies don't use language like that."

"Glad I'm not a lady, then."

"I *told* your mother to make you do ballet instead of baseball."

Jodie rolled her eyes. "I can swear just as effectively in a tutu."

"Here!" Jodie's mom came back in with the iPad and started fussing with it, trying to update the Instagram app.

"That's lunch over, then." Jodie started clearing the table. There was a mountain of food left over. "Sorry, Claude."

"Don't apologize to me." She sighed. "I could barely eat a mouthful." Together they cleared and stacked the plates by the sink. "Don't do the dishes now," she scolded Jodie when she went to fill the sink. "You'll miss the message."

"Screw the message. It'll play on a loop for the rest of my life. I'm in no danger of missing it." But she didn't fill the sink.

"Your parents wouldn't happen to have champagne flutes, would they?"

Jodie laughed.

"You can wash the wineglasses, then. But no plates."

When they got back to the table, they found everyone clustered around Jodie's mom, who'd propped the iPad up against one of Claude's gourd-filled vases.

"It's like they think it's a Skype call," Jodie said.

"I guess it's the next best thing."

"Jodie! Turn the music off!"

Fittingly the weather had worsened, Jodie thought grimly as

she dragged her feet to the living room to turn the music off. The wind was moaning and soughing like a restless ghost. Turning the music off only made the wind noises more unsettling. The rain was mixed with the clatter of sleet and hail and there was a branch scratching at the side of the house. Jodie peered outside. The day was gone, replaced with moody darkness. The bushes outside tossed their heads in silhouette against the poisonous orange streetlight.

Please let this rotten holiday be over.

"Jodie! Hurry! You'll miss it."

In her dreams.

Maybe she should go lock herself in the bathroom. Only the house was so small, she'd probably *still* hear the horrid video. Especially since her mom would probably have the volume turned up full.

"You going to open that?" Jodie asked Claudia, gesturing at the champagne.

"*Shhhhhhh,*" her mom hissed, flapping her hand, "it's almost five o'clock."

"I didn't want to interrupt," Claudia whispered. Claudia had started shivering again and she was as pale as milk.

They left the champagne bottle on the table, surrounded by the clean wineglasses. Moisture beaded on the green glass bottle.

Jodie found she was holding her breath as they waited for five o'clock. Mom kept refreshing her Instagram feed, looking for Bree.

Then, abruptly, there she was.

"Happy Thanksgiving!"

Bree had filmed this video late in the game too, by the looks of it, as she was as thin as paper and as transparent as glass. The yellow forsythia was still there behind her, frothing away in all its sunshiny glory. But Bree was less glorious. Her eyes were filmy and set in dark sockets. She was wearing the silk scarf Grandma Gloria had given her, knotted around her post-chemo bare head. The jewel-bright colors (purple, pink, green and blue) only made her skin look grayer, and the whites of her eyes yellower. When she spoke, there were lines around her mouth, like she was an old woman.

Jodie wrapped her arms around herself. God. This was ghoulish. She felt sick to her stomach and wished she hadn't just eaten all those sweet potatoes and parsnips.

"I hope there are lots of you watching." Bree waved at the screen. Her hand was skeletal. "Hopefully, I'm still popping up in your Instagram feed, even though I've been gone for a while now. I hope you don't mind, but I paid to boost some old posts, so I'd be visible again. So you'd see this special Thanksgiving post."

Gone for a while now . . . She'd known she was going to die. Even while the forsythia bloomed behind her and they all came in bearing gifts, assuring her things would be fine. Why was that so horrific? Jodie had to clench her teeth to stop from making a noise. Claudia took her arm and squeezed it tight.

"I need you all to watch because I have a *huuuuuuuuuge* favor to ask," Bree said. She was propped up in her hospital bed, looking like even sitting was an effort. But she still managed to smile. "I need you all to *keep* watching. As many of you as can. But this is going to take longer than sixty seconds, so I need you to click on the link in bio if you want to see the rest." She blew a kiss. Then the video restarted. "Happy Thanksgiving!"

Judging by the likes building up under her video, and the cascade of heart emojis, people *were* watching. What ghouls people could be.

They were probably clicking on the link in Bree's bio too, just like Mom was.

It took them to Bree's webpage, which had been inactive for a very long time. But now there was a video on the homepage.

"Thanks for joining me here!" Bree said, as soon as Mom pressed play. "I really appreciate it. I hope more and more of you come and watch this over the next little while and help me out with this little project."

Little project? *What* little project?

"People think dying is scary," Bree said, staring straight into the camera. She must have propped it up on her dinner tray. She certainly wouldn't have been able to hold it up by this stage. She was breathing like she'd run a marathon, just from sitting up in bed and talking.

Jodie's mom made a whimpering noise, and from the corner of her eye, Jodie saw Grandma Gloria place a hand on her mom's head, like she was a little girl. Jodie's mom leaned back into her own mother's body, for comfort. Jodie felt each and every one of her mother's whimpers in her bones. Watching her parents suffer was like being stuck with coal-hot needles. Jodie's heart was pounding so hard she could barely hear over it.

"And it *is*," Bree continued. "It is scary. It *was* scary. I was really scared at first, when I realized . . . that I couldn't get out of this one. That there wasn't any hope left."

Jodie's dad started crying now. He covered his face with his hands and gave in to big ugly sobs. And that set everyone off. Jodie's mom put her hand on the back of his neck but couldn't look away from the screen. She paused the video until he'd quieted down. Once he'd wiped his face on his sleeve and sat back up, nodding bravely, she started it again.

"But, you know"—Bree continued speaking, unable to see or hear their pain; they could pause her, but they couldn't stop her, because all of this had already happened, many months ago—"I was really just scared of the *not* knowing. Not knowing how it would feel, if it would hurt, how I would cope . . ."

Jodie had been dreading this video—but it was worse than she ever could have imagined. How was *this* a Thanksgiving video? It was more appropriate for goddamn Halloween.

"The closer I get, though," Bree said, melting back into her pillow, "the less scared I am."

She was telling the truth. Jodie already knew Bree hadn't been scared at the end, because she'd seen her through those last days. In person. She'd been there, sitting the horrendous death watch. She'd seen the complete and utter exhaustion, the overwhelming pain, which could only be drowned out by such huge doses of morphine that Bree wasn't really present at all. By the end, death had become a better alternative to life. To *that* life. It had been a release, a relief, a setting free. But a joyless one.

"I'm not scared for *me* at all," Bree said, staring through time, straight at them. "I'm scared for my family."

Jodie's mom let out a strangled sob.

Bree's eyes were suspiciously shiny. Jodie didn't think she could bear to see her cry. It would snap her in two.

Screw this. This was torture. Jodie flinched and almost ran for the kitchen. But Claude kept her arm held tight and wouldn't let her go.

"This is going to be so hard for you." Bree was talking to *them* directly now. Her family. "I hate the thought of you all in pain. I know you must be suffering."

She had no idea.

"I also know what a burden I've become."

"No," Jodie's mom wailed. "Not ever. Not *ever.*"

"I know the medical bills are insane." Bree pulled a face. "And that's my fault, because I never got a proper job and I never had any insurance."

Her fault? Jodie felt cold at the thought. What kind of country let someone die like this? What kind of country didn't let someone in the prime of their life get medical treatment without bankrupting them and everyone they knew? What kind of government made you pay and pay and pay, even after someone died?

"I should have sold the house while she was alive!" Grandma Gloria whispered. "I should have."

Pat hugged her tight. They were like a string of plastic monkeys, each one taking the other one in hand.

"My parents never once complained," Bree continued, mercilessly. "They got up and went to work; they took on extra shifts; they took out loans on their 401(k). My sister gave up her apartment and moved home to help with the bills. My grandma handed over most of her retirement money."

She had? Jodie hadn't known that.

"My Aunt Pat even sold her car."

"I thought you said you sold it because your doctor wouldn't let you drive anymore!" Jodie blurted, shocked.

"She would have stopped me, eventually." Pat blew her nose

loudly into a tissue, and then handed the box around. They all took tissues.

"But none of it even comes close to what it cost to try and save me." Bree's smile was sad. "I want you to know it mattered, though. That I was always deeply grateful."

"We know," Jodie's mom whimpered.

"I also know you *can't* pay off my debts. That without help, you'll lose the house . . . and everything."

Jodie started crying in earnest. Everything? They'd already lost everything, the day they lost Bree.

"Well, I can't have that." Bree smiled. She looked like a ghost in her own skin. "Which is where my Instagram friends come in."

Don't you dare ask them for money, Jodie thought in horror.

But she didn't. She did something far worse.

Something that involved Jodie.

"You all know what this is?" Bree reached off camera for something.

"Oh God, it's her bucket list," Claudia said, before Bree had even brought the damn thing into the shot.

And it was. It was her bucket list, written on the back of that stupid "Chili's kids" placemat. The front had a maze on it; the back was filled with Bree's loopy letters. The rectangle of paper was ragged and creased. She'd kept it in her wallet for a decade.

"I started this list when I was sixteen years old, in a booth at my local Chili's, with my BFF Claudia."

Now it was Claude's turn to flinch and try to leave. Jodie didn't let her. If she had to watch this, so did Claude.

"I'd been to the career fair at school and was told I'd make a great hairdresser." She rolled her eyes. Then gave a weak breath of a laugh. "Not that there's anything wrong with hairdressers. I *loooove* my hairdresser. Or I did." Her hand went to the silk scarf covering her bald head. "Not so in love with this look."

What was she up to? Jodie had no idea where this was going . . . but she had a bad feeling.

"I was determined to do something with my life. I knew there was more for me than Wilmington, as much as I love my hometown. I knew I wanted more than hairdressing or the

Pepsi factory or working a desk job. I just felt there was . . .
more somehow." Bree looked down at the back of the placemat. "That day I started my bucket list. At first, I only had
five things on there, the fifth of which was to graduate college.
Which I did," she said proudly. "First person in my family to
do so."

She hadn't just graduated, she'd made the honors list.

"Over the years I managed to finish ninety-four items on
this list!" Even wasted away and close to death, there was a
glow about Bree as she gazed down at her list. Memories chased
across her expression, like shoals of shadowy fish passing beneath the surface of a pond. "I guess I must have known time
would be short." She looked up again and the look of loss on
her face was profound. She turned the placemat around so the
camera could see the list. "I have six items left. Six I will never
finish. I know them by heart . . ." She began to recite them:

*17. Plant a tree that will live long after I'm gone. Some-
thing shady. That also has blossoms. (I can't quite believe
I never got to this one—it seems the easiest.)*

*39. Find Mr. Wong and finally have those piano les-
sons Mom and Dad paid for that I never took (long
story).*

*73. Eat a sandwich at Katz's deli in New York and
simulate the orgasm scene from* When Harry Met Sally.
Make sure to take someone to play Harry.

*74. Perform a walk-on cameo in a Broadway musical
(multitasking while I'm in New York—but probably best
to do this on a different day than number seventy-three,
as I don't think nerves and pastrami will go well together).*

*99. Fly over Antarctica (that's a thing people do—it's
very expensive but Iris Air have agreed to sponsor the
trip. It also means I get to add a bonus trip to Sydney,
Australia! I should have put that as number one hundred,
I guess, but I have another one I want to do last . . .)*

100. Fall in love.

Jodie had thought she couldn't cry harder than she'd cried when Bree died, but here she was, setting a new record. And she wasn't alone.

"This list," Bree told them, holding it up, "is how I'm going to save my family. Or rather, how my little sister is going to save my family."

That stopped the tears. *What?*

"I refuse to die without knowing this list will be completed. And I refuse to die without knowing my family will be okay. I will *not* be the ruin of you. I just *won't*. Jodie?" Bree leaned into the camera. "I know you're watching. I also know you'll pitch a fit about this. But you're my best shot. Iris Air has agreed to sponsor you to finish this list." Bree held the list up again.

Jodie wasn't crying anymore. She wasn't even breathing anymore. What in hell was her crazy sister talking about?

"They will fly you to New York; they will fly you to Antarctica. I bequeath you my Instagram account and all my followers. My dying wish is for you to finish my bucket list. Each time you finish an item, Iris Air will pay off some of my debts. And if you complete the entire list *and* manage to keep all my Instagram followers, they will pay off *all* of my medical debts. If you not only keep my followers, but manage to increase them, they will pay a thousand dollars toward the debts of every patient who was on my ward."

What the *hell?*

"I'm counting on you, Jodie," Bree said, her gaze unwavering. "Don't let me down."

"She can't be serious."

"Cheryl from Iris Air will be emailing you tomorrow with the password to my account and all the details." Bree smiled again and it sent ice through Jodie's veins. She *couldn't* be serious. "Happy Thanksgiving. You can open that champagne now, Claude." Her smile became a grin. "I love you all."

The video ended.

"Were they giving her *crack* in that hospital?" Jodie exploded. "If she thinks I'm doing the things on that stupid list, she's got another thing coming!" Singing on Broadway! Faking public orgasms! Flying to Antarctica! She *hated* flying. And what kind of sociopathic corporation thought *this* was a good look for them? Why not just donate the damn money? She turned to the family, only to find them all smiling. Laughing. Joyful.

"Oh my God, she's saved us." Mom was sobbing. "She's *saved* us."

Jodie's stomach sank all the way to her toes. "Now, hold on a minute."

But it was too late. They were popping the champagne. And as it sank in, Jodie felt a surreal mix of dread and relief. Relief because, oh my, they might be able to crawl out from under those medical bills . . . Dread because . . . piano lessons and all the rest of it.

Bree . . . you have no idea what you're asking of me.

This wasn't just a list. This was *everything.* This was everyone's future: her house, Grandma Gloria's house, her parents' retirement . . . Everyone was depending on her.

Jodie would do anything for Bree, and she'd do *everything* for her family.

Chapter 8
17. Plant a Tree

Jodie

Cheryl, the Iris Air representative, was a shiny coin of a person, with a knack for talking in marketing-speak. And she treated Jodie like she was a performing poodle. Jodie knew she was being unkind, and unfair, but she didn't care. It felt good to be unfair. Cheryl made her uncomfortable from the first, and Jodie hated being uncomfortable. Jodie felt drab and awkward and tarnished next to the woman's shininess. Cheryl had blown in the week after Thanksgiving, on a company plane, and come marching straight up to Jodie's car-rental booth. She'd barreled past the queue and slid directly in front of Jodie the moment the customer she was serving left with his key. Cheryl had given Jodie a brilliant smile and offered her deepest, most heartfelt, *sincerest* sympathies. (This was unfair too—Cheryl had probably been sincere.) For a moment Jodie couldn't understand why this sleek woman was apologizing to her. She hadn't been expecting Cheryl, so it took her a minute to realize who she was. In fact, she only realized because Cheryl slid her crisp business card along the counter. *Cheryl Pegler, Deputy Executive Assistant, Marketing, Iris Air.* Jodie stared at the card with rising dismay. Oh no.

Cheryl had emailed, as promised, and then she'd called, and now she was *here*.

Jodie had thought she'd been very clear with Cheryl on the phone: they could start the bucket list after New Year's.

"This is going to be the adventure of a lifetime!" Cheryl gushed, sliding quickly past deep, heartfelt and sincere sympathy and into sparkling enthusiasm. If you wanted to brand enthusiasm, you'd give it Cheryl's face. She was like a cross between Miss America and a TV executive's idea of a corporate lawyer (still very unfair; still not feeling guilty about it). When Cheryl smiled, her teeth were as white as mints against her fire-engine-red lips. And she smiled a lot. More with her mouth than with her eyes. Her eyes tended to dart around, taking stock.

"You'll need a makeover," she announced that first day they met in person at the car-rental counter. She'd didn't seem to care that Jodie still had customers waiting. "After we spoke on the phone, I assumed you might, so I've gone ahead and made bookings."

"Bookings?" Jodie said, taken aback. "Wait. What? How did you know I'd need a makeover just from talking to me on the phone?" Jodie felt too ambushed to even register the insult. Her head was spinning. She'd *definitely* told Cheryl to wait until the new year . . .

On the phone that day after Thanksgiving, Jodie had been expecting Cheryl to hand over the passwords for Bree's account and to let her get on with things—but that clearly hadn't been the plan. Jodie had stood in the kitchen, the phone clamped to her ear, her back resolutely to her family, who were eavesdropping madly. Her stomach had been in knots as she accepted the call from the unknown number. She'd known who it was, because the email that had come from Iris Air that morning hadn't included Bree's passwords or any instructions, it had just told her that Cheryl would be phoning her. She gave a precise time and called on the dot. After expressing her sympathy, Cheryl had swept right over Jodie, talking a mile a minute, bombarding her with a slightly nauseating mix of compassion and enthusiasm. And it was only after she'd hung up the phone that Jodie had realized that she *still* didn't have the passwords. All she had was a vague sense of vertigo. And now a week later Cheryl came marching in, in person, on her sky-high heels, with her mint-white smile, talking about makeovers and bookings, and a whole bunch of other things that Jodie couldn't quite take in. Things like baselines and bounce rates and engagements. None of it seemed to have anything to do with Bree or her bucket list.

"Do you need a car?" Jodie asked dumbly, watching the woman as though she was an escaped zoo animal. A dangerous one. She must be here for a car. Why else would she be standing here at the counter? It made *no sense*. They'd said after *New Year's*.

Cheryl smiled. Or rather, she *kept* smiling. Because she never really ever stopped. It was possible that the smile was Botoxed in place (definitely unkind; Cheryl looked naturally dewy fresh).

"Amusing." Cheryl laughed and tapped the back of Jodie's hand playfully with her red talons. "I'll wait here for you. As I said, I've made bookings." She checked the time on her phone. "You finish at four?"

"How did you know that?" Jodie had a sinking feeling. Something seemed to have slipped out of kilter. What had started as a normal day was feeling a bit nightmarish.

"I spoke to your boss. You've got some time off." Cheryl was way too pleased with herself.

"You what? I what?"

It was like being hit by a hurricane. Hurricane Cheryl. And she was at least a category five storm. Maybe higher. Did they go higher? If they didn't, they should.

"I can't afford time off," Jodie told her tightly.

"Paid leave, of course." Cheryl's smile was like a shield. "The rental company has come on as a sponsor. They're also giving us car rental whenever we need it. We just have to make sure we get the logo in shot. Shouldn't be hard. It's bright, isn't it?" She squinted at Jodie's neon-green shirt. "It's going to take time to finish this list, you can't possibly keep working." Cheryl had a picture of Bree's list on her phone. She zoomed in and held it up for Jodie to see. "This won't happen overnight; if we wait for your days off, it'll take us fifty years."

The sight of Bree's handwriting on the back of that placemat made Jodie's stomach fall out of her body.

"Your boss was very sympathetic," Cheryl said cheerfully. "And aware of the opportunities for the brand. So was your head office. They're sending you off with all the best wishes they can muster. Expressed on every platform, I imagine."

Jodie was having trouble keeping up. There was still a line of customers waiting to be served, and they were annoyed. Music festooned the moment with canned Christmas carols, which didn't help. It was all too surreal. Jodie stepped sideways so Cheryl wasn't blocking her, and gave the next customer a strained smile. "Yes, ma'am?"

Cheryl stopped talking for a moment. But only to take in the queue of cranky-looking customers. Jodie saw her job through Cheryl's eyes and winced. It was about as far from glamor as it was possible to get. Philly International was teeming with holiday traffic, gaudy with the plastic glitz of tinsel and baubles, scented with stale coffee, French fries and cleaning fluid, and drab with the reality of transit. Holidays were lovely; airports were not. Announcements cut through the Christmas music regularly, paging late customers in a flat, humorless monotone.

"I ordered an SUV." The woman who stepped up to the counter was rumpled from her flight and pulled a stroller with her. In the stroller there was a toddler, gumming on a chocolate bar, looking immensely self-satisfied. Jodie knew that look. She'd seen hundreds of toddlers with that look. It was the expression of a kid who'd thrown a colossal tantrum getting off the plane and had been bribed with candy. The kid's mother now had frayed nerves and a hair-trigger temper.

"Don't mind me," Cheryl told Jodie, blithely unaware of the temper, or the frayed woman who was barely containing it. Cheryl wheeled her compact travel bag around behind the counter.

"What are you doing?" Jodie watched as the coin-bright woman stowed her luggage under Jodie's desk.

"It's under the name Channing," Jodie's current customer, the rumpled mother, said tightly, irritated by Cheryl's constant interruptions. "I ordered the new model SUV with the child seats. My husband's taken Oliver to the bathroom. He had an accident."

Jodie winced. The SUV the woman had booked wasn't back in the parking lot yet. Jodie only had a sedan or a minivan to offer her. She was in the middle of explaining the situation to the increasingly irate woman, when she realized that Cheryl was taking photos.

"What are you doing?" Jodie asked, appalled.

"Getting some 'before' shots. People will want to see you in your real life. Before it all changes. You're like Cinderella in the cinders."

The frayed mother wasn't pleased with the interruption. "Do you *mind*?" There went the temper. The frayed woman was firing now. Jodie snapped back to attention before she caused a scene at the booth. *More* of a scene.

Cheryl managed to get some hair-raising footage of the travel-shattered mother tearing strips off Jodie.

"This will be perfect for the launch," Cheryl said, satisfied, once the woman had stalked off, with the key to a minivan at a discount price. "You'll have everyone's sympathy. Not that you didn't already," she added, hastily, aware that Jodie was still grieving.

"What launch?" Jodie demanded. "And why are you here? We said after *New Year's*."

"Think of me as your guide, Jodie." Cheryl gave her a kind minty-toothed smile.

"Guide to *what*?"

"To maximizing this experience, for you and your followers."

"Followers? This isn't a reality show. And I don't have any followers."

"For Bree's followers," Cheryl amended.

Jodie forced a smile for the next customer. But Cheryl wasn't going anywhere. As Jodie served the impatient queue, Cheryl held forth. Apparently she could "facilitate a smoother process" and "iron out kinks," she could "finesse the details" and "amp up the smart content."

"Smart content?" Jodie gave her another appalled look. "These are my sister's last wishes. It's not a marketing campaign."

"Of course not." For the second time Cheryl's minty teeth disappeared and she looked suitably grave. "Iris Air is passionate about honoring your sister's memory"—her voice caught and for a minute Jodie thought she might cry—"and so am I."

The woman was a ghoul, Jodie decided, in no mood to accept her sympathy or her kindness. She didn't want to be sympathized with; she wanted to be left alone.

"The makeover won't cost you a cent," Cheryl promised Jodie.

"I don't want a makeover."

"Not. A. Cent."

Jodie messaged Claudia. **There's a crazy woman here from Iris. She's talking makeovers. Help.**

What do you mean?

Jodie stared at Claudia's message, wondering how to even begin explaining Cheryl.

That woman. From the airline. Cheryl. She's here. Now. HELP ME.

Help you what? Get a makeover?

No. Not get a makeover. Jodie's thumbs hovered. She had no idea what to type back. What did she expect Claude to do?

She was trapped. No one could help her.

Maybe Cheryl didn't see how weird and inappropriate it was to barrel into someone's place of work and threaten them with a makeover. Maybe if Jodie explained to her . . .

But how? How did you tell Marketing Barbie that you didn't want a free haircut and a manicure? How did you explain that you just wanted to be *left alone*?

Jodie did her best to resist, she really did, but Hurricane Cheryl was irresistible. She whisked Jodie away from the booth as soon as Nena turned up for the afternoon shift. And careened Jodie toward the taxi rank.

"I've got a car," Jodie protested hotly, yanking her arm away from Cheryl's taloned grip.

Cheryl's eyes widened. "Fabulous! That's going to save time. Lead the way!"

Somehow Jodie found herself leading the way. In some ways Cheryl reminded Jodie of Bree. She'd never been able to stand up to Hurricane Bree either . . .

Jodie had so many questions. When had Bree first met Cheryl? Whose idea had this crazy bucket list thing been? Bree's or Cheryl's? When was the last time they'd spoken? What had Bree said? Why had she chosen Jodie to finish the list? Jodie: the least Instagrammable Boyd of all.

She could have picked Claudia. She *should* have picked Claudia. Bree and Claudia were as close as sisters; Claudia would have done it for her. And Claudia was more photogenic than a cover model; she would have made Iris Air very happy. But the question Jodie couldn't shake, and the one she was too scared to ask, was *why hadn't Bree told Jodie about this plan?* Jodie was her *sister.* Why hadn't Bree felt she could tell Jodie about Cheryl, about the bucket list? About her worries over the debts, and her worries over the family.

But also . . . the bone-juddering guilt and regret . . . why hadn't *Jodie* asked Bree about her worries when she was still alive? Maybe if she'd pushed her on some of these things, Bree would have spilled the beans. And surely that would have felt better than sitting alone with all of this? Better than taking her secrets with her to the grave?

That was the thing about death, it put someone out of reach forever. You could never, ever ask them a question, ever again. And now that Bree was gone, there were so many questions Jodie wished she could ask her . . .

"Did you know my sister well?" Jodie asked softly, eyeing Cheryl as they reached Jodie's old Honda Civic.

"This is yours?" Cheryl cocked her head and took in the modest hatchback.

Jodie sighed. "Yeah, this is mine." She was painfully conscious of her stiff ugly uniform and battered ski jacket next to Cheryl's power suit and luxuriant winter coat. Cheryl had called her Cinderella, still in the cinders. But she wasn't Cinderella. At best she was one of the house mice. One of the ones that got turned into a horse to pull the carriage. There was no prince and no ball for her.

Just a battered old Honda Civic.

Jodie bet Cheryl drove a fancy car, like an Audi or something. Jodie wondered if she'd even sat in a Honda Civic before . . . let alone an old one. One day Jodie would own something that wasn't thirdhand, she thought, as she put Cheryl's luggage in the trunk. But for now, at least she owned her car outright, and it ran. It was clean too. Jodie lifted her chin. Her car was nothing to be ashamed of.

"It's perfect." Cheryl had her phone up again and was snapping pictures.

Jodie ducked into the driver's seat to get away from her. But Cheryl was unperturbed and snapped another one as she slid into the passenger side.

"They're going to *love* you," Cheryl promised. She was fiddling about on the phone.

"You're not posting any of those," Jodie said in horror. She was at the end of a holiday-season shift and was looking her worst. Her hair was a limp mess, her unflattering uniform was rumpled, and she had all the energy of a deflated balloon. "Please don't."

"I'm not posting anything yet. I need to finesse things first."

Jodie gave her a sharp look. "I think we need to talk."

"We can talk while you drive. Let me just look up the address. It's in Philadelphia."

"Your hotel?" Jodie was hopeful.

"The salon."

The salon. For Pete's sake.

"Look, Cheryl, I'm sure you're very good at your job, and I know you're just here to help." Although Jodie didn't think their ideas of "helping" were at all the same. "But this is a really difficult time for me and my family."

Cheryl's face contorted into a look of deep, heartfelt, sincere sympathy again. "Oh, I know. Your mother told me how hard it's been."

"Wait. What? She what?" Jodie couldn't keep her footing with this woman. "You spoke to my *mother*?"

"Several times. You don't think I'd waltz in and disrupt her life without talking to her? She just lost her daughter." Cheryl clicked her tongue. "What do you take me for?"

"What did you talk to my mother about?" Jodie felt a stupid twinge of envy. Bree had spoken to Cheryl and now Mom was speaking to Cheryl . . . Why wasn't anyone speaking to Jodie?

"About you mostly."

"Me?"

"And about what kind of tree she wanted you to plant. We thought it would be nice to plant Bree's tree in your yard. *Plant a tree that will live long after I'm gone. Something shady. That also has blossoms.* Obviously, we didn't want to plant anything your mother wouldn't approve of."

Oh. Why hadn't Mom said anything about Cheryl? Or the tree? Why hadn't she asked Jodie what kind of tree would be nice in the yard? After all, Jodie was the one who was going to plant it.

"Here, this is where we're going." Cheryl tapped her phone and it started giving Jodie directions.

"Fishtown?" Jodie gave her a dubious look. "Are you sure?"

Cheryl looked momentarily nervous but then shook it off. "Yes, I'm sure. Look, Manatee, Frankford Avenue, Fishtown."

"Manatee?"

"You've heard of it?" Cheryl brightened. "It gets amazing reviews."

Of course Jodie hadn't heard of it. Did she look like she'd been to a salon lately? Or ever. "*Manatee?* As in the sea mammal?"

"It's a Pantone color, apparently. That's what their website says. They're all about color."

"What color is manatee?" Jodie asked dryly, as she drove out of the parking lot.

"Gray."

"I'm not coloring my hair," Jodie told her firmly. And then she realized she'd just implicitly agreed to the whole makeover thing.

"Of course not. We want you to look like you." Cheryl gave her a minty smile. "But a couple of highlights wouldn't go astray." She cocked her head. "Or maybe lowlights?"

"What kind of tree did Mom say she wanted?" Jodie changed the subject. She wasn't getting highlights or lowlights or any kind of lights, so there was no point in even talking about it. "And can you even plant a tree now?" Jodie peered out into the gloomy evening. The windshield wipers dragged against the sleet. "It's December."

"Your mother has her heart set on a dogwood, so long as we get one that doesn't get too big."

A dogwood? Why a dogwood? That seemed weirdly specific. "I think you have to plant trees in spring," Jodie said, feeling like she was on a runaway train. "Wouldn't the ground be too cold to plant now?"

"That's why I'm here, instead of waiting until the new year, like you wanted. We need to plant right now, or we'll miss the window."

Jodie thought she detected a faint sigh.

"If we wait any longer there's no way we could plant any-thing," Cheryl continued. "We wouldn't even be able to dig a hole. I wanted to beat the freeze." This time there was definitely a sigh. "I've picked out a dogwood and the tag says *late fall*. So, we should be fine. So long as we do it immediately. After all, it was still fall last week."

"You picked the tree already?" Jodie felt a stab. "You didn't think I'd like to be involved?"

Cheryl looked surprised. "Your mother thought it would be best if I helped."

Jodie felt more than just a stab. Right in the gut. Didn't Mom even trust her to pick a tree? Well, damn it, *Bree* had trusted her. Bree hadn't left the bucket list to Mom, she'd left it to Jodie.

God knew Jodie didn't ask for it, and it filled her with fear and dread, but she was *doing it*. Jodie felt tears rising. She fought them back. No self-pity allowed.

"Please don't do things without me," she told Cheryl tightly. "This is *my* bucket list. And don't consult anyone but me."

"Fair enough." Cheryl looked kind of relieved. "I have a picture of the tree here somewhere." She flicked through photos on her phone. "It's a red twig dogwood. I figured it'll pop in the shots, even though it doesn't have any foliage. I was a bit worried any tree we could find at this time of year would be drab, but this one is eye-catching."

It'll pop in the shots.

Jodie cleared her throat. "It sounds fine. I'll look at it." She paused. "Thank you."

She darted a glance at the photo of the dogwood when they stopped at the next traffic light. Denuded of leaves, it was a bristle of bright red stalks. Like a little kid had drawn leafless branches with a scarlet crayon.

"This is what the blossoms will look like." Cheryl flicked the photo sideways. The next image showed a ball made up of dozens of tiny white flowers. The individual flowers were delicate, but clumped together they blazed white against the kelly-green leaves.

"Bree would like that," Jodie said through a tightening throat. "She loved flowers." She loved everything. That was the thing about Bree. She saw beauty everywhere. "I think she'd really love the red branches too."

"They're amazing, aren't they? I almost hope it snows, even though it'll make it hard to dig the hole. The red would look stunning against snow." She peered out at the winter sky. Darkness had fallen and the streetlights illuminated a ceiling of cloud. Sleet was spitting.

Fishtown winked and glittered with Christmas lights and good cheer. The old town was festooned with decorations and there were Christmas-themed pop-up bars and an old-fashioned tree stand full of Christmas trees.

"Why did you think this wasn't the place for me?" Cheryl asked curiously. Her face was bathed in the twinkling light.

"You look more upmarket. This is for hipsters."

Cheryl gave her a cheeky look. "You haven't seen me out of work hours."

"Are you ever out of work hours?"

Cheryl laughed. "Not this month!"

"Your destination is on the left," Siri's weirdly warm robotic voice informed them.

The salon was in an old brick warehouse; *Manatee* was spray painted on the brick frontage in ornate graffiti. There were a couple of broken mannequins in Christmas hats out the front. They were naked other than the hats and were tied together in a quirky embrace with red and green lights.

"Here we are!" Cheryl checked the time on her phone. "Before we get started, I just need to go through some paperwork with you. We have twenty minutes until the appointment."

"Paperwork?" Jodie felt a spasm of dread. That didn't sound good.

"Let's grab a hot drink and do it inside in the warmth."

"What kind of paperwork?" Jodie chased after Cheryl, who was already out of the car and plowing toward a pop-up bar on the corner.

The door to the bar was framed with candy canes and the interior was a mad explosion of red and white tinsel. Cheryl ordered them a couple of hot cocktails, buoyantly called Sugar Plum Fairies, and took over a bench under a twirling mobile of actual candy canes. The candy canes clicked together as they spun in the air flowing from the heating ducts. Jodie wondered if the bar had been one of Claudia's jobs. Probably not. Claude would have used less tinsel.

Cheryl pulled a folder from her bag and flipped it open.

"Are these legal documents?" Jodie asked nervously. "Am I going to need advice?"

Cheryl's minty smile got mintier. "Nothing that scary. Just some media releases."

Jodie was glad Cheryl had ordered them spiked drinks. She needed the fortification. The Sugar Plum Fairy was a rum-laced hibiscus and berry tea. It was bright pink. Jodie was unsure about it, but the rum helped win her over.

Cheryl ran her through Bree's agreement with Iris Air, which was kind of legally binding, only Bree was dead and so couldn't be held to account anymore, so now Jodie was signing all of the same forms. It was scary. She felt like she was signing her life away. Which she kind of was . . .

Her mind spun as she listened to Cheryl talk about flights to New York, the deal with the theater on Broadway, the trip over Antarctica . . .

"I'm thinking New Year's Eve," Cheryl mused. "Don't you think that would be an amazing way to ring in the New Year, flying over Antarctica?"

Antarctica. Last year Jodie had spent New Year's at Bree's bedside, watching the fireworks on television. The year before, she'd spent it on her mother's couch, watching the fireworks on television. Pretty much every New Year's for her entire life had been spent watching the fireworks on television.

"Hopefully we've rustled up somebody for you to kiss by then . . ." Cheryl winked. "After all, we have to get to the final item on the list."

100. Fall in love . . .

Jodie drained her Sugar Plum Fairy. How on earth was she going to tick that one off? There weren't enough cocktails in the world to convince her that was possible.

Chapter 9

"It will be just like *The Bachelorette*," Cheryl promised. She seemed to think that was a *good* thing. She treated herself to a pedicure while Jodie was being groomed like a prize poodle. Cheryl was reclining, with her feet soaking in a great big sink of scented water, curls of lemongrass and basil steam rising lazily into Manatee's cavernous gray interior. The place was so stark it still looked like the warehouse it used to be. The mirrors were rimmed with lightbulbs, like backstage makeup mirrors, and there was a soaring arrangement of stripped willow branches cobwebbed with fairy lights, but otherwise the place was full of dramatic shadows and empty rafters.

Jodie had been waxed and washed, plucked and painted, by two very silent and very intimidating girls. Pet had thick black glasses and half a shaved head (the other half of her head was a mess of turquoise curls); Giselle had silver-white hair so straight it looked ironed, and her arms were sleeves of intricate tattoos. They were too cool. They made Jodie anxious. Luckily, they didn't deign to speak to her. They just went about their business.

"Don't change her," Cheryl had instructed them on arrival. "Just make her a fresher version of *this*. She needs to pop in photos."

Pop. Like the red twig dogwood.

"No one wants to see Cinderella in a ball gown at the *begin-*

ning of the story," Cheryl warned. Then she'd lounged back and enjoyed her foot bath and pedicure, keeping a somnolent eye on Jodie.

"You're not already in love, are you?" Cheryl asked as she watched Pet pluck a hair from Jodie's chin. Jodie had never even noticed that she *had* chin hair. It turned out she not only had it, but she had enough of it to keep Pet busy for a good few minutes.

"No," Jodie mumbled. She kept her eyes scrunched closed.

"Good, because that would ruin all the fun. Although it might make things quicker."

Jodie had thought she was in love once in her life, and it had been a disaster . . . She didn't relish doing it again. It had hurt like hell.

"I'll throw some eligibles in your way, don't fret," Cheryl continued cheerily. "I've already started compiling a list."

Jodie felt her stomach churning. A list? Oh God, she could only imagine the kinds of men Cheryl would include on a list. None of them would be men Jodie would pick. They wouldn't be men like . . .

No. Don't think about him.

Why couldn't Bree have put "swim with dolphins" as the last thing on the list? Why did it have to be something so impossible as *fall in love*?

It wouldn't have been impossible for Bree, of course. If she'd lived, she would have found a prince. Probably a real one, knowing Bree.

Jodie felt the airless suck of grief again, like a riptide pulling her from shore. Bree should be the one here finishing the list; *she* should be the one falling in love. Jodie should be the one . . .

"Do you need a break?"

Jodie just about jumped out of her skin when Pet spoke. She opened her eyes to see the half-bald, half-turquoise girl giving her a kind look. Jodie shook her head. But she realized to her horror that tears were leaking out of the corners of her eyes.

"We're just about done with the tweezers," Pet promised.

But it wasn't the tweezers causing the tears.

Jodie rubbed the tears away and took a breath. She was fine.

By the time they were done with her, she was more than fine. She stared at the woman in the mirror in shock. She looked the same but . . . better. Like an airbrushed, hypercolored version of herself. Her eyebrows were strongly arched and tinted a darker shade than her hair, which was glossy and subtly streaked, so the curls seemed sun-kissed, glinting with gold light. She looked . . . well, *good*.

"Perfect," Cheryl said. "We'll take the tinted moisturizer and lip gloss you used. That's all the makeup she'll need. We don't want to gild the lily."

Not to mention the fact that Jodie wasn't about to apply makeup even if Cheryl bought it. She was terrible at it. She always looked like a preschooler who'd got into her mom's makeup drawer. But, she conceded, as she took in the dewy glow of her reflection, she could probably cope with some tinted moisturizer.

"You like it?" Cheryl asked, her minty smile self-satisfied.

Yes, to her great surprise, Jodie did like it.

And so did her mom.

Mom couldn't stop touching Jodie's hair. It was OK for the first hour or so, but after a while it got wearing.

Cheryl had joined them for dinner and there had been more signing of release forms—this time by Mom, Dad, Grandma Gloria and Aunt Pat. And by Claude, when she turned up after dinner, bringing a pineapple upside-down cake with her. Claude eyed Cheryl warily. They were like two glossy tigresses sizing each other up.

"Does Russel Sprout need to sign one of these too?" Pat asked, squinting down at the forms.

"Who's Russel Sprout?" Cheryl looked around, as though expecting Aunt Pat had an errant husband.

"She's joking," Mom assured Cheryl, passing her a cup of coffee. "Russel Sprout is just the dog."

"He's not just a dog, he's part of the family." Pat was offended.

He was the part of the family intent on destroying Jodie's

shoes. He was currently in the doorway, snout deep in Jodie's running shoes.

"Oh, how cute." Cheryl pulled out her phone and snapped a picture.

"I can drive you to your hotel on my way home," Claudia told Cheryl brightly. Jodie could tell she was dying to get Marketing Barbie alone. She radiated possessive hostility. There weren't enough chairs for Claude, so she was standing at the counter, still fiddling with the cake knife.

"No need to worry, honey," Mom said, "Cheryl's staying here with us."

"She's not staying with us." Jodie couldn't believe how nuts her family was becoming. Did Marketing Barbie look like she belonged here? Dear God, imagine her using their shower, with its chipped tiles and supermarket shampoo. "She has an expense account," Jodie told her mom. "She'd rather stay in a hotel, I'm sure."

"No, I'd rather stay here." Cheryl beamed at them, all cherry-red lips and white teeth.

Why didn't her lipstick ever come off? Jodie wondered if it was tattooed on.

"It'll give us a chance to get to know each other," Cheryl said enthusiastically.

She meant it would give her a chance to take photos of them. The woman could snap a shot before you even realized she had the phone aimed in your direction.

"I'd like to do the tree planting tomorrow, if everyone is available?" Cheryl said.

"Already?" Claude blurted. She caught Jodie's eye.

Jodie shrugged helplessly. Who could stand in the way of Hurricane Cheryl? Besides, now that it was all happening, Jodie just wanted to get it over with.

"But what . . . where . . . we haven't planned anything," Claudia protested.

"It's all under control," Cheryl told her with a smile.

Jodie could see Claudia's fingers tighten on the handle of the cake knife.

"Can we put it off a couple of days, so Claude and I can be involved in the planning?" Jodie said quickly. She knew how much Claude liked planning things. "That's what Bree would want."

There was a murmuring around the table as everyone agreed that it was exactly what Bree would want.

"Let's see what the weather report says," Cheryl said, her smile unfaltering as she took a sip of her coffee. "The weather might not be right in a couple of days."

Jodie had a sinking feeling that the weather report wouldn't come out in their favor. There was something about the way Cheryl's gaze had narrowed as she met Claude's.

Jodie hoped the two big cats would keep their claws sheathed. This was already hard enough without a catfight.

Chapter 10

Jodie was in bed when Cheryl came knocking at her door. Cheryl was still fully dressed, even down to the sky-high heels. Jodie pulled the quilt up higher to hide her flannelette baseball pajamas.

"Sorry to disturb," Cheryl whispered. She had her laptop with her. "I just wanted to give you a heads-up that I'll be doing a launch post first thing in the morning. I have a string of posts ready to go, and I put out a media release. I'd like to have some press at the tree planting, if possible."

"Press." Jodie frowned. "No." She felt a spurt of anger at the way Cheryl was hijacking the whole experience. "I want it to be private."

Cheryl gave her a sympathetic smile. "I know. But you also want to pay off Bree's debts. Bree was part of all of this planning; I'm just here to help facilitate." Cheryl sat down on Jodie's desk chair and opened the laptop. "I don't want to share any of this without your explicit approval. After we've worked together for a while, I'm hoping you'll trust me enough to let me post without your direct sign-off. But for now, I think it's important we build trust."

Cheryl turned the laptop to face Jodie and Jodie flinched. Frozen on the screen was Bree.

"What's that?"

"A video," Cheryl said calmly. "Bree recorded some brief clips, to be released as you go through the bucket list." She leaned forward and put the computer on Jodie's lap. "This one is for the launch."

Jodie stared at the frozen image of Bree.

"I'll leave you in peace. The draft posts are all lined up here." Cheryl's red nail ran through the air above the open documents along the bottom of the screen. "I'm open to any improvements." She had the grace to retreat then, closing the door behind her with a soft click and leaving Jodie alone with the laptop. And with Bree.

Jodie's heart was racing. Her whole body had clenched, as though preparing for a blow. She was so tired of hurting all the time. And seeing Bree *hurt*. A lot.

In the frozen image Bree was wearing a pale pink beanie and had her yellow blanket pulled around her like a shawl. Her dry lips were coated thickly with Vaseline. By the end her lips had been so dry that they cracked and bled unless she slathered them with Vaseline. All of her looked dry. She was a husk.

With a trembling finger, Jodie pressed play.

"Hi." Bree smiled. It was a brittle smile but still contained a trace of the lively old Bree. "Thanks for coming along on this adventure. I love you, Jodie."

Jodie jumped. She'd thought this was a general post for Bree's Instagram followers, not one specifically for *her*.

The Bree in the video seemed to read her mind. "This one's just for you." The smile grew a little wider. "I figured you might need a pep talk or two."

Of course Jodie started crying. A pep talk. Resigned, Jodie reached for the tissue box. Trust Bree to be this thoughtful. Oh God, she missed her—so much it was physical, like someone had cut Jodie's leg off. Or her heart out.

"If you're watching this, you're just about to plant the tree. I hope you picked something beautiful."

She hadn't picked anything. Mom and Cheryl had picked it.

"I hope you think of me whenever it flowers."

She hoped so too. She hoped it didn't make her think of

Cheryl, swiping her glossy nails over the phone screen, peering at red-twigged dogwoods.

"I've got a few tips for you," Bree said.

Good. Jodie needed them. She didn't have the first clue about how to complete the list, let alone how to keep all Bree's followers interested.

"If I know you, you're tying yourself up in knots over all this."

Yep.

"But it's not that hard, you know. The first tip is just to *be yourself.* No one likes a phony."

Jodie mopped up her tears. Ha. It was easy being yourself when you were *Bree.* What wasn't to love about Bree? And how was Jodie supposed to be herself in such a weirdly artificial situation?

"Don't let anyone try and polish you up with spray tan and makeup. I've told Cheryl she's not to mess with you," Bree warned.

Jodie raised a hand to her newly highlighted curls.

"Just be you, and I guarantee people will love you."

Bree might be falling victim to her usual overoptimistic world view there . . . When had anyone ever loved Jodie for herself?

"When it comes to social media, people can spot a phony a thousand yards away. Don't try too hard, OK? Just post pictures of your experiences and give them the captions *you* want to give them."

Jodie glanced at the line of open documents at the bottom of Cheryl's laptop. She didn't even have the passwords yet for Bree's accounts, and the posts were already being done for her. Which was a relief, to be honest. Jodie's posts right now would be forlorn. Miserable. Heartbroken. No one wanted to see that. She'd chase off Bree's followers in droves.

"The second tip is that it's OK to be afraid." Bree had a look of such deep compassion that it set Jodie off sniffling again. "Doing new things is scary. You know that photo Mom has of me, the one on the mantelpiece? That was taken right before I jumped off the La Quebrada cliffs in Mexico. You have to time the jump just right, so you hit the water when the swells rise, and I was so scared. I kept imagining I'd screw it up and end up smashed to bits. And there's a restaurant right there, with all these tourists watching as you jump. It was terrifying! But the moment I jumped was just . . ." Bree's eyes shone. "The best. I'd do it again in a heartbeat."

Jodie didn't love the idea of jumping off a cliff. She didn't imagine it would be the best at all . . .

Bree smiled, almost as though she was reading Jodie's thoughts. She took another tack. "Remember when you were playing shortstop? Remember how nervous you'd get before games?"

Jodie did. She used to throw up before every game. It didn't help that she was the only girl on the team, so she was in a locker room by herself, and not with the rest of the guys. It just made her nerves worse. There weren't even cheerleaders for baseball games, so she was literally all alone in the girls' locker room. All alone with some giant-sized fears.

"And shortstop is, like, the hardest, right?"

Yes, it was. The shortstop had so much responsibility, so much pressure. And a lot of people (parents, supporters, even some of her own teammates) didn't love that a girl was playing at all, let alone in that position. Even in this century, girls were supposed to be cheerleaders, like Jodie's sister, not out on the field with the "boys' team." Maybe in a pinch they could play with girls, but Jodie had run out onto the field with the varsity boys' team and taken her spot just like she belonged there. And only Bree knew how vomitously nervous she felt as she ran out.

"And you *rocked*," Bree continued. "All those double plays! You were incredible. And you loved it!"

She did love it. And hated it. It was a weird mixed-up feeling of being utterly terrified and utterly exhilarated all at the same time. It was the time in her life when she felt most alive.

She'd been so *good* at it.

Jodie remembered the look on the coach's face when she'd turn a double play. He'd swell up with pride. Sometimes he'd shake his head, as though he could barely believe what he'd seen.

"Man, Boyd, if you were a guy, I'd put money on you playing in the majors one day."

But she wasn't a guy. So the coach had poured his energy into Kelly Wong and Mikey Nowiki instead of into Jodie, and both Kelly and Mikey got college scholarships.

That was OK. Jodie was never in it for a scholarship anyway. She prided herself on being a realist. Jodie was just glad Coach let her play while she could, instead of relegating her to the girls' softball team. The Junior and Senior Leagues only gave her the option of softball, so school was the only chance she had to play ball, in JV and then in Varsity. People looked at her like she was a freak when she trained and played with the guys, which normally would have sent her scurrying, but she loved baseball too much to run away. Baseball was *everything* back then. Well, baseball and Kelly Wong. She'd had such a searing crush on him. Kelly was the best pitcher she'd seen outside of the majors. And he was gorgeous. Breezy and cheerful, Kelly Wong always looked like his life was one long, good day. He was smart enough to make the honors list, talented enough to play in the school band, charming enough to always have a date, down-to-earth enough to be loved by the guys, popular enough to be encouraged to run for class president, confident enough to be on the debate team, and to top it all, he was the best pitcher in the high school league. Kelly Wong was *perfect*.

Jodie Boyd was not.

Jodie was awkward and shy, a straggler in class, someone who sucked at playing music even after years of lessons, and who wouldn't have been able to keep up in the school band, even if she'd had the courage to join. Jodie had never even thought about running for student council or joining the debate team. God, even the thought of debate made her break out in a cold sweat. She'd just wanted to be invisible and play baseball. As long as she got the grades to graduate, she was happy. She had her own small group of friends and her own way of being. And that was OK. In her yearbook, she wasn't voted most likely to do anything. Under her name, was just one achievement: shortstop. And she'd been thrilled when she saw it. Kelly Wong, however, was voted most likely to succeed.

And he was succeeding. Kelly went on to the University of Miami, to play with the Hurricanes and get a Business degree, while Jodie was working at Philly International at a car-rental booth and inching her way through an associate's degree at the local community college. Kelly played AAA baseball for the Tacoma Rainiers, after being a first-round pick into the minors after college, while Jodie wasn't even playing local softball anymore, because she spent every waking hour working to pay off her family's debts. One day, no doubt, Kelly Wong would be playing at T-Mobile Park in the majors, while Jodie would be . . . what? Working her way up to regional manager in car rentals?

"Jodie," Bree said, snapping her back to the moment and to the recording. "The point is, fear is just part of life. It's a normal feeling. So, when you step out onto that Broadway stage soon, you're *supposed* to be afraid. All those actors are too, even though it's their job. Do it anyway. Because it's worth it. And beyond the fear is something else—and it feels *amazing*."

Oh God, Jodie had managed to repress the fact that she had to go out on a Broadway stage soon . . .

"Good luck, Scaredy Smurf," Bree said. She looked so happy. How could she look happy when she was so sick? When she was *dying*. "I'm cheering you on. I love you."

The video stopped. And Jodie was alone in her bedroom, swollen with sadness. If only Bree *was* here, still able to cheer her on. But she wasn't. There was just Jodie and the laptop.

And all of Cheryl's posts. Jodie clicked them open one by one.

She had to admit, Cheryl was good. The draft of the first post featured Jodie at the car-rental stand, a clear figure in a blurred rush of humanity. The picture was edged with smears of Christmas lights, caught mid-twinkle. The neon green of Jodie's uniform drew the eye, but it was the look on her face that filled the post with pathos.

Is that what I look like?

She looked like a puppy locked in a cage at the pound. Her eyes watched the customer in front of her with a deep sadness, and her face was drawn and tired. She looked abandoned.

Cinderella in the cinders.

The post had a caption: *Life after Bree*. Seeing it was like being stabbed in the heart with a boning knife. Because it was keenly, flayingly *true*.

Chapter 11

Jodie hadn't really slept. She'd lingered over the draft posts until Cheryl came back for her laptop.

"They're very good," Jodie told her. And they were. They were a hypercolored version of their day together. A hypercolored version of Jodie looking glum, anyway: as she got told off by cranky customers; as she sat at the wheel of her Civic, in heavy traffic; as she stood in the sleet in Fishtown, the merriness of the Christmas lights contrasting with her slumped shoulders and defeated expression. Hell, even when she was sitting in the cozy pop-up bar, haloed by candy canes and cradling a steaming hot-pink cocktail, she looked *limp*. Didn't she ever smile? She looked like a total misery.

Somehow Cheryl made her misery look poetic, at least. Cheryl's photos were like works of art. The shots of family dinner were beautiful, although not at all reflective of the actual loud and chaotic experience of it. In real life, Grandma Gloria and Aunt Pat had been bombarding Cheryl with questions, and pressuring her to eat more, while Russel Sprout had been nosing around the garbage bin like a muscular rat. Mom had insisted on bringing out the family photo albums and had then dissolved into tears. Dad didn't say a word but at least he stayed at the table and didn't go turn the television on. But in Cheryl's photos . . . it was hard to describe. They were tableaux of profoundly sinewy emotion. There was one of Mom and Dad and Jodie under the spill of light from the kitchen range hood; Mom was in the center of the frame, staring down at the photo album, her face suffused with memory; Jodie's gaze was locked resolutely on her hands, her body rigid, exuding a refusal to look at the photos; while Dad was staring sideways at Mom, his face spasmed into a bruising expression. He looked . . . ravenous. Starved. *Ferocious* with sorrow. Jodie had never seen that look before. It was naked, raptorial, ravaged. Had it been a momentary flicker of expression, one that Cheryl's phone just happened to catch and fix in place? Or did he wear it often, and they just never noticed, because they were too caught up in their own subterranean sorrows?

"I haven't captioned them all yet," Cheryl said gently, breaking the silence. "You can help. If you want to?"

"I wouldn't know what to say," Jodie told her honestly as she handed the laptop back.

"Well, if you think of anything . . ."

Jodie had tried to sleep after Cheryl left, but it was useless. Her mind was too busy, and her body was too full of emotions. She didn't even know *which* emotions; it was all a great big mess. All those images. Dad's expression. How had she never *seen* it before? Bree would have seen it. Jodie reached for her phone and tapped the Instagram app. She'd never posted anything on Instagram. Which made her a complete freak. But what would she post? The car-rental stand? A cup of horrible coffee from the doughnut stall at the airport? Her childhood bedroom, where she still lived, in her twenties, like a total loser?

She'd never even set up a profile picture. She was a circle with the default silhouette of a head and shoulders. There was no profile description. No posts. As far as Instagram went, she barely existed. She was a nonperson. A ghost, haunting other people's feeds. Well. Not even.

Jodie had only ever followed three accounts: Bree's, the Phillies' . . . and Kelly Wong's. That was a pretty limited ghost, haunting only three feeds. And she barely even haunted *them*, especially since Bree's death. She'd hidden the app in a folder, because just the sight of the icon on her phone had been overwhelming; the spikes of grief had been too acute. The only time she'd opened the app since Bree's death was on Thanksgiving when Bree's message had popped up. Now that Bree was gone, there was no one to haunt but the Phillies and Kelly. Right now, her feed was all Phillies. It was the off-season so there wasn't much interesting happening, just a bunch of marketing filler. Jodie scrolled down, trying to get past the Phillies to find Kelly Wong, the only real human she followed anymore. The last time she'd properly looked at Instagram, Kelly had been in the Mariners' farm system; he'd gone from team to team, the way players did in the AAs, posting pictures of long bus trips and local baseball fields. He'd been with the Arkansas Travelers for a long time. But Jodie hadn't checked in on him since spring training, since before Bree . . .

It looked like he was still in the AAA team in Tacoma, Washington, now, at least according to his profile. He was still gorgeous. He had a square jaw and full lips and he squinted into the sun in a way that was so familiar it made her stomach turn over. He looked the same but . . . better. There were deep lines crinkling out from the corners of his eyes; those incredible red-brown eyes the color of sunlit rosewood. His lower lip still had that crease right in the middle, and his teeth gleamed as he smiled. Kelly always smiled. And he had the slightest nick of a dimple in his cheek, which flickered an instant before he grinned. She could see it now in his profile picture, a coy indentation, like a sideways comma. She looked at his feed, feeling the old buzzing feeling; it was like nerves but floatier. His most recent post was a picture of a homemade burger; it was a towering structure, in jewel-bright colors. The caption read *three different kinds of cheese*. He'd always been obsessed with food. And he ate more than anyone she knew, although you'd never know it. While some of the guys on the team worked out like demons and still had trouble keeping their weight down, Kelly was lean and hard, even though he ate like a pig. She went to his profile and clicked on his most recent story. Her heart jolted when she saw him cradling a child. For a minute she thought it was his. And why wouldn't she? He'd been dating that gorgeous girl a while ago; the blonde who looked effortlessly stunning, whether she was in workout gear or formal wear. Her name was Jessica. Jodie knew because once she'd been stupid enough to stalk her feed. Only once. But it had been painful. She didn't need to see their date-night pictures, or the photo she posted of Kelly sleeping in her bed.

Seeing the child in Kelly's arms, why wouldn't she think it would be his? That's what people did, wasn't it? Fall in love, date, buy diamonds, get married, have kids. The blonde was the kind of woman you gave diamonds to, for sure. But as the story flicked through, Jodie saw that the baby wasn't his and her heart calmed down again. He was visiting his family, and the kid was a niece. It looked like Kelly's brother had a couple of kids. They were cute too. One of them even had a copy of Kelly's dimple.

And there was no sign of the blonde.

Jodie hunted through his older posts. Wow. No sign of the blonde for quite a while . . .

She went right back to baseball season. There were photos of him pitching. God, look at that form. Look at the balletic muscularity of him, frozen in action. Look at the intensity. The green of the field was a luminescent blur behind him. She could see the sheen of sweat on his skin. She could practically hear the low murmur of the crowd and the snap of gum, smell the cut grass and the pine tar on the bats, feel the heat of the summer sun.

Jodie felt a bolt of visceral jealousy.

But no blonde. Not for months. Jodie finally found her, way back at the tail end of spring training. She was wearing a Mariners cap and poking her tongue out. Before that she was in a shot taken at Kelly's parents' house. The two of them were posed awkwardly in the dining room; they didn't look so happy. Behind them, Jodie could see the familiar piano, an old upright Steinway, and it gave her a sick feeling in the pit of her stomach. Soon she'd have to take those piano lessons on Bree's bucket list.

Why did it have to be piano? Why couldn't she have asked

Jodie to take lessons in another instrument . . . *any* other instrument? Jodie would rather learn the tuba, the harp, the kazoo . . . anything else. She'd suffered through hours and hours of piano lessons with Mr. Wong when she was young. It didn't matter how many lessons she took, she was *terrible*. The metronome was still the soundtrack of her nightmares. If only Bree had taken the lessons at the time, like she was supposed to, instead of skipping out to go shopping with Claude . . . Jodie's throat was swollen. None of this was fair.

Jodie clicked on Bree's profile. There was the video again. Before it could start playing, she scrolled past the Thanksgiving message that had kicked off this bizarre adventure. She didn't need to see it again; Mom had played it so many times, Jodie had it memorized. It was a relief to get past it and to the feed before Bree's death.

Bree's last few posts were sunlit. There was the branch of forsythia, exploding with yellow happiness; there was a pool of light collecting in the folds of Claude's buttery blanket; there was a spangle of raindrops glittering on the window. There was a close-up of Bree's stuffed cat Ginger with the caption *my bae*. There were no selfies. Jodie scrolled back. The last selfie Bree took was two dozen posts or more back; in it she was wearing Jodie's lucky Phillies hat and was hooked up to an IV. Even then she had the look Jodie had come to associate with death. There was a thinness to her skin, a look in her eye. Like she was half somewhere else already. The very last post—Jodie caught herself; she meant the very last post before they started getting Bree's messages from beyond the grave—featured a single raindrop. Its convex swell was fragile, the membrane stretched almost to breaking point. It looked like Bree had caught the moment before it burst and spilled itself down the windowpane. Suspended inside the raindrop was an upside-down world in miniature: whorls and eddies of cloud at the bottom, with a horizon of inverted trees rising from their churn. Contained in that serenely swollen membrane was a roiling, gusty day; upside-down and behind glass, captured through a phone. Bree had been so many steps removed from the wind that had tossed those trees and churned those clouds, but she saw it clearly. Saw it and captured it and captioned it: *my gift to you.*

That had been her very last living post: an upside-down world, the moment before it burst.

Jodie had stayed up long into the night, lost in the labyrinthine tunnels of Instagram, moving from post to post and feed to feed, following breadcrumbs to moments long past, heading toward something she couldn't name, but which pulled her forward, mesmerized. It was like being in a trance.

When she woke the next morning, she still had the phone in her hand. Through the gap in her curtains she could see a heavy swirl of snow; the kind of snow that belonged on romantic Christmas cards. Fat lazy snowflakes twirled and tumbled in wide arcs. The first real snow of the season.

Cheryl wouldn't waste it. As soon as Jodie saw that snow, she knew that the tree was being planted today, whether Claude liked it or not. Because the red twigs would *pop* against the snow. And Cheryl wasn't one to waste a good photo.

Phone still in hand, Jodie pulled herself out of bed and padded to the window. She unlocked it and pushed it open. Deliciously icy air flooded in. The ground was already frosted white with powder snow and the trees were rimed with white. Curtains of snow fell in great shivering sheets and low clouds made everything foggy and soft.

On impulse, Jodie stepped back and took a photo of the open window and the wintery day beyond. Bree would have approved, she thought, as she uploaded her very first post to Instagram. *Snow day*, she captioned it. It wasn't very poetic . . . but it was true. She took a deep breath, feeling the gelid air flood her. *OK, Bree. Here we go . . .*

Chapter 12

Everyone wanted to be involved. It was a total circus. Mom changed her mind five times about where she wanted the tree planted. Front yard, so you could see it from the dining room. Back yard, in front of the kitchen window, so she could see it when she was doing the dishes. Around the side, where she could see it from her bedroom. Maybe right in the middle of the lawn, so it was a feature? No, definitely out by the front door, so it was the first thing you saw when you came home.

In the end, it went in the middle of the front lawn, because Cheryl insisted it would make a good shot.

"You'll be able to glimpse it from both the dining room *and* the living room," she told them cheerily.

Glimpse. Just. If you craned your neck.

Cheryl was all decked out in her luxurious coat and Mom's borrowed old yellow snow boots and was pink cheeked and bright eyed. She'd wanted Jodie to change her hat and coat, but Jodie refused. She hadn't got to pick which tree, or where to plant it, or even *when* to plant it, but she could damn well pick her own clothes. And her lucky Phillies cap was nonnegotiable.

Grandma Gloria and Aunt Pat were there, and so was Claudia, who looked like a thundercloud. Jodie could tell that she was itching to push Cheryl into a snowdrift. Jodie's mom had told all the neighbors about the tree planting, and they'd gathered around like it was a memorial service. Mrs. Tavoulareos even brought a plate of brownies. Mom took the brownies inside and then invited everyone to stay for coffee afterwards. It was becoming a regular bucket list launch party.

"Don't you think Jodie should be the one to dig the hole, Joe?" Mr. Schields called out. He was leaning on his fence, watching Jodie's dad scrape the snow away from the earth.

Jodie's dad stopped and thought about it. "Maybe." He met Jodie's gaze. "But the ground's pretty frozen, it's not an easy job."

"Let's get a photo of Jodie breaking the ground," Cheryl suggested, "and if she runs into trouble, you can help out. That's what fathers are for, after all."

Jodie felt Cheryl's hand in the small of her back, pushing her forward. She was well aware that Cheryl was snapping photos of her as she took the shovel from her father.

The snow had lightened to the odd flake, but there was fog rolling through, making the yard seemed cut off from the rest of the world. Christmas lights glowed here and there through the shifting fog; it was so dark it almost felt like evening, rather than late morning. Sound was muffled. Jodie could hear her own heartbeat as she stood in the cleared patch of ground. Her family was clumped in front of the dining room window, haloed by the yellow light spilling through the glass. Claudia was slightly off to the side, her hands shoved deep into the pockets of her black parka, her expression dejected.

"Use the sharp edge," Mr. Schields called, "and put some muscle into it."

Jodie was aware of Cheryl circling to get the perfect shot.

None of this felt right. It felt rushed and . . . hijacked, yes, that's how it felt. Jodie would have preferred to do it in quiet, without the audience. This didn't feel meaningful at all.

At least she'd talked Cheryl out of calling the local papers or the evening news. She didn't care how much of a "human interest" story it was, this was her life, not a reality show.

The ground was hard as hell. It was like trying to carve a hole in a slab of rock.

Cheryl had gone out early to collect the dogwood; Jodie had driven her. It was a pretty spectacular tree. Cheryl had found an established plant; it was as tall as Jodie and they had to wrestle it into the back of the Civic, over the folded seats.

Here in the snowy yard, the vigorous branches were as bright as coals. If you had to plant a tree in winter, this was the one to plant.

Because it *popped.*

In the end, it took a team of them to dig a hole, passing the shovel back and forth whenever they wore themselves out.

"There's no way that poor tree will survive," Jodie's mom fretted.

"I looked up some tips," Claudia ventured, inching into the circle around the tree. She pulled out her phone and called up a gardening website she'd been consulting. She'd clearly been itching to get involved. "The main thing is to keep it well watered."

"It's going to be covered with *snow,*" Jodie pointed out.

"Well, this says that plants get desiccated in winter from lack of water." Claudia held the phone up to show her.

"What else does it say, Claudia, honey?" Jodie's mom all but took the phone from her. Claudia didn't seem to mind; the dejected left-out look was gone from her face.

"Jodie?" Cheryl steered her attention back to the hole. "It's time." She clapped her frozen-looking hands together. "Everyone! I need the family all in place."

As if on cue, it started snowing again. Jodie stood by the hole, watching Cheryl boss her family around through veils of snowfall. She fussed with their positions, trying to get them framed by the Christmas lights winking through the window. Claudia retreated to the porch and tried to look like she was absorbed in reading about plants, but Jodie could see the defensiveness in her posture. It was the same way she'd stood in school, when she was keeping her head high, while the kids teased her about her thrift store clothes. Or the way she stood when she was on the phone to her mother. Claude was proud. Bruise her and she lifted her chin and acted like she was a queen at her own coronation. But inside . . . Jodie could tell she felt as far from a queen as it was possible to feel.

"Hey," Jodie called over to the family and Cheryl. "You forgot Claude! Bree would kill you if you left Claude out!"

Mom and Gloria and Pat let out horrified exclamations and turned as a group, waving Claudia over.

"Come on, honey! What are you doing over there on the porch?"

"You heard the lady: she wants all the family together!"

Jodie saw the wave of relief wash over Claude. She looked as though she'd been granted a reprieve on death row or something. She ducked her head as she jogged across the yard to join the family, and Jodie wondered if she was blinking back tears.

"OK, everyone ready?" Cheryl had her phone ready. "Jodie, away we go!"

"Are you *filming* this?"

"Only a little. For the Instagram story."

Right. Great. Now she was going to be miserable in action, as well as in still life. She tried to arrange her face into something less miserable, but for all she knew that looked worse. She bent over the dogwood and let the brim of her hat hide her face. Luckily the sheeting snow would help hide her too.

It was hard to get the tree out of the pot. Dad moved to help but Mom held him back.

"She has to do it herself," Mom scolded him.

"Whack the bottom of the pot with the shovel," Mr. Schields suggested, his voice muffled by the weather.

Jodie whacked it and the dogwood came thumping out.

"Watch the branches," Cheryl warned.

There were too many cooks. Jodie turned her back on Cheryl as she lowered the ball of roots and dirt into the hole. The wind was picking up, whipping snow into Jodie's eyes.

Is this what you pictured, Bree? Once the tree was snug in the hole, Jodie shoveled frosty earth in and stomped it down with her boots. The scarlet branches shivered in the wind. In spring they'd unfurl radiantly green new leaves, and this season of darkness and ice would be a long-distant memory. Jodie reached out and touched the fragile tip of a slender red branch. *Don't die on me, OK?*

She turned to face her family, huddled against the snow. Her mom gave her a wobbly smile.

"That's one down!" Aunt Pat said with a sharp nod. The pom-pom on her beanie wobbled.

"One down, and a chunk of debt paid off." Dad came and took his shovel from Jodie and dropped a kiss on the top of her head. She could feel the pressure of it through her cap.

Planting that tree had taken all of ten minutes. Not counting digging the hole. All in all, it maybe took an hour. She'd just paid off more of their debt in an hour than she would in dozens of hours of work at the airport. Jodie glanced up at the foggy sky. *Bree?* Snow spiraled down. It was like being inside a snow globe. *I don't know how you did it, but wow. That's a lot of hours I won't have to work . . .*

"Let's get inside and out of this wind," Grandma Gloria said briskly, ushering everyone in for coffee and brownies. Jodie watched the stream of neighbors clomp up the porch steps.

Claudia joined Jodie by the dogwood. "It is very pretty," she said grudgingly. "Bree would definitely have liked it."

"Yeah," Jodie agreed. "She would." She felt Claudia's shoulder bump hers.

"You did good."

Jodie swallowed hard. She didn't know why Claudia's praise mattered so much, but somehow it did. "Thanks," she said huskily.

"You sure did," Cheryl gushed, darting through the snow toward them like a playful squirrel. "That was *beautiful*."

"Beautiful isn't the word I'd use," Jodie said dryly. "Cold, maybe." Staged, definitely. But the tree was planted and that was all that really mattered. Wherever she was, Bree could be happy that her bucket list was one step closer to being finished.

"That's number seventeen down!" Cheryl cheered. "Now, time for those piano lessons with Mr. Wong!"

Ah. Yes. The piano lessons . . .

"Um . . ." Jodie cleared her throat. "That's going to be difficult." Her late-night Instagram safari had found a hole in the plan.

"Why is that?" Cheryl cocked her head. She was still smiling mintily.

"Because . . ." How did you break news like this? Quickly, Jodie decided. Like ripping off a Band-Aid. "Because Mr. Wong is dead."

Chapter 13

39. Piano Lessons with Mr. Wong

She was in the *paper*. Jodie stared at the image Mom had messaged through, her toes curling in horror. Right there in *The News*. And it was a big picture. It took up most of the page above the fold, by the look of it. There was Jodie planting the damn tree, the snowflakes suspended in white speckles all around her. The red of the dogwood branches was stark. The red of Jodie's vintage Phillies cap popped too. The photo captured the moment she'd touched a gloved hand to the scarlet branch, her face shining with sadness and . . . something else. Something soft and suffused with . . . what? Hope?

Wilmington Local Grants Celebrity Sister's Last Wish.

"You took this photo," Jodie accused Cheryl. They were on a flight to New York, courtesy of Iris Air, even though the train would have got them there just as quick (given all the rigamarole of airports). But no trains for them, not with Iris as a sponsor. Instead they were on a thirty minute flight, first-class to New York. To eat a sandwich. Because that's how crazy her life was now. "And Bree wasn't a celebrity."

"Close enough to one," Cheryl said with a shrug. "I didn't claim she was a celebrity when I sent out the press release. But I can see why they went with it." Cheryl was deep in her second gin and tonic. She looked a little less Marketing Barbie and little more human. Her hair was ruffled, and her eyelids were heavy. Her crimson mouth opened in a wide yawn.

It had been a long couple of days for Cheryl, as she tried to salvage the bucket list after Jodie's shocking revelation about Mr. Wong. Because how were the piano lessons going to happen if the piano teacher was dead?

Poor Kelly. Every time Jodie thought about Mr. Wong, the image of Kelly standing in front of the piano swam to the surface. In the picture, there was an unnaturally starched look to him. Stiff. He was trying to smile but there was no trace of his sideways-comma dimple. And although he had his arm around the blonde—Jessica—it wasn't a warm gesture. His arm was rigid, like a plank of wood sitting on her shoulders. She looked tense too.

Grief was a bitch. It screwed everything up.

Jodie had stumbled onto the discovery about Mr. Wong deep in her labyrinthine night on Instagram. She didn't discover it through any big announcement on Kelly's feed; there was just a card propped up on that piano behind Kelly and the blonde. A card from a funeral service. Jodie had been zooming in on the photo, trying to parse the body language between Kelly and his girlfriend (Were they looking awkward because they were breaking up? *Had* they broken up? And when?) when she noticed the enlarged funeral card. It had an oval-shaped photo of Kelly's dad on it, she realized. And a set of dates . . . *That* was when she realized what she was looking at.

Kelly's father had passed away.

Jodie zoomed in closer. The dates were fuzzy, but she could just make them out. Mr. Wong, her old piano teacher, had died around the same time that Jodie had donated her bone marrow to her sister. God, poor Kelly. Jodie had then madly scrolled back through Kelly's feed. She found confirmation about two weeks before the piano post with the blonde: a memorial post to his father. Then there were sad photos of the empty piano bench; of Mr. Wong's car, with the line, *First time it hasn't been washed on a Saturday morning*; a bowl of eggs and a loaf of bread on a counter, *No one made French toast like Dad*. There were posts of the family packing up the house. The piano being loaded into a moving van.

Jodie did not have fond memories of that piano, or of Mr. Wong. He'd been strict and humorless and his presence standing behind her piano stool had filled her with dread. But he'd been a dedicated teacher. And he'd raised a magnificent son.

"I guess that means no piano lessons," Jodie had said after breaking the news, as she'd stood with Claude and Cheryl in the snow after the tree planting. Her mind kept wandering back to sitting on Mr. Wong's piano bench, her clumsy hands fumbling every few notes. Now and then Mr. Wong would tap her on the shoulder, to remind her to sit up straight.

"Take pride in yourself," he'd say, in that quiet but intractable way he had.

Pride. Jodie didn't see what pride there was in turning Bach into an offensive mess of accidental sharps. The more mistakes she made, the more uptight she got, and then the *more* mistakes she made. It was a vicious circle. And Mr. Wong exuded mounting tension as she sharped her way through the mess. It was as though her errors caused him physical pain.

"What does this mean for the bucket list?" Claudia had said, worried, as the three of them stood around the newly planted red twig dogwood, like it was a campfire. "What does it mean if she can't finish the list?"

"It doesn't mean *anything* for the bucket list," Cheryl had told her briskly. She'd lost her minty smile by that point. "Worse comes to worst, we'll move on to the next item on the list, until we sort this one out."

And now Jodie and Cheryl were on a plane to New York. But Jodie didn't see how Cheryl was going to "sort this one out," certainly not in the time it took them to have a sandwich at Katz's Delicatessen.

And it was all in the *paper*. Hell. Imagine the follow-up story. *Wilmington Local Fails Celebrity Sister.* Everyone would know what a waste of space she was.

"I'm going to have a nap." Cheryl turned off her light. "Wake me when we get to New York."

New York. Jodie had hardly ever been to New York, even though it was less than an hour from Philly by plane. Technically just over thirty minutes, on a direct flight. Which this wasn't. They'd had to go via Washington, D.C., which stretched it out long enough for Cheryl to fit in a nap.

Jodie was too wired to relax. She hated flying. It made her feet sweat with sheer terror. Every bump made her grip the armrests. As Cheryl snoozed, she fidgeted. Maybe she should watch something, even though it seemed silly, given there was only fifteen minutes of cruising time between ascent and descent. She flicked through the menu on the screen. *When Harry Met Sally* was there in the list of rom-coms. It made her feel a bit ill. She didn't watch it. She *should* watch it; she was supposed to act out that mortifying scene. But just the thought of watching Meg Ryan growling throatily and writhing and moaning in the middle of a crowded restaurant made Jodie feel hot and sick and poisonous with terror. Maybe they could do the orgasm thing after hours? Maybe the people at Katz's would be kind enough to clear the restaurant so that she could humiliate herself in private?

She was glad that Cheryl had let her have the window seat on the plane. She liked to see the ground. When the plane bumped it was reassuring to see the earth wasn't rushing up toward them. She turned off her screen and stared out at the night sky, trying to distract herself by watching the glitter of distant cities and highways slide by. When the flight attendant came through, she asked for a beer. She tried to relax. It wasn't happening. The pressurized hum of the cabin added to her anxiety. Her ears were all blocked and weird.

Manhattan emerged from the night, like something out of *Peter Pan*, magical, glittering in the cold clear winter air. Jodie felt a spiral of nerves shoot through her. But not entirely bad nerves. Sparkly, fizzy nerves. As they flew lower, Jodie craned her neck. She felt like she was in a movie. The shining towers. The dark serpentine ripple of the Hudson River. The winding flow of cars lit up red and white like streams of molten lava. The fact that she didn't have to go to work tomorrow, or the day after, or the day after that. The cliff edge of adventure at her feet . . .

It was overwhelming. Jodie felt like a pinball machine; things were pinging and lighting up inside her.

Bree had always loved New York. *You should come with me! There's nowhere in the world like New York!* But Jodie couldn't afford New York. Hell, she could barely afford her daily life, let alone a vacation. *We could see a Broadway show*, Bree sang. *I can't afford a show*, Jodie had replied, never really taking her seriously. Never really even considering the idea. Bree's suggestions had always just rolled over her, like a daydream, like a fantasy game of what-if. *We could do touristy things, like catch the ferry out to the Statue of Liberty and walk the High Line. We could go to the Met!* Jodie didn't even know what the High Line was. It sounded expensive. *We'll go see a ball game*, Bree teased, knowing baseball was the key to Jodie's heart. *We could see the Phillies play the Mets at Citi Field and drink beer and eat Cracker Jacks.* But it had always been cheaper to watch the game on TV. Cheaper, and less intimidating. Jodie was comfortable in her groove; she knew what to expect from it. There wasn't much anxiety in her groove; it was safe. So, she had never taken Bree up on her offers. Not that they'd been concrete offers. Bree was always busy, and the offer of New York had remained hypothetical, but if Bree had forced Jodie's hand and booked the tickets, she would have gone. Which, Jodie supposed, was exactly what Bree had done to her now . . .

Because here she was. Bree had not only found a way to make it free of charge, but she'd made an offer Jodie couldn't refuse. There were no excuses this time.

But now Jodie was here, and Bree wasn't. And there would be no baseball game because it wasn't even baseball season.

There *would* be a Broadway show, though. Bree had made sure of that.

Right, Jodie thought, as she watched Manhattan loom large in the window. Bree had gone to a lot of trouble to get her on this plane, and into this city. She'd kept secrets and made plans and found a way to get them out of debt, to boot. So the very least Jodie could do was try and enjoy it. As terrifying as some of these things were (Oh God, she had to fake an orgasm in public . . .) she'd face them head on, just the way Bree would have if she were here. When Bree tackled her bucket list, she did it wholeheartedly. So, Jodie would be wholehearted too.

Fear is just a part of life.

Did Bree think Jodie didn't know that already? She'd been scared her whole life. You'd think she'd be used to it by now, she thought, draining her beer as the attendant came around for the garbage.

Well, she wasn't. But fear didn't seem to be going anywhere, so she'd just have to carry it along with her. No matter how scary it was, she was going to do this. Fake orgasms, Broadway shows and all.

Alright, New York, here I come. I might not be the Boyd you deserve, but I'm the Boyd you're going to get.

Chapter 14

Cheryl had booked them into an incredible hotel. It was a pagoda of pale amber glass, which glowed like a lantern rising into the night sky. There were doormen in expensive coats, whisking their bags away on brass trolleys, and pots of orchids with blooms almost the size of Jodie's head. Were they real? They looked real.

Cheryl led Jodie into a soaring foyer, across a gleaming veined-marble floor. Over the void of the foyer hung an enormous, fringed, art deco chandelier. It was like a big starry jellyfish. Cheryl kept apologizing that the hotel was only three stars, but Jodie didn't have much to compare it to. It was a million times fancier than the motels she'd stayed in as a kid on her family vacations. It looked like something a Kardashian would post a selfie in. Although it was nowhere near as fancy as some of the luxe resorts Bree had posted about on her travels, so maybe that's why Cheryl was apologizing.

"It's a pretty standard business hotel." Cheryl sighed as she handed over her company credit card.

Jodie craned her neck, staring at the starry jellyfish overhead. What kind of business thought *this* was standard? The kind of business that mined diamonds?

"I picked Midtown because I thought you might want to do some sightseeing," Cheryl said as she clicked across the marble foyer on her sky-high heels, the key cards to their rooms in hand. She punched the elevator button. "Most people want to see Times Square and Rockefeller Center and Central Park and all the rest of it; it's all pretty easy from here."

"Central Park is nearby?" Jodie perked up. She'd brought her running shoes, thinking she could find a hotel treadmill, but Central Park would be way better.

"It's a ten-minute walk uptown. We're on the zoo end."

Jodie wondered how much time she'd have to look around. She wasn't even sure how long they were going to be in New York. Long enough to fake an orgasm, eat a sandwich, and then go ruin a Broadway play . . .

"Are we anywhere near the High Line?" Jodie asked. She'd looked it up. It wasn't expensive; it was free.

"No, that's over on the Lower West Side. But it's not hard to get to."

Even the elevator was fancy. It was walled with brassy-toned mirrors and had an art deco lamp on the ceiling. As soon as the doors slid closed, Cheryl slumped a little against a mirror. Even after a nap, she looked tired.

"You know," Jodie said as the elevator zoomed skyward, "I assumed you lived in New York." She didn't know why, except that New York seemed to be where fancy people like Cheryl belonged.

"No, ma'am," Cheryl drawled, with a half smile. "Dallas, Texas. It's where the company is based. But, originally, I'm from Vegas. Which is one big old suburb with a fancy road right through the middle."

The elevator stopped on the thirtieth floor, and they stepped out into a heavily carpeted and muffled corridor. Cheryl checked the numbers on the key cards and then plunged ahead. Their rooms were opposite one another. Cheryl unlocked both and peered around; she pulled back the filmy curtains and looked out at the views, which consisted of skyscrapers in every direction.

"Here, you take this one," she said, ushering Jodie in. "It has a better view."

How could she tell? One sparkly skyscraper looked much the same as the next.

Cheryl paused in the corridor. She bit her lip. "I was supposed to take you out to dinner, but do you mind if we stay in? You can order room service and help yourself to the mini bar. It's all on the company." She pulled a slight face. "I mean, not French champagne or anything. They do audit my receipts."

Jodie laughed. "I'm not a champagne kind of girl."

Cheryl smiled and this time it looked different. Less minty and more genuine. "Yes, you are. You just don't know it yet. *Everyone* is a champagne kind of girl, Jodie."

"If you say so."

"I say so."

"Hey," Jodie said as Cheryl went to leave. "This might be a really stupid question . . . but would it be OK if I went for a walk? Maybe went out to find some food?" It seemed a waste to come all the way to New York and stay in a hotel room. Especially since the energy of the city pulsed behind those windows; the streets spangled and swirled with lights, even though it was frigid bleak midwinter.

"Of course." Cheryl looked surprised. "You're not a prisoner."

Jodie laughed again. "No, I meant I didn't know if it was safe or not."

Cheryl really grinned now. "Yeah, it's safe. As much as anywhere. You've got my number, right? Call me if you get lost. And try to be back by morning; I have plans for tomorrow." Cheryl seemed to think Jodie was planning on finding a party to join. She winked as she left.

God. If only her life was that interesting. Her only intention was to find something to eat and to soak in a bit of the city. Jodie bundled up in her ski jacket and her woolen beanie, pocketed the key card, and headed out into the evening. She smiled shyly at the doorman as he opened the door for her and only afterwards realized that she was supposed to tip him. She'd have to find him when she got back and apologize.

Outside a glacial gust blustered down the wind tunnel between the buildings. Jodie lowered her head and started walking deeper into Midtown. She'd leave the park for tomorrow. She felt nervy and exposed but also exhilarated. She took a deep breath of the chilled air. Everything sparkled. Or so she thought, and then she turned onto Fifth Avenue, and that's when she learned what sparkling *really* meant. The whole street was decked out in full holiday glory. Right on the corner was Harry Winston, bedazzled with lights that looked like giant jewels. It was like something out of an old Audrey Hepburn movie. Jodie half expected a big band to start serenading her. It was impossibly enchanting. *Magical.* She felt like a kid on Christmas morning, convinced that reindeer could fly; anything seemed possible. It was almost nine o'clock on a weeknight, but Fifth Avenue was bustling. Stores were open, spilling light into the sparkling street; there were chocolate shops and jewelry stores; Irish pubs and Belgian beer bars and French brasseries. People walked quickly, dashing through the night, looking like they were on their way to busy and important things. Jodie couldn't bring herself to walk faster; she wanted to take it all in. It didn't seem real: the Ferragamo store, wrapped in a giant stripy ribbon; Louis Vuitton, projected with lighting designs in candy colors; Cartier, collaged with a tumble of enormous red presents, as though they were falling from an upper-level window toward the earth. It was excessive and majestic and luxurious beyond measure. Jodie found it hard to believe that people really lived and worked here. They certainly weren't people like *her.*

She turned slow circles as she walked, unsure where to look. And then when she thought it couldn't get any more excessive, she reached the glitz and stardust of Rockefeller, with its ice-skating rink and its one-hundred-foot Christmas tree. Just think how much electricity was used by that one tree . . . let alone the rest of Fifth Avenue. No wonder the planet was in trouble.

Jodie spent a good hour wandering around, watching the skaters, and the people coming out of Tiffany's with their distinctive robin's-egg-blue shopping bags. She bet at some point in the past Bree had come and eaten a croissant in front of the

Tiffany's window, pretending she was Audrey Hepburn. Jodie could imagine it clearly. She could also imagine Bree skating on that ice rink, in the sparkle of the lights, her warm breath pluming in the cold air.

You should go have a skate.

Jodie imagined Bree's voice so clearly it was as if she'd spoken. She had to stop herself from looking over her shoulder.

Go on. Go have a skate. You love skating.

Jodie shook her head. *Not tonight, sis. Maybe next time.*

Next time? Bree's imagined voice sighed, dissolving into the wind.

Next time. Because the thought of skating out there alone wasn't really appealing. There were a lot of couples out there, holding hands and enjoying the magic. She'd just be out there by herself, skating circles, with no one to talk to, and no hand to hold.

She'd rather keep walking. And she was hungry. It was way past dinnertime. Jodie doubted she could afford to eat around here, though. Not when the closest deli had a sign advertising beluga caviar. Jodie dug out her phone and looked up cheap eats nearby. Luckily, she didn't have to walk too far; there was a Korean hole-in-the-wall just a few blocks away. Manhattan blocks were a little bigger than she was expecting, but it was worth the walk for the steaming hot tofu bibimbap at the unpretentious counter. *And* the fact that it cost her under twenty bucks. Cheap enough to afford a beer as well.

She could get used to this, she thought as she sat with the last mouthful of beer, her stomach full of great food, watching people pass by on the street outside. She'd had three days off from work in a row, something that hadn't happened since the week of Bree's funeral.

Wish you were here with me, sis.

Jodie left a tip in the jar on the counter and rugged up to head back out into the streets. The song didn't lie, this place really didn't seem to sleep. She checked the time. The thought of going back to an empty hotel room wasn't very appealing. According to Google Maps, Times Square wasn't too far away, and that seemed like a place you'd want to see at night, all lit up. As she walked, Jodie realized she felt lighter, easier. *Happier.*

You know what, Bree, this might be kinda fun.

She bet Bree was rolling her eyes, wherever she was. *Of course it's fun, Brainy Smurf. Why do you think people travel?*

To feel free. Because that's how Jodie felt right now. She didn't have to be anywhere, do anything, please anyone but herself. There was no work, no responsibility. There was just the night and the streets and . . . *Times Square.*

She'd come here once as a kid, but her memory hadn't done it justice. Wow, it was tacky. Gloriously so. Energetically so. It was like an explosion of neon and advertising and cheap tourist stands; there were people in costume and street performers and general chaos. Jodie stood in the middle of it and just let it happen around her. It was great.

She meant to go back to the hotel after that, she really did. But on her amble back, she happened to pass a French champagne bar. Who knew such things even existed?

Everyone is a champagne kind of girl, Jodie.

It was a sign. What else would you call it?

She wasn't dressed for a fancy place, but even dressed up she wouldn't fit in, would she? Her kind of dressed-up wasn't *New York* kind of dressed-up. So, despite her jeans and old ski jacket, she went in.

Now, she'd never been to Paris, but she guessed that in a Hollywood movie version of Paris, the champagne bars would look like *this*. It was dripping with chandeliers, a rosy vision in dusty-pink velvet and polished wood. Mirrors bounced the softly glowing light around, and everything looked like it was in soft focus. There were giant palms in brass pots and candles flickering on linen tablecloths.

She was definitely not going to be able to afford this place.

But when the maître d' greeted her, she was too embarrassed to back out. She'd just have to order the cheapest thing on the list. And hope they did champagne by the glass. Was that a thing?

"Table for . . . one?" His gaze flicked over her shoulder, registering the empty space behind her.

Jodie's chin went up. "Yes." There was nothing wrong with drinking alone. Nothing at all. Bree would have been fine doing it. She'd done it a lot. Jodie had seen her posts.

My own best date. That had been one of her captions. At a French restaurant, no less. So if Bree could do it, Jodie could too.

The maître d' took her jacket and beanie and then led her through the plush room to a table for one, nestled between the folds of some pretty impressive brocade curtains. The guy did a pretty good job of pretending like she belonged. Jodie ran a hand through her curls, knowing she had atrocious hat hair from her beanie. Not like the women in here. They looked like they'd just stepped out of salons. Didn't they wear hats? And if they didn't wear hats, how did they keep those glossy heads unmolested by the winds gusting down the tunnels between the skyscrapers? There must be a trick to it.

The maître d' pulled out the plush pink velvet chair for her. Jodie sank into it, feeling awkward. This had been stupid. It was just reinforcing that she *wasn't* a champagne kind of girl. Especially when he handed her the menu and she got a look at the prices. Dear God, one of the champagnes was a hundred and five dollars *a glass.* Was Krug really that much better than Ruinart, which was "only" forty-five dollars? Hell, her whole dinner had been half that, including the beer and the tip.

The maître d' had now been replaced by a waiter, who looked like he came from central casting. He was dark and gorgeous and elegant as hell. He should be sitting in this chair and she should be waiting on *him.* He poured her a crystal tumbler full of sparkling water and she hoped there was no charge for it . . .

"Is mademoiselle looking for a champagne by the glass today?"

She almost snorted at that. Of course by the glass. Even if she could drink a whole bottle by herself, she'd have to sell a kidney to pay for it.

"Yes, please," she said instead, trying to keep her expression from showing her dismay at the prices. He could probably tell anyway, just from sizing her up by her clothes. "Um . . . what do you recommend?" As if she'd take his recommendation. He was probably working on commission.

"What flavor profiles does mademoiselle prefer?"

What did she say to that? *Wet ones?* Oh, to hell with this, they both knew she had no idea what she was doing. Jodie closed the menu. "I don't have a clue what a flavor profile even is," she said honestly. She thought she saw a twinkle in his eye at that. "I haven't had much experience with champagne." She hadn't even had the champagne at Thanksgiving. Her stomach had been roiling from Bree dropping the bucket list on her; champagne had been the last thing she wanted to drink. "Once I had wine in a can, *that* had bubbles in it, but I don't think that counts?"

He was definitely twinkling now.

"I don't have much money." Since she was being honest, she might as well be *brutally* honest. "But a friend of mine told me today that everyone is a champagne kind of girl, so when I saw your place . . . well, I thought I'd see if that was true or not."

The waiter cleared his throat delicately and pressed his lips together. He was trying not to laugh at her in public, which was nice of him.

"Leave it with me," he said, backing away. "I know just the thing."

She almost groaned. Great. He was probably going to bring her the slop from the leftover bucket and tell her it was worth the ninety-dollar price tag. She was such an idiot.

But when he came back, he brought an unopened bottle with him, along with a fancy glass, which had a swirl etched into it. A swirl which matched the label on the bottle. Did every champagne get its own etched glass? Jodie snuck a careful look at the table next to her but couldn't make out the etching on their glasses.

"Some people prefer to order from the upper end of the list," the waiter told her quietly, as he presented the bottle, "as though price dictates quality. But champagne is like art: there's no right or wrong, it's all personal taste. Now, I'm not saying this isn't expensive," he warned her, "because this *is,* after all, a champagne salon. But this is one of the wines from the middle of our price point."

Jodie couldn't quite keep her concern off her face, clearly, because he bent forward and whispered the price in a low voice.

"Forty-nine dollars a glass."

Forty-nine dollars for a drink.

Not just a drink. French champagne! In Jodie's imagination Bree sounded giddy with the thrill of it.

Fine for you to say, sis. You're not the one having to pay for it. And it wasn't just forty-nine dollars . . . it was forty-nine dollars *plus tip.* And a place this nice would expect a twenty-percent tip.

"This is the classic Billecart-Salmon Brut," the waiter was telling her with great solemnity. Really almost with reverence. "It's a pinot noir, chardonnay, pinot meunier blend from, of course, the Champagne region of France."

Of course.

Jodie hadn't had to pay for her flight, or for the cab from the airport, and she wouldn't have had to pay for the room service (if she'd ordered it), and she didn't have to pay for that fancy hotel room she was going back to. So far it had been an inexpensive trip. She could splurge on a glass of fermented grapes, couldn't she? Because *everyone* was a champagne kind of girl. Even the girls who couldn't afford the stupid stuff; sometimes even they deserved it too.

"I'd love a glass," she said huskily. She'd better be careful not to spill it, because it cost about twelve dollars an ounce, she thought as she watched him uncork the bottle. He did it with a slow graceful twist. There was no pop, like she was expecting, like you saw in the movies. Instead there was a near-silent sigh as the gas escaped the bottle.

"You don't want to bruise the wine by popping it," he informed her. She doubted he'd bother saying that to his other customers. They probably already knew.

"How do you bruise wine?" she asked, unable to restrain her curiosity. "It's a *liquid.*"

The waiter had that twinkle back again. "I think it has something to do with the sediment, or the cork."

"You think? You don't know?" Jodie was genuinely surprised.

"Inexcusable, I know."

She laughed. She liked him. Bree would have liked him too.

He had a deft way of pouring, so the pale gold liquid didn't fizz up too much. "This is a mature wine, with a lasting mousse, floral perfume and flavors of ripe pear."

Right. Jodie wondered what mousse had to do with wine. Or whether it went well with pears.

He stood back and waited. Clearly he wanted to see what she thought of it.

Gingerly, Jodie picked up the glass. *Don't spill it.* She took a careful sip.

He was too expectant. She didn't know what to say without disappointing him. It tasted like . . . wine. Bubbly, slightly sour. Nice.

"It's good."

"Your palate will acclimatize to it," he said. "At first you'll just get all the top notes. Let it unfold."

"Right." She took another sip. The bubbles tickled her nose.

"Enjoy." And off he went, into the refracted chandelier light, weaving between the linen-covered tables and shiny people.

Jodie took tiny sips, holding the champagne in her mouth and trying to work out what all the fuss was about. What was weird was that she *could* taste ripe pear, but she probably wouldn't have been able to if he hadn't pointed it out. And maybe the mousse referred to the creamy sensation? Which was odd, wasn't it? That something could be sharp and fruity, but also creamy? Maybe it was bruised.

She didn't want to rush it. Not for forty-nine dollars. She tried to sit back and relax, but it was pretty hard when you were sitting all alone in a romantic French bar, with horrid hat hair and sneakers on your feet, surrounded by glossy-headed women in heels, who were most definitely *not* alone. After a while, she felt too conspicuous, so she pulled out her phone.

She didn't have any messages, so she looked at her news apps.

It was grim, as usual. This was why she didn't check them very often; they made her anxious. And now they'd also managed to make her finish her champagne too quickly.

"What did you think?" The waiter was back. He whipped away her empty glass and replaced it with a fresh one.

"Oh no," she blurted. "I can't afford another one."

"This one is on the house," he said. He bent forward so he could talk more discreetly. "I know who you are," he whispered.

"What?" Jodie didn't think so. *She* didn't even know who she was.

"I follow your sister on Insta." He gave her one of those compassionate looks people gave you when your sister had died. "So does Cady." He nodded toward the curved marble-topped bar. The bartender was polishing glasses and watching them like a hawk. When she saw Jodie look her way, her eyes widened.

"We know why you're in New York." He was whispering like she was a secret agent and he didn't want to blow her cover.

"Oh wow. Right." Jodie didn't know what to say. It was too surreal.

"Cady and I miss your sister so much." The waiter's eyes had the shine of tears.

"You knew her?" Jodie felt a bolt of happy surprise. How lovely to find a trace of Bree still in the world.

"Not personally," he said quickly. "Only online. But we *love* her."

Bree had *fans*. For the first time the reality of that hit home. She knew Bree had hundreds of thousands of followers, and she'd seen the likes and the comments, but she'd never *met* any of those people before. Somehow seeing this waiter's genuine emotion for Bree made it real. How many people like this waiter were out there in the world, missing Bree, and now watching Jodie stumble her way through the bucket list?

That wasn't a helpful thought. God. She was going to fail them. She was going to fail this poor, beautiful, dark-eyed man, and his friend behind the bar, who was still watching them closely.

"We just want you to know that we're with you all the way,"

he assured her. And then he poured her a glass from "the oldest champagne house in the world," with notes of "citrus, white flowers, and peaches." He gave her a sympathetic smile. "Great choice of tree, by the way. That red . . ."

It popped.

"Thanks." Jodie took a gulp of the champagne. She could hardly tell him she hadn't chosen the tree. Cheryl wasn't part of the public story, was she? The whole feed was set up as though Jodie was posting. Cheryl didn't exist for the rest of the world. It was all such a lie. Kind of. Maybe *lie* was unkind. Maybe *fantasy* was a better word. It was just a Technicolor fantasy version of things.

"I don't think it matters that it's not really a tree," he confided.

Wait . . . *what*?

He caught her shocked look. "I know it's all blowing up online, but you should just ignore it. You know what people are like. They can be total trolls."

Jodie's stomach clenched. *What* was blowing up online? She held off until the waiter had glided off to the next table, and then punched open the Instagram app. Cheryl had posted some beautiful pictures. Full of emotion, as always. There was even the same picture that *The News* had printed. This was probably where they'd got it, Jodie realized. She was such an idiot. It hadn't sunk in until today how public all of this was going to be.

Oh God, look at all the comments on the tree post. Hundreds of them. Jodie scrolled through them, the champagne turning to vinegar in her stomach. There was a vigorous and not always polite debate unfolding over whether the dogwood was a tree or a shrub. Which was just stupid because everyone knew a dogwood was a tree.

It was while she was reading the comments that she noticed the red notification on the direct message icon. She never got messages.

Expecting it to be some crazy person wanting to contact her directly about the shrub/tree debate, Jodie opened it. And almost died.

Because it was a message from Kelly Wong. The actual Kelly Wong. The Kelly Wong she'd played varsity with; the Kelly Wong who'd taken her to prom (as a friend); the Kelly Wong she hadn't spoken to in years. The Kelly Wong who was the most perfect specimen of manhood she'd ever encountered, so perfect that he made all her subsequent boyfriends seem so lacking that they hadn't stayed boyfriends for long. *That* Kelly Wong.

And all his message said was . . . **Hey.**

Jodie took a big sip of the citrussy/flowery/peachy champagne, the one that she couldn't really tell apart from the last champagne. What should she do?

What kind of question was that? There was only one thing *to* do. She wrote back.

Hey.

And waited, staring at the stupid screen like he was hanging around, waiting for a response. Only the green dot did say he was online *now.* He'd messaged right back.

I'm sorry to hear about your sister.

Why was he messaging her? She hadn't spoken to him in years. Had he seen the newspaper? But why would he? He didn't live in Wilmington anymore. She glanced at the waiter, who was now standing at the bar with his friend Cady. They were giving her surreptitious looks. *They* knew all about her and they didn't live in Wilmington. Jodie's heart was pounding so hard that she was surprised it wasn't shaking the chandeliers. Her hands were trembling as she tried to type back.

Thanks. I'm sorry to hear about your dad.

Maybe he followed Bree on Instagram, just like the waiter and the bartender did. Maybe he'd seen all of those posts, the ones where she looked like a pathetic kicked dog.

Grief's not fun, he typed back.

No, it sure wasn't. She tried to calm herself down. She couldn't believe she was messaging Kelly Wong. After all these years.

I've missed you, Boyd, he wrote.

Jodie felt like her bones had been removed. He'd *missed* her? No, no, no. Don't read too much into it. That was just something you said to an old friend. But what did she say in return? Did she say she'd missed him too?

She couldn't. It was too true. He might be able to tell it was true and then things would get weird.

But then he typed something else, and things got weird anyway.

Looking forward to seeing you tomorrow. Tell Cheryl 11 a.m. is fine.

Chapter 15

"Why the hell are we seeing Kelly Wong tomorrow?" Jodie burst into Cheryl's room the minute Cheryl opened the door. She'd been pounding on the stupid door for a good five minutes. The doors were thick, and her knocks were muffled. She didn't care if she woke up the whole corridor. She was furious. "How do you even *know* Kelly Wong? Where do you get off? What does he mean *Tell Cheryl 11 a.m. is fine!*"

"Jodie! It's the middle of the night." Cheryl tried to push her out of the dark room, but Jodie wasn't about to be pushed.

"For God's sake!" The lights went on and Jodie saw that there was a woman in Cheryl's bed. A very pissed-off looking woman. "Just one night, Cher. *One night.* Is that too much to ask?" She was older than Cheryl, but even rumpled and mostly naked she looked glamorous as hell. She had dramatic winged eyeliner, which only looked sexier for being slightly smudged, and a cloud of tight curls. The woman yanked the quilt up to cover herself and fumbled for her glasses on the nightstand. She put them on and glowered at Jodie. "You got any idea what time it is?"

Jodie was caught between her righteous rage at Cheryl and her shock and chagrin at interrupting this woman's night. "Sorry," she mumbled.

"You *will* be sorry if you don't get out of here. Who do you think you are barging in on us like this in the middle of the night? You think you own her? Just because she works for you doesn't mean she's at your beck and call."

After the initial shock of finding the woman in Cheryl's room, Jodie remembered why she was there. And why she was mad. "*Me?*" she gasped. "Her at *my* beck and call?" She could feel the blood rush to her face. "You've got it completely backwards, lady."

"Calm down," Cheryl sighed, tightening the belt on her hotel robe. She pushed her hair back. "That's enough, Tish. Leave her be. I don't work for her, and you know it, but I *am* at her beck and call. That's my job."

"Oh no. *No!*" Jodie wasn't letting that slide by. "*You're* the one bossing *me* around. If anyone's beck-and-called, it's *me.*"

"Well, your job sucks." Tish ignored Jodie completely, leaning back on her elbows and giving Cheryl a poisonous stare.

"I know you're capable of holding that thought until I get back," Cheryl said dryly. "Let me just sort this out and I'll be back to hear all about it."

Jodie didn't want to be *sorted.* She'd come here to do the sorting. But here she was, somehow caught in the middle of Cheryl's domestic argument.

Tish snorted. "I might not be here when you get back. Not after the way tonight's been ruined."

"Well, I'm sorry we're ruining your night," Jodie snapped, "but I'll have you know my whole *life's* been ruined." That was melodramatic but it sure felt good to say. She was overdue for a tantrum, given how bossy Cheryl was. Jodie fixed Cheryl with an icy glare. "I'll leave you in peace with your girlfriend, or whoever she is, but I'll be talking to you in the morning." And then she slammed the door. It felt so satisfying that she was tempted to slam her own door too.

"Wait!" Never one to be daunted, Cheryl unslammed the door and followed Jodie into her room. "Now, what's all this about Kelly Wong?"

Jodie's ire leapt back brightly. "You contacted *Kelly Wong*! What the *hell*?"

Cheryl rubbed her eyes. "You mind if I hit the mini bar while we have this conversation?" Without waiting for Jodie's answer, she pulled a tumbler off the shelf and opened a tiny bottle of scotch. "I contacted Kelly Wong's *mother*. She was kind enough to put me in contact with Kelly." Cheryl squinted at Jodie over the rim of the glass. "You know Kelly Wong well?"

Yes. No. Ugh. Jodie didn't know. And it was beside the point. The point was Cheryl's meddling. Her managing. Her Marketing Barbie evil ways.

"I used to play baseball with him in high school," Jodie said tightly. "But that's not what we're talking about."

Cheryl drank her scotch thoughtfully. "Right. Well, I called Mrs. Wong because I had an idea. A really brilliant idea, which you can thank me for as soon as you've calmed down."

Jodie didn't think she was going to like this brilliant idea and she had no intention of "calming down."

"Now, you—"

"Number thirty-nine is piano lessons with Mr. Wong, right?" Cheryl said, cutting Jodie off. "But it doesn't specify *which* Mr. Wong . . ."

Oh no. *No.*

"Yes, it does," Jodie told her firmly. "It says *Find Mr. Wong and finally have those piano lessons Mom and Dad paid for that I never took.* Mom and Dad paid a very specific Mr. Wong, who is now no longer available to give piano lessons." Her palms were sweating. Because Cheryl had that look, that immovable, implacable, impossible look.

"Indeed." Cheryl took another sip of her scotch. She'd gone all sly. "Your parents paid Mr. Wong for lessons, which he never delivered. You could say Mr. Wong is in your parents' debt, couldn't you . . . and now he's passed, rest his soul, that debt belongs to his estate . . ."

"Oh no. No, no, no. Debt doesn't work like that."

"Doesn't it?" One of Cheryl's perfect eyebrows arched. "Then why have you been working double shifts all these months?"

Goddamn it. There was no answer to that one.

"While the original Mr. Wong may no longer be with us, he

does leave two sons, both of whom can play piano." Cheryl was triumphant. "So, there we have it. A Mr. Wong can deliver the piano lessons, as owed!"

Jodie was speechless. She tried to muster an argument, but Cheryl plowed ahead.

"I explained everything to Mrs. Wong, and she said that both of her sons are capable of teaching you piano, but that you'd probably prefer Kelly." If Cheryl's eyebrow went any higher it would disappear into her hairline. "She didn't say why . . ."

"We played baseball together," Jodie reminded her snappily.

"And went to prom together, apparently."

"I thought she didn't say why." Jodie scowled. "Besides, that wasn't romantic. We only went as friends. We were teammates, that's all."

Cheryl swirled the scotch in her glass and tried not to smile. "She didn't tell me about prom; Kelly did."

Oh God, what else had he told her? How did Cheryl manage to get so much information out of people?

Cheryl shrugged. "I don't care which Mr. Wong you pick. Bailey will be there tomorrow too."

Right. Bailey. Kelly's stiff and boring older brother.

"I've organized for us to meet the whole Wong clan at Bailey's place out at Great Neck tomorrow morning. Apparently, the infamous piano is at his house. We can work out the details when we get there. They're all more than happy to help you complete the list. Kelly and his mom were visiting for the holidays anyway—isn't that lucky?"

Yes. Lucky . . .

Cheryl drained her scotch. "I'd best get back to Tish." She nervously adjusted her bathrobe and glanced at the door. "I'm sorry Kelly messaged before I had a chance to speak to you."

It was only once Cheryl was gone that Jodie realized that, despite her ire, she'd barely said a word. Damn, that woman was good at her job. Jodie felt completely managed.

She sat on the bed and stared at the muffled shimmer of the city through the gauze of the curtains. *Kelly Wong.* He was right here, in the same city she was in.

Jodie fumbled for her phone and opened Maps. Where was Great Neck?

It was in Long Island. So, he wasn't exactly in the same city.

Jodie flopped back on the bed, the weight of memories falling on her like a rockslide. That godawful prom. It had started out so well and ended so badly. Jodie pulled the pillow over her face. *Don't think about it.*

The slow dance to that ridiculous '80s power ballad, his hands on her back, her cheek on his shoulder . . . Hanging out with the baseball team, feeling like one of the guys. Kelly getting crowned Prom King, next to his ex, Ashleigh Clark. The after-party . . . with everyone except Jodie in the pool in their underwear. Kelly disappearing into a bedroom with Ashleigh.

Oh my God, it was years ago. Who even cared anymore? What kind of loser was she to still be thinking about *prom night* at her age?

She wasn't some spinster virgin. She'd dated. She'd moved on. And it wasn't like Kelly had been her boyfriend or anything. Really, if she was going to be ruminating over man problems, she should be ruminating over Cooper, who was still popping up on Messenger in the middle of the night, a perennial not-boyfriend. At least he was *almost* a boyfriend, unlike Kelly . . .

Stop thinking. Please stop thinking. Jodie rolled out of the bed and headed for the shower. She'd wash herself clean of today and get some sleep. She took in the bathroom. It was *fancy.* She'd never showered in a marble bathroom before, under a mini chandelier, with designer shampoo that smelled like a flowering jungle. Jodie stood in the falling water, inhaling the exotic smell and trying to focus on the positive. Just like Bree would have done.

And in the morning, when she rolled out of that downy soft bed, she'd pull on her running shoes and go running in Central Park. Something she'd never done and never imagined doing.

And she wouldn't think about Kelly Wong.

Chapter 16

Tish came with them to Great Neck. Because it turned out the one person Cheryl couldn't manage was her own girlfriend.

"I took time off work for this," Tish said stubbornly, climbing into the car Cheryl ordered.

"I'm working, Tish," Cheryl complained. She stood on the sidewalk, holding her takeaway coffee, refusing to get in the car until Tish got out.

The three of them had gone for breakfast at the diner across the road from the hotel. Jodie had completed an epic run just after daybreak and was starving. She polished off an omelet with a side of pancakes while she listened to them argue. Cheryl barely ate. She seemed to subsist on coffee. Jodie pinched her uneaten Danish as they left the diner.

"I don't mind if she comes with us," Jodie said, more than happy to needle Cheryl. Tish had offered Jodie a pained apology over breakfast; Cheryl hadn't. Jodie took a bite of the Danish as she watched Cheryl glare into the car. The car that Tish most definitely wasn't getting out of.

"You hear that? Your client doesn't mind." There was a snap from the dark interior of the car as Tish buckled her seat belt.

"*She* isn't my client," Cheryl snapped. "This is company business. You want me to get in trouble? Who's going to pay the mortgage then?"

There was an ominous silence from inside the car.

Cheryl ran a hand through her hair, mussing her blowout. "We've been having some trouble," she confided to Jodie under her breath.

There was a snort from inside the car. Then Tish's curly head popped out. She strained against the seat belt. Clearly something had hit a nerve. "*We* haven't been having trouble." She spoke directly to Jodie. "*She's* been having trouble. Keeping her *word.*"

Jodie froze, with the Danish half in her mouth. She didn't know what she was supposed to say or do.

"This weekend was supposed to be our weekend away," Tish continued. The seat belt looked like it was about to cut her in two.

"Weekend?" Cheryl looked skyward, as though the skyscrapers might have an answer for her. "It's *Tuesday*, Tish."

"Yeah. A full two days after our weekend. A weekend that included me sitting alone in a McKinney bed-and-breakfast, just so you could go plant some shrub."

"It's a *tree* and I didn't plant it. Jodie did."

"Hey." The driver stuck his head out the open window. "You girls planning on going anywhere, or you just paying me to sit here?"

Cheryl sighed. Then she fixed Jodie with a fretful stare. "I know this is highly unprofessional."

Jodie hastily swallowed the last of the Danish. "It's fine." And it was. Tish actually made Jodie feel a lot less nervous about going to see the Wongs. So long as Tish was here to argue with Cheryl, Jodie wasn't the only attraction in the three-ring circus. She appreciated not being the center of Cheryl's attention.

Cheryl pressed her cherry-red lips together. "If you could not mention to anyone . . . that my girlfriend came with us to New York . . ."

"Who am I going to tell?" Jodie rolled her eyes. Then she remembered the whole Instagram thing. "Oh. I get it. Don't post anything with Tish in it. OK. I don't really post anything anyway." Only that one shot of the snow. And it was a pretty bad shot. Not like Cheryl's fancy ones.

"Thank you." Cheryl still looked fretful as they slid into the car next to Tish. Jodie found herself in the middle. She was well aware of Tish and Cheryl pointedly ignoring one another. There was a charged silence in the car as they pulled away from the hotel.

"How long does it take to get to Great Neck?" Jodie asked eventually, too uncomfortable with the silence to keep it.

"Half an hour or so," the driver said cheerfully. "This your first time in New York?"

"I've been here a few times. But only for a day or two." Jodie leaned forward, away from the frosty couple and toward the driver, who was clearly practiced in ignoring couples having a spat.

Jodie rested her elbows on her knees and let him play tour guide as they headed out of Manhattan and toward Long Island. Vaguely, she heard Tish and Cheryl start whispering behind her. Then she caught the word *shrub*.

"Is this about the dogwood?" Jodie apologized to the driver and leaned back into her seat. "Are you talking about Bree's tree?"

"You mean Bree's shrub," Tish corrected.

Cheryl turned her face to the window. She emanated sourness. "There still seems to be some debate about whether it's a tree or not."

"Of course it's a tree. It's a *dogwood*." Jodie shook her head. People online could get upset over the dumbest things.

"It's a *red twig dogwood*," Tish corrected, holding her phone up so Jodie could see the Wikipedia page she was scrolling through. "Which is apparently a *shrub*." Tish's nimble finger clicked on a link to a gardening encyclopedia before she handed her phone over to Jodie.

"Oh God, it *is* a shrub."

"It's a *tree*," Cheryl disagreed snappily. She lowered her sunglasses and was looking mulish.

"Not according to this." Jodie scrolled through the page, past photos of dramatic, red-branched *shrubs*. "According to this it's most definitely a shrub."

"It is deer resistant, though," Tish said dryly, "so that's something." She took her phone back.

Jodie groaned. "Does that mean we have to return the money? We can plant another tree, can't we?" Then she swore. "But not until spring! It's way too late to be planting trees now. Dad said it snowed all night." Just when she'd thought she could get this bucket list over with quickly . . . although there was still the problem of number one hundred on the list . . . there was no way *that* was happening quickly. Maybe waiting until spring was a blessing in disguise?

"Of course you can plant another one," Tish reassured her. "There's always a do-over."

"That is *not* your call," Cheryl warned her girlfriend. "Don't promise her things—I don't know whether there *is* a do-over or not. I'll have to talk to Ryan."

"*Ryan.*" Tish rolled her eyes. "Sure, call Ryan. I'm sure he'll sort it out."

"Who's Ryan?" Jodie asked.

"A god, according to Cheryl," Tish snapped.

"I never said he was a god," Cheryl snapped back. "I said he was a *genius.*"

Jodie probably should have kept her mouth shut. What good did it ever do, getting in between a warring couple? Especially when you were *literally* in between them.

"*Sir Ryan Lasseter,*" Tish told Jodie. She had her phone out again and was typing into her browser. "The owner of Iris Air." She showed Jodie the image on her phone.

Oh. Jodie should probably have known that. After all, he was the one paying off their debts. If she could ever get this list done. Which she wasn't doing so well at now the dogwood was revealed to be a shrub. In fact, she was right back at the beginning. She'd struck out in the first inning. Hopefully this Sir Ryan guy would let her take another swing at it.

The guy in the image was posed on a runway in front of a commercial airplane. He was flanked by wings of attendants in the tailored teal-blue uniforms of Iris Air. He had a whiter than white grin (he could have given Cheryl a run for her money in the minty teeth stakes) and a devilish expression.

He was the pinup for a billionaire playboy.

"He's a total blowhard," Tish muttered under her breath, so only Jodie could hear.

"He's a genius," Cheryl told Jodie, glaring at Tish. She knew something had been said and clearly guessed it wasn't good. "Self-made. Innovative. *Visionary*. And a really nice guy."

"Self-made?" Tish hooted. "He went to Eton and Cambridge!"

"His father was a grocer," Cheryl said tightly. She was looking mulish again.

"His father owned a *chain* of grocery stores in England," Tish told Jodie.

Jodie didn't really care if the guy owned every store in England, so long as he paid her every time that she finished an item on Bree's list. If she ever actually finished one . . .

A shrub. Damn it, she should have picked the tree herself. It would have to be a proper dogwood tree because her mom wanted a dogwood. *Your sister had a corsage of dogwood for Homecoming, remember, Jodie? The year she was crowned queen.*

Jodie hadn't remembered. But Mom had lit up as she pored over the photo album, as Cheryl had sat there stealthily snapping photos. That was about when Cheryl had snapped the photo of Dad looking ravaged.

Poor old Connor McAvoy bought her that corsage, not realizing it was fake. Remember, Jodie?

Nope. No memory of it at all.

He looked crestfallen when I told him it wasn't real. Poor boy. He'd spent ages choosing it at the florist. Shame on them too for not telling him. But Bree loved that thing. She kept it with her crown on her shelf. It's still there.

It was too. Jodie had gone to look. A stiff old cloth corsage, with one big white dogwood flanked by two smaller ones, all in a bed of silky fake leaves and threaded on a filmy white wrist ribbon. It sat in the circle of the Homecoming crown, which

was a silly glitzy thing. Jodie didn't remember a thing about
Bree winning Homecoming Queen. Bree was queen of everything and always had been. It just didn't seem that special, she
supposed. Not special enough to remember. Now she wished
she'd paid attention.

She looked so beautiful that night. Mom had gone all
dreamy. *She had a strapless white dress and wore her hair
down. She bought that dress for less than forty dollars, but you
never would have known. And even if they weren't real, those
dogwoods were perfect for that dress. She was like an actress
walked out of one of those old Hollywood movies.* Mom had
sighed. *If we'd had a real dogwood tree, we could have pinned
a flower in her hair . . .*

*Well, now you'll have one, and you can pin a flower in Jodie's
hair for her wedding day,* Grandma Gloria had said, winking
at Jodie across the table. Jodie had pulled a face at her. Wedding day? Gloria was all too excited about that last item on
the bucket list. Jodie wondered how they were going to judge if
she'd fallen in love or not . . . Did they just take her word for it?

Jodie didn't go to her Homecoming, did you, Jodie? Mom
had sighed again.

No, she hadn't. And if she had gone, she wouldn't have worn
a white dress or a dogwood blossom in her hair. Although she
had worn a dress to prom. But it hadn't been strapless or white.
And Kelly Wong *had* brought her a corsage. Not dogwoods, and
not fake. His mom had made it, he'd told her; she'd picked freesias because they smelled nice. *Sorry, she picked yellow,* he'd
apologized. *I told her it might not go with your dress.* It didn't,
but Jodie didn't care. She was too overwhelmed at even getting
a corsage, and from *Kelly Wong,* to care what color it was.

Later that night she'd thrown the stupid corsage in the trash
on her way home. Her friendship with Kelly had pretty much
gone in the trash that night too. And she couldn't stand the
sweet smell of freesias anymore. God, she'd been so stupid. It
curdled her stomach to think about how she'd nestled her cheek
against his jacket as they danced. While all the guys had been
laughing at her . . .

She can't honestly think that Kelly asked her to prom for reals?

Ugh. Like an idiot, she honestly had.

"We're nearly there," Cheryl said, breaking into the freesia stench of Jodie's unpleasant memories. Cheryl peered at herself in the reversed camera phone and reapplied another coat of cherry-red lipstick.

Nearly there. She wasn't ready. Jodie's palms were sweating. Maybe she should have put a bit more effort in? She was just in her usual jeans and hoodie. It was her nicest hoodie, but still . . . She wished she had her lucky cap with her, but Cheryl had drawn the line at the beat-up Phillies hat.

"You look great," Tish said, reading her mind. "You look amazing in every photo she's taken of you."

Of course. Tish thought she was worried about the photos. But Jodie was worried about something much stupider than the photos. Like whether she looked worse than she did in high school.

"Put some of that lip gloss on," Cheryl ordered, casting a quick eye over Jodie to make sure she'd used the tinted moisturizer.

Jodie ignored her and instead focused on her breathing. *It's just like those baseball games, Sporty Smurf,* she heard Bree's phantom voice say. *A little fear never stopped you from turning a double play.*

No, it hadn't. And it wouldn't stop her today.

"Great Neck sure is pretty," Tish said, trying to distract Jodie. They could both feel the pressure building; Hurricane Cheryl was picking up speed again. Her thumbs were thudding quietly against the screen of her phone as she typed messages.

"Look at this main street," Tish whistled, "it's like something out of a Disney cartoon."

It was. Jodie tried to take it in, but she was too anxious to do more than let it slip past the window in a wintery blur.

"I half expect to see cartoon dogs sucking on spaghetti in these alleyways." Tish laughed. "It's almost too pretty to be real. How much you think you have to earn to live around here?"

"More than I'm ever likely to earn at the rental booth," Jodie said.

"Oh yeah." The driver joined in. "You're looking at well over a million for a place around here."

Jodie felt a bit ill. Bailey Wong was rich. Of course he was. And Kelly was on his way to the majors. While she worked in a car-rental booth and lived with her parents.

Fumbling, Jodie hastily slicked on some lip gloss.

She was relieved when the driver pulled up in front of a brick tower. It wasn't a fancy-looking apartment building from the outside, but that didn't mean anything here in New York, did it? Things could cost a fortune without being fancy.

"Thank you," Jodie said to the driver as Cheryl dropped a cash tip over the seat as she slid out. She felt weird that Cheryl was paying for everything. She didn't like it. It made her feel like she was in Cheryl's debt. Or rather, Iris Air's debt. That Lasseter guy's debt.

"Feeling OK?" Tish asked Jodie.

"Of course she is. Why wouldn't she be feeling OK?" Cheryl took Jodie's arm and started hauling her toward the building. "Look, Kelly's already come down to meet us."

Jodie balked. She didn't mean to. It just happened. It was like her whole body locked up and refused to move.

Because sitting on the low wall by the front path was *Kelly Wong*.

"Looks like you have a love of hoodies in common," Cheryl said dryly.

God, he looked good. His hair was super short, showing off the sculptured lines of his jaw. And he made the slouchy gray Rainiers hoodie sexy as hell. How did he do that?

Tish gave a low whistle. "He's got some shoulders on him, doesn't he?"

Cheryl shot her an evil look as she pulled Jodie forward. She was strong.

"He's a pitcher," Jodie said numbly, as she took a moment to appreciate those shoulders.

"I may have to start watching baseball."

"You hate sports," Cheryl snapped.

"Maybe I just haven't watched the right sports," Tish said primly.

At that moment Kelly looked up and caught sight of them, and Jodie lost the capacity to listen properly. All she could hear was the blood rushing in her ears.

Kelly sprang off the wall, his face lighting up. "Boyd!" he called, waving.

"Boyd," Tish drawled. She poked Jodie in the back. "Looks like he remembers you."

Jodie felt her face burning as they reached him.

And then, to her shock, Kelly Wong *hugged her.* Jodie was too surprised to hug him back. She just stood there as his long arms wrapped around her and he hauled her against his body. His hard, fit body.

"I was so sorry to hear about Bree," he said, when he finally pulled away. She met his gaze and her shock turned to something much, much worse. Something melty and fluttery and shivery—a feeling she hadn't felt in a very long time. His eyes were that same red brown, all glowing like they were lit up by inner sunshine. They were warm with sympathy and concern. And he still had his hands on her arms as he peered down at her. "It was such a horrible shock to hear. She was always so . . . alive." He gave a shrug and pulled a face at the stupidity of his words. "That's the only way I can think to say it."

Jodie should say something. This is the bit where you said *Thank you,* or, *Yeah, it's been hard* or something equally inadequate. But she couldn't talk. In fact, to her horror, she found her eyes flooding with tears. It was his sympathy that did it. Or rather, it was the fact that it was *genuine.*

"Hey," he said, his voice husky. A frown line between his eyebrows flickered into existence.

"It's been really fucking horrible," Jodie blurted. And the tears fell, just splattering away down her face.

"Ah, Boyd, it is. It's really fucking horrible," he agreed.

"Sorry," she apologized, rubbing her face.

"Don't apologize. I cry at the drop of a hat these days." He sighed. "The other day I was at the supermarket, and I just started bawling in the toilet paper aisle. Grief is just a bitch."

Yeah. It was.

"It's a bit chaotic up there at Bailey's," Kelly warned as he led them into the lobby of the apartment building. "It's pretty crowded."

"We like crowded," Tish assured him. She pushed Jodie into the corner of the elevator next to Kelly. "Cheryl's one of a family of eight. You don't know crowded until you've been to a Pegler family dinner."

Cheryl gave Tish another one of her poisonous looks.

"What?" Tish graced Cheryl with a sunny smile.

"This is my *professional life*," Cheryl hissed, turning her back on Jodie and Kelly as she corralled Tish in the corner of the lift.

"Bailey's got a couple of kids now," Kelly told Jodie, politely pretending he couldn't hear a word of the conversation in the corner, which consisted of a lot of hissing.

"I saw on Instagram," she admitted. Then she blushed, aware she'd confessed to looking at his feed. But that's what Instagram was for, wasn't it? He wouldn't have posted if he didn't want people to look.

"They're pretty cute. Harper is a bit of a handful." He grinned. "Mom thinks she's possessed. But she's keen to start Little League in the spring, so that should run some of the energy out of her."

As the doors to the elevator slid open, they could hear squealing.

"That's her," he said. The sideways comma dimple flickered to life. He sounded so absurdly proud that Jodie laughed. "She's just turned four. Her party was yesterday, and the place is still a bit of a mess," he warned as he opened the front door.

It sure was. The small open-plan kitchen living space was an explosion of purple streamers and silver foil helium balloons shaped like unicorns.

"She likes unicorns," Kelly said as they took in the herd.

Harper herself was decked out in a purple mermaid costume, complete with sequined satin tail, and a tiara perched on the brim of a Mariners' baseball cap. She was jumping up and down on the white leather couch, squealing happily as her grandmother blew bubbles into the air.

"You remember my mom, Jodie? Mom, you remember Jodie Boyd, don't you?"

"How could I forget?" Mrs. Wong didn't get up from the couch, but she lowered the bubble wand and gave Jodie a smile. "No one butchered Bach like Jodie Boyd."

Jodie winced.

Mrs. Wong's smile turned gentler. "I was sorry to hear about your sister, Jodie."

"Thank you," Jodie mumbled. The goddamn tears were back again.

Mrs. Wong looked exactly the way Jodie remembered. She was immaculate in tailored navy slacks and a white blouse, and she wore glossy dark jade beads around her neck and gold hoops at her ears. She even had her hair cut in the exact same pageboy she'd had when Jodie was a kid, although these days it was streaked with gray.

"I was sorry to hear about Mr. Wong too," Jodie told her.

Mrs. Wong nodded gravely. "Not as sorry as he was."

Jodie didn't know what to say to that.

Kelly groaned. "Mom, stop freaking people out. Just say thank you."

"I'm supposed to be thankful for his death?" Mrs. Wong picked up the bubble wand and blew a stream of bubbles at Kelly.

"Hey! Those are my bubbles!" Harper shrieked, launching herself off the couch and straight at Kelly. He caught her effortlessly.

"Harps, this is my friend Jodie. We used to play baseball together." Kelly flipped her upside down and lifted her up so her face was level with Jodie's. Her legs flopped over his shoulders.

"But there aren't any girls on your team." Harper sized Jodie up.

"In high school, Harps. And *this* girl was the best at it. You never saw so many double plays. Jodie was the queen of the double play."

"I can play baseball too," Harper told Jodie. "I'm the baseball *princess*."

"Your uncle Kelly said you were starting Little League next year," Jodie said a little awkwardly. She'd never had much to do with kids.

"I'm going to be a pitcher," upside-down Harper told her imperiously. "Pitching runs in the family."

"Indeed it does." Kelly spun around so he and Harper were facing the other direction. "And this here is Cheryl and . . . ?"

"Tish," Tish supplied helpfully. She was beaming. "Happy birthday," she told Harper. "If we'd known it was your birthday, we would have brought cake."

"We *have* cake!" Harper squealed. "A *unicorn cake*."

"A rainbow unicorn cake," Mrs. Wong agreed. She was as calm as Harper was hyperactive. "Why don't you and your uncle make some coffee and cut up some of that leftover birthday cake for our guests."

"Good idea," Kelly agreed. "Come on, short stop." He hauled her over to the kitchen in the corner.

"Bailey and Faith took the baby for a walk," Mrs. Wong told them. "You'll have to do with instant coffee, I'm afraid, as neither Kelly nor I can work their machine."

"Oh, Cheryl can probably work it," Tish volunteered. "As a bona fide coffee addict, she can work every machine known to humankind." She gave Cheryl a push toward the kitchen.

"Wonderful." Mrs. Wong put the bubble wand away under the side table. "Why don't you lovely ladies take your coats off and come and join me on the couch while they organize the coffee."

Jodie was glad Tish was there. She was nervous as hell, and she couldn't tear her gaze from the kitchen, where Kelly had dumped Harper on the counter and was chatting to Cheryl. Cheryl was barely paying attention to him as she dealt with the coffee machine. Cheryl's cherry-red lips were framing their usual minty smile, but her perfect brows were in an arrow of annoyance. Jodie guessed she didn't like being relegated to coffee duties.

"Gene and I were married for thirty-three years, you know," Mrs. Wong told Jodie and Tish as they perched on the edge of the leather couches. "I told him if he died before me, I would make his afterlife a misery, and I intend to keep my promise." She laughed. "It seemed a good place to start to have Jodie come and torture his Steinway again."

Jodie winced.

Mrs. Wong patted her on the knee. "Not everyone is a musician," she said cheerfully. "Gene always liked you," Mrs. Wong confided, to Jodie's surprise.

"I doubt it," Jodie blurted. "I was probably his worst student."

"Oh no, not his worst," Kelly called from the kitchen. "There were lots way worse."

"But you always turned up," Mrs. Wong said, "and you'd always done your practice."

"Not that it helped." Jodie sighed.

"I bet you could play better than your sister," Mrs. Wong assured her. "She never came to a single lesson. I know because I found his record book! Not one lesson."

No. No, she hadn't. And she'd made Jodie lie to Mom and Dad, which still made Jodie's stomach curdle with anxiety.

"I hope you're hungry, because Harps has cut some giant-size pieces of cake," Kelly announced. He and Harper crossed the short distance from kitchen to couch, each holding plates. On each plate was an enormous rainbow-striped wedge of cake.

He winked at Jodie as he handed her a plate and she felt her stomach twist, and not with anxiety this time.

As Cheryl brought the coffee out, Kelly's brother Bailey came home with his wife and baby and the already full apartment hit breaking point. The stroller just about filled the kitchen. The baby started crying. Mrs. Wong took the baby away from its tired parents and started singing a lullaby. Somehow Harper got rainbow cake all over the carpet and started howling. Her mother scolded her, and her father got her more cake. Cheryl was pulling release forms out of her bag. Jodie felt like she was caught in a storm.

And then Kelly was sinking into the couch beside her.

"It's always like this," he reassured her, as he ate a third of his cake in one forkful. "Best to just let it happen."

Right. Jodie ate her cake too and, side by side, they watched the storm sweep through. Somehow Cheryl managed to get everyone to sign a release form, even in the midst of the chaos.

"It's good cake." Jodie didn't know what else to say. She felt awkward beyond belief. She kept her gaze on Harper, who was bent low over a new wedge of cake, frosting all over her face. Kelly was so close. She could feel the heat from his body.

"I saw the thing about your tree," he said.

"You mean my shrub?"

"Yeah. Is that going to be a problem?"

"Probably."

He nodded. "Dad left the most horrific medical bills, and he wasn't even sick for very long. It's cool you have a chance to pay them off like this." He grinned. "Although it's pretty weird."

Just the mention of the bills made Jodie tense. That damn shrub.

"Look, here's Gene's record book!" Mrs. Wong bent over the back of the couch, directly between Kelly and Jodie. She'd offloaded the baby onto Tish and was holding a cheap accounts book, the kind you got in a dime store. She opened it and pointed gleefully at Jodie's name, which was written in Mr. Wong's careful handwriting. "There you are. And see, he kept a record of every piece you worked on. Right at the end here, it was Gershwin."

Jodie remembered the Gershwin: "Our Love Is Here to Stay." Mr. Wong had wanted her to play it as a moody, dreamy piece, mellow, full of longing. But when she played it . . . love sounded like an uneven, restless cacophony, full of wrong notes.

"Your father sure could play the piano." Mrs. Wong sighed, leaning forward to rest her cheek on Kelly's head. He reached up and squeezed her arm with his big hand.

"You play it, Kelly." Mrs. Wong snapped the book closed. "I'd ask Bailey but he's busy with the baby."

Bailey blinked, pausing with a forkful of cake halfway to his mouth. "I don't have the baby."

"Give him the baby," Mrs. Wong ordered Tish, "we have things to do."

Tish obeyed and Bailey sighed, looking longingly at his cake.

"Bailey's a much better pianist than Kelly," Mrs. Wong confided in Jodie. "Shame he's busy with the baby."

Kelly groaned. "Don't you start. Dad never let me forget I was second best."

"Kelly never practiced enough. Too much baseball."

"Yeah, what a waste." Kelly rolled his eyes. But he stood up. "Come on, Boyd. Looks like it's time to hit the piano."

Jodie felt a bolt of panic. Already? She almost balked again, but Tish was right there, like some kind of emotional support animal. She fixed Jodie with a sympathetic look and held out a hand to pull her up from the couch. Jodie was aware of Cheryl snapping photographs as they moved into the tiny cupboard of the room, where the piano was kept. It was clearly a guest room as well as the piano room. There was a very narrow single bed and Mrs. Wong's suitcase was open on the quilt. There wasn't much room between the bed and the piano. And there were a lot of them crammed into that very small space.

"Stay out of frame," Jodie heard Cheryl hiss at Tish as they crowded in. "You're not supposed to be here."

"It's a pretty small room," Tish hissed back.

"It's a pretty small *apartment*," Mrs. Wong agreed. Tish looked embarrassed but Mrs. Wong didn't seem upset. "But look"—she pointed at the window—"if you bend all the way that way, you can just see a bit of water."

They bent, and sure enough there was a sliver of water.

"Waterside apartment," Mrs. Wong said with a nod. "Very valuable."

"It's lovely," Tish assured her.

"But Great Neck is a terrible name for a neighborhood," Mrs. Wong complained. "I couldn't live anywhere with such a terrible name."

"Where do you live?"

"Coral Gables."

"She picked it for the name," Kelly said dryly. "When I went to college in Miami, Mom and Dad followed me, and she just picked a neighborhood with a nice name."

"It sounds like a nice place to live, doesn't it?" Mrs. Wong sounded pleased with herself. "And it *is* a nice place to live. Lots of old people like me. Now, get playing, Kelly, before we run out of oxygen in here." Mrs. Wong zipped her suitcase closed and took it off the bed. Then she made everyone sit. Except for Jodie, who was told to stand next to Kelly and turn the pages.

Obediently, Kelly sat down on the piano bench. "Hell. I haven't sat at this since he died." He sounded a bit wobbly.

"We don't have to do this now," Jodie said hastily. Like everything since Hurricane Cheryl had arrived, this felt rushed. They'd come crashing into the Wongs' apartment and everything had been chaotic and loud; there was no time to process things as they happened. "We don't have to do it here either," she assured Kelly. "I'm sure we can find another piano."

"Don't be silly," Mrs. Wong scolded. "Of course he has to do this now. You want them to have to schlep all the way to Great Neck again, Kelly?"

"We don't mind," Jodie assured her.

"Well, actually . . ." Cheryl was wielding her minty smile again. "We're so grateful to you for squeezing us in, because we have a lot to get through this week. We have two more items to tick off the list after this."

"It's OK," Kelly told Jodie. "I'm happy to help."

Jodie didn't feel right about any of this.

Gently, Kelly lifted the piano lid. The ivory keys shone from years of finger oils. She heard him let out a shaky breath. "God. It's like he's right here behind me. You know how he always used to stand behind you while you played? Reading the music over your shoulder."

Jodie did.

He held his fingers in the air over the keys. "It used to make me tense."

"Me too." Jodie sighed.

They heard a sniff and turned to see that Mrs. Wong had started to cry.

"Mom . . ."

She held up an impatient hand. "No! Ignore me. I'm just leaking again. Play the Gershwin."

Kelly took a deep breath and scanned the sheet music quickly. Jodie heard him mutter under his breath. *Don't fuck up.*

And then his long fingers spread over the keys, and he started to play.

And Kelly could *play*. The music started slow and low, almost sad, with a trill here and there promising something, a shiver of expectation. His playing was like a caress. It swirled through the room in currents, eddying around bodies that had grown still and pensive. The notes were thoughtful and wistful, shimmering with a whimsical and fanciful *yearning*.

This was how Gershwin should sound, Jodie thought with an inner sigh, as she turned the page for him. How did he make the notes sound like questions? They swirled in bittersweet pleading refrains, beseeching, entreating, beguiling.

As the final phrase hung fading in the air, long after he'd played the last low note, there was appreciative silence.

"Was it that bad?" Kelly asked huskily.

"It was *amazing*," Tish breathed. "I hope you got all of that." She elbowed Cheryl, who of course had her phone up, recording every second.

"Third best in the family," Kelly's mother said proudly.

Kelly laughed and plonked the keys. "Third best. Story of my life."

"She's joking," Bailey said, poking his head into the room. He was jiggling the baby, who was still fretful. "Kelly's a thousand times better than me. Trumpet's my instrument."

"So loud," Mrs. Wong complained. "We took it away. He was always blowing it." She still held the accounts book. "According to this, we owe the Boyds more than half a dozen piano lessons. You're in New York for the week? So is Kelly. Perfect timing."

"Half a dozen?" Cheryl paled. It made her lipstick look even

starker. "I thought it was only a couple?" She gave Jodie a panicked look.

Jodie pulled a face. "Bree made me lie to Mom and Dad *a lot*."

"You best start now," Mrs. Wong said. "They paid for an
hour a lesson. We'll go in the other room and get Bailey to make
us some more coffee."

"No, I need to take some photos," Cheryl protested.

"Take them at the end. No one hears music in photos. They
won't know she's not really playing. And that way you won't
have to listen to her racket." Mrs. Wong wasn't taking no for
an answer; she ushered everyone out like a snowplow clearing a
road. "Play extra bad," she called over her shoulder. "Remember I told Gene I'd make him suffer if he left me."

"Your mom has a weird sense of humor," Jodie mumbled, as
Mrs. Wong closed the door, leaving her alone with Kelly and
the piano.

"Yeah, she really does." Kelly's long fingers noodled on the
piano keys. "You know when I made the AAAs, she sent me a
congratulations email? Or rather, she sent it to the club and had
them read it out on the broadcast as I pitched my first game. You
know what it said? *We're very proud of you, son. Don't forget
to wash your jockstrap after the game.* You know she laughed
so hard she pulled a muscle? Had to go to physical therapy after
to sort it out. 'They read it out, just like I wrote it!'" He mim-
icked his mother's voice perfectly. "Trust me to get a mother
who thinks she's a comedian. You know what my nickname was
after that, right?"

Jodie pressed her lips together. She could only imagine.

"That's right. *Jockstrap.* And then it became J. Strap. Now
it's just Straps. For the rest of my life the good people of Tacoma
will know me as Straps, because of my pain in the ass of a
mother."

Now Jodie did laugh.

"She looks like a classy lady, but she's not." Kelly slid over to
make room for her on the bench. "Come on, Boyd, we'd best get
you started on that piano lesson."

What are you waiting for? Bree's voice just about squealed in Jodie's head. She sounded like Harper, who was ramping up the noise out in the living room again. *You get to have a piano lesson with Kelly Wong!*

Not just one piano lesson, but *half a dozen* of them.

Gingerly, Jodie took her place on the bench. She looked at the keys, feeling the old sinking feeling. "I'm really bad at this," she warned him.

"I remember." He laughed. "Do you know how hard it was to study for a trig test with you bashing away at the piano downstairs?"

Jodie blushed. She bet he didn't know how many of her wrong notes were caused by the thought of him upstairs, listening.

"OK, Boyd. Let's show Gershwin how it's done. You remember how to read music?"

Poor old Gershwin, she thought as she put her fingers on the keys. He and Mr. Wong were about to suffer together.

Chapter 17

By the time the lesson was over, Hurricane Cheryl had struck again. Jodie was stunned to find that in the course of a single piano lesson Cheryl had hijacked Kelly too. According to her, he was coming along with them on this insane ride.

"It will be *amazing*," Cheryl promised, as she snapped some photos of the two of them at the piano bench. Now and then she ordered them to crowd closer so she could take a better shot. "Won't it, Mrs. Wong?"

"There's no room for you here anyway," Mrs. Wong told Kelly, who seemed as bemused as Jodie felt. "You'll be much more comfortable in a hotel than on the couch."

"I can't afford a hotel, Mom. Especially not one in Manhattan. I'm not in the majors yet," he said ruefully.

"All expenses paid," Cheryl and Mrs. Wong parroted together.

"There are still five hours of piano lessons to go," Mrs. Wong told Kelly. "And Bailey can't do it; he has a *baby*."

Kelly exhaled slowly. "I thought this was a one-afternoon kind of thing."

"I'm so sorry," Jodie apologized. She felt about an inch tall. They were forcing *Kelly Wong* into spending time with her. It was mortifying. "You really don't have to do this."

"Yes, he does," Mrs. Wong disagreed. "A debt's a debt."

Kelly rubbed his face. "But I came to visit the family, Mom."

"And you've visited. Besides, piano lessons don't take the whole day. We'll come in and see you in Manhattan. I promised Harper the zoo and the children's museum anyway."

"The zoo!" Harper started up squealing again. "Just like in *Madagascar*! I can see Alex the Lion!"

"The hotel is near the zoo," Jodie found herself saying. But she was cringing inside. Oh God, imagine what he must be thinking.

"There you go," Mrs. Wong said brightly. "Harper can go and be disappointed that there's no cartoon lion. And it'll give you a chance to catch up with Jodie—you haven't seen her since high school."

"But what about you?"

"What about me? I'm not leaving Great Neck. I've got a baby to cuddle." Mrs. Wong ran her hand over Kelly's head. "And you can't abandon Jodie, can you? Cheryl told you how much she needs this."

Jodie tried to catch Cheryl's eye. *Abandon Jodie.* What exactly had Cheryl told the Wongs? Cheryl had a way of spinning things, so they didn't quite resemble the truth. Although the truth was already pretty extreme . . .

"Right." Kelly sounded completely blindsided, and who could blame him? He turned to Jodie, who was still right beside him on the piano bench. "Guess we're having some piano lessons then."

And that's how Jodie found herself bundled into a car with Kelly Wong, headed back to Manhattan. Cheryl exiled herself to the front seat, so she could get to work on the Instagram account, and left the three of them in the back. She'd hired a fancy private car service again.

Kelly drummed his fingers on his knees and stared out the window. Was he angry? They'd pretty much kidnapped him. God, he must think she was a complete nightmare. Tish gave Jodie a sympathetic look, which only confirmed Jodie's fears. He *did* think she was a nightmare, didn't he?

"So, you play ball for a living, Kelly?" Tish said gamely. Once again, Jodie was grateful she was along for the ride today.

Kelly turned back away from the window, pasting a polite expression on. But before it fell into place, Jodie caught a glimpse of a frown. "Yeah. Pitcher. Just made the AAAs last year."

"Wow." Tish clearly had no idea what any of that meant.

Kelly grinned. He could tell. "And what do you do? Do you work for the airline too, or are you also accidentally caught up in this circus?" He felt Jodie flinch at that and shot her a gentle look. One which said, *You aren't to blame. You're just as caught up as I am.*

That was why he was such a good pitcher, Jodie remembered. Because he could communicate without ever saying a word. And he could read people in a nanosecond. He saw you more clearly than you saw yourself.

"Oh no, I'm an ethical hacker," Tish said cheerfully. "And I'm here of my own free will."

"What?" Jodie blurted. A *hacker*? Why hadn't Jodie thought to ask Tish what she did?

"What's an ethical hacker?" Kelly was burning with curiosity. He leaned forward and gave Tish his full attention.

"I test software for companies. You know, try to hack it. See what the weaknesses are."

"Wow. That sounds cool."

"It is. I love it."

Jodie stared at Cheryl's girlfriend with new eyes as she held forth on the joys of hacking. Tish's face lit up as she talked about her job. Jodie sat like a lump between Kelly and Tish and felt like the single most boring person on the planet. There was Cheryl, turning everyday life into the stuff of magic on social media; there was Kelly, pitching his way up to the majors, with a college degree paid for; and now here was Tish, like some kind of crazy cool spy. While Jodie was . . . completely sick of herself and how useless she was. She'd best finish her Exercise Science degree when this bucket list wrapped. She didn't want to be this boring forever.

They were still chattering away about Tish's job when they reached the hotel. Jodie trailed after them as they followed Cheryl through the sliding doors, past the giant orchids, and up to the front desk, where Cheryl set about booking Kelly a room. Kelly and Tish were joking around like old friends and Jodie felt like the boring kid at school. She could never think of anything interesting to say. Certainly nothing as interesting as ethical hacking.

Jodie moved away from them and pretended to be absorbed in staring up at the sparkly jellyfish chandelier. She tried to push down the rising tide of jealousy that was rushing through her. Why couldn't she be like Tish?

"Is there something wrong?"

Jodie jumped a mile. Some guy had joined her in staring up at the chandelier. He was craning his neck, as though trying to see what she was looking at. He was an expensive-looking guy, in a charcoal suit and a pair of stylish spectacles. Behind the spectacles he had clear blue eyes, the color of a July sky. His English accent was like something out of a movie. Jodie wondered if he was the concierge.

"No, nothing wrong," she said nervously. "I was . . . uh . . . just wondering how they cleaned it. The jellyfish. I mean . . . uh . . . the chandelier."

As the man in the suit looked back up at the chandelier, his foresty scent wrapped around them. He smelled like warm leather and rain-swept woods. "I imagine they have a chandelier guy," he said. "Why, are you looking for one?" His blue eyes sparkled.

Jodie wasn't sure if he was joking or not. "What, a chandelier guy?"

"I know a good one, if you need one."

She still wasn't sure if he was joking. "Right." Did she *look* like the kind of person who needed a chandelier guy? Jodie put her hands in the front pocket of her hoodie and gave him a polite smile. "Thanks, I guess."

"You're very familiar," he said, cocking his head and giving her a quizzical smile. "Have we met? In the Hamptons, perhaps?"

Jodie was almost startled into a laugh. "I don't think so."

"I never forget a face."

Jodie felt a sudden shock as an idea dawned. Did this British guy recognize her from social media? She was never going to get used to that. "Are you on Instagram?" she asked warily.

He looked pained. "Ah, you recognize me." He pulled a face. "Can't go anywhere these days." He seemed genuinely embarrassed.

Oh no. She was supposed to know *him*? Who was he? She didn't follow anyone, how was she supposed to know who he was?

"Ryan?"

"Cheryl!"

Ryan? Jodie almost groaned as she saw Cheryl click hastily across the marble floor on her heels, her smile enormous and genuine as she closed in on the British guy in the suit. *Ryan* could only mean . . . *Sir Ryan Lasseter.* The man who was paying her to finish this list. And she hadn't known who he was.

The British guy seemed thrilled to see Cheryl. He gave her a smacking kiss on each cheek and then one more "just to be all European," he said laughingly. Cheryl was pink and beaming. Jodie saw Tish back at the check-in counter, her face like a storm cloud. Kelly was watching curiously, his duffel bag still slung over his shoulder.

"What are you doing here?" Cheryl asked breathlessly.

"I asked Maya to book me into your hotel, so I could touch base about the project."

Cheryl's gaze jumped to Jodie. That's when Jodie realized *she* was "the project."

"Ah, Ryan." Cheryl gestured to Jodie. "This is Jodie Boyd. Bree's sister. The one who's finishing the bucket list."

"I knew I knew you!" He was delighted. Then he was peppering her with "European kisses" on each cheek. "How are you enjoying New York?"

"She just had her first piano lesson," Cheryl said proudly.

"Great. Wonderful. Good to hear. Shame about the shrub." He pulled a face.

Cheryl blanched. "I'll get that sorted."

"I know you will. You're a whiz, Cher, a total whiz." Sir Ryan Lasseter could out-enthusiasm Cheryl herself it seemed. He beamed at Jodie. "I *knew* I recognized you," he said again. "I never forget a beautiful woman."

Jodie blushed. She couldn't seem to help it, even though she knew she wasn't beautiful and that he was just being "all European."

"I thought I could take you ladies out to dinner tonight," he declared. "Catch up on the plans. Get a couple of photos taken with the talent." He winked at Jodie.

There was a pointed clearing of the throat from Tish at this point. Ryan turned. Tish and Kelly had joined them under the jellyfish. Kelly was holding a key card to a room, Jodie noticed.

"Sorry," Tish said with acid sweetness. "But we already have plans."

"And who do we have here?"

Cheryl's eyes went wide with panic. She seemed to freeze. Tish crossed her arms and watched, waiting to see what Cheryl would do. She couldn't seem to do anything.

Tish wasn't supposed to be there, Jodie remembered. Cheryl was supposed to be working, not hanging out with her girlfriend. Jodie's gaze flicked back and forth, trying to work out the undercurrents. Ryan didn't seem to know who Tish was . . .

"Ah, this is my friend, Tish," Jodie blurted. She didn't know why she was helping Cheryl out after the whole Kelly Wong stunt. But she was. "She's here for moral support."

Cheryl gave Jodie a look of profound gratitude.

"Tish!" Ryan was now doling out the European kisses again. "Welcome!"

Tish faked a smile but Jodie could see she didn't enjoy Sir Ryan and his kisses.

"Thank you," Cheryl mouthed to Jodie.

"And is this your partner, Tish?" Ryan had moved on to Kelly now.

"No, I'm the piano teacher." Kelly shoved his hand out for Ryan to shake, before any more kisses could be forthcoming.

"The piano teacher!" Ryan marveled. "Excellent." He shot Cheryl a teasing glance. "Am I paying for all of their rooms?"

Cheryl flushed. "We're only in the standard rooms. And some of us are sharing." She avoided Tish's cranky stare.

"I'm only joking. Of course we're paying for everyone's rooms. And there's no need to share! Just make sure you get lots of photos," Ryan said cheerfully. "I've been following along. It's been a bit grim so far; can you throw in some fun here and there too?"

"Cheryl's a great photographer." *Why* did she keeping jumping in to help Cheryl? Jodie didn't know why she found herself offended on Cheryl's behalf. "Her posts are works of art."

"She's a *whiz*," Tish agreed sourly.

"And don't I know it," Sir Ryan Lasseter agreed. "She's worth every penny. But happiness can be just as artistic as suffering, can't it?" He clapped his hands together. "So, dinner for five? Is this it? Or are there more?"

"This is it," Cheryl said quickly.

"Table for five it is. I'll have Maya book Alodie. You'll love it. It's divine." He checked his watch. "I have a meeting now, so I'll meet you there, shall I? Maya will book for eight p.m. *Ciao*." And then he was off.

That was clearly where Cheryl had learned her hurricane tactics.

"*Ciao*," Tish growled. "What was that? I thought *we* were having dinner tonight?" She fixed Cheryl with a black stare.

Cheryl shrugged helplessly. "I can't say no to my boss."

"Clearly." Tish stalked off to the elevators.

"Tish!" Cheryl ran a hand through her hair. "Jodie, can you show Kelly up to his room?" she begged. "I'm sorry." And then she was clicking off, just managing to catch the same elevator as Tish.

Jodie took in Kelly's sheer bemusement.

"Welcome to my life," she said.

"Is it always like this?"

"Yeah. Lately it is." She couldn't imagine what he was thinking. "What room are you in?"

Kelly showed her his key card. He was on the same floor as she was. Well, that was easy anyway. They punched the button for an elevator. Jodie tried to think of something to say. There was nothing. And too much.

Kelly was the one to break the silence, as usual.

"You want to go get a drink before dinner?" he asked when the elevator arrived, and they stepped in. "It's a long time between now and eight p.m. I might go work out now. But later? We could go for a walk and get a drink?"

Had Kelly Wong seriously just asked her out for a drink?

"Sure," she said, sounding way calmer than she felt. "That sounds like a plan."

"What about that champagne bar you went to last night? We could go there?"

"How do you know I went to a champagne bar?" she asked, surprised. She hadn't mentioned it to anyone.

"It's on Instagram."

Chapter 18

Once she was alone in her room, Jodie punched Instagram open. Sure enough, there she was, with her horrid hat hair, sitting in the candlelight alone with a glass of champagne. She looked like a total wallflower. Pitiable. And the waiter had tagged her, as well as Bree's official site: #DefinitelyAChampagneGirl. So much for her meager privacy. And now she had followers. More than a hundred of them. She scrolled through the comments under the photo. They were a mix of kind cheerleaders and horrible trolls. Jodie groaned and flopped back on the bed.

It wasn't only the waiter, either. Cheryl had been busy. Bree's Instagram was a photo essay of Jodie's twenty-four hours in New York. As usual, Cheryl had captured the sheer pathos of the situation. But also something else . . .

A something else called Kelly Wong . . .

And, oh God, the way Jodie was looking at him in some of the photos. And the video of Kelly playing Gershwin, the way Cheryl had zoomed in on Jodie . . .

Everyone was going to see how she felt about him.

Screw this. Jodie called Claude.

"Hey." Claude sounded surprised to hear from her. "How's New York?"

"Insane." Jodie could hear crowd noises in the background. "Where are you?"

"Hopper's." Claude was trying to sound flippant about it.

"Really."

"I shop here every week," Claude reminded her primly.

"You're shopping?"

"I'm having a double espresso."

"Say hi to Thor for me."

"Oh, shush and tell me about how you're enjoying New York instead."

Jodie laughed. "I miss you, Claude." She did. So much. It crashed over her in a painful wave. What she wouldn't give to have Claude here with her now. She'd probably be rearranging the throw pillows or something.

"I miss you too." There was a catch in Claude's voice. "Tell me what's happening. I'm dying of curiosity."

"Order one of those espresso martinis," Jodie told her. "There's a lot to tell." Of course Claude didn't get a martini. But she did order another coffee and Jodie unloaded about her last couple of days.

"You met *Sir Ryan Lasseter*?"

"Why does everyone say it like that?"

"Because he's *Sir Ryan Lasseter*."

Jodie heard someone in the background. "What was that?"

"Thor . . . I mean, Hopper. He wants to know what Lasseter's like."

"He kisses people a lot. Like *a lot*. Like three times each. Left cheek, right cheek, left cheek. Or maybe it's the other way round . . ."

Claude laughed and Jodie heard her repeat it back to Thor. "Hopper says he sounds like a blowhard."

"Tell Thor I'll let him know after dinner tonight." Jodie listened as Claude relayed the message. "But to be honest, he seems lovely." She remembered the warm sparkle of his July-blue eyes.

"What are you going to wear to dinner?" Claude asked. "It sounds fancy."

Jodie's stomach sank. "Oh God, I don't know. I don't do fancy."

"Go to your closet and tell me what you see."

"Everything's still in the suitcase," Jodie said guiltily.

"So, look in the suitcase, then." Claude sighed. "And while you're there, why don't you unpack it. They have closets in hotel rooms for a reason, you know."

As Claude went into a stress attack over Jodie's bound-to-be-creased clothes, Jodie kicked the unzipped suitcase open and pawed through the clothes she'd brought. Blue jeans. Hoodies. Black jeans. A woolen sweater.

"You must have *something*." Claude sighed in disgust. "What were you thinking? You must have known you'd go out to dinner while you were in New York?"

"I went out to dinner last night and my jeans were just fine," Jodie said defensively. "I had bibimbap."

Claudia groaned. "But now you're going to *Alodie*."

"It's fancy, huh?"

"Haven't you looked it up?"

"I called you first," Jodie snapped. Honestly.

"Alright, don't panic, you've got time."

"I'm not panicking. Black jeans are fancy, right?"

"You are *not* wearing jeans."

"I think I am. There's not much else to pick from."

"I'm going to put you on hold, Jodie. Don't you dare hang up. I'll be right back."

"Why? What are you—" Goddamn it, she'd gone. Jodie glared at the phone. Jeans were *fine*. Even celebrities wore jeans, didn't they? Although they probably wore designer jeans, not Levi's. Jodie rummaged through her suitcase. Black jeans and black sweater. There, outfit sorted. But the only shoes she had were sneakers. That might be a problem.

"All organized!" Claudia was back chirping on the phone.

"What do you mean, all organized? You mean I'm OK to wear my jeans?"

"Nope." She sounded too pleased with herself.

Jodie had a sinking feeling.

"Have a bath and relax for a while. You've got a delivery coming. It should be there in a couple of hours."

"A delivery? What?"

"You're welcome!" Claudia sang and then she hung up.

What had that woman done? Jodie tried calling her back, but Claude wouldn't answer. Hell. Jodie snatched up her black jeans and her black sweater. She wasn't playing this stupid game. She would have a bath, though. Because how often did a girl have dinner with Kelly Wong and *Sir Ryan Lasseter*? God, she was even *thinking* of his name in that stupid way.

The bath was enormous and took forever to fill. Jodie dumped the tropical body wash in until it foamed up into a mountain of bubbles. She got in and sat there for a bit. She didn't feel the slightest bit relaxed. Jodie washed her hair with the tropical-jungle-scented shampoo and took the time to do a proper conditioning treatment. Then she shaved her legs. Stupidly, because who was even going to see them? What did people do in the bath? She was just sitting here like a bump on a log.

Screw this. It wasn't at all relaxing. Jodie climbed out, deciding she was more of a shower girl. Now she had to deal with blow drying her wet curls, which she still hadn't mastered. The Manatee people had given her an anti-frizz spray, which she tried to use, but it was still potluck how things would turn out. Yet another thing she could blame on Bree's cancer. She hadn't had curls *before* she shaved her head.

Jodie put on her tinted moisturizer and lip gloss. And then considered herself in the mirror. The black jeans and sweater didn't look the slightest bit dressy. Hell. If only she had some jewelry or something to glitz it up a bit. Maybe she should ask Cheryl if she could borrow her red lipstick?

Oh, don't be stupid. She'd look ridiculous in red lipstick. Like a little kid playing with her mom's makeup.

The hotel room phone burred, and she just about jumped out of her skin. She snatched it out of its cradle. "Hello?"

"Ms. Boyd? A package has arrived from Macy's for you. Shall we send it up?"

Macy's.

Claudia, what have you done?

"Ah, yes, OK. Send it up." What else could she say? She reached for her wallet. She'd have to tip the bellhop. What was the right amount to tip a bellhop?

After she'd closed the door, she considered the Macy's bags like they were snakes coiled to strike. She and Claude didn't have the same taste, so she wasn't hopeful. Only, she thought, glancing at her reflection again, this probably wasn't the time for *her* taste, was it? This was probably the time for a bit of Claude.

Oh my God, Scaredy Smurf, would you just open the packages?

She did and heard the phantom sigh of Bree's admiration. *Oh well done, Claude.*

Well done, Claude, indeed. She'd shown great restraint, Jodie admitted, as she pulled a sleeveless black jersey dress from the tissue paper. It was simple, unfussy, and high necked.

It'll show off your arms, Bree whispered. *You've got great arms. And not many people can get away with a dress that clingy. That's the best thing about being a jock, hey?*

Jodie rolled her eyes. No, the best thing about being a jock was playing the sports, but she had never had any luck in convincing Bree of that.

Claudia had also sent a black tuxedo jacket and a pair of ankle boots. The only concession to Claudia-ness was a pair of lacy tights.

Sexy. Phantom Bree gave a breathy whistle.

She'd also sent a pair of big silver hoop earrings. Jodie had never owned such a fancy outfit. She fussed through the bags looking for a receipt but there wasn't one. God, she hoped Claude had bought all this on sale.

Send me pictures when you're dressed, Claude messaged.

Right. Pictures.

Jodie wriggled out of her jeans and sweater and into the black jersey dress. God, it clung. But the soft wool didn't feel tight at all. It felt . . .

Sexy.

Oh, shut up, Bree.

But she was right. Sexy was the exact right word for it. Even more so once she'd rolled on the lace tights and zipped up the ankle boots.

Wow. Who knew she could look like *this*?

Claudia, that's who.

Jodie's fingers were trembling as she removed her stud earrings and replaced them with the hoops.

You've got amazing arms, Hefty Smurf. Michelle Obama-level arms.

Thanks, Bree. Jodie stared at herself through her sister's eyes. Her arms were pretty good. And she could carry off this tight dress thanks to years of running.

But she'd *never* looked this good before. Not in her whole life.

Nervously, she snapped some pictures and sent them to Claude.

OMFG!!!!!!!!!

Jodie laughed.

Thor says to tell you you're smokin'!

You're a genius, Claude.

I know.

Jodie laughed again. God, she wished Claude was here, instead of back in Wilmington.

Pics with jacket 2 plz!

Jodie pulled on the tux jacket. The material slid, cool against her bare arms. She sent Claude a photo.

Claude sent back a meme. *Slay, Queen!*

Jodie laughed.

I'll be watching Insta. Have fun.

Yeah, that's right. Instagram. Oh well, at least tonight she wouldn't have hat hair.

Chapter 19

Jodie wished she could have snapped a photo of Kelly Wong's face when he saw her. It would have been nice to have proof, because she was sure she'd doubt it had ever happened come morning, but Cheryl wasn't present to capture a stealthy picture.

Jodie had been nervous as hell waiting for him to knock on her door. They'd said six thirty and she'd been ready way too early. She'd spent the time pacing. It wasn't calming. By the time he had knocked on her door, she was coiled as tight as a spring.

She flung the door open way too energetically. It slammed against the wall, and he jumped. But then he caught sight of her.

And she'd never forget his face as long as she lived. She might doubt it, but she wouldn't forget it.

His mouth literally fell open, like something in an old movie. His eyes went all big and he looked her up and down in a breathless moment that seemed to last forever. She wouldn't have been surprised to see cartoon birds circling his head, like he'd just been hit by an anvil.

"Wow," he said eventually. He didn't seem capable of much else. "Wow." He cleared his throat. "I mean *wow*." He seemed to have glitched. He ran his hand down his T-shirt, clearly feeling underdressed. "I looked the place up," he finally blurted. He dragged his gaze to her face. He still looked a bit stunned. "It's just over an hour's walk. You want to get a drink and then catch a cab there, or just walk?"

"Walk," she blurted back. She grabbed her ski jacket. It was the only winter coat she had, and it was too cold to walk anywhere without a coat. "Let's just take a walk to the restaurant. It'll be good to see more of New York," she babbled.

He seemed more comfortable now that she'd dressed down her fancy outfit. "You're OK to walk?" He glanced down at her feet, as though expecting to see heels.

Jodie didn't wear heels. She thought they were equivalent to foot binding. Thank God Claude hadn't pushed her on it; if Claude had ordered heels, Jodie would be wearing her old sneakers right now with this fancy new dress. The ankle boots Claude had ordered were flat and comfortable. "I can outwalk you any day," she told him, as she yanked the hood up on her ski jacket. She wasn't about to wear a hat tonight; it wasn't worth the hat hair.

Kelly grinned. "We'll see, Boyd. It may be the off-season, but I'm still in training."

It was just like old times, Jodie thought, as the two of them powered down Sixth Avenue, headed in the direction of Lower Manhattan: always a competition. They fell into talking about baseball, just like the old days too. And Kelly fell into treating her just like one of the guys. She packed away the memory of the stunned look on his face, and the way he couldn't stop saying wow, to pore over later, when she was alone, and surrendered to being one of the guys again. Her cheeks were still flushed from the thrill of his gaze, and she walked with her shoulders back and a swing in her stride. She felt sexy as all hell, and more confident than she'd ever felt in her life. Thank you, Claude.

Now that they were walking through the bustling neon night, facing the city and not each other, conversation came easy. They talked about the boredom of traveling in the minor leagues, about the roach motels and terrible food, about getting traded at a moment's notice and having to pack up your life. Jodie peppered him with questions, dying to know every detail. It was a snappingly cold night and their breath frosted in the air as they walked. Jodie wished the walk could last forever. Every inch of her felt alive.

They paused a few times to take in the sights—Radio City Music Hall, a retro neon dream in primary colors; Bryant Park winter village, with its ice-skating rink, glittering with carnival spirits; and the Empire State Building, a spike of red and green for Christmas—but even with all their pauses, Jodie and Kelly clearly walked faster than Google Maps anticipated, because they reached the restaurant way too early.

Alodie didn't look that fancy from the outside. It was just a little shopfront in Tribeca.

"Do you want to keep walking for a bit, or shall we get out of the cold?" Kelly asked. His eyes were twinkling, and his face was nipped by the cold. Jodie opted to head into the warm. Inside, the restaurant was intimate. There was a lot of brass and milk glass. Leather booths. A long wooden bar. The maître d' took their ski jackets and led them to a spot at the bar, to wait until their table opened up. Jodie didn't think she imagined that the name *Lasseter* got them a slightly warmer welcome.

"Cocktail?" the bartender suggested, sliding them a drinks menu.

"You know what, why the hell not?" Kelly said. "Seems appropriate to the situation." He grinned at Jodie. "How often do you get kidnapped by your old teammate and roped into dinner with a British billionaire?"

"Don't forget roped into giving piano lessons," Jodie reminded him.

Kelly laughed. "I wouldn't dare forget. My mom would kill me." He turned to the bartender. "We'll have whatever you recommend."

"Isn't that dangerous?" Jodie murmured, as the bartender whisked their menu away and disappeared down the other end of the bar. "Did you look at the prices?"

"Ah. No. How bad?"

"Bad."

"Best make it last, then. You got any idea what ballplayers earn in the AAAs? This is probably my whole food budget for the month."

"Bryce Harper got 330 million dollars out of the Phillies," Jodie teased him.

"I ain't Bryce Harper, baby." Kelly said it cheerfully enough, but he winced imperceptibly.

"One day."

Kelly laughed. "I like your optimism but, trust me, now that I'm playing with the big boys, I don't seem that good. They're *good*."

"So are you." Jodie meant it. He could tell and got bashful.

"What about you?" he asked, switching the subject. "Are you still playing?"

Jodie rolled her eyes. "Where? In the softball leagues?"

"They have women's baseball."

"Not for the likes of me. How would I pay the bills?"

"You didn't play at college?"

"I'm still at college. Part-time at Delaware Tech. But they don't have a women's baseball team. Only softball."

Kelly tilted his head. "But you're at least playing softball?"

Jodie was glad their cocktails arrived at that point. She didn't want to talk about how much baseball (or softball) she wasn't playing. Or how much she missed it. Or that she was still in college, when he'd already graduated.

"Le Soixante-Quinze," the bartender crooned as he slid two champagne flutes across the polished bar. The drinks were frosty yellow, with twists of lemon curling exuberantly across the rims. "A classic French cocktail, invented in World War One, named after the seventy-five-millimeter weapon. Because it hits you hard." He gave them a cheeky smile.

It sure did. It was so strong Jodie's face just about collapsed in on itself when she took her first mouthful. "What's in it?" Her voice sounded a bit strangled.

"Gin, champagne, lemon juice, sugar syrup."

"Quite a lot of gin?" Jodie guessed.

The bartender winked and moved on to the next customers.

"Well, I guess at least this'll knock my nerves on the head," she said to Kelly, as she slid onto a bar stool.

"You're nervous?" He seemed surprised. He pulled the lemon twist garnish off the glass and twirled it between his long fingers. "You don't look it."

Jodie scoffed. "Now you're just being polite. I look like a rabbit caught in the headlights. Perpetually."

"No." He smiled and seemed to relax a bit. He stayed standing but leaned against the bar. His warm brown gaze fell to her legs as she tried to cross them. She wobbled on the stool, gracelessly, and grabbed hold of the bar for balance. He seemed appreciative of the lace tights. Good call on Claude's part, as they drew attention to her legs, which were also one of her best features. Jodie was glad she'd spent the season of grief running. It was about the only thing that had kept the howling sadness at bay. And she'd run *a lot*. Which meant she could pull off a pair of lace tights pretty well, she thought gratefully.

"But you never seem nervous," Kelly told her. "You were the only one who stayed cool during some of our toughest games."

Jodie was so shocked she just about fell off the stool. "I did not. I was a *wreck*."

He rolled his eyes. "Sure you were."

"No, really," she said, astonished. "I was a complete basket case. I used to throw up before every game, not just the tough ones." She didn't know why she was telling him this. She was just so shocked. "You thought I was cool? I mean . . . calm?"

"Everyone did. You were famous for it. We all thought you had ice in your veins."

Jodie was speechless now. She took a mouthful of the lethal cocktail.

"You really threw up?" He didn't sound like he believed her.

"Yes! It's just that I was off in the girls' locker room all by myself, so none of you ever saw it."

The narrow frown line was back between Kelly's eyebrows. "No way." He shook his head. "But . . . you used to just amble out, looking cool as anything."

"Looking stone-cold *petrified*, you mean." Oh God, just

thinking about it brought the feeling back. Her stomach had been roiling; she'd chewed gum madly to get rid of the sour taste of vomit; and her face had felt like it had frozen into some kind of mask. The long white howling mask from the movie *Scream*.

But now Kelly was telling her everyone had thought she was cool, calm, and collected? Is that what petrified looked like from the outside?

"You have no idea how intimidating you were," Kelly said, shaking his head again. He took a mouthful of his yellow drink.

"Me?" Jodie was feeling the effects of the cocktail. *"Me?"* For the first time all day, her nerves were fading. A lovely loose feeling was unwinding, starting in her shoulders, and working its way down her body.

"Yeah, you." The drink was working its magic on Kelly too. He was loosening up, slouching against the bar. "You were always so composed."

Shut down, Jodie corrected silently, not composed. Packed away deep inside herself, terrified of screwing up, or making a fool of herself. *Composed?* She'd been in hiding.

"You looked like nothing could faze you," he said.

Jodie couldn't believe what she was hearing. *Everything* had fazed her. She had lived her high school life in a state of constant anxiety.

"Even when people were yelling at you—I have no idea how you coped with that, by the way—even when they were yelling all those awful things, you just played like it was you and the ball." He gazed at her with wonder. Jodie felt her stomach turn over. "You'd just take it all in your stride. You'd turn a play, and tug on the brim of your cap, and never blink an eye."

Is that what it had looked like? Because that wasn't how it *felt*. It wasn't even close to how it felt. If she hadn't blinked, it was only because blinking would send the tears tumbling.

"And I don't know how you coped with being the only girl on the team, because those dudes could be gross." Kelly pulled a face. "Even I found them gross, and I was one of them."

She'd coped by completely withdrawing into herself. It hadn't been fun.

"Granted, all the guys were half in love with you," he was saying now, "but none of them could get up the courage to ask you out." Kelly grinned at her, completely unaware that she almost fell off the stool again. She had to hold on to the edge of the bar with white knuckles.

What?

Jodie listened, floored by Kelly's alternate reality.

"You know they almost flushed my head in the toilet when we went to prom together." He laughed now.

"What?" She really couldn't keep from blurting it aloud this time.

"Oh yeah. They were *pissed*. Particularly Josh. He'd been gearing up to ask you out for months."

"Josh?" Jodie couldn't take that in. *"Josh* Josh? As in Josh Sauer?" As in their outfielder? The six-foot-three rock star? The one Bree and Claudia thought was "too good-looking." *There's good-looking and then there's* too *good-looking, and that boy is* too *good-looking.*

"Can I get another drink?" Jodie asked the bartender, draining the cocktail.

"I'll have one too." Kelly followed suit. "Man, it's good to see you again. It's been too long, Boyd. Why didn't we ever catch up after high school?"

Because you ditched me for Ashleigh Clark at prom and I was so pissed off I never wanted to see you again.

But she didn't say that. What she said instead was, "Because you moved to Miami."

"But we didn't even stay in touch on social media."

"I'm not really on social media." Jodie was feeling the effects of that drink. Her tongue was loose. "Besides, you never called me."

He winced. "I didn't, did I? I guess I was embarrassed about prom."

Luckily, Cheryl and Tish turned up and spared Jodie the humiliation of talking about prom.

"What happened to *you?*" Cheryl gasped, looking Jodie up and down.

"You look amazing!" Tish claimed the bar stool Kelly wasn't using. "What are you drinking? It doesn't matter, I'll have one," she told the bartender. "I don't care what it is, so long as there's booze in it."

"There's *a lot* of booze in it," Jodie warned.

"Even better."

"What have you done?" Cheryl complained. She looked distraught.

"Ordered a drink," Tish snapped. "Like a normal person would on a date. Oh wait, this isn't a date. It's a dinner with your boss."

"Not you. *You.*" Cheryl fixed Jodie with her black look. Jodie was getting used to that look.

"Me? What have I done?"

"You're supposed to look like you! Not like *this.*"

"Oh, shut up, Cher." Tish sighed. "She looks great." Tish had well and truly seen Cheryl in action today and was completely on Jodie's side.

"Yes, she does! She's not supposed to look great! Not yet! We have to save it for later down the list. Honestly, Jodie, you can't peak now, or we'll have nowhere to go later."

Jodie flushed, painfully aware that Kelly was watching. *Cinderella in the cinders*, she remembered. That's what Cheryl had called her back at the car-rental stand on the day they met. Well, screw that. She had no desire to play Cinderella to Cheryl's fairy godmother.

"So, don't take any photos of me, then," she said sharply.

Tish laughed. "Good response." She took the cocktail the bartender delivered and held it up in a toast to Jodie. "Don't let her boss you around."

"It's my *job*," Cheryl growled.

"It's after hours, princess," Tish purred. "Get a drink and stop hassling the pretty lady."

By the time *Sir Ryan Lasseter* arrived—almost an hour late—they were all a few drinks in, and Cheryl had loosened up considerably.

"I'm so completely, dreadfully sorry!" He cut through their

conversation, and pretty much *all* the conversation in the restaurant, with his juicy Britishness. "Terribly poor form to keep you waiting." He liberally doled out European kisses again and then scooped the group of them from the bar to the table. His hand was warm on Jodie's elbow and she was enveloped in that heavenly warm-leather-and-rainy-woods scent. Jodie found herself squeezed next to His Sir-ship on a leather banquette, opposite Kelly, who was scanning the menu with vague horror. Jodie looked down at the menu in her hand to see what the horror was.

Oh.

It was hard to tell what the prices were for, as the menu was in French. But something was fifty-nine dollars.

"Um"—Jodie cleared her throat—"I don't speak French . . . Is there anything vegetarian?"

"You're vegetarian?" Sir Ryan lit up. "So am I! Although I do eat fish."

"Aren't fish animals?" Tish asked with faux sweetness. Then she jumped a bit in her seat as Cheryl kicked her under the table.

"Let me order for you?" His Sir-ship asked Jodie, his blue eyes twinkling like he was suggesting a grand adventure. "Trust me?"

"Sure. But I'm the kind of vegetarian who doesn't eat fish." God, he was charming.

"Because they're animals." Tish withstood another kick from Cheryl.

In the end Sir Ryan ordered for everyone, and he was generous. Jodie saw how Kelly watched warily. She knew he was tallying up an imaginary bill in his head. But the wine Ryan ordered took the edge off his anxiety, and Jodie's too, because Ryan ordered wine *in volume*.

Almost in as much volume as he ordered food. There were truffled eggs, eggplant steaks, caramelized carrots, gnocchi in basil oil. It was a feast. The meat eaters on the other side of the table demolished a whole bass and a crispy-skinned duck too. And there was so much wine.

Jodie was glad her dress was stretchy.

"You look like you're having fun," Tish said, when they absconded to the ladies' room before dessert.

"I think I am," Jodie admitted. Sir Ryan had been charming and funny (and he smelled good), and Kelly had been . . . well, Kelly.

"You think?" Tish laughed.

"It's been a while."

"Yeah, I hear you on that." Tish rolled her eyes. "All I ever do is hang around waiting for Cher to finish work."

Jodie paused to wait for her while Tish reapplied her lipstick. The room was a bit wobbly. She put one hand on the wall to keep it steady. "You having fun tonight, even if it is just waiting around for Cheryl to finish work?"

"Yeah," Tish said, but she looked a bit flat.

Jodie felt a wave of sympathy for Tish, who wanted such a simple thing. Time. *Cheryl's* time, specifically. And time was so limited, wasn't it? You ran out of it eventually.

"Tish," Jodie said as they left the ladies' room. She was aware she was slurring slightly. She stopped and blocked Tish's way.

"Yes, honey?" Tish looked rather amused by Jodie's tipsiness.

"You're amazing, you know that?"

"Uh-huh." Now she looked *completely* amused. "You didn't think so last night."

"No. *You* didn't think so. Of me, I mean." Jodie remembered Tish's fury when Jodie had barged into their room. "Sorry about ruining your time with Cheryl last night," she said.

Tish laughed. "Yeah, well, you had every right to be mad at her."

"She's lucky to have you. You're better than amazing. You're *the best.*" Jodie went with an impulse and gave Tish some of *Sir Ryan Lasseter's* European kisses.

Tish laughed. "Thanks, honey."

Chapter 20

"I'm a bit drunk," Jodie admitted.

"Me too," Kelly said as he threw his jacket at the hotel chair. He missed and Jodie giggled.

"I thought you were a pitcher."

"I am. But I don't pitch jackets." He fiddled around with the television and his phone. "I hope this works," he muttered.

"Do you want some snacks while we watch the movie?" Jodie yanked the basket of snacks off the bench above the bar fridge. She tore open a candy bar. Drinking always made her hungry.

"Here it is!" Kelly was triumphant.

The Metro-Goldwyn-Mayer lion roared. And then the jazzy sound of a piano filled the room. Jodie and Kelly were watching *When Harry Met Sally*. It had been decided around the time the second trayful of cognacs arrived at the restaurant. Cheryl had been regaling Sir Ryan with her plans for Bree's bucket list.

"I've booked the *exact* table from the movie," she'd told her boss, flooding him with enthusiasm.

Ryan had been delighted. "And who's playing Harry?"

Jodie had glanced at Kelly.

But before Cheryl could answer, Sir Ryan Lasseter had sat up ramrod straight and gasped. "Wait! I have an amazing idea! *I'll* play Harry!"

Jodie had almost spat her wine all over the table, laughing. He *what*?

"But it'll have to be tomorrow," His Sir-ship told them cheerfully. "I'm off to London the day after."

To Jodie's horror, she found the whole orgasm thing was going to happen *the next day*. And with *Sir Ryan Lasseter*. For once, Cheryl might have been even more horrified than Jodie was, as now she had to try and move the booking to the very next day. "They don't take bookings for less than ten people," she mumbled once His Sir-ship had said his goodbyes and left them to finish the final round of drinks. Jodie had felt a warm buzz when he squeezed her hand. He was larger than life, that was for sure.

"Do you know the strings I had to pull to get that booking? I can't call them and ask to move it."

Jodie started laughing. This was getting too stupid. "I haven't even watched the movie again to see what I'm supposed to do." She hiccupped.

And that was when Kelly volunteered to watch it with her. Tonight. She was drunk enough to think that was a *great* idea.

"Bree *loved* this film," Jodie said around a mouthful of candy bar as Kelly fiddled with the volume. She shucked off her tux jacket and tossed it on the chair. "See that? *That* was a pitch."

Kelly glanced her way and did a double take. He was also more than a little worse for wear and wobbled on his feet. His expression was a bit dazed.

Jodie groaned. "I've got chocolate all over my face, don't I?"

"No," he said tightly. "No, you're good." His gaze dropped down her body.

"These old couples!" Jodie pointed at the screen. "Remember them?"

"I've never seen the film before," Kelly reminded her.

"Oh right. I'll be quiet." Jodie reached over and snapped the lights off, so it was more like being at the movies. She tossed Kelly a pack of M&M's. He'd always loved M&M's.

Then she unzipped her boots and collapsed on the bed. "You should take your shoes off too."

He sat down gingerly on the edge of the bed, glancing at her. She was still drunk enough that it didn't occur to her that "we can watch the movie in my room" might be a loaded thing to say to a man. As was "take your shoes off."

He took his shoes off and joined her on the bed, but far enough away that he was out of reach. Jodie threw a pillow down the far end and stretched out on her stomach. She rested her chin on her crossed arms. She must have seen this film a hundred times. Bree had loved it *soooooo* much.

"I love this bit," she said, as young Harry and Sally argued over whether men and women could be friends.

After a while she heard Kelly tear open the M&M's and then heard the crunch of the candy. A while after that he stretched out beside her. The next morning, she realized that was probably when he decided she wasn't hitting on him. That "watch a movie" meant "watch a movie." Mortifying. But, in the moment, it didn't even occur to her. She was blissfully happy, here in this room, on this bed, simply watching a film with him.

He seemed to enjoy it too. He laughed a lot. Especially when they got to the orgasm scene.

"You have to do *that*?" he said in disbelief, turning his head to stare at her. He was very close, Jodie realized. So close she could feel the warmth of his breath as he spoke.

Her heart skipped a beat. "Yes," she breathed. "Apparently I do." Imagine if she had the courage to kiss him, right there and then, when he was only a few inches away from her. Up close the crease in his lower lip was sexy as hell.

He shook his head. "Man, I'm glad I'm not you."

Yeah. Jodie wished she wasn't her too. She wished she was the kind of person who had taken the chance to kiss him before he turned back to the screen. The kind of person whose mind didn't skip ahead to think about consequences. Like the consequences for kissing him. Consequences which included Kelly being horrified, and her total humiliation. And then she'd have to face him over piano lessons, her vulnerability painfully obvious. All documented by Cheryl and her guerilla photography.

No. Best to just let the impulse pass and watch the movie.

But there was one weird moment, right at the end, when Jodie felt the mood in the room shift. The atmosphere thickened and slowed. It was during the New Year's Eve scene right at the end of the film. Frank Sinatra was lazily crooning—*For nobody else gave me a thrill . . . With all your faults I love you still*—and there were fairy lights spangled in the background as Sally plunged through the crowd to leave before midnight, and Harry came running in to find her.

She sees him. A look crosses her face: immediate, uncontrolled pleasure; a frown; a glimmer of something vulnerable and naked. And then he sees *her*. And a whole mess of stuff happens. Relief, softness, resolution. She's proud and angry and hurt. He sees it all.

Before the characters even spoke, Jodie felt the slowing of time, breathless stillness falling in the hotel room. She felt Kelly's body beside her on the bed. Heard his breath catch. Felt tingles of anticipation spiral through her.

I've been doing a lot of thinking, Billy Crystal said. *The thing is, I love you.*

How do you expect me to respond to this?

How about, you love me too?

Jodie's stomach was weak. Kelly was so close she could touch him with just a twitch. She barely heard a word as Harry and Sally argued their way through their "I love you" moment. All she could hear was her own heartbeat. The last few moments of the film felt like they lasted forever.

But then the credits were rolling, and it was all over.

"That was great," Kelly said eventually, after they'd lain in silence as Harry Connick Jr. reprised "It Had to Be You." "I can't believe I've never seen it before."

"Me either. How do you get to your age and not see *this*?" Jodie herself had forgotten how great it was. But it had never been *that* great before. Watching it with Kelly Wong was a million times better than watching it without him.

Kelly turned his head, so his cheek was resting on his forearm, and he was looking straight into Jodie's eyes. Jodie felt a little light-headed.

"You're a brave woman, Boyd," he said quietly.

No, she really wasn't. A brave woman wouldn't be lying here frozen, next to the man she'd once dreamed about. A brave woman would seize the moment . . .

She was a coward.

"You really think you can do it, that orgasm scene, in the middle of a busy restaurant?"

Oh God. That was tomorrow. Jodie was sobered up enough now for the reality to hit hard. "No," she said honestly. "No, I really don't."

"You want me to come along for moral support?"

Yes.

No.

Which was worse, having Kelly witness her shame live? Or having him watch it on Instagram?

Say yes, Scaredy Smurf! You don't have him for long. While he's here, you might as well spend every minute with him that you can.

Bree was right. When the piano lessons were over, Kelly Wong would disappear from her life again. And there were only five more piano lessons to go.

"Yes," Jodie said huskily. "I'd love you to come."

Good work, Scaredy Smurf.

Was it? Or was it insane? This sexy ghost from her past was about to witness her complete and utter public humiliation.

Along with more than a million people online . . .

Oh God.

Chapter 21

73. Sallying at Katz's

"What the hell is this?"

Jodie woke up to a raging hangover and an even more raging Hurricane Cheryl. Jodie couldn't get a handle on Cheryl. Sometimes she was polished and minty fresh, sometimes fiery and insecure, sometimes kind, and sometimes (like now) explosive. Jodie wondered who she was underneath. Because a lot of the time she seemed to put all her energy into performing, into being someone she wasn't. Someone who would impress Sir Ryan Lasseter, Jodie guessed, judging by the way Cheryl fell over herself around him.

When Hurricane Cheryl blew in, Jodie had stumbled out of bed to find she was still fully clothed in her black jersey dress and tights. She'd fallen asleep after Kelly had left, too boozy to even climb out of her clothes.

"Jodie!" Cheryl was there at an ungodly hour. The minute Jodie opened the door, she found Cheryl's phone shoved in her face. "What the *hell*?!"

The "hell" in question was an Instagram post featuring Jodie and Tish at the restaurant the night before. It was a *video* post, no less, in which Jodie was kissing Tish passionately on the cheeks, European style, like the good Sir himself. Cheryl turned the volume up.

"You're better than amazing. You're *the best*," Jodie-in-the-video was saying fervently.

"Who took that?" Jodie said now, peering blearily at the screen.

"Someone at the damn restaurant." Cheryl shook the phone at Jodie. "It's gone viral!"

"Really? Why? It's not very interesting." Jodie couldn't work out why Cheryl was so upset. Was it because she'd got so drunk? Jodie felt a little embarrassed about it. And a lot sick from it.

"People think you're a couple!"

Wait. Was Cheryl *jealous*?

"They what?" She was. She was poisonously jealous. Jodie's head hurt. Cheryl's screeching wasn't helping matters.

"They think you're a *couple*." Cheryl played the video again.

"Oh." OK. Looking at the video again, Jodie could see why people could think that. Especially with the way she was showering Tish with those "European kisses." Hell, those cocktails had been a really bad idea. Everything after that had been an inevitable downward spiral.

Except for *When Harry Met Sally . . .* Jodie remembered the way Kelly had stared into her eyes, only inches away, looking too kissable for words. That had been worth every second of this hangover.

"Look at the comments," Cheryl growled. "People think Tish is going to be number one hundred on your list! Tish. *My* Tish!"

"Well, clearly she's not, so I don't know why you're so angry."

Cheryl glared at her. "I'm so angry because of *Ryan*."

Ryan? What did *Sir Ryan Lasseter* have to do with anything?

"He thinks this is excellent," Cheryl seethed. "He wants Tish to join us for the rest of the bucket list."

"But that's great." Jodie brightened. "You two can spend time together!" Tish would be over the moon.

"No, you idiot, he wants *you two* to spend time together. He thinks this is marketing gold."

"But you'll be there too."

"Jodie," Cheryl said, clearly struggling, and failing, to control herself, "I was going to ask her to marry me."

"But that's *great!*"

"Oh my God, you're really not getting this." All trace of Marketing Barbie was gone. Cheryl seemed tired and brittle. "Ryan thinks I don't know Tish, remember? That's fine if he only meets her once, but now I'm going to be *lying to my boss* for as long as this stupid list takes. Longer! How do I bring Tish along to work functions now? And how do you think Tish will react when I ask her to take more time off work? You think she's going to enjoy getting caught up in this circus?"

It was too early for this conversation. Jodie rubbed her forehead. "Hold on. Haven't you already screwed yourself by pretending she's not your girlfriend? Whether I've kissed her or not in some video, he's going to think it's weird if you propose to some woman you've just met."

Cheryl looked like she'd been slapped. Was it possible she hadn't thought this through? More than possible. As Cheryl opened her mouth, Jodie held her hand up to stop her.

"Hold it," she said firmly. "I'm going to need a cup of coffee before we continue."

"There's nothing to continue." Cheryl sighed. "Ryan wants it, so it has to happen. But I'd appreciate it if you can remember you're in the public eye now. Everything you do has *consequences*."

Insane ones, in Jodie's opinion. She didn't see how she could predict how a bunch of strangers online were going to react to things.

"I didn't know I was being filmed," Jodie said defensively.

"Clearly." Cheryl shook the phone at her again. "From this point on, assume you're being filmed at all times."

Jodie didn't like the sound of that.

"And stop kissing my girlfriend." Cheryl straightened her jacket and pressed her red lips together, composing herself. "We'll meet you in the foyer at midday. Somehow between now and then I'll magic up the Sally table at Katz's. *You're welcome.*" Cheryl spun on her heel and then caught herself and turned back. She looked Jodie up and down. "And can you please come as yourself and not as . . . whatever this is. We're still too early in the piece for you to be looking this put together. We need somewhere to go." She slammed her hotel room door as she disappeared.

Somewhere to go . . . Jodie wasn't sure she wanted to go wherever it was Cheryl planned to take her. Hell. She might just go in her own direction, thank you very much.

Chapter 22

Even though she was feeling seedy, Jodie put on her workout gear and went for a run. She needed the fresh air and some space from the circus back at the hotel. The temperature had plummeted overnight, and it was icy out. Literally. There was a lacework of ice crocheting the edge of the pond. The ducks were fluffed up against the cold. Jodie hadn't brought her phone; without her playlist, she could only listen to the slap of her feet on the path and the rasp of her breath. Running felt hard today. Her whole body was toxic from the wine.

Jodie loved Central Park. Even in the arctic cold it was beautiful. A world unto itself.

Told you.

No need to be smug, she scolded her absent sister. I'm here now.

You're welcome.

Jodie did a pained circle around the pond, but soon she found herself loosening up, finding a rhythm, settling into her body. She took winding paths, not caring where she was headed. It was all new to her. Her hot breath formed great white clouds in front of her. Her thoughts circled like a flock of birds, flicking past her, taking flight. Now and then, one would settle.

Josh Sauer had wanted to ask her out.

What the hell had that been, huh? Jodie could see Kelly as

clear as if he were right here in front of her, leaning against the bar. *All the guys were half in love with you.*

Jodie didn't know what to do with that. It couldn't be true. But Kelly wasn't mean; he wouldn't make fun. Even on prom night he'd been kind. It had been the other guys, including Josh Sauer.

Jodie stopped dead in the middle of the path.

Josh Sauer.

God, did you see the way she was looking at him? His voice had come at Jodie like a slap on prom night. She'd been coming out of the bathroom upstairs. Josh and some of the guys were downstairs, their voices rising to Jodie on the landing. *She can't honestly think that Kelly asked her to prom for reals?* Josh's voice had been dripping with scorn.

Jodie's body reacted as though she was a teenager again, standing on that landing in her stupid prom dress, with that stupid freesia corsage on her wrist. Her stomach turned sour and she went hot and prickly, like she was being stung by ants all over her body.

You know Jodie, one of the other guys slurred. They'd been hitting the beer pretty hard. *She's not like normal girls.*

Not like normal girls. That had ripped her up inside. She'd held on to that for years. Every time she tried on a dress. *You know Jodie.* Every time she even thought about trying makeup. *She's not like normal girls.*

Jodie didn't even know who'd said it. It could have been Mike, or it could have been Tyler. The slurred voice was hard to pick. But whoever had said it had knocked her feet right out from under her. She'd already been insecure, but after that she was shattered.

All the guys were half in love with you.

God, did you see the way she was looking at him?

Jodie was still standing on the path, like she'd been stuck with superglue. Because an idea had struck her. An idea so crazy it couldn't possibly be true.

Was it possible that Josh had been *jealous*? Because she'd gone to prom with Kelly Wong and not him?

No. No *way*.

Not her. Jodie Boyd. The girl shortstop. The shy mess.

You were always so composed.

Jodie shuffled over to a bench. She had to sit down. This was too much on top of a hangover. They'd thought she was composed, like some kind of ice queen?

No *way*.

But for the first time, Jodie started to take a different point of view. Sure, she'd thrown up before every match, but how were any of them to know that? They were nowhere near her. She was secluded away by herself, in her locker room for one. And how was she to know what her face looked like when she was anxious? Maybe she *had* looked cool, calm and composed, even though on the inside she was all screaming nerves.

You were famous for it. We all thought you had ice in your veins.

Well, hell. Jodie slumped back against the bench. What if it was true?

What did it change?

Everything.

Shut up, Bree.

It *would* change everything. She'd felt shy, but maybe she came across as standoffish? She'd felt stone-cold terrified, but maybe she looked icily confident? She'd been so busy concentrating on the vivid mess of feelings on the inside that she'd never stopped to consider how she seemed from the outside.

Now that she thought about it, Josh Sauer had nearly always been her training buddy. That couldn't have been a coincidence. Jodie had barely noticed, because she'd been too busy trying not to stare at Kelly Wong. And because it never occurred to her that any of the guys would like her in that way. Because she was Jodie, not Bree. She wasn't the kind of girl who . . .

Who what?

Got noticed.

Uh-huh. Imaginary Bree sounded like she was rolling her eyes. *Only turns out you did get noticed. You might need to rethink some things.*

Jodie felt like the world had turned upside down. If she *was* the kind of girl the guys had noticed then . . . what did that mean?

It means you're all wrong about yourself.

The wind kicked up and Jodie shivered. She glanced up at the sky, which was ominous with clouds. She didn't fancy getting rained on when it was this frigid. She got up and started walking back the way she'd come.

She didn't like these thoughts. They had her feeling all messed up. More messed up than usual, anyway. Jodie kicked into an easy run.

You can't outrun the truth, sis.

Watch me. Jodie picked up the pace, headed back to the hotel. Where there was more than enough stark reality waiting for her.

Chapter 23

Jodie hadn't eaten and had a serious case of the hangries by the time they got to Katz's Delicatessen. It was her own fault. She'd made the mistake of looking at Instagram when she got back from her run. The place was a madhouse. A madhouse in which Jodie had gone viral. Her feed was flooded with posts which tagged her, some from Bree's official page, courtesy of Cheryl, but most not. Most of them were from randoms she didn't know. There was some kind of crazy scavenger hunt on, where people were snapping photos of her without her knowing. #JodieSighting was trending. As was #BucketList and #Kelly-Wong and #MysteryWoman. The mystery woman was of course Tish.

The video of Jodie showering Tish with European kisses appeared over and over again. People loved it. Bree's official page had collected thousands more followers, and even Jodie's sad little page, with its empty feed, had exploded with followers. They seemed to love everything she did. The other post that had gone viral was the one where Kelly played "Our Love Is Here to Stay" and the stupid camera zoomed in on Jodie's face. But even the most banal posts had thousands of likes. Jodie eating rainbow cake. Jodie staring out the window of the car at Great Neck. Jodie with suspiciously shiny eyes, like she was about to cry.

What on earth did all these complete strangers find so interesting about her? She'd done nothing more than eat breakfast, go for a ride, take a piano lesson and have dinner.

Her family were just as baffled as she was. She knew, because they all called to tell her so, one by one. Mom particularly was at a loss.

"It's not like you're jumping off a cliff or climbing the Himalayas."

"Bree didn't climb the Himalayas, Mom, she only trekked them."

"You wore a dress!" Grandma Gloria exclaimed. Pat yelled something in the background. "Patricia says you looked frisky."

"I bet she also says not to call her Patricia."

They ate up her whole morning. She barely had time to jump through the shower and get dressed, let alone time to eat. She snagged a bottle of juice from the mini bar. Without it, she might have killed someone.

"You're late," Cheryl snapped at her when Jodie stepped out of the elevator. Her mood clearly hadn't improved since their early morning run-in. Cheryl was dressed to kill in a sleek power suit, her hair swept up in a tight French roll, her lips matte red, her heels vertiginously high. She was standing on the veined marble like some kind of Valkyrie. "There's no time to lose if we want to get a table at Katz's."

"Where's Tish?" Jodie knew she was asking for trouble, but she was feeling cranky and didn't appreciate Cheryl's tone.

"She's not coming," Cheryl said tightly.

"Oh yes she is." Tish looked about as hungover as Jodie felt as she crossed the foyer, takeaway coffees in hand. "It's black." She handed Jodie a cup and then rummaged in her pocket. "Sugar? Creamer?" She held out a handful of sachets.

"You're my savior." Jodie sighed as she dumped sugar and creamer in her coffee.

"You didn't get me one?" Cheryl sounded wounded.

"That was yours." Tish took a sip of her own coffee. "You didn't deserve it after talking to her that way."

Cheryl scowled. "Let's go. We have to get to the deli before Ryan." She stalked off, her heels clicking an irritable tattoo against the marble.

"She hasn't booked the table." Tish sighed. "They wouldn't let her. So, it'll be potluck whether we can get the right one or not. It's put her in a mood."

"She was in a mood before that," Jodie said mildly, wondering if Tish had seen the video.

"She's jealous." Tish gave her a sly sideways glance and winked at her. So, she'd been on Instagram then.

Outside the day was gray with winter rain. Cheryl had a car already waiting for them and she was in the front seat, stabbing her phone with her talons.

Jodie's stomach was in knots. She didn't know if she could go through with this.

"Hey!" Kelly came running toward them, through the misty rain, out of breath. "Sorry I'm late, I had brunch with Mom and Harper. Mom's taking her to be disappointed about the lack of cartoon lions at the zoo." He was damp, diamond raindrops glinting in his hair.

Jodie had no idea how he looked so sparkly, when she was this hungover.

"How are you feeling?" he asked. "Ready for your orgasm?"

Tish jabbed Jodie with her elbow. "Are you, Jodie? Ready? For your orgasm?"

Jodie blushed.

Tish laughed. "Come on, princess, your carriage awaits." Tish bowed in the direction of the car.

They all piled in. She was gathering an entourage, Jodie thought weakly. More and more people to witness her humiliation.

Oh, she was going to be sick. Maybe it was a good thing she hadn't eaten. She felt worse and worse as the car crawled through traffic on its way downtown.

"You OK?" Kelly asked.

"No, I don't think so." She closed her eyes. This felt exactly like before a game . . .

"Here." He reached across her and lowered the window. "Fresh air will help." The sound of the city rushed in with the icy breeze.

Jodie leaned into the stream of frigid air and gulped in big breaths.

"Try and breathe normally."

She felt his big hand settle on her back, rubbing soothing circles. Jodie tried, she really did, but her head was full of Meg Ryan faking a loud graphic orgasm in the middle of a crowded delicatessen.

Bree, you suck.

You can do it, Scaredy Smurf. It'll be fun!

Says the woman who jumped off a cliff.

"Oh, my goodness, look at the queue." Tish gasped as they pulled up to the curb. "It's literally down the block."

The line of people stood huddled in the rain, wrestling to keep their umbrellas from being turned inside out by the wind.

Cheryl swore. "Wait here," she instructed. They watched as she teetered through the rain on her red-soled heels, making a beeline for the deli's crowded door.

"Well, I don't know about you two, but I don't like her chances." Tish sounded a bit smug.

Maybe Jodie wouldn't have to do it. There wouldn't be a table for them. They'd have to turn back the way they'd come. She slumped against the headrest, still breathing the cold air in jerky breaths.

"You know, Boyd," Kelly said, "you don't have to do this."

Jodie looked at him, startled. *Of course* she did. She had no choice in this at all.

"I mean, I know there's a lot riding on it. But no one's going to lock you up if you don't do it. It's not life and death." His red-brown gaze was warm. Comforting. "You can ditch this madness anytime you choose. It wouldn't be easy, but you aren't trapped. You can go." Then his brown eyes glinted with mischief. "But if you *do* want to do it, I can give a mean pep talk."

Jodie took a steadying breath. Rain was misting through the

window. She thought of the medical bills stacked on her parents' dining table. Of the crumpled Chili's placemat Bree had carried in her wallet for a decade. "Pep talk," she said quietly. "Please."

He grinned. "Do you want the Al Pacino or the Matthew McConaughey?"

His smile was irresistible. Despite her topsy-turvy stomach, Jodie couldn't help but smile back. "Pacino?" she hazarded.

"Alright. Here we go." He cleared his throat and stretched. Then he fixed her with an intense Pacino-like stare. "'We're in hell right now,'" he told her in a weird raspy voice. "'We can stay here and get the shit kicked out of us. Or we can fight our way back to the light. We can climb out of hell, one inch at a time.'"

Jodie laughed. His whole body had taken on the hunched, smoldering energy of Al Pacino. Not that his impression was good . . . but it wasn't bad.

"'When you get old,'" he told her roughly, "'things get taken from you. I mean, that's part of life. But you only learn that when you start losing stuff.'"

Jodie swallowed hard. Yes. That was so true it cut.

"'You find out life's a game of inches. On this team we fight for that inch.'"

"*Any Given Sunday*!" she blurted, recognizing the speech.

He wagged his finger at her to shush her. "'Because we know,'" he told her, his voice getting more gravelly by the moment, "'when we add up those inches that's going to make the fucking difference between winning and losing. Between living and dying.'" He took her hand in his. His skin was warm against hers. "'Because that's what living is. The inches in front of your face.'" He squeezed her hand.

Jodie nodded. She felt weirdly choked up. She tried to swallow the lump in her throat.

Kelly dropped the Pacino and his sideways comma dimple flickered to life. "Shall we go take some inches?"

"You got it, Coach." Jodie heard the wobble in her voice.

"Atta girl." He reached over and opened the door.

"Wow," Tish murmured, "I feel like I could take it to the end zone." She paused. "Is that a thing, or did I make it up?"

"It's a thing." Jodie stepped from the car, feeling marginally less sick. *We can climb out of hell, one inch at a time . . . one medical bill at a time.* A few minutes of humiliation would knock thousands of dollars off the debt. Jodie remembered the look on her father's face after the tree planting. The *shrub* planting. He'd looked easier than he had in years. Every dollar took a weight from his back. So, Jodie would go in there and do this thing. Inch by inch.

"Let's just get in line," Tish suggested. "In case Cher can't work her magic."

They followed the snaking line to the end and took their places, huddling together against the wind and rain.

"Ho, team!" a bouncy British voice bellowed.

Tish groaned.

Sir Ryan Lasseter was bounding down the street underneath a teal Iris Air golf umbrella. His glasses were speckled with rain, but he was in his usual good cheer. He looked thrilled to be here, in the rain outside Katz's. Thrilled to see them. Just generally thrilled. There were more European kisses. Then he handed Kelly the umbrella and spread his coat to show off his outfit underneath. "Look what I had Maya hunt down! It's the same as Billy Crystal wore in the movie!"

It wasn't exactly the same, but it was pretty close. A plaid gray wool sweater and dorky blue jeans. Jodie hated to think the morning his PA had spent trying to put that outfit together. Did they even make jeans like that anymore? She must have combed through vintage sites to find them. Whoever she was, the woman deserved a raise.

It was impossible not to smile at how much pleasure Sir Ryan took in his costume. His enthusiasm was catching.

"Wow," Jodie said, grinning. She didn't know what else to say. "Should I have dressed up like Meg Ryan too?"

Sir Ryan laughed like she'd told an excellent joke, then took the umbrella back and rocked jauntily on his heels. "I had

Maya print out the script for us too." He pulled a folded sheet of paper from his pocket and handed it to Jodie. "This one is yours."

"You look pretty excited about this," Tish observed.

"What's not to be excited about! It's a hoot! And have you seen the hit rates on this campaign? People love it."

Jodie flinched. All those people, watching . . .

"Just take his money and ignore his bullshit," Tish whispered to her as soon as His Sir-ship had bounced off looking for Cheryl. "You know why you're doing this. Who cares what he thinks?"

Tish was unkind about him. She was jealous of the claim he had on Cheryl's time. And maybe of how much Cheryl seemed to need his approval. Jodie liked the zesty Englishman. He reminded her of Bree, the way he bounded around, relishing every little experience.

"He could have left us his umbrella," Tish grumped. She was looking a little like a drowned cat.

"Wait here," Kelly said, then he darted off into the rain.

"Where would we go?" Tish asked. Then she grinned at Jodie. "So, what happened last night?"

Jodie flushed. She had a vague memory of drunkenly saying goodnight to Tish and Cheryl in the hotel corridor outside her room. And of Tish's face as Kelly followed Jodie inside. "Nothing happened. We watched *When Harry Met Sally*."

"Uh-huh."

"We did." He'd been close enough to kiss. Just like that night at prom. But she hadn't kissed him, just like that night at prom . . .

"Oh my God. Is he for real?"

Jodie followed Tish's gaze to see Kelly jogging through the rain. Under an umbrella. A giant bright yellow umbrella. He was grinning from ear to ear.

He was for real. Jodie almost had to pinch herself as she stood next to him, under the sunny umbrella. Somehow, she was standing here in New York City, next to *Kelly Wong*.

"On this team we fight for that inch!" he growled in his silly

Al Pacino voice. "Even if that inch is just buying an umbrella big enough for us all to fit under."

Tish laughed. "Good lord. You're like something out of a movie."

"Nah, that's *him*." Kelly gestured to Sir Ryan Lasseter, who was now standing at the head of the queue, beckoning them. "And I know which movie he's out of, Boyd, and it's your turn to do impressions."

Jodie took a shaky breath. Yes. It was time.

They guiltily jumped the queue, aware of the shivering line of people glaring at them.

"Thank you, good people!" Sir Ryan Lasseter was heartily bellowing at the poor damp people. "We appreciate your understanding. We have a scene to shoot."

"Like it's actually a movie," Tish muttered.

Inside, Cheryl was guarding the table. *The* table. There was a sign dangling above it, which read WHERE HARRY MET SALLY . . . HOPE YOU HAVE WHAT SHE HAD! ENJOY!

"Good luck, Boyd." Kelly winked at her. "Go take those inches."

Jodie straightened her spine. She wasn't going to be sick. She *wasn't*. "Yes, Coach."

"Shall we?" Smiling, Ryan led her to the table. Tish and Kelly stayed back by the door. Jodie wished they were coming with her.

"The strip lighting in here is going to make the photos difficult," Cheryl murmured to His Sir-ship as they sat down. She hovered for a moment, her matte-red mouth pursed. She was looking pinched. "Thank you for getting the table, Ryan," she said meekly.

"Don't mention it." He grinned. Then he turned his attention to his script, which he had spread in front of him. "Now, there's one problem," he said. "In this it says that Sally is eating turkey and I'm eating pastrami. But we're both vegetarians."

"Oh." Cheryl blinked. "I don't think we need to be that fastidious. Bree's list simply said, 'Eat a sandwich'; it didn't specify what kind of sandwich."

"Right." He nodded. "Let's order then and get this show on the road." He winked at Jodie.

Flustered, Cheryl rustled up a waitress. Jodie glanced over at Kelly, who was standing with Tish against the wall, trying not to get in the way. He gave her the thumbs-up.

"You know there's room at our table for them too," Jodie said. "It seats four."

"Oh no, it has to be just the two of us." Ryan showed her the script. "If we're going to do this, we should do it properly. I'm sure Bree would have wanted it that way." He ordered himself a lox and cream cheese bagel and waited for Jodie. She hadn't even looked at the menu.

Hell. This place was for meat eaters. Of course it was. It was famous for pastrami. "I'll have the egg salad sandwich," she said hurriedly, choosing the first thing she saw that didn't have meat in it. She threw in a Dr. Brown's cream soda too. She needed the sugar.

"Did you know my sister?" Jodie asked, curious.

"I met her a couple of times." He leaned back in his chair and shrugged off his coat. Somehow he made the dorky sweater look charming. "She was one of our brand ambassadors, so I had the pleasure of meeting her at some of our events. Such a natural on social media; the kind of person who seems full of light. And a really sweet person." He sighed and sat back in his chair. "It's hard to believe she's gone."

"Yeah," Jodie agreed, "it is." She had no plan to get emotional in the middle of a crowded deli, so she pushed her feelings down as they reared up. "Although, she's not completely gone, so long as I have to finish her bucket list . . ."

He gave her a sad smile. "No, I guess not." Then he cleared his throat and smoothed his hand over the wool sweater. "Shall we rehearse?" Sir Ryan asked.

"Rehearse? Oh, please no. I don't want to have to do this more than once." She gave Cheryl a panicked look.

Cheryl took pity on her. "We don't want to lose the freshness, do we?" she told her boss. "Let's just try it when the food comes. If Jodie needs a second take, we'll deal with it. But she might nail it first time."

She was definitely nailing it first time. Even if she didn't nail it, she wasn't doing it more than once.

"Your sister had nerve, didn't she? Planning to do something like this," Ryan said admiringly as soon as Cheryl had retreated. She'd wrangled a table nearby for her and Tish and Kelly and had her phone out, ready to record the moment.

"She was a lunatic," Jodie told him. She was so nervous she felt ill. And the food arriving didn't help. She was too queasy now for food. And the sandwich was enormous, a great creamy stack of egg between rye.

"Do you know your lines?" Sir Ryan asked her.

"Ah, no." To be honest, she hadn't thought she was going to be saying the lines; she'd thought she'd just have to fake the orgasm and then be out of there.

Sir Ryan kindly suggested she hide the script in her lap and just look down at it when she needed a line.

It was totally surreal.

Jodie kept glancing sideways at Kelly and Tish as Sir Ryan launched into being Harry. Kelly and Tish were holding menus but staring, riveted, at Jodie and His Sir-ship. Both of them looked enthralled. Jodie guessed it was like watching a car wreck in slow motion.

The delicatessen was crammed and loud. Maybe no one would hear her . . .

"'This is not about you,'" Sir Ryan said. Jodie jumped, confused. But then she realized he'd started "acting." He didn't sound in the least like Billy Crystal.

Jodie glanced down at her script. "Um . . . 'Yes, it is. You're a human affront to all women and I am a woman.'"

Sir Ryan grinned, giving her an encouraging thumbs-up. He cleared his throat and continued with the scene. "'Hey, I don't feel great about this, but I don't hear anyone complaining.'"

At first Jodie read her lines like a grade schooler reading a primer, but Ryan's enthusiasm was infectious. She relaxed. And then started enjoying it a little too. It was such a ludicrous thing to be doing.

"Eat your sandwich," Sir Ryan whispered, his blue eyes summer-warm. "In the scene, they're eating."

Jodie did as she was told and took a bite. A big hunk of egg salad fell out and landed on her script. Right on the bit where His Sir-ship's PA had helpfully written out the orgasm noises.

"You don't think that I can tell the difference?" Sir Ryan asked around a mouthful of bagel.

Jodie put her sandwich down. Oh, here it came . . . "No," she whispered. She took a deep breath.

Come on, Smurfette, show them how it's done!

She could do this. It was just like playing ball. Block out the fear. Focus on the game.

Don't think.

Jodie pretended she was the only person in the room. She still felt stupid. But she did it. She moaned and writhed and built to a crescendo. She heard the restaurant quiet, but only for a moment. They were clearly used to people acting out the scene in this place. In her head she heard Bree start to giggle.

Hey, you're good!

Damn straight. Jodie let loose with a throaty scream and pounded the table. "'Yes! Yes! Yes! Yes!'" And then, just like in the movie, she sat up, pushed her hair out of her face, and scooped up a forkful of coleslaw.

Sir Ryan was staring at her with his mouth open. Behind his spectacles, his blue eyes were dazed. "Wow," he said. There was something in his voice that made her shiver.

She'd done it. She'd actually done it. Blushing, terrified, Jodie glanced around. Cheryl was filming madly; Tish was grinning like a Cheshire cat; and Kelly was wearing an expression she'd not seen before. It made her toes tingle.

"'I'll have what she's having,'" Kelly said huskily.

Then a slow wave of applause spread through the deli. It built until it was an ovation. Jodie thought she heard laughter, but it wasn't mean.

"That was the best one we've seen since the flash mob," the waitress said. "Dessert's on us."

"Smile," Sir Ryan said cheerfully, waving to the crowd, who were snapping pictures on their phones.

Jodie stared at the sea of phones. Bree had told her to be herself. That people could spot a phony.

She didn't smile.

Chapter 24

74. Broadway Cameo

According to Tish, Cheryl had a hell of a time finding a musical that would let Jodie on stage. In the end she found a beleaguered revival of *West Side Story*.

"They've lost four people to injuries," she said, scrolling through articles as she listened to Jodie butcher Gershwin on the hotel piano. "You know Cher wanted you to sing 'I Feel Pretty'? But then she found out they cut the song from the show. She's not having much luck."

"'I Feel Pretty'?" Jodie's nose wrinkled. Well, that wasn't going to happen.

"That's exactly how Stephen Sondheim felt about it, according to this. Which is why it's not in this version."

The piano was in the corner of the ballroom. There was a swarm of sparkly jellyfish chandeliers swirling from the ceiling, their spangles reflecting in the glossy parquet dance floor. Outside the floor-to-ceiling windows, the city glittered in the rain. Jodie had just finished her third piano lesson with Kelly. It hadn't gone much better than her first two. She seriously had zero musical ability. Luckily, Kelly had infinite patience. Although now and then she'd heard him make a pained noise when she stumbled a few notes in a row.

Tonight he'd left her to torture the instrument, while he ran off to have dinner with his family in Great Neck. He'd set her homework, but Jodie was having trouble keeping her mind on the task. It was hard to concentrate when his body was beside hers on the bench, his long fingers brushing hers and sending fizzes through her, but it was even harder to concentrate with him gone. When he left, he took something with him. Some secret magic that made this bucket list bearable.

What was it about Kelly Wong? Hell, he was just a *guy*. He slopped about in jeans and hoodies and ate junk and told dumb jokes and lived and breathed sports. He wasn't special. Except he could pitch a no-hitter and play Gershwin with so much soul it made people cry. And he *listened* when Jodie spoke. Like really listened. What guy did that? Not to mention that he'd fetched an umbrella when she got rained on; taken time out from his family vacation to teach her piano so she could clear her sister's debts; put up with being dragged all over the city on this insane quest, and even managed to seem cheerful about it. *And* he did bad sports-movie impersonations on top of all that. Impersonations that somehow made everything OK.

"Do you sing as well as you play?" Tish asked, as Jodie *spanged* another wrong note.

Jodie had forgotten where she was. It was amazing she'd hit any right notes at all. She'd been staring at the sheet music without even seeing it. "I sing exactly as well as I play," she admitted, thoughts of Kelly eddying away like smoke clearing. "In choir at school, Mrs. Harris told me to mime."

"Maybe they'll let you mime on Broadway?"

"We can only hope." Jodie hit a sharp. If faking an orgasm had been daunting, the thought of getting up on a Broadway stage was keeping Jodie up nights. They wouldn't make her actually do a solo or anything, would they? Because she really couldn't sing.

West Side Story had a lot of dancing too, didn't it? She couldn't dance either.

"Oh my God." Tish's shocked voice filled the ballroom.

Jodie glanced up. She knew it wasn't going to be good. It was never good when people said *Oh my God* while looking at their phones. She wished people would get off their cells. It only made her life a mess.

Tish's expression was torn between horror and glee. "This is ridiculous."

"I don't think I want to know."

"Oh, I think you do." Tish crossed the dance floor. "Look! There are Teams!"

Jodie didn't understand.

"Teams!" Tish shoved her phone in front of Jodie's face.

Teams? Oh God. *Teams.* As in . . . Team Tish. Team Kelly. And Team *Ryan.*

"They've made T-shirts!" Tish laughed. "Look!" She flicked through her Instagram feed. There was a string of posts, featuring people in their team T-shirts: #100 #TeamKelly; #100 #TeamTish. "I'm doing pretty well so far," she told Jodie. "Coming second."

"Who's coming first?"

"Ugh. Sir Narcissist." Tish didn't sound pleased. "I bet it's only because he's a billionaire. People have a whole Prince Charming narrative that's completely divorced from reality." She paused. "Oh no, wait. They're tied. Kelly and Ryan are tied. That means I'm coming *last?* Come on. After the European kisses and everything? Maybe I need to do a Pacino impression too."

Jodie laughed. Kelly's Pacino impression had gone viral. Someone in the queue outside Katz's had filmed them through the open car window. #JodieSighting. The sound hadn't been great, but it was good enough. The footage was blurry in extreme close-up, but also good enough. Poor Kelly. He never thought he was signing up for this when he agreed to a few piano lessons.

"Hey, Jodie?" Tish gave her an impish look. "Want to do me a favor?" She sat down next to Jodie on the bench. "Want to serenade me with that Gershwin number?"

"Are you planning on filming it?" Jodie already knew the answer.

"Of course. It'll drive Cheryl crazy."

Jodie laughed. "I'll play it, but I'm not serenading you, I'm just practicing." As she returned her fingers to the keys, Jodie wondered what Kelly was doing right now. She pictured him in the middle of a herd of unicorn balloons, his niece dangling from his back. Happy.

He was always happy. Infectiously so.

He kind of reminded her of Bree in that way. She realized she'd thought the same thing about Ryan. They were both enthusiastic—just as Bree had been. People who dived into the crashing, shining sea of life headfirst.

Jodie was still pondering sisters and billionaires and baseball players when Cheryl came clicking in to collect Tish for dinner.

"We can't leave her here by herself," Tish whispered to Cheryl. She wasn't much of a whisperer; her voice seemed to fill the ballroom.

Jodie felt a familiar curdling in her stomach. She hated it when people felt pity for her. She kept her gaze fixed on the keys.

"You're the one who keeps bitching that we never spend time together." Cheryl sighed. "I don't mind if she comes with us."

Jodie spoke before they started fighting again. "I'm happy here. I have heaps of homework." She *plunked* her hands on the keys.

"You need to eat," Tish scolded.

"I really don't. Did you see the size of that sandwich at lunch?"

"I saw that you didn't eat it."

"Tish, stop fussing," Cheryl grumped. "She can order room service if she gets hungry."

"You sure, honey?" Tish gave Jodie a concerned look.

"Oh my God, no wonder people think you're a couple!" Cheryl scowled at them. She clearly wasn't on Team Tish. And she was clearly still jealous as hell.

Jodie noticed Tish looked rather pleased about that.

"OK, we'll leave you here." Tish capitulated. "But call us if you want us to bring you some food."

"Tish! She has free *room service*."

"Maybe she doesn't like what's on the menu."

"Then there's Uber Eats. And *New York*." Cheryl gestured at the city glittering like a fairyland outside the sweeping windows.

"Eat, OK?" Tish gave Jodie's arm a pat. "Good luck with your practice."

"I'll need it." Jodie sighed.

"I need to freshen up," Tish told Cheryl. "I'll meet you in the lobby." She disappeared with a skip, plainly looking forward to a night alone with Cheryl.

Jodie felt Cheryl hovering as she turned her attention back to the sheet music.

"You look tired," Cheryl observed as Jodie haltingly began to play.

"It's been a big day." Jodie struck a wrong note. "Don't worry, I'll put on my tinted moisturizer so I don't look like a hag in the photos."

Cheryl winced. She pressed her red lips together. "I wasn't worried about the photos. I was worried about you."

Jodie shot her a dubious look.

Cheryl sighed and seemed to slump. "I promised Bree I'd make this work," she said, sounding glum. "But it's not working, is it? I've screwed it up. She wouldn't like seeing you like this."

"Like what?" Jodie was startled. She hadn't seen this side of Cheryl before. The veneer was flaking away and underneath the gloss was a regular self-doubting person. Someone very much like Jodie herself.

"Sad," Cheryl said.

Jodie took her fingers off the keys. Of course she was sad. She was here doing all the things Bree was supposed to be doing.

"I think I lost sight of the fact this was supposed to be fun . . ." Cheryl admitted slowly. "I got so caught up in . . . well, work."

"I don't know how fun it can be," Jodie told her bluntly. "My sister is dead."

Cheryl flinched.

"That's *all* I think about," Jodie said flatly. "That it should be her here, not me." She took a breath and straightened her spine. "But you're right, *she* wanted it to be fun."

"I think about her too. I do . . ." Cheryl joined Jodie at the piano. She leaned against its shiny ebony flanks. "She asked me to help. I want to help . . . How do we make this fun?"

Jodie was startled into a laugh. "God, I don't know. I barely know how to keep breathing without her."

There was a moment's silence. Then Cheryl persisted. "We had fun the other night at dinner, though?" Cheryl prodded. "With Ryan?"

"There was a lot of wine involved," Jodie said dryly, "and some very strong cocktails."

"So, the answer is to liquor you up?" Cheryl joked wryly.

Jodie shrugged. "I've had some good moments," she confessed. She remembered the freedom of her first night in New York, walking through the sparkling icy city, down the carnival of Fifth Avenue. The champagne bar. Watching *When Harry Met Sally* with Kelly Wong. The weird euphoria of playing Sally opposite a gleeful Sir Ryan Lasseter. It hadn't been all bad. In fact, maybe now that she thought about it, it had been mostly good.

"Tomorrow morning we're going to the theater," Cheryl told her softly. "I'll do my best to make it better. I promise." She ran her hand over the piano as she left. "Eat, OK? Order room service. Even if it's just so Tish doesn't kill me?"

Jodie's stomach tumbled over as she listened to Cheryl's heels click out of the room. The theater. Bree, you complete maniac. How could you do this to me?

It'll be fine. You know when you're under those lights you can't even see the audience.

No, but you can hear them laughing at you.

Oh, she didn't want to think about that now. She couldn't do anything about it, could she? So, she might as well leave it to the future.

Sitting in the empty ballroom, alone with the piano and her thoughts, Jodie felt melancholy settle over her like a misty rain.

There were so many things she was leaving to the future. Too many things. Everything.

What *did* the future hold for her?

Jodie stared at the raindrops running down the enormous windows. The lights of the city were smeared and sad. Funny how you could feel so alone in the middle of millions of people.

She had a lump in her throat. It was also funny how sad the Gershwin sounded as she played it. It was supposed to be a love song. She remembered listening to versions of it when she was trying to learn it with Mr. Wong. Some artists made it sound playful and teasing; others filled it with longing; some made it cozy, others breathless. But tonight, when Jodie played it, it was the saddest song in the world.

It's very clear, our love is here to stay . . . but her notes said love was already gone, that nothing stayed, that all things passed away.

Things pass, Jodie. But love stays. Nothing disappears, things just transform. You still love me, don't you?

Oh, Bree. She would love her sister until her last breath. But the love that remained was sad in the same way the end of fall was sad. Transformation wasn't always good. Spring and summer had flown, and winter was falling like a long shadow. She hurt. All the time. Like she had a phantom limb that ached and ached, even though it wasn't there anymore.

Jodie didn't realize she was crying until the tears started splashing onto her fingers. The clumsy sad notes stumbled to silence.

What did you do when you had all this messed-up powerful love and no one to give it to?

Chapter 25

Jodie was in her pajamas when there was a soft knocking on her door. She almost ignored it. She didn't want to see anyone. She'd cried in the ballroom for a while, under the swarm of jellyfish, then she'd gone upstairs to her room and cried some more. Once she was all cried out, she'd taken a shower. She was out of tears, but still deeply despondent. She'd spent the night alone with her thoughts and the rainy New York night, sinking into the melancholy, surrendering to it. She'd yanked the curtains wide open, pulled a chair up to the hotel room window, propped her feet on the sill, and stared out at Manhattan in the rain.

The ragged bellies of the clouds were brushed orange by the city lights, and the streets glistened, slick with rain and oil and headlights. The sheeting raindrops caught the city lights and glittered as they fell. The buildings were diamond crusted with rain, spires of dark magic in the winter night. Jodie felt like she was cocooned away from it all. A world apart. But maybe that was just the hermetic effect of the hotel room. Or maybe it was another stage of grief. Whatever it was, it was alarmingly comfortable. Jodie felt a vague fear that she would be trapped in this muffled sadness forever, the way Dorothy was trapped by sleep in the poppy fields in *The Wizard of Oz*.

There was something swollen and magical about the feeling of sadness she sat inside. It was like being caught inside that raindrop that Bree had posted on her Instagram, in her very last living post: suspended, upside down and about to break.

She hadn't had time alone like this since Bree died, she realized. She'd been dealing with her devastated parents, with Claude and Gloria and Pat, and she'd worked a million hours at the car-rental stand, every spare moment, suffering long, numbing shifts in order to pay the bills. She'd had no privacy or solitude. Or time.

The sorrow swelled and filled her and overflowed, forming a bubble around her. It was silent and calm and weirdly holy. Not that Jodie was into that kind of thing. But *holy* was the only word she could think of to describe it. It shimmered with something spiritual. She sat in the dim room and watched the rain blur the unfamiliar city. She missed Bree so much that it was hard to breathe. But it was a clean kind of feeling. Razor sharp, but a clean cut.

I miss you, Bree.

She didn't answer. Because she wasn't there. There was only the empty room and Jodie. Jodie, who was alone . . . and profoundly, but not unpleasantly, lonely.

For this suspended time, in this infinite sorrow, profound loneliness didn't feel *bad*. It was just a feeling. Like stepping out into a freezing night and having the air go as dry as powder in your lungs. You could still breathe. It just felt different.

By the time the knocking came at the door, she'd settled into the deep freeze of her sadness. But there was something about the knocking, the gentle inquisitiveness of it and the fact that it didn't stop, that made her get up and pad over to the door. She thought it was probably Tish, bringing her a doggie bag with leftover food. She wouldn't mind seeing Tish—she wouldn't smash through the membrane of her bubble. She'd be quiet and gentle and hand over the food. She'd be kind. Cheryl was lucky to have found someone like Tish, Jodie thought.

But it wasn't Tish.

It was Kelly.

His hair was wet from the rain, sticking up in damp clumps,

and his sideways comma dimple was a deep groove as he smiled at her. "Nice pajamas."

Jodie looked down at herself. The bubble broke and her grief evaporated. Oh God, she was in her baseball pajamas. They were so old, covered in cartoon baseballs and bats. She crossed her arms over her chest, feeling painfully conscious that she wasn't wearing a bra.

"I hope I didn't wake you up?"

She shook her head. "No. I've just been . . . looking at the city." Ugh. It was true, but it sounded lame. Kelly always made her feel so awkward. She was hyperaware of her body when he was around. And of his. Which was very close.

How had she gone from profound spiritual melancholy to trivial crushing idiot in such a short space of time? How did he do this to her? Jodie felt a little dizzy. A broken raindrop, spilling herself out onto the floor.

"Mom sent some food back for you. She seems to think room service is some kind of punishment." He rolled his eyes. "I don't think she's ever actually had it." He held out a paper sack.

Gingerly, Jodie took it and peered inside. There was a neat stack of plastic containers.

"It's just leftovers," he said. "I told her you wouldn't have a microwave, but she insisted. I have no idea what cold eggplant curry tastes like . . ."

"Thanks." She was touched, even though she suspected cold eggplant curry might taste less than ideal. She wasn't really hungry anyway.

"How did it go after I left?" He was hovering in the doorway and didn't seem in any rush to leave. "Did you get through the Gershwin OK?"

Should she ask him in? But she was in her pajamas. And not really in a social mood. "I got through it," she said carefully, "but I don't know that anyone would call it OK."

She couldn't ask him in. Could she? It seemed too intimate. Especially because she was *in her pajamas.*

But he wasn't moving. In fact, he leaned against the doorjamb. "Cheryl said you're going to the theater to tackle *West Side Story* tomorrow?"

"Oh, please don't remind me." Her knees felt watery.

"That bad, huh?"

"It's the worst one on the whole list," Jodie said honestly. "You have no idea. I think I'd rather eat spiders."

"You know it's still early . . ." He gave her a rueful smile. "We could always have another movie night? I'd be up for watching *West Side Story*. You know, if you felt like it. If you wanted to brush up on it or anything . . ." He seemed a little bashful. "I mean, it worked pretty well with *When Harry Met Sally*."

Jodie was astonished to see that he was blushing.

"You were amazing today." He cleared his throat. "At the whole fake orgasm thing, I mean." He was definitely blushing.

Jodie was startled into a laugh. "Amazing? I sounded like an ambushed parrot. Don't deny it, I've seen the video online."

"You did *not* sound like a parrot. You sounded . . ."

"Sounded like what . . . ? A poodle with separation anxiety?"

"No."

"A toddler who lost her pacifier?"

"*No.*"

"A geriatric goat screaming to be let out of its pen?"

"You sounded sexy." He met her eye and then looked away, his gaze darting downward before she could quite work out his expression.

Sexy.

Kelly Wong had just called her sexy.

What was *happening*?

OMG Smurfette, please tell me you're not going to waste this! Ask him in to watch the stupid movie! Bree had been nowhere to be found an hour ago, but now Kelly was here, she came rushing back into Jodie's consciousness, in full force.

But the baseball pajamas!

So, take them off. Or let him take them off.

Now Jodie was the one blushing. A flood of images swept over her, all of them involving her losing her baseball pajamas.

"*West Side Story*, huh?" she kind of squeaked.

He grinned, the sideways comma back in his cheek. "I downloaded it already," he admitted. "I was hoping you'd be up for it."

Kelly Wong had downloaded *West Side Story*. To watch. Tonight. With her.

This was too surreal. He actually seemed happy to hang out with her.

Let him in, you idiot!

Jodie held the door wider so he could come inside. She had a moment of déjà vu as he crossed the room and made for the television. She put the eggplant curry in the bar fridge and then sat on the chair by the window and pulled a pillow into her lap, wrapping her arms around it. Really trying to hide behind it, so she didn't feel so naked. Stupid to feel naked in neck-to-ankle flannelette, but she wasn't wearing any underwear and she was intimately aware of her nipples brushing against the fabric.

"I got the old sixties movie. My mom said she loved it, but I can't vouch for it. I haven't seen it . . . have you?" he asked as he sat on the edge of the bed and yanked his sneakers off.

He was taking his clothes off. Okay, shoes. He was taking his shoes off. But it ignited a little flash of excitement, right in the pit of her stomach. Or lower.

She liked the way he looked, sitting on the edge of her bed, taking his shoes off.

"No. Never," she admitted, trying to keep her mind on the movie. She'd taken too long to answer the question—what if he could tell what she was thinking?

"It won like a million Oscars. According to Mom. You want to get any snacks before it starts?"

She shook her head. No. She wasn't about to get up from the chair and cross the room in front of him, wearing only her pajamas.

"Alright then." He grinned at her, pressed play and stretched out on the bed. The room was lit only by the sparkles from the city and the flood of blue light from the television. Then the light blazed red and the overture started. Jodie's gaze kept drifting to Kelly. The flickering light cast his fine-cut features into sharp relief.

"Not going to join me?" His voice was husky as he turned his head and caught her staring at him.

Jodie felt her nipples tighten. What *was* happening? Was this a come-on? Or a movie?

What do you want to happen, Smurfette?

Nothing! Everything. Anything . . .

Cautiously, Jodie moved to the bed, bringing her pillow-shield with her. Kelly gave her a slow grin and then turned back to the film.

It was a really long overture. Like really, really long. Jodie sat cross-legged on the bed beside Kelly, who was stretched out on his stomach, resting his chin on his hands. She hugged the pillow tight. She had a clear view of his broad shoulders, his lean back, his waist . . . best stop there. She forced her gaze to the screen just as the title card was replaced by a shot of a basketball court.

"Which bit of the show do you have to appear in?" Kelly asked as the opening number unfolded.

"I have no idea," she admitted. "Tish said something about 'I Feel Pretty'? But then I think she said it's not in the revival. They cut it."

To her discomfort, Kelly rolled over on his side, toward her, propping himself up on his elbow. He divided his attention between the screen and her. She wished he'd just watch the screen. "Do you have to sing?" he asked.

"God, I hope not. Bree's list just said, 'walk-on cameo.'" Jodie hugged the pillow so tight it collapsed in on itself.

He noticed, because he noticed everything. He reached out and stroked her foot with his thumb; Jodie jumped a little at his touch. "You'll be great."

"Everyone says that, but you know I might *not* be." All of Jodie's being seemed fixed in the small thumbprint of skin he was touching. She didn't know how she managed to talk like nothing was happening. "I might fall flat on my face."

Kelly looked like he was considering that carefully. He shrugged. "Yeah, that's true, you might."

"And everyone in the stupid audience will have their phones

out, recording it, and I'll be immortalized online forever. Flat on my face." Oh God, his thumb was stroking the back of her foot. It was doing weird things to her insides. Fluttery, shivery, earthquaky things.

He nodded. "Yeah, alright. That's all a thing."

She was appalled. "That's supposed to make me feel better?"

He grinned. "Not better. Just less crazy. All of those things could happen. I'm validating you." The stroking stopped, but only because he wrapped his hand around her ankle and held it. Then he turned back to the movie. But he didn't let go of her ankle.

Jodie'd had no idea her ankles were an erogenous zone. Turned out they were. It was ridiculously erotic to sit here, fully clothed, with a weird '60s movie playing, as Kelly Wong held her ankle.

That small circle of skin felt burning hot. It sent tendrils of warmth through her, long lazy curls of shimmering heat. She felt a wild desire for him to move his hand, to rub it over her skin, up her leg, over her whole body. She'd never been so aroused in her life, she thought, as she sat there, stock still, with his hand around her ankle. Fantasies flickered in her mind. Ones involving bare skin and wet mouths and the width and breadth of this king-size bed.

She barely noticed the movie, she was so distracted by her thoughts. At least until the blackface happened. "What is *that*?" She was genuinely shocked.

The guy on the screen had thick greasy brown makeup on.

"I think he's supposed to be Italian . . ." Kelly eyed the screen with distaste.

"But . . . that's . . ."

"Yeah." He cleared his throat. "Mom didn't say anything about that."

It got worse. A scene or two later the heroine appeared. "Now, that's definitely blackface," Jodie said, appalled.

"Technically, I think it's brownface. She's meant to be Puerto Rican."

"Seriously? But the other girl is Latina? Why isn't she?"

Kelly shrugged. "I'm going to guess racism?"

"Wow."

"We might stop this." Kelly's hand disappeared from her ankle and Jodie felt a plummeting sense of disappointment. He turned the film off.

"You don't think the show is like that too? The one I'm supposed to be in?" All her fears about number seventy-five on the list came crushing back in.

"No. Noooooo. No, surely not." He sat on the edge of the bed and stared at the blank screen. He glanced over at her. His was barely a silhouette in the dim room now that the light from the television was gone.

Oh. The light from the television was gone. Without the movie, there was no reason for him to be here.

He looked a little glum that the film hadn't worked out.

Jodie held the pillow breathlessly. What was he going to do? She didn't want him to leave. She wanted him to hold her ankle again . . .

OMG Smurfette, would you just jump him already!

Oh. Oh my.

She could make a move, couldn't she . . . she didn't have to wait for *him* . . . If she wanted him, she could . . .

Jodie's whole body was tingling. She didn't know if she felt hot or cold. She felt overwhelmingly . . . something. *Zingy*, that's how she felt. The thought of taking charge of the situation was swirling around her head. Imagine if she did . . .

"We could just listen to the soundtrack?" he suggested. His voice sounded tight. Husky. Jodie wondered if he felt a little zingy too. "You'd get a fair idea of the story from the soundtrack? Maybe I can find one where they're not dressing WASPs up as Italians and Puerto Ricans?"

He wanted to stay.

Kelly Wong wanted to stay. Here, in her room, with her.

God damn, he was gorgeous. He had the sexiest way of sucking on his lower lip as he fished Spotify for the soundtrack. She wondered what would happen if she did kiss him. Would he kiss her back?

"Aha, this looks good." He was triumphant. The overture started playing.

"We could skip that," Jodie suggested. "It went on for ages." She regretted saying that as soon as he skipped it. She *wanted* it to take ages. The sooner it ended, the sooner he'd leave . . .

Without the television on, the room was dark except for the city lights twinkling beyond the glass.

"Have you ever seen the play?" Kelly asked softly, as he leaned back on his hands. Jodie felt a stab of disappointment that he wasn't lying down again.

"No," Jodie admitted. "Actually, I've never been to the theater except in school. I went to a few school plays."

"*Our Town?*" He laughed. "Remember that one?"

She did. Bree had been in it.

"So corny."

It was corny. And boring. School plays were always so *loooooong*. Interminable. And you had to be quiet and sit still. Jodie had been dragged along by her parents and she'd spent the whole night wishing for it to be over. She couldn't remember any of Bree's lines, or even what her costume looked like. For the hundredth time, Jodie wished she'd paid more attention. At the time it hadn't seemed important. Just like Bree's dogwood corsage. But then things ended, and all those little moments were gone, and you could never get them back.

"They used to get me to play the piano sometimes for the drama club rehearsals," Kelly said. "Tommy told me it would be a great way to meet girls." He laughed. "It was a *boring* way to meet girls."

Ashleigh Clark had been in the drama club, Jodie remembered. She took the lead in musicals, all fresh-faced ingenue. She was the nice girl. She was pretty.

"They ever do *West Side Story?*" Jodie asked, her throat tight. Don't think about Ashleigh Clark now, she told herself. On the soundtrack, some guy was singing about the air humming and something great coming. This particular memory lane that she and Kelly were going down didn't feel so great and it certainly wasn't humming.

"Nah. They did *Oklahoma!* once." Kelly shook his head. "I must have played 'People Will Say We're in Love' a million times. They really struggled with that one."

"My sister played Ado Annie in *Oklahoma!*" *That* Jodie did remember.

"Yeah, that's right. 'I'm just a girl who cain't say no.' She was loud as hell."

Jodie laughed. "Yeah, she never was one to be meek." Jodie jumped when Kelly's hand found hers in the darkness. His touch was shy and gentle. There was a question in it. Jodie answered by not refusing it.

"I'm sorry about your sister. She was one of the world's shiny people. The kind you remember."

"Yeah," Jodie agreed, not daring to move in case he took his hand away. "She really was." Jodie felt his fingers curl around hers, until their hands were entwined. His skin was warm. The shadows of raindrops rolling down the window fell across the bed.

"You were pretty memorable too," he blurted. She felt his fingers shiver in hers.

It was dim, but the refracted city lights showed her enough of his face to see that he was earnest. Earnest and vulnerable.

Now her palms were sweating. He'd be able to feel that, the way she'd been able to feel him shiver.

"Because I was the only girl on the team?" She couldn't help herself. Defensiveness was like a second skin.

"No. Well, yes. But not just that." He squeezed her hand. "You were the most . . . I don't know . . . you were just you. I didn't know anyone else like that. I still don't. You didn't seem to care what anyone thought. There was no fake smile, no inane small talk. If you had something to say, you spoke; if you didn't, you stayed quiet."

He had no idea. She'd cared so much she'd made herself sick. She'd cared so much she'd spent most of high school hidden in her room, out of fear of doing the wrong thing, saying the wrong thing, *being* the wrong thing. "I was quiet a lot," she admitted. And she didn't see that it was a great thing to admit.

"You just did what you wanted. Like being the only girl on the team. I thought that was so cool."

She did what she wanted . . . ugh, when had she *ever* done what she wanted? Half the time she didn't even make it to the plate, let alone take a swing at the ball. Let's face it, most of the time she didn't even suit up. She stayed in the locker room. Would she be working at the car-rental stand if she did what she wanted? Truth be told, she didn't know. She wasn't even sure *what* she wanted . . .

Well, right now she wanted to kiss Kelly Wong. She wanted to feel what that dent in his lower lip felt like under her mouth. She wanted to know what he tasted like. She wanted to kiss him until neither of them remembered their own names. Would he think *that* was cool? Here he was, right in the strike zone. If she didn't swing now, she'd regret it for the rest of her life. She knew it deep down in her bones.

Hell. You only lived once.

It was the bravest thing she'd ever done. Braver than being the only girl on the baseball team. Braver than faking an orgasm in a busy restaurant. Maybe it was the music they were listening to, the *I saw you and the world went away.* Maybe it was her melancholy before he'd arrived. Whatever it was, Jodie swung at the ball.

Everything slowed as she leaned toward him; the moment narrowed to a single heartbeat in time. The aquatic deep blue light, shivering with nets of coruscating city sparkles, made the moment surreal. Bewitched. Out of normal time.

Jodie could feel the warmth of his breath, could hear the hitch as he realized what was about to happen. She felt his fingers tighten around hers. His eyelashes flickered as his gaze dropped to her mouth. The dent in his lower lip was a shadow. He didn't flinch or say no.

Jodie closed her eyes as her mouth met his.

She'd imagined this moment a million times. But no fantasy lived up to reality.

It was like being struck by lightning. The electric force of it just about stopped her heart, the voltage sending sparks flying through her body and heat shooting to every square inch of her. And then he started kissing her back. She reached for him, sure she was about to melt away, needing to find support.

He pulled her close, his athletic arms easily holding her, which was good because she was incapable of holding herself upright anymore.

His mouth slanted over hers, parting her lips. The kiss deepened, blossoming, opening, questioning. Jodie heard herself moan as his tongue slipped across her lips and then into her. He tasted like sweet citrus, smelled like herbs and salt. His arms were sinewy against her back. His mouth was as hot as summer.

By the time they came up for air, Jodie's heart was hammering as though she'd run for home. She felt like a curtain had been ripped aside and the world was laid bare. Behind the drabness of her everyday reality was a humming neon radiance.

Kelly seemed equally astonished.

They sat in spellbound silence, still tangled in the embrace. Jodie could feel his heart beating. He stared at her in mute confusion, but there was something else there. Something Jodie couldn't name. Something a bit like wonder.

She didn't want to break the spell by speaking, and she hoped with all her might he wouldn't break it either.

He took a breath.

No. Not yet. She didn't want this to end yet.

So she kissed him again.

Chapter 26

Can we talk? Kelly messaged her first thing in the morning. Jodie was already up, dragged out of bed by Cheryl at an ungodly hour. She'd barely slept and looked it. Fortunately, Cheryl had brought strong coffee. Jodie wouldn't have been functional without the coffee.

The sight of Kelly's name on her phone made Jodie's stomach float, and somersault, and do things a stomach had no right doing. *Can we talk?* Jodie didn't like the sound of that. *Can we talk* was never good, was it? She and Kelly hadn't talked at all the night before. Well, only one word: Goodnight. And that was after hours of kissing, when the hotel was silent, and the rainy night was waning. Neither of them had wanted to break the spell.

Jodie would have done more than kiss, but nothing more had happened. Somehow that had been OK. It had been a long, slow sorcery. Trancelike. She could still feel the way his hand had cupped her face as his tongue had drugged her senseless.

God, he was a good kisser.

But now, in the dull not-quite light of the very early winter morning, Jodie wasn't sure she hadn't imagined it all. It had been too perfect. Too charmed. Like a dream.

Can we talk?

It was the chime of midnight at the ball, wasn't it? When the magic horse turned back into a common mouse. And Cinderella went running home in her rags.

Jodie didn't want to hear that last night had been a mistake. That it shouldn't have happened. That he didn't want to ruin their friendship . . .

Friendship. *What* friendship, Kelly? Jodie lapsed into an imaginary argument with him as she showered, as Cheryl waited outside the bathroom door. *What* friendship? He'd moved away to college and never looked back. There'd been no messages, no calls, no emails, no nothing. What was there left to ruin with a kiss?

By the time she was dried and dressed, the imaginary argument she'd had with Kelly left Jodie grumpy. She took it out on Cheryl. "I don't see why I have to be up so early," she complained. She wondered if she could avoid Kelly so she could hang on to the magic for just a bit longer.

"We have to get to the theater before *Good Morning America*."

That hit Jodie like a brick smashing through a plateglass window. "We *what*?"

Cheryl was chagrined. "I know I should have warned you, but it happened late last night. Ryan's friends with the producer—he set it up."

Jodie was appalled to hear they'd organized for Jodie to be interviewed live on television, in the theater, about her "Broadway debut."

"I'm not doing it."

"It will be OK. The interview will be quick. Over before you know it."

"And it's just the interview?" Jodie was suspicious.

Cheryl looked guilty. "They also want to get some footage of you backstage. And they'll be following us through the rehearsal and performance. They'll air a package about it on Thursday."

"What day is it today?" Jodie couldn't remember for the life of her. Things were too abnormal for things like weekdays to matter anymore.

"Wednesday. You can rehearse today and tomorrow and be on stage on Thursday night." Cheryl checked the time.

"I'm not doing it." Jodie planted herself in the chair by the window and crossed her arms. "I refuse."

"You can't," Cheryl said miserably. "You're contractually obligated."

"I'm what?"

"Remember those forms you signed in the pop-up bar?"

Jodie felt her stomach plummet. What had she signed? And why hadn't she read the pages more carefully?

Because they were in legalese, and she couldn't understand a word of it . . . Suddenly she felt a little less like she was in *Cinderella* and a little more like she was in *The Little Mermaid*. Had she really signed away her voice?

"I want to see those contracts. And I want to talk to Ryan."

"He's in transit."

"I'm sure his phone works on his private plane," Jodie snapped.

Cheryl was tense with stress. "Please, Jodie. I'll get you the contract. I'll minimize what you have to do for *GMA* . . . but Ryan called in a favor to get this interview. I can't cancel it." Cheryl seemed sick at the thought.

Jodie crossed her arms. She didn't want to go on television. But she also didn't have time to wade through all that legalese before the interview. "Fine. I'll do it. But this is *it*. From now on, you don't arrange anything without clearing it with me first."

"Yes." Cheryl exhaled. "Thank you."

Jodie's phone buzzed again. Kelly.

Message me when you're up?

Jodie waited until she and Cheryl were in the elevator before she answered.

Sorry, Cheryl's dragged me off to the theater. Talk later?

She turned her phone off before he could reply, feeling like a coward. How did you hide from the inevitable? If Cinderella couldn't stop time, the mouse-turned-horse pulling the pumpkin-carriage certainly couldn't do it.

"We're walking?" Jodie was surprised when Cheryl headed out into the street rather than waiting for a car. She should have noticed that for once Cheryl wasn't wearing sky-high heels.

"It'll be quicker," Cheryl said as they headed toward the theater district. It was so cold her words puffed in front of her like dragon's breath.

Jodie was glad. She needed to walk off her anger. And her anxiety about Kelly.

The street was icy, littered with cloudy and rimed-over puddles, and the shop windows were fogged up. It was a magic hour between night and day; the lights in all the skyscrapers were winking on as the city powered up for the week ahead, and the holiday decorations twinkled in the misty blue morning. The traffic was only just beginning to fill the streets. Steam billowed from subway vents, smearing the twinkling lights.

Jodie still had a hard time believing she was in New York. The magic of the place rubbed the edge off her feelings. She crammed her hands into her pockets, wishing she'd brought her gloves. Despite the coffee, her stomach was complaining especially loudly because she hadn't fed it dinner the night before. She guessed a real breakfast was off the table until after the interview. Although maybe it was good that she hadn't eaten much . . . there'd be nothing for her to throw up when the nerves hit. As they hastened down the frosty early morning streets, Jodie's mind wandered back to her hotel room and the night before.

Maybe this was all a weird dream. It had to be because there was no way she'd just kissed *Kelly Wong.* Not just kissed him but kissed him *all night long.*

If she was dreaming, let her stay asleep just a bit longer. And maybe have a bit more of the kissing and a bit less of the nightmarish walking into a Broadway theater to humiliate herself live on national television. Oh. And not just *a* Broadway theater, *the* Broadway theater, she saw, as they turned onto Broadway and she saw the marquee. Proving this might actually be a dream, the lights flicked on, as if on cue, slicing through the watery gray-blue morning with vivid neon pink and blue. The old art deco building beckoned in Technicolor glory, shining like a beacon.

There was a white van parked right out front; it had a cheery yellow *GMA* logo on the side. Jodie glanced at Cheryl.

"You'll be fine," Cheryl promised. "I'll be with you every step of the way."

Inside, the place was fancy beyond words. The velvet and chandeliers and deep crimson chairs made the jellyfish back at the hotel seem paltry. And then Jodie noticed all the seats.

"How many people does this place fit?" she breathed, as she crept down the aisle between the banks of seats. She turned and craned her neck to look at the balconies and upper stories.

"That would be 1,761," a chirpy voice answered from a box above. A young woman was up there, gazing down at them.

Cheryl gasped in outrage.

"Is that not enough people?" Jodie asked her dryly.

"Maya!" Cheryl was turning red as she glared up at the gilt-edged box. "What are you doing here?"

The young woman leaned over the railing above. She was perky looking, with her hair in a messy knot; she wore thick black-framed glasses and bright coral lipstick. She was younger than Cheryl and less glossy. But somehow cooler.

"Ryan asked me to come along. Didn't he tell you?" The woman tilted her head.

"No," Cheryl growled, "no, he didn't."

"Oh well, you know him." The woman waved a dismissive hand. "He's got so much on his mind." She gave a bright coral smile. "I assume this is Jodie?" She waved.

Jodie found herself waving back. Cheryl glared at her. Jodie shrugged. "I was just being polite."

"I'm Maya, Ryan's right-hand person."

"His assistant." Cheryl seethed.

"Nice to meet you," Jodie said warily, nervous because of Cheryl's extreme response. "I assume you're the one who dressed him up like Harry for the whole orgasm scene at Katz's?"

"You assumed right. Wasn't the sweater a *find*? Wait there and I'll be right down. *GMA* wants you down there in the stalls, with the stage in the background, so I'll come to you."

"You've been talking to *GMA*?" Cheryl sounded ready to explode. But she was talking to thin air, as Maya had already disappeared behind the thick velvet curtains at the back of the box. "Where does she get off? This bucket list has nothing to do with her!"

Jodie didn't see that it had that much to do with Cheryl either, but Cheryl was powering off down the aisle, in a fury, as though she'd been personally slighted.

Jodie sat down in one of the comfy velvet seats and waited for someone to tell her what to do next. The theater was OK when she was all alone. It didn't feel so scary. In fact, it was kind of soothing. It was a bit like being inside a cushion.

She took it all in. All 1,761 velvet seats of it, raked in tiered balconies. It was a red-and-gold palace. The stage was deep and dark, the floor the color of a chalkboard. Jodie imagined Bree writing number seventy-four on her list on the back of the Chili's placemat, full of sunny optimism. This would have been exactly how she imagined a Broadway theater. Shame she wasn't here; she would have been beside herself. Probably running up there on stage and doing an impromptu dance number.

As Jodie stared at the stage, a figure emerged from the wings. A young guy. Carrying two takeaway cups of coffee and a paper sack.

"Jodie?" He stood center stage and smiled down at her. He was good-looking, lean and loose-limbed and clearly comfortable up there. "Ready to take Broadway by storm?"

Jodie's stomach plummeted, the peaceful sense of being safe inside a cushion evaporating. Oh no, it was time for the roller coaster again.

She must have looked alarmed because he frowned. "You are Jodie, aren't you?"

"Yes," she said, guardedly. She didn't get up from the chair.

"I'm Jonah." He smiled at her like that should mean something.

"Hi . . . ?"

"Jonah Lourdes." He *definitely* thought that should mean something to her. Was he one of the talking heads on *Good Morning America*? She didn't watch it, so how was she to know?

"I play Tony," he said.

Tony. Oh. *Tony.* Like in the play. He was the guy who sang about something humming and something great coming. "Oh *hi*." Jodie got out of the chair and ran her hand nervously through her hair; her fingers snagged in the curls. "Nice to meet you," she said lamely. "Or it would be, if I wasn't stone-cold terrified."

Jonah Lourdes laughed. "Terrified is normal."

"So my sister told me."

He adopted that face everyone made when they offered condolences. "I'm very sorry to hear about your sister." People meant it, but they also looked kind of shifty with discomfort. No one ever knew how to act. Even actors, apparently.

"Thanks." Jodie didn't bother pulling a face back. The *you're so kind* face. What did he care, he'd never even met Bree. He was just being polite.

"I brought you coffee," Jonah-the-actor told her, holding up the cups. "And some pastries." He was smiling again.

Jodie's stomach growled. Despite her reservations, she gave in to the hunger and accepted his offering. "Thank you." She watched as Jonah navigated around the orchestra pit and joined her in the front row of the theater.

She took the coffee gratefully.

"It's black," he apologized. "I didn't know what you liked."

"As long as it's hot, I'm happy. Thank you. It's really nice of you." Although, as Jodie looked down at the cups, she saw a name scrawled on them in metallic marker. *Maya.*

Jonah stretched his long legs out as he flopped back in the chair. He gave her first choice of the pastries and then fished a Cronut out of the sack and ripped it in half with a single bite. He groaned. "Man, I love these."

You wouldn't know it, judging by how lean he was. Jodie took in the musculature of his thighs, visible through his tight jeans. Jodie guessed eight shows a week would burn off a lot of Cronuts.

"So you're not looking forward to your cameo, then?" he asked once he'd polished off the pastry. He licked icing sugar off his fingers.

"I would rather ride a shark."

He laughed. "I once read public speaking is the number-one fear. Over death even."

"Did they say anything about public singing and dancing?"

"It's the best rush in the world."

Now it was Jodie's turn to laugh. "You would say that. You sing and dance."

"Your sister liked it though, I assume?"

"My sister liked everything. She was weird that way."

"I looked up her Instagram. She did some wild things." He didn't pull the odd face this time. He sounded admiring.

"Yeah. And then she left a bunch for me to do." Jodie liked this guy. He was direct. She offered him the sack of pastries again. "There's another Cronut in there."

He gave her an impish look. "My trainer would kill me." Then he took it.

Jodie definitely liked him.

As they sat sipping their coffee, there was a commotion at the doors. Jodie turned to see Cheryl and Maya coming down the central aisle, flanking a camera crew and a cranky-looking producer, who was carrying an armful of equipment. They were all talking over each other.

"There's no need for anyone but Jodie," Cheryl was insisting.

"Of course there is," Maya argued, "this is bigger than just her Broadway cameo. This is about the whole bucket list."

"I don't care who you want to put in front of the camera, but the live cross is in fifteen minutes, so you'd best decide soon," the producer snapped.

Jodie ignored them and took the paper sack back off Jonah. He'd put his coffee down and was adjusting his clothes. Jodie pulled out a Danish and took a bite. She was a sucker for a good Danish, and these were *good*. If she had a trainer they'd be horrified. She'd had pastries every morning so far. Oh well, she would probably get an attack of nerves and throw it all up anyway. Jodie settled back in the velvet chair and enjoyed her breakfast as the camera crew chose angles and set up equipment and Cheryl and Maya argued.

She remembered sitting with Kelly on his brother's couch, eating rainbow unicorn cake. *It's always like this . . . best to just let it happen.* She took his advice again now, and let it happen while she ate. At least by the time they mic'ed her up she'd have sugar and caffeine in her system to combat the brutality of the early morning and the lack of sleep.

"Now, Jodie," Maya said, sliding between the camera and Jodie, "I have just a couple of talking points for you." She handed Jodie a card.

"What talking points?" Cheryl wedged herself in too.

"Just be sure to name-check *West Side Story* and the Broadway Theatre, and to say that you'll be here for Thursday night's performance." Maya's short, clear-varnished fingernail pointed to the black-marker list on the card. "And don't forget to mention Iris Air's generous sponsorship of the bucket list. And just here at the bottom are some handy hashtags for people who want to follow along with us."

Us? Jodie met Cheryl's gaze and wrinkled her nose.

"The *GMA* people will mention all of this in their questions, but just in case."

Cheryl took the card out of Jodie's hands and ripped it in two. "She doesn't need this," she said tightly. "It's better if she's natural. Just let her be herself."

Maya made a noise that somehow managed to be dubious, patronizing, pitying and annoyed all at once. Cheryl looked like she wanted to push her over.

"I'll help you, if you forget," Jonah whispered to Jodie. He was being mic'ed up too and was apparently joining her for the interview.

Jodie had a crazy urge to laugh. This was degenerating into

one big advertisement. Name-checking companies? Listing
hashtags? None of it had anything to do with the bucket list, or
with Bree, not really. It was just about getting Iris airtime, on
Bree's platform, co-opting her brand and her established audience. Ostensibly to put a few more millions in His Sir-ship's
already overflowing bank accounts. They were taking Bree's
death, and Jodie's roller coaster of grief, and turning it into an
ad. It was sick. But weirdly, it made Jodie relax as she faced the
camera. Who cared if she screwed this up? This wasn't about a
promo for some dumb airline. This was about her sister, and the
last six items on the bucket list that she never got to finish. This
was about Bree's wide and shining smile as she faced the world.
And about the world Jodie faced, now Bree was no longer in it.
Jodie might be paying off Bree's debt with these crazy stunts,
but the list wasn't really about money, not for Jodie. No matter
what happened in this interview, Jodie would be getting up on
that stage and ticking off number seventy-four on the bucket
list. And she wouldn't be doing it for Iris Air. She'd be doing it
for *Bree*.

She had a moment of horror when the lights fixed on her and
the producer counted them in, but she needn't have worried.
The interview itself was over before she'd quite realized it was
happening. Jonah did a lot of the talking. He was more than
comfortable on camera, and he seemed to know an awful lot
about Jodie's bucket list for someone she'd just met. He was the
wingman she never knew she needed.

"I think we can all agree that Jodie's a born actor, after her
Sally impression at Katz's." He laughed.

Oh God, that's right. He'd been looking at Bree's Instagram.

"She'll be equally amazing on stage on Thursday," he said,
giving Jodie a reassuring smile.

He'd watched the orgasm. Jodie realized every guy she'd ever
meet from here on out would be able to look at her writhing in
that deli . . .

"Now that you mention it, Jonah, we have some footage of
Jodie's adventures the other day, from Instagram," the anchor

said chirpily in the tinny earpiece in Jodie's ear. And then Jodie had the mortifying experience of listening to herself fake an orgasm. She felt herself turning red. No one had warned her *that* was going to happen. God, she hoped no one she knew was watching. Her parents. The guys from the car-rental stand . . .

Oh, who was she kidding, you could bet they'd all see it on Instagram anyway. She had no privacy left. Cheryl and the #JodieSightings had seen to that.

"Good luck, Jodie, from the *GMA* family!" The anchors were getting saccharine as they wrapped up the interview. "We're all cheering you on, and we should remind our viewers that our cameras will be following Jodie for most of this week, as she rehearses for her Broadway debut."

And then it was over. At least the interview bit was. It turned out they still had hours of filming ahead. The camera crew was glued to Jodie, like she was some kind of reality TV star.

"I didn't agree to any of this," Jodie told Cheryl, during the "walk around," where the *GMA* camera crew followed as Jonah took Jodie on a tour of the theater. The camera had followed Jonah into the dressing room. He'd stepped into the role of host and tour guide, to Jodie's immense relief. Jodie had taken the opportunity to pull Cheryl aside, letting him have the cameras to himself for a moment.

"I know," Cheryl said miserably. "I'm so sorry."

"Not sorry enough to stop it," Jodie snapped.

"This is the last time," Cheryl reminded her. "I promise. After Broadway, everything gets cleared with you first."

"You keep making all these promises," Jodie said angrily, "but they only count if you actually keep them."

Cheryl flinched.

Jodie didn't bother to hide her annoyance when they filmed Jonah leading her out onto the stage. She felt like a performing seal.

"Can you sing something?" the producer called out from darkness of the audience.

"God no!"

"Not you! Jonah. *Tony.* Sing something romantic at her."

Because girls loved being sung *at.* Jodie couldn't help but roll her eyes.

"Do you mind?" Jonah asked her softly. He pulled a face at the pushiness of the producer.

"As long as it's you singing and not me, I'll cope." But she didn't like it and it was plain.

Jonah gave her a sympathetic look and then gently launched into "Tonight." Which Jodie had a vague memory of as a duet. But he found a way to make it a solo without embarrassing either of them.

He took her hands and led her center stage, singing with swirling passion. *Tonight, tonight, there's only you tonight . . .*

He was really good. So good that Jodie got goose bumps. In her head she could hear Bree squealing with delight. She would have loved everything about this, and everything about him.

Jodie fell under his spell as he sang. His voice filled the theater, achingly beautiful and full of love. He moved behind her, turning her to face the empty seats. His muscular dancer's body was warm at her back, and his breath smelled sugary, like Cronuts.

When it was over, there was a thin smattering of applause from the empty theater.

"Oh, bravo," Maya called.

"Is that what we're doing on Thursday? That song?" Jodie asked, pulling out of Jonah's grip. Her heart was skidding. No one had ever serenaded her like that before.

"Oh no." Jonah seemed amused. "That's one of the most important songs in the whole show. The production wouldn't let us mess with it."

Right. Wouldn't want to ruin that one.

"We'll go to rehearsal now," Cheryl said hurriedly, "and you can learn your song."

Her song. Here they went again, off with the circus . . .

"Don't worry," Cheryl assured her, "you don't have to sing the main part."

"I'm not singing anything," Jodie said firmly. "The bucket list says *walk-on cameo* and that's all you're getting."

"It's a musical," Maya called from the audience, her voice sharp, "of course you have to sing."

"You can just talk your bits," Cheryl told her quietly.

"No."

Cheryl glanced at Maya and then turned her back to her, so Maya couldn't read her lips. "Please," she whispered.

"No."

"Come on," Maya called, "the car's waiting to take us to the rehearsal studio."

Cheryl made a soft hissing noise. Jodie couldn't work out why Cheryl didn't just tell Maya to take a hike.

"I'm not singing," Jodie said as she jumped down from the stage.

Cheryl glanced at Maya. "OK." She sighed. "I'll work it out."

Chapter 27

She should never have turned her phone on. There were more messages from Kelly. Mostly of the *we need to talk* variety, and then one telling her he was available for a piano lesson later but was heading off now to see his family for lunch. Just reading them made Jodie feel light-headed. Piano lessons. She'd see him later. When he'd tell her in person that it was all one great big mistake. That he'd let her kiss him last night, but, you know, now it was the next day . . .

Ugh. She couldn't even.

Her phone vibrated in her hand. It was a message from Cheryl. **Where are you?**

She was locked in the bathroom across from the rehearsal studio, that's where she was. She'd holed up here the minute they'd reached the studio, after the farce with *GMA* at the theater. It had been a long day and it was still only morning.

The bathroom she'd locked herself in was a long narrow change cubicle with a toilet in it, rather than an actual bathroom. There was a wooden bench down the long wall and a bunch of pegs for people to hang their clothes on. A worn-out ballet shoe hung from one peg; the shoe was so ravaged that it made Jodie worry for the dancer's foot. The whole place smelled of stale sweat and cheap deodorant. Jodie had locked herself in to take advantage of the privacy. She'd needed a few minutes alone. She wanted to check her phone but hadn't wanted to open Kelly's messages in public. You know, just in case he'd decided to pull the pin via text message. Which wasn't unheard of. It happened. It had happened to Jodie before. More than once. She might have also been guilty of doing it herself. But in her defense, it had been a very bad date.

Had *she* been a bad date last night?

It hadn't even been a date . . . it had been a truncated movie, followed by a lot of kissing to the soundtrack of *West Side Story*.

Had she been a bad kisser?

He hadn't seemed to mind it at the time.

Jodie's phone vibrated again. Cheryl.

Don't look at Instagram.

Well. That was a red rag to a bull, wasn't it? Jodie punched open the app, steeling herself for what she'd find.

It turned out there was a lot to find. Hell, it wasn't even eleven o'clock in the morning, how was there this much material already? And who the hell had taken it all? Jodie scrolled through the images on Instagram. There were HD shots of her morning at the theater: Jonah on stage holding up the coffee; Jodie taking the coffee from his hand; the two of them alone in the immensity of the luxurious theater. It looked like an ad for Cartier or Tiffany or something, it was so labored in its romance. #TeamJonah was already trending.

Team Jonah? Ha. Jodie had been more interested in the Danishes in his paper sack than in him. But the photos made it appear otherwise. In one close up, Jodie's eyes seemed to glisten with the magic of attraction.

For the *Danish*, but of course the Danish had been edited out. The footage of Jonah singing at her on stage was real enough. Jonah was every inch a romantic hero. He looked like a boy band pinup. Maya didn't waste any time, did she? And Jodie knew this was Maya's doing. Firstly, because these images didn't have any of Cheryl's sinewy visceral truth. These were just glossy fashion-magazine-style splashes. Secondly, because of the name scrawled on that coffee cup. Maya had set the whole Jonah thing up. She was looking for Team Jonah to trend.

But she hadn't taken the photos herself, because at the time they were taken, Maya had been off waging passive-aggressive warfare with Cheryl. She must have had someone planted in the recesses of the theater. A sniper photographer.

Jodie scrolled through the comments beneath one of the images. They were pretty funny, at least the ones that didn't call her a fat pig or a useless slut.

I wouldn't say no to Jonah Lourdes!

No chance. Look at her face! She's faking it.

Not faking it. The man had a voice to make a girl weak at the knees. And the rest of him wasn't bad either. Close-ups made things look more dramatic than they actually were, that was all.

"Why does Maya have access to the account?" Jodie demanded, after she'd hunted Cheryl down and hauled her back to the bathroom. She locked the camera crew and Maya out. The cubicle felt like a prison cell, but at least it was a *private* prison cell. Provided they didn't have secret cameras wired up. Jodie found herself scanning the room, like a paranoiac. Bare bricks. Floorboards. An old cistern toilet. A square old ceramic sink. A chipped and flyspecked mirror. No cameras. "How does she have the passwords?"

Cheryl was white-faced and hollow-eyed with stress. She was gripping her phone like it was a stress ball. "I don't know!"

"Did Ryan send her? Or is she just barging in on her own?" Jodie would think a lot less of Sir Ryan and his July-sky-blue eyes if he *had* sent her.

"I don't know that either." Cheryl's blood-red lips had gone very thin and there was no trace of her usual minty-white smile.

"Well, what *do* you know?"

"I know that she's an undermining attention-seeker and I'll get her out of here if it's the last thing I do," Cheryl said grimly.

None of that sounded helpful to Jodie. Why couldn't any of this be *simple*?

It didn't get any simpler when they left the bathroom. The rehearsal studio was full of dancers. The studio itself was an oblong windowless box, with mirrored walls. There were dance barres and worn floorboards and the smell of old sweat. The dancers were all women, lithe and muscular as hell. They were standing around the old upright piano in the corner, holding sheet music and chattering away.

Jodie felt like holding on to the doorjamb and refusing to move. Her nerves came back full force, like a swarm of bees. Her ears were humming and her skin felt hot and prickly. This didn't look like preparation for a simple walk-on cameo. And she'd be damned if she was doing anything more than that.

Cheryl crossed the room like a conquering general and was shaking hands and greeting everyone mintily, wielding her smile like a weapon. Jodie hoped she was using her powers for good and not evil.

Cheryl turned and beckoned her, but Jodie couldn't move. The pianist had started playing softly and Jodie was riveted to the spot. She knew that song.

"Cheryl . . ." Jodie ground out. "What the hell is this?"

Cheryl smiled gamely, only her darting gaze revealing her guilt. "I convinced them to value add to Thursday's performance. People will love it, and this way we won't disrupt their usual numbers."

"Value add . . ." Jodie felt a spike of anger.

"This was all arranged before we spoke this morning," Cheryl said hurriedly.

Well, it could be *unarranged*, then.

The pianist was gaining vigor and there was no doubt which song it was. "I Feel Pretty." Which wasn't even in the damn show anymore.

"They *cut* 'I Feel Pretty,'" Jodie protested. "Sondheim didn't like it. Tish told me."

"Tish?" Maya's gaze narrowed at Tish's name. A wolfish smile played around her lips.

She knew, Jodie realized. She *knew* who Tish was, that she

was Cheryl's girlfriend and that they were all lying to Ryan Las-seter. It was there in the sly sideways look Maya gave Cheryl.

Jodie decided she didn't like Maya at all. "Yes. *Tish*," she said bullishly, "the girl who was my date the other night." What did another lie matter at this point?

"The company agreed to do the number on the proviso that we do it the way it was done in the last revival," Cheryl told Jodie, turning her back on Maya, pulling the conversation away from Tish. "In Spanish."

"In Spanish . . ." Jodie repeated, sounding like a slow-witted parrot. "Even if I was going to sing—which I'm not—I don't speak Spanish."

"You don't need to. You can learn it by rote," Maya said. She was unfazed by Jodie's protests.

Cheryl pulled sheet music from her bag. "No singing," she promised. "The cast can sing. You can do your walk-on while they sing."

Jodie stared at the music like it was covered in spiders.

Maya's coral smile fixed on Jodie. "I feel I have to give you my two cents on the choice of the song."

"Why?" Jodie crossed her arms.

Maya blinked. "Pardon?"

"Why do you feel you have to give me your two cents?" Jodie demanded. "I didn't ask for it."

A peeved look flickered across Maya's face. "*Ryan* asked me. I'm here to *help*. And my advice is: this is the wrong number to do. It's a complete waste of an opportunity to do an all-girl number in this show. Don't forget we're working toward number one hundred on the list."

Number one hundred? What did . . . oh. Team Jonah.

This chick was really getting under Jodie's skin. "*We* are, are *we*?"

Maya didn't pick up on Jodie's tone. "And this is the perfect opportunity to do a duet with Jonah. People will *love* it."

"I'm not singing," Jodie said flatly. "The bucket list says *walk-on cameo*."

"Just imagine"—Maya gestured with her hands, as though conjuring an image—"you and Jonah, alone on stage, spotlit. The theater is hushed. The music comes in, faintly. And you sing 'Tonight.' One of the most romantic songs in Broadway history . . ."

"That's not happening." Jodie looked at Maya like she had two heads. "And neither is 'I Feel Pretty.'"

"'Me Siento Hermosa,'" Cheryl corrected.

"Pretty . . . *hermosa* . . . I'm not singing anything at all. The bucket list said *walk-on cameo*. I'm doing the bucket list, not whatever circus act you two are putting together."

Maya cocked her head and narrowed her eyes. She seemed to be sizing Jodie up. Then she just bulldozed on ahead. "Don't blame *me* for this circus. If it was up to me, it would be a simple act. Just the two of you."

"No acts!" Jodie snapped at her. She was over being pushed around. "Forget the damn acts. Just let me walk on, like Bree wanted."

Cheryl sighed. "She has a point."

"No, she doesn't."

"Yes, I do." Jodie was done. She turned and headed back through the door. "I'll find my own stage to walk onto. I don't need this garbage."

"Jodie!" Cheryl was hot on her heels. "Not you!" she heard Cheryl snap at Maya when Maya moved to follow them. Cheryl all but slammed the door in Maya's face, and then Jodie and Cheryl were alone on the landing to the stairwell. "Wait, just listen, would you?"

Jodie waited, but not patiently. She had one foot on the first step. And she was barely listening.

"I'm doing my best," Cheryl said, her minty smile nowhere to be seen. "This isn't as easy as it looks."

Jodie didn't think it looked easy at all. But most of it didn't look necessary either. Cheryl was twisting herself inside out turning Bree's list into a circus it didn't need to be.

"The extra song was a solution, OK? The company wasn't

keen to let you walk on during the performance." Cheryl gripped the banister at the top of the stairs. "It's a safety issue for you and for the dancers."

"They can't all be dance numbers," Jodie snapped. "There must be a scene I could walk in on."

"It's a pretty intense show. Athletic."

"So pick a different show."

"I tried. I really did. But it's short notice. And *this* show said yes and have been very accommodating. I'm just trying to find a solution that works for you *and* for them. A little extra number, where you're not in danger from a flying kick, and they're not in danger of you accidentally injuring someone. It was the best solution. And the audience will be happy because they get something no one else does—a one-night-only number."

"But it *doesn't* work for me," Jodie told her firmly. "I only want to *walk on*. I've told you over and over: I don't sing. I won't sing. I'm not here to be unnecessarily humiliated. This is my life, Cheryl. I'm not a clown."

Cheryl nodded. "OK. Fine. No singing. I said no singing, and I meant it."

"Maya didn't."

"Screw Maya," Cheryl said through clenched teeth. "This is my rodeo, not hers."

"No," Jodie told her sharply. "It's *mine*."

Cheryl was suitably abashed.

Jodie glared at her. "No singing. And no dancing either."

Cheryl nodded. "No singing. No dancing."

"I walk. I stand. That's it."

Cheryl sighed. "OK."

Jodie couldn't believe it. Had she actually contained Hurricane Cheryl?

"But you still need to come in and rehearse," Cheryl told her. "They'll need to choreograph it around you." Cheryl seemed wilted. "There are rehearsals tomorrow morning too, here again, and then we'll do a dress rehearsal in the theater, before the performance." She bit her scarlet lip. "Would that be OK?"

Jodie gave a short nod.

"I thought we could multitask and drag Kelly along," Cheryl suggested, "and he can cram a few piano lessons in on the piano here and at the theater." Cheryl forced a smile. "How's that, two items ticked off at once?"

As Jodie went back into the rehearsal room, she didn't feel very smiley, even though she'd got what she wanted. There was so little time left with Kelly. He'd be heading back to Tacoma, to his life. And she'd return to watching him from a distance. Being someone that he used to know.

"Ready for Broadway?" Cheryl asked gently.

No. But she'd do it anyway.

Jodie was getting used to doing things she wasn't ready for, but her stomach still went south when Cheryl opened the door and all the dancers turned to look at her.

Chapter 28

"Do you have to sing?" Tish was a welcome gust of fresh air at the end of rehearsals. She and Kelly arrived together, clomping up the stairs just as the dancers skipped past them. Maya and the camera crew had left hours ago. Cheryl snagged Kelly at the door to talk piano lesson schedules, and Jodie's whole body was zipping with nerves at the sight of him. She was grateful he hadn't arrived fifteen minutes earlier, or he would have seen her miserable attempt at the choreography. Today Jodie had learned that she couldn't even *walk* properly.

"No singing. But they seem determined to get me to mime," Jodie told Tish, unable to tear her gaze away from Kelly. Luckily she could watch him stealthily in the mirror. "The choreographer is ready to pitch a fit about it."

"What do they want you to mime?" Tish asked cheerfully, pulling off her scarf and snooping around the studio.

"Ah ah. Lala la la la. And then there's a bit in Spanish. *Po que soy amada / Por un maravilloso chico.*"

Tish laughed. "I meant which song."

"'Me Siento Hermosa.'"

Tish looked confused.

"'I Feel Pretty.'" Jodie sighed.

Tish gave a startled, horrified laugh. "She didn't!"

"She did."

"Want me to shortsheet her bed tonight to get back at her?"

"It's your bed too," Jodie reminded her.

Tish rolled her eyes. "Not that you'd know it, the way she pretends not to know me when her boss is around."

"Well, *he* may not know, but Maya knows," Jodie told her.

"Maya?" Tish went still. "Maya's here?"

"Didn't Cheryl tell you?"

Clearly not. Tish made a beeline for Cheryl and Kelly. "Maya's here?" Her voice echoed in the empty dance studio. "Are you *OK*?"

Kelly looked over and met Jodie's eyes. She felt like a shaft of sunshine had struck her on a cold day. Everything went warm.

What should she do? Say hello? Go over there? Wait for him to come to her? Apologize for not answering his messages? Act like nothing had happened?

Kiss him.

Hell. She wanted to. Look at him. Who wouldn't want to?

In the end she didn't do anything. He came to her. "Hey," he said softly. He looked shy.

"Hey," she said back. She didn't know what to do with her hands. What did she normally do with her hands? Why was she noticing them now? She tried putting them on her hips but that felt weird; it felt weirder just letting them hang by her sides. What was *wrong* with her?

She always forgot how stunning his eyes were. They were lit with red sparkles. Best not to look at them, she thought, as she caught herself staring.

"How did it go? Was it as bad as you feared?" he asked.

"Yes," Jodie blurted. He looked surprised. He might not have been expecting honesty. "It turns out I can't walk, let alone dance."

"I've seen you walk," he said mildly. "You walk just fine."

"You'd think so, but you'd be wrong. At least according to the choreographer."

Kelly looked like he was trying not to smile. "Oh yeah? What are you doing wrong?"

"Apparently I need to walk *earthier*." Jodie rolled her eyes. "He says I spend too much time on the balls of my feet."

Kelly nodded. "Right. Well, you're an athlete, so that makes sense. You want to hit the ground with the ball of your foot when you're running. Which is the opposite of 'earthy.'"

Jodie was startled. She hadn't thought of it like that. She'd only heard that she was doing it wrong. That there was something wrong with her.

"From what I saw in the movie last night, this is a pretty 'earthy' kind of choreography. It's not like fancy ballet or anything. I think they probably just want you to match the style."

"Well, they can dream. They're all so good at it," she said, examining her feet. Kelly was right. They were fine for running. So maybe it wasn't her. "The dancers, I mean."

"Sure, they are. It's their job." He laughed. "You'd hope if you got on Broadway you'd be good at your job."

"Good point." Jodie straightened up. He was right. They were the best in the world at what they did. She shouldn't compare herself, even if she'd just spent the day staring at herself in the mirror in their midst, looking like a pigeon in a field of peacocks. "You should see the state of their feet," Jodie said, just talking now to fill the silence. The longer they talked about this, the longer she could delay talking about his message. *Can we talk?* Look, they were talking. "Their feet really taking a beating."

"Dancers are pretty amazing athletes," Kelly agreed. "I dated a dancer. She was stronger than I was."

He'd dated a dancer. Who? Was that Jessica, the blonde? And dat*ed*. Past tense. Why had they broken up?

"Piano lesson time?" Cheryl asked. She pulled a copy of the sheet music from her bag as she crossed the room.

"Do you carry a library of sheet music in that thing?" Jodie asked. "You got *The Sound of Music* in there too?"

"I brought it just in case. Any time there's a piano, we should probably have a lesson," she told them. "We've got just enough time to do one now and then go back the hotel and change."

"Change? For what?" Jodie blinked. The whole day was being hijacked again. She'd wanted to get to the High Line at some point . . .

"We've got tickets to *West Side Story*. I might have forgotten to tell you. It's been a bit of a day," she said sheepishly. "I know this whole Broadway thing is out of hand—I swear the next item on the bucket list won't get hijacked like this."

Cheryl had made so many promises. Jodie would believe it when it happened.

"*GMA* wants to film you watching the show," Cheryl updated her, "and then talking to the dancers backstage. For the package. It's probably wise for you to have seen it before you appear in it anyway."

Jodie supposed so.

Tish wasn't pleased. "You're ditching us *again*? What are Kelly and I supposed to do while you guys are at a show?" She said it like Kelly and Jodie were a couple, just like she and Cheryl were, as though of course they'd be hanging out tonight if Jodie weren't being dragged to a show.

Jodie glanced at him. He didn't say anything either way.

"Stop whining," Cheryl said tersely. "You're coming too."

Tish brightened. "I am?"

"You both are."

"We are?" Kelly sounded pleased.

"Is it free?" Tish was suspicious. "Or is this going to cost us?"

"It's free." Cheryl's regular enthusiasm was tarnished this afternoon.

"Are they good seats?"

Cheryl rolled her eyes.

"Hurry up with the piano lesson," Tish ordered, changing her tune. "I want to get back in time to sort my hair. We should all go for dinner after. I'll look for somewhere." She had her phone out and was punching up websites.

"You guys ready?" Cheryl asked. "Is it OK if I snap a couple of photos and a video or two? You can pretend I'm not here. It doesn't have to be a long lesson. Once through should do."

"Does it upset you that Bree's bucket list got hijacked like this?" Kelly asked softly, once Cheryl had snapped her photos and retreated to join Tish in the corner. The studio piano had a stool, not a bench, so Kelly was standing behind Jodie as she fumbled her way through the Gershwin.

"Does it upset me?" Jodie repeated, wincing as she hit a sharp. "Yes, it upsets me. It *infuriates* me. But then . . . Bree set it up like this, so I don't know if it *has* been hijacked. She's the one who got Cheryl involved. But . . . yeah . . . I don't love it."

"You could just go rogue and do it all by yourself."

Jodie laughed. "Fly over Antarctica all by myself? I'll just warm up the jet." She pulled a face. Like she could afford Antarctica without Sir Ryan Lotsofcash. "I think I'm stuck with it for now."

For a while there was just the sound of Jodie clunking away through "Our Love Is Here to Stay." Kelly turned the page. Then cleared his throat. "So, you met the guy from the show? That Jonah guy?"

Damn Instagram. Jodie stumbled over the final phrase and the piano made a tortured noise. But . . . did he sound *jealous*? "I did," she agreed, "he gave me a coffee. He didn't *buy* the coffee, but he definitely gave it to me."

"Right."

"Lesson over?" Tish was on her feet and ready to go. "You stopped playing. It's over, right? Because my hair takes ages."

"Can you guys fit in another lesson before you go to bed tonight?" Cheryl asked. "The ballroom at the hotel is available. I checked. So, you could use their piano again. And can you selfie it for me? I promised Tish I'd turn in early, otherwise I'd do it."

"Sure," Kelly said quickly. "More than happy to."

Jodie wasn't happy to at all. The quicker they got through the lessons, the quicker her time with Kelly would end.

She dragged her feet as they headed back to the hotel and soon Cheryl and Tish had pulled ahead. Kelly slowed his pace to stay beside her. It was late afternoon and getting dark already. Jodie wondered when she'd get some time to see New York. In daylight.

"You OK?" he asked.

"Yeah."

"Nervous?"

"Always." She sighed. "But no, right now I was just wondering when I can take some time and go see some things. Bree once told me she'd take me to see the High Line and I'd like to get there before I head back to Wilmington."

"Oh. You mind if I ask a question?"

Sure, so long as it's not *Can we talk?*

"Why don't you just go do it? Why do you need someone's permission?" He said it gently enough, but Jodie still felt stung.

"I don't need permission," she said defensively.

His silence was disbelieving.

"I *don't*." Jodie quickened her pace. Maybe she should have opted for the *Can we talk?* conversation.

"So, let's go see the High Line."

"It's *dark*."

"Tomorrow, then."

"Rehearsals," Jodie said tightly.

"Play hooky. Or be late. Or finish early."

"I need to finish this list." Jodie didn't like the feeling of being annoyed at Kelly Wong. He was making her feel like a toddler about to throw a tantrum. He was just so calm and reasonable. He didn't sound judgy, he sounded *curious*. How did you get mad at curious?

"It's not either/or," he said gently. "You could do *both*. Finish the list *and* see the High Line."

Jodie scowled at the sidewalk as she walked. She hated be-ing . . . what? Called out for being passive?

God. He was right. She *was* passive.

"Let's go tomorrow morning. Early." He nudged her with his elbow as they walked. "We can eat breakfast while we walk it. My treat."

"It's free," Jodie said. "I looked it up."

"I meant the breakfast."

Was this a date? Was he asking her out on a date? What was all the *can we talk* stuff then? Jodie was confused, but she wasn't about to look a gift horse in the mouth. She'd take every second of this she could get and store it away to remember when the inevitable Life After Kelly arrived.

"OK," she said. "Breakfast on the High Line."

"Before we get back to the hotel, I was wondering if we could talk . . ."

Oh, *here* it came. Fortuitously, Jodie's phone started vibrating in her pocket. She scrabbled for it before Kelly could blurt out that he meant could they have breakfast *as friends. It was all a mistake, sorry to lead you on, you sad, desperate, lonely person.*

"It's my grandmother," Jodie apologized to Kelly, cutting him short. "Sorry, I'd better get this."

"You were on *Good Morning America*!" Grandma Gloria shouted gleefully in her ear. "Why didn't you tell us? I turned on the television and there you were!"

"Talk later," Jodie mouthed at Kelly. He nodded, but she thought he didn't look very happy about it. Like a complete and utter coward, Jodie kept Grandma Gloria talking until she and Kelly had reached their separate hotel rooms. She gave him a wave and disappeared inside. Total and utter cowardice. As usual.

Chapter 29

Jodie only had the black dress Claudia had given her to wear to the theater, so she wore it again, remembering as she wriggled into it how Kelly had looked when he saw her. She shivered. Would he look that way again?

"You know what you need?" Tish said when she came knocking at the door to tell Jodie the car was on its way. "Lipstick!" She fished a tube from her fancy mesh evening bag and tossed it to Jodie.

Instinctively Jodie caught it. Sure, why not? Kelly had already seen the dress, but he hadn't seen her in lipstick, had he? Jodie uncapped the tube. Bright red. Well, she might as well go big or go home. Jodie carefully applied the shock of red to her lips.

Tish whistled. "Girl, you're *owning* that." She opened her bag and pulled out another small shiny tube. "No trip to a fancy-ass theater is complete without a little Chanel." She took her travel sized perfume and sprayed it all over Jodie, who sneezed. "Ta da! You'll be ready for the paparazzi tonight!"

Ugh. The endless photos. Who needed so many photos taken of themselves?

"Now, come on, I want to hit the bar before the show." Tish yanked Jodie from the room.

Cheryl and Kelly were waiting out in the corridor. Jodie

darted a glance at Kelly's face. He was staring at her again. If he'd looked stunned the other night, tonight he looked . . . well, like he might just kiss her right in front of Tish and Cheryl.

Jodie would have kissed him back. And they might never have made it to the theater.

Cheryl probably wouldn't have noticed, as she was too busy typing on her phone to look up, but Tish definitely would have. Tish was smirking *now*, and there wasn't even any kissing happening.

"Kelly," Tish ordered, "when we get out of the car, you and I are going to stay close to Jodie. Let's give them all conniptions. They won't know whether Team Kelly or Team Tish should be trending."

"No problem," Kelly said, his voice husky. "I won't leave her side."

"And what about me?" Cheryl asked.

"You talking to me, or your phone?" Tish sniffed as she sashayed toward the elevator. "I can't always tell."

"You look incredible," Kelly whispered to Jodie as she stepped past him into the elevator.

"It's the same dress."

"I said *you* looked incredible, not the dress." His dimple flickered but his gaze was intensely serious.

For a hot minute Jodie wished they were alone. If they'd been alone, she might have lost her self-control and yanked him close and kissed him senseless. It's all she wanted to do.

As the elevator whooshed downward, memories of the night before made Jodie tremble. That floaty helium feeling was back. Every nerve in her body was singing. She could feel her thighs pressing together under the woolen dress, she could feel the weight of her breasts and the tightening of her nipples, she could feel the swirl of air against her throat. Every inch of her wanted to be touched. By him. *Now*.

The car ride was torture. Trying to keep up with the conversation over drinks was impossible. Sitting in the theater, right in the middle of the stalls, Jodie couldn't think of anything but Kelly's body beside hers.

"No holding hands," Tish told Kelly jokingly, "or everyone on Team Kelly will think they've won! I'm not losing that easily."

Kelly laughed. "Like this, you mean?" He reached over and took Jodie's hand. She felt the sizzle from her palm to . . . other places.

"If you're not playing fair, I'm not either." Tish leaned over and placed a smacking kiss on Jodie's cheek. She held it for a moment. "Think anyone got a shot of that?" she asked cheerfully as she pulled away.

"I did," a buttery voice said. It was Maya. At some point she'd slid into the empty seat beside Cheryl. She leaned forward and showed them the image she'd snapped. It was in glorious color, a close-up of Tish's kiss, her eyes closed in rapture.

Cheryl made a strangled noise.

Jodie pulled her hand away from Kelly's. She didn't want her own look of rapture going viral. And she couldn't guarantee that she wouldn't look rapturous. Kelly's touch made her itchy with desire.

"The *GMA* crew are over there," Maya stage-whispered to Jodie, leaning so far over Cheryl that she eclipsed her. She nodded to the far wall of the theater. "They'll get some shots of you in the audience and then we'll go backstage after the show."

"Thank you, Maya," Cheryl said, sitting forward so Maya had to move. "I already told her the running plan for tonight."

The bell began dinging for people to take their seats and the lights flickered. The orchestra began tuning up.

"This is cool," Kelly said, grinning.

Jodie was startled. She'd been so keyed up that she'd barely taken in what was happening. She guessed it *was* pretty cool. She'd never been to a Broadway show before. She felt a flutter of excitement as the din from the orchestra pit grew. The lights dimmed and there was a rustle of expectation from the crowd.

As the overture swelled, Jodie was startled to feel the featherlight brush of Kelly's hand on hers. His palm covered the back of her hand and his fingers slid between hers. Jodie's heart thundered. As always, his touch was electric. She felt like she'd just grabbed hold of a live wire. She gave him a furtive glance, but he was staring at the stage, which was still dark. He seemed engrossed. She glanced around. Someone would notice their hands. It would be all over social media before the show was finished. As though he could read her mind, Kelly pulled her hand off her knee and under the arm rest, between their bodies, hidden by the darkness.

And he didn't let go.

The touch of his hand tangled with her experience of the show. The syncopation of the songs matched the skidding and stopping of her heart as Kelly's thumb stroked hers. The breathlessness of Tony's love for Maria mirrored her breathlessness at being here, in this moment, with Kelly Wong. The darkness of the story, of the tortured lovers, took her fears and turned them into something real, into something that made sense. The show was sinewy, played against a screen that projected images from social media and livestreamed private moments. It felt keenly true to Jodie. But while those characters were doomed by circumstance and feuds, she was doomed by . . . what? An ordinary life. Debt and a car-rental stand.

Today the world was just an address, a place for me to live in, no better than alright . . .

Jodie found tears flooding as the actress playing Maria sang the words on stage, and it wasn't because of the play. It was the thought of returning to the airport and the car-rental stand. She hated it. She hated her whole life.

But here you are and what was just a world is a star . . .

Jodie closed her eyes and concentrated on the feel of Kelly's skin against hers. Sparks flowed from his hand into her veins. She could feel the hot fizz of them through every last tributary of her blood stream. *This* was how life should feel. Terrifying, magical, wonderful, risky . . . She didn't know what their tangled hands meant, she didn't know what he was thinking, or where this was leading, but standing on the cliff edge of this feeling was miraculous. It was the polar opposite of her dreary life. Here, in this wobbly moment, buffeted by winds on the edge of a cliff, not able to see or trust what she was jumping into, Jodie felt alive.

The show ended too quickly. Kelly released her hand in order to applaud. Jodie would have been happy to keep holding hands and to skip the applause, even if everyone in the theater had snapped a picture of it on their phones. Reluctantly, she rose to her feet and applauded too. The performers came skipping out for their curtain calls, wave after wave, until it was only Tony and Maria standing there.

The applause died out in a spatter as Jonah Lourdes lifted his hands to quiet the crowd. "Thank you!" Even in full costume and makeup, with a neck tattoo and a scar shaved into his eyebrow and all the paraphernalia of Tony's gang membership, Jonah looked weirdly clean-cut. The joy he took from being on stage was palpable; he shone with it. "If you watched *Good Morning America* today, some of you may know that we have a special guest in the audience tonight."

Jodie's stomach went sour. Oh no.

The sourness grew sharper as he launched into a moving speech about Bree. It was heartfelt. Sincere. To Jodie's horror she found herself on the verge of tears as the screen behind him projected an image of her sister. It was the photo from Mom's mantelpiece, of Bree standing on that cliff edge, with her arms spread, a blindingly joyful smile shining brighter than the sun sparkles on the sea behind her. A series of hashtags ran down the bottom of the screen. Most of them mentioned Iris Air.

Jodie sat down. She felt like someone had poured icy water over her head.

"Are you OK?" Kelly whispered, as he sank into his seat beside her.

All around them, people were following their lead and sitting down, realizing that Jonah's speech wasn't going to be quick. The sight of Jonah Lourdes standing up there, in front of a giant picture of Bree and a bunch of marketing hashtags, brought the surreal ludicrousness of the situation home to Jodie. The grossness of it.

Who the hell were these people? And why did they keep hijacking her bucket list?

Jonah was inviting the crowd, and the *GMA* audience, to

"Join us on this crazy adventure." *Us.* Like he was more than merely a tangential part of it. If Jodie had been standing up there with him, she would have pushed him into the orchestra pit. But she wasn't up there. She was down here. In the audience.

"I'd like to dedicate this song to Bree." Jonah said it so earnestly, like he'd known and cared for her sister, like she was more to him than a picture on a screen, and an orgy of free self-promotion. "And to Jodie . . ." His voice dropped shyly, his arm sweeping in a fluid dancer's arc to where Jodie sat.

A spotlight followed his gesture, finding Jodie in her seat.

Fuck.

The theater was hushed, every eye on her. Jodie had rolled the playbill into a stubby bat. She gripped it in white-knuckled hands, wondering how much damage she could do with it.

Then the strings swept in, rising from the orchestra pit, fragile and sad. And of course Jonah started singing. As the spotlight blinded Jodie, singling her out in her chair, Jonah stood poised on the very lip of the stage, gazing down at her, the way he'd gazed at the actress playing Maria all through the show. He was liquid with tenderness, not a drop of it real.

There's a time for us, someday a time for us . . .

He'd better hope not. The moment she got him alone, she was going to show him how much damage a playbill could do. Let him post that on his story.

As he finished his balladeering, the final word—*somewhere*—trembled in the air, fading to the silence of the hushed theater. And then the crowd was on their feet again, their applause thunderous. The whole theater sounded like it was going to come down around them.

Jodie stayed seated, the playbill a crushed baton in her hands.

Kelly and Tish stayed seated too. Jodie kept her gaze fixed on the back of the plush red seat in front of her.

"Well," Tish said eventually, barely audible over the wild applause, "I'm glad he gets killed every night. I'm looking forward to seeing him get shot again on Thursday."

Chapter 30

Jodie didn't feel like going out after the show. She felt like a zoo animal—and an enraged one, at that. A tiger prepared to maul the first person she saw. She couldn't turn around without someone snapping a photo of her. Jodie didn't know why they bothered. #JodieSightings weren't rare. It seemed like everyone in New York had snapped a photo of her. And in most of them she looked terrible.

Jodie's thoughts were so tangled together that she couldn't find their heads or tails. She needed some peace and quiet. And she was sick to death of all these people.

"I'm so sorry," Cheryl said, the words flooding out as soon as they escaped the smothering red cushion of the theater.

Jodie was sick of Cheryl's apologies. She turned her back on Cheryl and the Broadway Theatre and faced the honking, light-spangled street. The icy night air was sharp in her lungs.

"I didn't know anything about that stunt with Jonah," Cheryl said desperately. "It was an ambush."

In the reflection of a cab window, Jodie could see Maya playing with her phone. Uploading videos, no doubt. To *Bree's* account. Maya had stalked Jodie like a hyena during the back-stage *GMA* safari, snapping away, trying to get as many photos of Jodie and Jonah as she could.

"You guys go ahead to dinner, I'm not in the mood," Jodie

said sharply. She shut their protests out. "Go," she snapped. She didn't look at them. She was too angry.

Kelly, being Kelly, respected her wishes, even though he looked back regretfully as he followed Cheryl and Tish off to dinner. "I'll be back for the piano lesson after?" he asked softly as he said goodbye. She shrugged. She didn't know how she'd feel or where she'd be by then.

Once they were gone, Jodie headed for the stage door. As she passed Maya, she flipped the phone out of her hands, caught it, and pocketed it.

"Hey!" Maya was indignant.

"You can have it back when I'm done." Jodie stalked to the stage door and rapped on it. When the doorman opened it, she barged through and then pushed the door closed before Maya could get in. "Don't let that woman through!" she ordered the doorman, who was bewildered. He knew who she was from the *GMA* filming but was in no mind to be taking orders from her. "She's a stalker," Jodie told him, as she headed for the dressing rooms. "If she tries to follow me, call security!"

"I am security," he protested.

Jodie got lost in the maze backstage and only found the right room by luck.

"Jodie!" Jonah Lourdes was already out of costume. She'd caught him in the middle of lacing up his shoes. He looked pleased to see her.

Idiot.

She closed the door and scanned the room. His phone was on the counter; she pocketed that one too.

"Hey," he protested, confused.

"Just for security," she told him. "This is between us; I don't want it online."

"I wouldn't do that." He stood. His confusion had turned to genuine bewilderment.

Jodie snorted. "Sure, you wouldn't."

He frowned.

Jodie crossed her arms. "What was all that tonight?"

"All what?"

"All *what*? *That!* Turning my sister's bucket list into a public freakshow."

Jonah went very still. He looked like a kid being dressed down by his mom.

"I mean, I know for you this is just a jaunt," Jodie said tightly, "a sideshow. A chance to get your pretty face on *Good Morning America*. But for me . . . this is everything. This is my sister's last goddamn wish. And a chance to get my parents out of debt. Despite what you and Maya and Cheryl and Sir Ryan-goddamn-Lasseter think, this isn't a circus. This isn't a marketing campaign; it's not about hit rates and bounce rates and how many followers I can get. This is about my *sister*, do you understand? And I resent you using her for your own ends." Jodie was breathing hard. God, it felt good to say.

Jonah Lourdes was wide-eyed. "My own ends . . . but . . . they told me . . ." He groaned. "Jesus. They told me this was what you wanted."

Jodie gave a harsh laugh. "What I *wanted*—what I *want*—is to just walk on and walk off, like the bucket list says. And I want a moment's peace to actually honor my sister while I do it." Oh God, here came the tears again. They flooded in at every inconvenient moment, every time she wanted to look strong. Jodie dashed them away. They were hot against her cold hand. "I don't want my grief paraded before a bunch of strangers. I don't want to be humiliated and embarrassed. I don't want to be pushed into being someone I'm not. And I don't want someone I've just met serenading me, in front of a giant picture of my dead sister. Do you have any idea how much that *hurt*?"

Jonah was grave and shaken. "I'm so sorry," he said. "I thought . . . I was told . . ." He took a shaky breath. "That's no excuse. I should have asked you directly."

"Yes." Jodie couldn't stop the tears. But they didn't make her weak, she realized. If anything, right now they made her feel stronger. More certain. "You should have."

He nodded. "I really didn't mean to hijack anything. I'm very sorry."

Jodie nodded, trying to accept his apology graciously. But she was still a swirling tide of rage and grief. "Who asked you to do it?" Although she already knew.

"Maya. She said it was what you wanted." He was shame-faced.

As the tears fell, Jodie swiped them away angrily.

"Can I buy you a drink to say sorry?" he asked.

The kindness in his voice made a mess of her. She felt herself crumpling, the tears an unturnable tide. The chaos of the past few days had well and truly caught up with her. She felt like a tired and overwhelmed child: angry, overstimulated, depleted. She tucked her chin into her chest and tried to draw a shuddering breath.

"Hey," Jonah protested. He radiated concern. "You need a hug?"

Jodie shrugged. Ah hell, she was going into the full ugly cry. She just kept thinking about that photo of Bree up there on the big screen in the theater, that smile of joy, those arms flung wide. Bree trapped in a moment. Always there, never *here*.

She surrendered to the tears; not just tears, great big strangled sobs.

Then she felt Jonah Lourdes wrap his arms around her. He was taller than her, and her head tucked under his chin. She pressed her cheek to his soft wool sweater and closed her eyes. He smelled powdery, and like cold cream. She felt his hand on the back of her head, stroking her hair. He made soft soothing noises.

Eventually she calmed and grew embarrassed. God. She'd barged in here, railed at him, and then melted down. She was a lunatic. She pulled back and rubbed her face.

"Sorry," she mumbled.

"God, don't apologize. I need to apologize to *you*."

"You already did," she reminded him. She groaned as she caught sight of herself in the mirror. The rim of lightbulbs illuminated the shocking state of her. She was all red and swollen. Even her lips were all puffed up, and her eyes were bloodshot. "They'll have a field day with photos of me coming out of the theater like this," she moaned.

"Nah, you can wait here till it calms down." Jonah smiled and pulled a bottle of bourbon off the counter. "Look, we don't even need to leave to get a drink." He poured a measure of bourbon into a couple of coffee mugs. "I really am sorry. I never would have done it if I'd known it would upset you. It was dumb. I should have thought . . ."

"Thank you." Jodie took the mug. She felt like she'd been hit by a truck. She sank into the chair by the wall. It was a tiny dressing room. When he sat in the chair by the makeup counter, their knees almost touched. "Dutch courage before you go on stage?" she asked, taking a sip.

"Kentucky courage." He laughed. "But no, never before a show. It makes me too mellow. You need the nerves to put in a good performance. I save it for after, when I'm winding down."

Jodie sighed and leaned back in the chair. A phone buzzed in her pocket. She fished it out. "Is this yours or Maya's?"

"Not mine. How many do you have in there?"

"Not enough." Jodie pulled his out and handed it to him. "Don't Instagram this, OK?"

"Promise." He took the phone and threw it into his backpack. Then he took a sip of bourbon and threw her a cheeky smile. "You think I have a pretty face, huh?"

Chapter 31

Once she was back at the hotel, Jodie retreated to the sanctuary of the ballroom and the grand piano. She left most of the lights off. There was so much light spilling in from the city outside that she barely needed the jellyfish chandeliers anyway. She dropped her bag on a table and went to stand at the windows.

Jodie rested her forehead against the cold glass, her breath forming a fog cloud on the window. She let the silence of the ballroom fill her. She still couldn't get that giant image of Bree out of her head. The smile, the arms thrown wide, the ocean glittering over her shoulder. Jodie thumped her head gently against the glass. She missed her so much.

Bree would have loved tonight. If the spotlight had found her in the audience, she would have shone, as incandescent as a firework. She also would have loved Jonah. He would have matched her, firework for firework. Jodie could imagine them together. Two beautiful, shiny people, up there in the spotlight.

Jodie was happier in the audience, in the dark.

She sighed and the window in front of her bloomed white with condensation. With the clouds hanging low, it was the kind of night that meant snow back home. Jodie felt abruptly homesick. She imagined her parents at home in front of the television, under the ugly blanket Aunt Pat had knitted for them. They didn't like it but couldn't bring themselves to throw it away. Just like the marshmallow casseroles. Mom and Dad would be side by side on the couch, sharing a block of chocolate, watching some police drama. Mom would fall asleep before it was finished, and Dad would stay still so he wouldn't wake her, and quietly turn the channel over to sports. For a moment Jodie could almost see them in the reflections on the window, and she missed them so much it was like a toothache.

She fished her phone out of her bag. There were a zillion messages. Claude. Gloria. Pat. Some from her friends from college, and some from her friends at the car-rental stand. Even from Cooper, who was still fishing for a hookup, even though she hadn't responded in months. Aside from the messages, there were a flood of notifications from Instagram. Jodie ignored them all and called home.

Please pick up. She needed an anchor. Something to remind her who she was.

"Hello." Her dad's low bass grumble sounded in her ear. He'd answered it on the second ring, which meant Mom was probably asleep and he was trying not to let the phone wake her.

"Hi, it's me." Jodie sank onto the piano bench, facing the city.

"Hey." He sounded so pleased to hear from her that Jodie felt tears pricking. She missed him. It had been a long, long time since he'd seemed pleased about anything.

"Your Grandma Gloria says you were on the TV today. You didn't tell us that was happening."

"I didn't know it was." Jodie kicked her heels against the parquet floor. "I don't seem to know anything that's happening anymore. It all just seems to happen *to* me."

"Sounds like life to me," he said in his usual placid way. She could hear him grunt as he got up from the couch. She heard him shuffling into the kitchen, getting a glass from the cupboard, and opening the fridge. He'd be pouring himself a glass of milk and helping himself to the cookie tin. She could see it so clearly. Her dad was like a tired bear at the end of the day, grizzly but kind of cuddly. She missed him so much.

"Things didn't just happen to *Bree* . . ." Jodie paused. She had so much to say, but her dad was still so wounded by talk of Bree. It felt like kicking a puppy. But she needed to talk, and only her parents understood the hole that was in her life now. But also . . . there'd been kind of a hole even before Bree died. Now she had *two* holes. One Bree-shaped, and one Jodie-shaped. "*Life* didn't just happen to Bree. She made it happen."

There was silence, then Jodie heard a slow exhale. "Well, no, that's true enough," he rumbled.

Jodie continued. "I've been thinking about it a lot." Argh, this felt hard. Jodie craned her neck and stared up into the dark glint of the unlit jellyfish over her head. "About Bree . . . and just, well, life I guess."

She heard the sound of the cookie tin being prized open. "Yeah, me too," he admitted, almost too quiet to be heard.

Jodie felt her eyes growing hot. "I think I've wasted my life," she blurted. God, that was hard to say. Because it was so *true*. It should have been Jodie. Jodie should have been the one who got sick. No one was going to miss the loser from the car-rental stand. The tears came, and they were burning hot. They stung her eyes. No one would miss her the way they missed Bree . . .

"Hey," her dad rumbled. "Hey, hey, hey." It was the voice he'd used when she was a kid. That astonished, slightly fearful tone. He'd always hated it when she'd cried. "What's this?" She heard him sit down heavily at the kitchen table.

And it came spilling out. Bree up on the screen tonight, the spotlight, the hijacking of the bucket list.

"Well, that's a lot right there, peanut," her dad said mildly once she'd trailed off into hiccups.

"I'm sorry."

"Don't be sorry."

"I am, though. I *am*." The tears were still falling. Then Jodie heard her mother's voice in the background. She wiped her tears away with the palm of her hand. "Oh God, I'm sorry, did the phone wake Mom?"

Her dad grunted. "That woman doesn't sleep anymore."

Jodie heard her mother pick up the extension. "Jodie?"

"Hi, Mom."

"Why didn't you tell us you were going to be on *Good Morning America*?"

"Not now, Denise," Jodie's dad said. "She doesn't want to talk about that now."

"Oh no, why? What's gone wrong? Did something go wrong with Jonah?"

"Jonah?" Jodie pressed her hand over her eyes. Oh God. Instagram. Of course her mom had seen everything. "*Nothing* happened with Jonah." Nothing much. Just a hug and a drink. And a bit of casual flirting.

"Nothing except the fact he serenaded you! On *Broadway*. Did you know he has a solo album out? I just downloaded it."

"Denise!" Jodie's dad snapped. "Not now."

"It's very good. He was in *Phantom of the Opera* too. There are clips of it on YouTube. He wasn't the phantom; he was that other one, Whatshisname, the one that sings the love songs." Jodie's mom kept talking like her dad didn't even exist. "Well, I know what will cheer you up. Did your dad tell you the news?"

"What news?"

"Denise . . ."

"Iris Air paid off the bone marrow transplant today—the whole procedure!" Her mom sounded buoyant. "You're doing an amazing job, Jo-Jo! Bree would be so proud."

Jo-Jo. Her mom hadn't called her that since before Bree died. Jodie couldn't swallow for the lump in her throat. "They paid it off, huh."

"Jodie . . ." Her dad sounded at a loss.

"I'm fine, Dad." She was sorry she'd dumped on him. He didn't need her angst. Not now. "That's great news. By Thursday night I'll have finished two more and there'll be more payments. Oh hey, I have to do this piano lesson now," she lied. "Sorry to love you and leave you, but I'd better go. I'll call you tomorrow." She hung up as quick as she could, feeling as small as an ant. She shouldn't have told her dad all that. He was sad enough. Stupid. So stupid.

Jodie swiveled on the bench so that she was facing the piano. She lifted the lid. She should practice, she thought listlessly as she stared at the shining ivory keys. Her phone vibrated in her hand. She looked down. Claude.

"Hey," she said, trying to sound like she hadn't been crying.

"OK, what's wrong?" Claude had her bossy voice on. Jodie contemplated hanging up.

"Nothing."

"Nothing. Sure. *Nothing.* Which would be why I got a message from your father. The first message he's sent me. Ever."

Jodie scrunched her eyes closed. She felt awful. She was a terrible daughter. "What did he say?" she asked in a small voice. Oh, she hated the thought that she'd made him worry.

"It's your dad, so not much. But let's just say, it's pretty clear he's concerned. He thinks you need to talk to another girl."

Jodie groaned. "It's nothing. I was homesick. I shouldn't have called."

"He said no matter what you said, I should stay on the phone, so fess up. What's going on?"

"Nothing. Seriously. I just had a bad night, that's all."

"Oh, I saw. That hot Broadway star. Horrendous. You poor darling." There was a pause and then Claude sounded gentler and more genuine. "Come on, Jodie, what's up?"

Jodie didn't have the energy to say it all again.

Claude listened to the silence. "You're feeling like you wasted your life," Claude said softly. "That you've let life pass you by . . . in a way that Bree never did."

"He wrote you quite a bit then." The tears were falling again.

"You think it should have been you, and not Bree."

"I didn't tell him that." Jodie was crying hard now.

"You didn't need to. You don't need to tell *me* either. I think it every day." Claude's voice was husky. "Why wasn't it *me*? Answer me that, Jodie. No one would care if I died, except your family. My mother probably wouldn't even notice. I don't even have a cat to miss me. I could die tomorrow, and the only people in the world to notice would be *Bree's* family."

"We sure would," Jodie said hotly. She was horrified to hear the frigid bleakness in Claude's voice. "You're our *family*."

"You have parents who love you," Claude reminded Jodie. "Sure, they're a little wrapped up in their grief right now, but they'll come out of it. Your dad just sent me a text message which was the equivalent of *War and Peace* for him, he loves you so much. He also wants me to message him back after I talk to you, to let him know that you're OK."

"Why doesn't he talk to me himself?" Jodie wailed.

"Because he's garbage at it and he's always been garbage at it? What he *does* is take you to ball games and bring you Pepsis and he sits next to you on the couch. He can barely breathe without Bree, and it would have been exactly the same if it had been you. And if it *had* been you, Bree would be feeling the exact same way you are now. She'd be beating herself up and thinking it should have been her instead."

That stopped Jodie cold. It was true. She knew it, deep in her bones. Because if she was sure of one thing, it was that her sister had loved her. And despite the fears and irritations, she knew her parents loved her too.

"Grief is just horrible." Claude sighed.

Yes, it was. "But this isn't just grief," Jodie admitted, feeling raw, unvarnished terror as she spoke the words aloud. "This is from before Bree."

"What is?"

"I work in a car-rental stand." Jodie didn't know how that had happened. How was *that* her life? She was Jodie Boyd, the girl who kicked ass on the varsity team. She could turn more double plays than anyone. She was the *best* at it. But here she was, hitting her midtwenties and she didn't even play anymore. She didn't do *anything*.

"I know you work in a car-rental stand." Claude sounded baffled. "So?"

Jodie didn't know how to say it. "I . . . gave up," she blurted. "No one fought for me . . . and *I* didn't fight for me. I just let it pass me by. I gave up. Right at the beginning."

"Gave up? On what?" Claude sounded even more baffled now.

"On *me*. On everything. I mean, 'gave up' is generous. I never even *tried*. And now I'm stuck." Somehow, she'd frozen in time. She couldn't have baseball, she couldn't have Kelly, and so she hadn't tried for anything much. How self-hatingly stupid was *that*?

There was another pause. Jodie could almost hear the penny drop. There was an intake of breath and then another pause. Eventually Claude spoke. "Give me a minute here, because it's hard to know where to even begin."

"I work in a car-rental stand," Jodie said numbly. "And I don't even know how I got there."

"It's a good job," Claude said flatly. "Don't you dare beat yourself up for working a decent job. Do you know how many people don't have jobs? You have worked hard for as long as I've known you. Even as a kid, you went and mowed lawns, remember?"

"Dad got me into it," Jodie whispered. "I didn't do it myself."

"You certainly mowed all those lawns yourself."

"But I've never done anything on my own steam," Jodie said. "That's what I mean. I've never . . ." What was she trying to say . . . "Bree decided what she wanted out of life and she went and got it . . ."

"Well, you can do that too. What do you want?"

"I don't know," she admitted, feeling like a fool.

To her astonishment, Claude didn't laugh. "Well, you can work it out." She paused. "What about your degree? You must have picked that for a reason."

Jodie swallowed.

"Jodie?"

Yeah, she'd done it for a reason. A crazy one. One she was too scared to tell people. One that she could barely admit to herself, let alone to Claude.

"C'mon, dweeb," Claudia coaxed. "It's only me."

"Baseball," Jodie blurted.

"What?"

"Baseball," she said, louder. "I want to work in baseball." It felt like saying she wanted to be an astronaut. "I want to work for the majors," she admitted, waiting for Claude to laugh.

She didn't laugh.

"Scouting. Or coaching. Or something . . ." Jodie was blushing, even though there was no one to see her. It was crazy, wasn't it? I mean, who was she to think she could work for the majors? Nobody. "I thought Exercise Science might be a way in," she admitted, "somehow."

Baseball had been her whole world as a kid. Just the thought of it made her heart pinch and her breath catch. The smell of clay and cut grass, the feel of the ball in the glove, the crack of a line drive coming right at you. She loved the stats and the strategy, the training, the heightened energy of game day. She even loved the goddamn nerves that had her vomiting before a game. Everything about baseball made her feel alive. Sitting in the stands with her dad, pen in hand as she filled in the score card, was the next best thing. Following the trades, watching spring training, spending the season living and breathing with the team . . .

She wanted in. More in than being a spectator allowed. She wanted to be part of it. Somehow . . .

"If anyone can do it, it's you." Claude was firm. "I know I've been the first one to call you a dweeb and a doofus, but that's only because . . . I learned it from Bree . . . it's what sisters do. The fact is you were always tough. You were an anxious kid, but you still went out there and played. Not just played. *Won.* You've always been too hard on yourself, you know. If this is something you want, go for it. *Someone* does those jobs. Why not you?"

Jodie was leaking tears again. "Bree said something similar," she confessed.

"Listen to her then, huh? She was a smart cookie. Now, I better go message your dad that it was more a baseball talk than a boy talk."

"Boy talk?" Jodie squeaked.

"Yeah, your mom's been stressing him out by updating him on which Team is winning."

"Winning?" Jodie's heart plummeted. "How do they know who's winning?"

Claude giggled. "There's a league table! People are actually placing bets."

Jodie closed her eyes. "I don't want to know."

"Any tips on who I should place a bet on?"

"No!" Jodie hung up on her. But then messaged.

Thanks, Claude. I love you.

Love U 2. Dweeb.

Chapter 32

Jodie sat at the piano for a long time, staring sightlessly at the keys and thinking about her life. She could see the inertia. The burrowing away. The fear. She'd lived in fear for a very long time. But what had she been afraid of? Failing?

You're too hard on yourself. Bree's voice sighed. *Lighten up, would you? You're no more scared than anyone else.*

But that wasn't true. Bree had been braver.

Not braver. Just quicker to act, Smurfette. Your turn now.

"Uh-oh. That doesn't look like it's going well." Kelly's voice made her jump.

He was here for their late-night piano lesson.

"Hey," she said, trying to act normal. "How was dinner?"

"Fancy. I would have preferred a burger." He took his jacket off and draped it on the back of a chair. He moved like a big cat, all slow, packed energy. He cocked his head and fixed her with a sympathetic stare. "Rough night, huh?"

"Yeah. No veggie burgers either." She turned back to the piano. "Shall we do this?"

He sank down on the piano bench beside her, but facing into the room, not toward the piano. He leaned back so he could see her clearly. "You know I don't mind if you want to snap a selfie and call it a night. We can just say we did it, we don't have to actually do it, if you're not in the mood."

Jodie was startled. "No. I have to do it. I promised I would."

He looked sad, she realized. Tired. Abruptly, Jodie remembered that he was grieving too. He smiled, but it didn't quite reach his eyes. "OK, then." He spun around to face the piano.

The piano. Oh God, the piano. Imagine what it was like for him to sit at the piano, finishing the lessons his father had started. Jodie remembered the look on his face as he'd sat down at his father's instrument, in his brother's apartment. His grief had been raw.

And yet Kelly had played for them. And he'd let himself be dragged into Manhattan, made to wait around until Jodie deigned to take a lesson, filmed and fetishized and turned into a team captain. And the whole time he must have been thinking about his dad and feeling his own tectonic shifts of grief.

She'd been so selfish. And he'd been so generous.

"You must miss him," she blurted.

Kelly met her gaze, startled. She saw the flow of feelings in those honest red-brown eyes. Surprise, then the deep bruise of pain. "I do," he said huskily. "I miss him very much."

Jodie couldn't imagine life without her father. And she didn't want to.

She reached out and put her hand over Kelly's, which rested lightly on the keys. He entwined his fingers with hers and squeezed.

"It must be hard to take his place in these lessons," she commiserated.

"I'm not taking his place," Kelly said, smiling faintly. "No one could take his place, least of all me. I'm just sitting on his piano bench. And I think he'd be very happy about that—he always did want me to live and breathe piano."

He smelled so good. Citrusy and herby and fresh, and something else that was just him.

"I know this can't be fun for you," Jodie told him, trying not to get distracted by the scent of him. "I really appreciate the fact that you're helping me."

"My pleasure, Boyd." He lifted her hand to his mouth and pressed a kiss to the back of her hand. "Now stop trying to wriggle out of it. It's time to take your lesson."

He fished his phone out of his pocket.

"Just still photos," Jodie begged. "No one needs to hear this."

"Let's do it as a duet?" he suggested, propping the phone up in front of them on the sheet music ledge. "You move down an octave, and I'll move up one. We'll do a practice run before I film it. How's that?"

Jodie did as she was told. She was still terrible, but less so than when she played alone.

"Slow it down," he suggested. "Make it lazy, like you never want it to end. Drop the notes heavy and slow."

God, he could play. Jodie found herself falling into his rhythm. It had the languidness of late nights, of moonsets and slow-moving clouds. The last notes hung on the air.

"Nice," he said. And he sounded like he meant it. "Alright, Boyd. Now for the camera."

Ugh. Lucky the lights were still off. The screen just showed dark silhouettes. Behind them the crystals of the unlit jellyfish chandelier glinted from the lights cast by the city outside.

"Cheryl will complain that no one can see us," Jodie told him.

"Nah. They'll be able to *hear* us. And the chandelier looks nice. Ready?"

"Nope. But press record anyway."

He did and they played. Jodie jumped when Kelly started singing. "*It's very clear our love is here to stay . . .*" His voice was a gentle husky tenor. It made her shiver. "*Not for a year, but ever and a day . . .*"

He was no Jonah Lourdes. But then, he wasn't doing it for a career. He was doing it just for her.

Jodie turned to watch him. He was staring straight at her. Every word he sang fell into her like a stone sinking into a pool. Her fingers forgot what they were doing. She clanged a sharp and then couldn't manage to play at all. "*But oh my dear, our love is here to stay . . . Together we're going a long, long way . . .*"

She couldn't breathe. His eyes were as black as a night sea. The music was caressing her, the words were stealing her thoughts. And all she could think was *yes*.

The final twirls of the keys spiraled into the open ballroom and then faded. He didn't look away. He tilted his head sideways, questioning, and held her gaze. Nothing happened for a long breathless time. And Jodie realized this was up to her. And there was no question; she knew what she wanted.

"Kelly," she breathed. "I'm going to kiss you now."

"Jodie," he whispered back, his darkly liquid eyes full of promises, "I'm going to let you."

She felt like she was moving through water, compelled by invisible currents; time slowed, viscous as honey. Jodie closed her eyes as her lips touched his. It was soft, gentle, careful. A slow kiss. Jodie felt like she was filling with helium, floating. She held on to him as his mouth opened under hers. He tasted sweet and salty.

She'd never been kissed this well in her life.

She didn't know how long they spent tangled together on the piano bench. Forever. Not long enough.

"Wow." Kelly sighed as they pulled back. He drank in the sight of her, like he was trying to memorize every detail. She pushed his short black hair back from his hairline. He cocked his head and gave her a look that was equal parts wickedness and bashfulness. "Have I told you how much you featured in my fantasies when we were in high school?"

Jodie was stunned. "You had fantasies about me?" *Kelly Wong* had fantasies about *her*?

He groaned. "Did I ever." He bent and pressed a kiss to her neck, where her pulse leapt against his lips. "I remember one of my favorites involved the locker room."

Jodie was too stunned to think straight as she listened to him talk between kisses.

"I imagined I was in the locker room after a game . . ." He changed to present tense. "All the guys have gone home, but I'm running late. I'm just getting out of the shower when you come in. It's just me, naked except for a towel, and you . . ."

Jodie could picture it clearly. She closed her eyes, imagining the locker room, still steamy from the showers.

He'd had fantasies about her. *Her*. Jodie Boyd.

But maybe it was just because he was a boy and boys had fantasies about everyone when they were horny teenagers? Oh, who cared. He'd fantasized about *her*.

Had he known that she'd fantasized about him too?

She felt like she'd stepped through the looking glass. If anything was a fantasy, it was tonight. Best not to question it, best to surrender to bewitchment and enjoy it. Maybe this time, there'd be no chime of midnight, and no unravelling of the spell. Maybe she could keep the prince.

"I was so in love with you." Kelly sighed, running his fingertip down her nose.

Jodie felt like he'd dropped an anvil on her. He *what*?

"You have no idea." He gave her that look of wonder again. "And now here I am, in New York, kissing Jodie Boyd . . ." He smiled. "I keep thinking I'm going to wake up and this will all have been a dream."

Jodie couldn't get her thoughts together.

He laughed. "I must have been so obvious."

"No," Jodie blurted. "I had no idea."

"Sure." He laughed again.

"No," Jodie said, shaking her head. "I didn't. I literally had no idea."

"But I asked you to prom."

"Because your mom told you to." Jodie had overheard Mrs. Wong in the kitchen, urging Kelly on. Forcing him to go talk to her before she left after her piano lesson. She hadn't cared at the time why Kelly was asking her. The fact that it had happened at all had seemed like a miracle.

"Yeah. She told me to because she knew I was dragging my feet." Kelly laughed. "She said if I didn't do it, she'd do it for me." He pulled a face. "And then I fucked it all up."

Oh God, did they have to talk about Ashleigh Clark now?

"I was like the worst date ever. I was just so nervous. And then the guys got me drunk . . ." He went on, describing his experience of their date, of prom, and the party afterwards.

It was like listening to some bizarre alternate reality. Jodie's past was flipped upside down and back to front. The night Kelly described bore little resemblance to the night she remembered. She hadn't noticed his nerves at all—she'd been too tangled up in her own. And Kelly's version didn't seem to include Ashleigh Clark at all.

"Wait," she interrupted him, when he started talking about throwing up in the garden. "When was this? After I left?"

"No, I ran off and left you when I knew I was going to vomit. I didn't want you seeing *that*. It was the bourbon that did it." He pulled a face. "I'd only ever had beer before that."

"But Ashleigh . . ." Jodie cleared her throat when her voice broke. "You went off with Ashleigh . . ."

"I what?" Kelly frowned.

"You disappeared into the bedroom with Ashleigh Clark." She knew what she'd seen.

"Ashleigh?"

"Yes," Jodie said tightly. "The prom queen. Your ex."

"Wait. You left because you thought I went into a bedroom with Ashleigh Clark?" He straightened up. "You were jealous?" The sideways comma dimple flickered. "You didn't leave because I was a drunken ass?"

"You were a drunken ass who *went off with your ex*. It was pretty clear our date was over. Besides, you were only there because your mom felt sorry for me."

"No, I was there because my mom felt sorry for *me*. She got sick of me mooning around when you were over for piano lessons, and the fact that I never got around to asking you out."

None of this could be true, could it?

Only . . . he was here now, his lips all swollen from being kissed. By *her*. And he'd looked at her with such wonder tonight. And last night. And *now*.

"And I cross my heart I never went off with Ashleigh on prom night. I was too sick for that."

"I *saw* you."

"What did you see?"

"You went into the bedroom."

"Was she showing me to a bathroom by any chance? Because I tried the family bathroom and all the en suites, but they were in use." He gave her a rueful look. "I don't have a great memory of that night. But I do remember feeling desperate and not wanting you to realize how drunk I was. I climbed out a bedroom window when I found the last en suite was locked and went and vomited in the garden. When I eventually came back, you were gone."

"I don't remember you being that drunk." Jodie was having trouble reconciling their two versions of the night.

"It happened quick, after we got to the party. When everyone was swimming in the pool."

She remembered *that*. It seemed like most of the people at the party had stripped off to their underwear and jumped in the heated pool. They didn't seem to care it was still only March, which in Wilmington was super cold. Jodie remembered steam rising from the pool into the cold night air. She'd freaked out a bit when they all stripped off. The last thing she wanted was to get semi-naked with all these people. And *Kelly Wong.* She'd gone and hidden in the upstairs bathroom. Ugh. The same bathroom she'd come out of to find Josh Sauer and the guys talking about her. *She can't honestly think that Kelly asked her to prom for reals?*

She had. Even knowing his mom had pushed him into it, Jodie had fallen into a fantasy version of her life, where she was on a date with Kelly Wong, and he actually seemed to be enjoying it. The guys had found her exposed nerve and twisted it. Because she'd known Kelly hadn't asked her for reals. That they were just friends, teammates. She'd known his mother had pushed him into it. She'd felt the whole night had been delusional on her part. And she was humiliated that other people had seen her delusion too.

After hearing the guys, she'd been expecting something like the Ashleigh Clark incident . . .

But now Kelly was saying it hadn't happened. That he'd *wanted* to be there with Jodie. *I was so in love with you . . .*

"Josh gave me a drink"—he sighed regretfully—"and then another . . . and then someone brought out the bourbon. And I was so nervous, I just kept drinking. It was the pool that did it. I was scared you'd want to swim." He pulled a face. "I was terrified you'd take that dress off and be in your underwear and I'd get a boner and you'd see it . . . It sucks so much being a teenage boy." He was rueful. "By the time I saw you again, I was messy drunk and afraid I'd completely fucked it up. And I had. Because you left and didn't really ever talk to me again."

"*I* didn't talk to *you?*" Jodie was shocked. But as she looked back, she realized she hadn't. She'd never gone to another piano lesson. And she'd avoided him at training and games. He was a senior and she was a junior, so they didn't have any classes together. And then he graduated and went off to college. And that was it.

"You're still mad at me," Kelly said softly.

Jodie realized she was scowling. "No." She sighed. "I'm not mad at you. I'm just *mad*. I didn't know you . . . I mean, I thought . . . I left because of Ashleigh Clark . . ."

What would have happened if they'd had this conversation years ago? Jodie felt the maze of her life snap into focus. So many directions she could have taken. So many avenues that didn't lead to dead ends. What if she'd been brave enough to talk to Kelly then? To *act*. Even if she'd yelled at him for going off with Ashleigh . . . if she'd confronted him, he would have told her about vomiting in the garden. And she wouldn't have carried the humiliation of Ashleigh Clark for all these years . . .

He would have gone off to college anyway. But maybe she would have felt differently about herself . . .

"You were jealous of Ashleigh Clark." Kelly was grinning again.

Jodie's scowl deepened.

"Boring Ashleigh Clark who didn't know a baseball from a football." He laughed.

"Beautiful Ashleigh Clark who was the star of every theater show and queen of everything."

Kelly's grin was so huge that he looked like the Cheshire cat. "You were *jealous*."

Jealous? She'd been *humiliated*. It had reinforced everything she believed about herself. But now she found out it hadn't even been true. *She'd* reinforced everything she believed about herself. All on her own.

"How stupid were we?" Kelly marveled. He lowered his forehead to hers and rubbed the tip of his nose against hers. His lips found hers. He was gentle. Lingering. "You were the sexiest girl in school," he whispered against her lips. "The hottest, most composed, most tantalizing, intimidating, spellbinding . . ." He deepened the kiss, keeping it slow and tender. "You were *perfect*. And I have never met anyone like you since."

Jodie melted under his words and his touch. She surrendered and let the novel feelings close over her like warm water.

"And I was an *idiot* not to tell you how I felt." He sighed.

She couldn't take anymore. There was too much to think about already. So she kissed him, and stopped thinking altogether.

Chapter 33

Jodie woke to Kelly joyfully knocking at her door.

"Come on, Boyd," he said cheerfully, "up you get. We have a date."

Kelly was a morning person. He was cheerfully wide-awake, up, and dressed and ready to drag her through the cold morning to walk the High Line.

"I promised you breakfast," he said, as he ushered her off to have a shower. His hands wandered a little as he ushered, and he sounded regretful that he didn't have time to join her in the shower. "Later," he promised, kissing her. "We have to get out of here before Cheryl is up. If she catches you, we're never getting to the High Line."

It had snowed overnight, and the already magical Christmas-decked city had turned into a fairyland. They picked up coffee and bagels and took a long ambling walk through the snowy streets, winding through the grid toward Chelsea and the High Line.

"It's probably not the best time of year to see it," Jodie admitted. "I bet it's beautiful in spring and summer. Even fall." In winter they were probably just going to see a snowscape.

"Oh, I don't know. Winter is pretty beautiful. And romantic." He winked at her. "Misty rain, snow, fog, cozy nights in. I missed winter when I was in Miami."

"What's Miami like?" Jodie asked curiously.

"The weather's exactly what you expect. It doesn't get colder than about sixty degrees and it's sunny. It was a fun place to go to college. It's pretty. Lots of beaches and tourists. Great weather to play ball. Bit steamy but you get used to it." He laughed. "You'll think I'm weird but I kinda missed Wilmington. Especially during the holidays. It never seemed right without snowdrifts and floods and generally shitty weather."

Jodie laughed. "Yeah, we do that well."

"Here we are, Boyd. The High Line."

Jodie smiled at his enthusiasm. He squeezed her hand.

Here I am, Bree, she thought as they climbed the stairs, emerging onto the old railway line, which had been turned into a city garden. *I made it.*

The High Line was an undulating landscape of snow. Bristles of dried flower heads poked through the crust, looking like blown dandelions. Icicles hung in spiky bunting along the railings and in shiny fringes from the tips of the tree branches.

They were the only people there.

Jodie and Kelly headed along the line, their footsteps soft crunchings in the snow. Thick fog blanketed the city beyond the barriers; it felt like they were in a private cocoon. Now and then a skyscraper was revealed by the shredding fog, its lights veiled, like the lights of a distant ship on a becalmed ocean. The sound of traffic was muffled, a world away. They passed through copses of silver birches, boughs lined with snow, and clumps of holly and winterberries, the fruit blazingly red against the winter starkness.

Jodie paused as they reached a narrow path beneath an archway of branches. The trees, which had twisty trunks of swirly silver-brown, stretched out, meeting the trees across the way. They were veiled and laced with snow, their fingertips spindly, touching overhead. Shreds of fog tangled in their limbs. They were like a line of ghostly bridesmaids.

"I gotta give it to you, Boyd, you picked a romantic place for a date." Kelly was standing just behind her. His arms closed around her, and he nuzzled into her neck. Jodie's heart was skittering in her chest. The magic of the morning was febrile. For a moment, she felt a stab of dread that something would come and snatch it away from her, this snowy fragment of time, and the entire night before.

It was too good to be true.

The stillness of the morning was rippled by a gust of wind, and she shivered.

"Cold?" Kelly asked, pulling her tighter.

Scared. Scared to lose this. To lose him.

"I'll keep you warm," he promised.

"What kind of trees are these?" Jodie asked, leaning back into the strength of his body.

"I'm not great at trees, but they might be crepe myrtles? They have a lot of them in Miami. They're pretty. They're covered with frothy flowers in spring, pinks mostly, and their leaves go all red and orange in fall."

Jodie turned in the circle of his arms and kissed him fiercely. Whatever happened, she was grateful for this moment. For the miracle of being here in the snow on the High Line with Kelly Wong, talking about trees. For being able to kiss him whenever she wanted. For him kissing her back.

Eventually he pulled away. "Want to spend the day in bed after this?"

"*Yes*. But I can't. I have rehearsals." She sighed.

"Can I come along?"

"To rehearsals?"

"Yeah. I can be on hand to kiss you as needed. Besides, I think Cheryl wants us to finish our piano lessons whenever you have a free moment."

Jodie's mind flashed to the change room at the rehearsal studio, and all the uses they could put it to. "You can come." She grinned at the double meaning, and he laughed.

Arms wrapped around each other, they drifted under the veiled arms of the ghostly bridesmaids, and down the line. As they walked, she heard Kelly humming softly under his breath. She knew that tune. *Our love is here to stay . . .*

Chapter 34

The romance of the day was well and truly frayed by evening. Jodie sat rigid with nerves in the corner of the dressing room. She'd finished all her piano lessons and survived a grueling day of rehearsals and dress rehearsals. She was about to pay off a big chunk of debt. She'd had good-luck messages from every single member of her family. Now she was sitting here, dressed in gang colors and a baseball cap, her face painted, the smell of makeup and foot powder a miasma around her. The room was bustling with the chorus of dancers, who were stretching and chatting and putting on their makeup. Jodie felt like she might vomit. She didn't know how they could be so blasé about the ordeal ahead, or how they did it *eight times a week*.

No matter how much they'd rehearsed, Jodie couldn't get it right. She couldn't walk *earthy*. She couldn't do anything well enough for the cranky choreographer. If Kelly hadn't been there in the rehearsal studio and then at the disastrous dress rehearsal, winking at her and cracking jokes, she might have locked herself in the changeroom again. But she kept her chin up, because she didn't want Kelly Wong to think less of her. And she'd be damned if she'd let a musical get the best of her. Even though she was steadily getting more toxic with nerves.

No one seemed to understand the scale of her terror.

"Is Jodie in here?" Cheryl came looking for her, just in time to catch the peak of Jodie's nerves.

Jodie didn't think she could move. She was like the remains of one of those volcano victims in ancient Pompeii, frozen in place, in their last act before death.

"Oh." Cheryl looked a little freaked out by Jodie's condition. She was carrying her laptop and tottering on spike heels, but somehow she still managed to squat beside Jodie. "Hey. You OK?"

"I can't do this."

Cheryl's hand settled soothingly on Jodie's knee. "I have something that might help."

"A plane ticket home?"

Cheryl slid the laptop onto Jodie's knee. "Another message from Bree."

Oh, that didn't help at all. It just filled Jodie with *more* adrenaline. She was a jittery mess. Cheryl handed her a pair of earbuds to listen to the message with a degree of privacy. She opened the laptop for Jodie. Jodie found she was so full of chemicals that her teeth were chattering.

There on the screen was her sister. She was wearing a silk scarf around her bald head and her face was puffy and her eyes exhausted. Cheryl turned away to give Jodie some privacy. Jodie couldn't actually move to start the video. Her hands were frozen into claws. This felt *exactly* like before a game.

Cheryl glanced over and saw the state of her. Gently, she reached over and pressed play.

"Hey, Scaredy Smurf, I'm guessing you're feeling pretty on edge right now?" Bree smiled but it didn't quite reach her eyes. She was clearly having a bad pain day.

On edge didn't cover it. Jodie was hitting a wall. There was a speaker in the room that was linked to a mic on stage, so the actors could hear their cues. That speaker was currently playing the sound of an audience filing into their seats. It sounded disturbingly like an ocean rising. An ocean that was going to suck the life right out of Jodie.

"Jodie? Are you listening to me?"

Jodie blinked. Video Bree was staring patiently into the

camera. There was a mix of kindness and irritation there. She seemed to expect Jodie to be in a fog of nerves. Which she was.

"When I wrote this list, I never dreamed *you* would have to do it," Bree said, leaning back on her pillow. She turned her head and stared out the window. Jodie wondered what she'd been looking at. "If you're watching this, I assume you've already faked an orgasm in public. I bet that one was hard for you too."

It had been. But it wasn't like this. Listen to *all* those people out there. And there was a camera crew out there too. Oh God, she was going to throw up.

"I wish I was there." Bree sighed. And the resounding sadness in her voice broke through Jodie's panic. Video Bree was still staring out the window, her expression distant. "New York," she said faintly. "Broadway." She made them sound like mythical places. Out of reach. Except in dreams.

Jodie felt like someone was squeezing her heart in their fists. Oh, Bree.

Bree tried to shake off her mood and adjusted her expression before turning back to the camera. She smiled. But her eyes were still distant and sad. "I'd give anything to be there with you, Jodie."

Me too, Bree.

"Enjoy it for me, would you?" Bree's smile turned dreamy. "What does it smell like, a stage like that? Can you hear the audience breathing? Are the lights hot? When the nerves wear off, does it feel *amazing*?"

Jodie was arrested by Bree's manner. Bree hadn't seemed so sad in the other videos. It struck Jodie that this item on the bucket list might have been far more important than the others. Or maybe this video had been filmed later than the rest . . . As Bree sat there in that hospital bed, in pain, knowing the end was coming fast, she was mourning the loss of her Broadway dream. And more.

"I wish more than anything that I could be walking on that stage tonight," Bree said. "Please don't waste this. Enjoy it. Even if you're terrified. You can be more than one thing. I am." That sad smile again. "I'm scared and sad and also full of gratitude and joy. I'm all the things at once. And that's life, Smurfette. Being everything at once and not trying to fix it. Or escape it." Bree stared into the camera, trying to see through time to where Jodie sat now, terrified in a chair in a corner of the busy dressing room. "Break a leg." She blew Jodie a kiss. And then the video ended.

All the things at once. Now Jodie was slashed with grief *and* full of nerves. It pulled her inside out to see Bree sick and sad and scared.

And full of gratitude and joy, Smurfette. All of it at once.

Jodie closed her eyes and tried to breathe. She was still sick with all the chemicals. Adrenaline and cortisol and all the toxic nerves. But that was how it felt to be *alive.* And one day, like playing baseball, this would be in her past. And she would miss it.

So she would do this. For Bree. And for herself.

She just had to throw up first.

She thrust the laptop at Cheryl and ran for the toilet, where she crouched for the next fifteen minutes, throwing up everything she'd ever eaten. There was even a damn speaker in the toilet. Jodie could hear the orchestra tuning up over the sound of her own vomiting. The sound of the audience made her vomit even harder. She could also hear Cheryl and Maya, whispering behind the toilet door. They didn't think she could do it. They were making contingency plans.

They didn't know her. She'd do it. She'd just be very, very sick first.

Over the speaker she heard the announcement about the "special event" and "additional number." That was *her.* Then she heard the overture start.

Jodie flushed the toilet and washed her hands and rinsed her mouth. She checked she hadn't messed up her costume. Oh God, the overture was swelling to a crescendo.

She threw up again.

When she eventually emerged, the show was well underway, and Cheryl looked like she'd chewed through her fancy red nails. Maya, however, had her phone out, pointed at the toilet door.

"Did you film the sound of me vomiting?" Jodie asked suspiciously. She wished she'd never given Maya her phone back.

"You'll have everyone's sympathy."

"Oh, get fucked, Maya." Jodie didn't have another second to spare for that woman. "I'll post my own damn photos."

"You OK?" Kelly asked quietly. He'd been leaning against the wall beside the door. He held out a bottle of fresh water. "Sip it, don't drink too much."

Jodie sipped it and gave him a wobbly smile. Oh great, Kelly Wong had been listening to her vomit too. Excellent.

"You can do this, Boyd. Just keep your eye on the ball."

She nodded. Yes. Eye on the ball.

"'Great moments are born from great opportunity,'" Kelly told her, pulling her into a hug.

"Pacino again?" Jodie asked. Her teeth were back to chattering.

"No, that time it was Kurt Russell. *Miracle*."

"I can see I've got a lot of sports movies to catch up on."

"Cheryl!" Tish snapped when she saw Cheryl filming Kelly and Jodie. "Not you too! She said *no*." Tish took Cheryl's phone away from her.

"It's my *job*. And Jodie didn't tell *me* not to take photos."

"*I'm* telling you. Leave her alone." Tish led Cheryl from the room. "Good luck, Jodie. Go kick some Broadway ass. Maya, you get out too." She swept Maya along with them.

The stage manager gave Jodie her call and Jodie felt like she was falling from a great height.

"You can do it, Boyd." Kelly told her, dropping a kiss on her tense lips. "Inch by inch."

"Inch by inch," she repeated. And then she she he was gone too, and she was all alone. Just her and that whole audience full of people . . .

Jodie balked as she got to the side of the stage, when she saw the dancers jumping around in front of the big screen. Oh God, Bree, you *can* hear the audience. Breathing, coughing, moving. An ocean of people, a wave coming right at you. *No, no, no, no, no*. She couldn't do this.

At the exact moment she was about to turn and flee, Jonah
Lourdes appeared. He was in full costume and shiny with sweat
from his last number. "Hey," he whispered. "You alright?"

She shook her head.

He took her by the arms and stared closely at her. "You'll be
OK."

Jodie started shaking so hard her teeth were chattering. She
made a low moaning noise. She sounded like an animal. This
was a million times worse than before a ballgame . . . She'd
never been so afraid in all her life.

Jonah swore.

On stage they were up to the big fight, which was the last
scene before her number. All around her the women in her scene
were gathering. *No, no, no, no, no.* Jodie was sweating through
her costume.

"Hold it together," Jonah told her softly. "I'll be back."

Hold it together? *How?* Listen to all those *people.*

"Break a leg," the actress playing Maria whispered to her.
"Just remember: walk earthy."

She was going to be sick. Or faint. Or scream. *Bree, help.*

"Ready?" one of the other dancers took her by the arm.

"No."

"Yes." Someone else took her by the other arm.

"Jonah?"

Jodie didn't have time to freeze. She was too shocked to find
Jonah Lourdes sweeping onto the dark stage beside her. He
wasn't supposed to be in this number. What was he doing here?
This was an all-girl number, and it certainly wasn't supposed to
feature Tony. Only . . . he wasn't dressed as Tony. He'd swapped
his gang colors; now he was in black Adidas track pants and a
red hoodie, like the girls in the number. That had been one hell
of a quick change. He had the hood pulled up and had painted
his lips red. His feet were bare. Maybe from a distance he might
pass as one of the gang girls gathered around Maria, but up
close he was all man.

The spotlight was on Maria, at least, and she shone in her

white dress. The audience should keep their attention on her. With any luck.

Jonah winked as he followed Jodie to her position upstage. Jodie felt a wave of hysteria and had to bite her lips to stop laughing. The distinctive music began and there was a wave of delighted applause from the audience.

"*Me siento bonita* . . ." Maria's soprano filled the stage, and the number was off and running. Nothing Jodie did now would stop it. Thank God she wasn't mic'ed up, she thought. She almost hyperventilated when the spotlight hit her as the other women sang their *ah ah*s and *la la la*s. Her heavy breathing would have drowned everyone out.

Jonah hadn't seen the rehearsals and had no idea how the number went. He tried to copy the earthy walking and screwed up the choreography. And then things went really wrong. He turned left as everyone else turned right. And he did it with vigor. One poor girl almost went flying; Jonah caught her and tried to turn it into a move but in doing so crashed into Maria. The dancers were having trouble keeping straight faces as the number deteriorated. They got the giggles. It was catching. Maria struggled to keep singing, the laughter bubbling in her voice. He was ruining the number. It was Jodie's worst nightmare. But Jonah only gave Jodie an impish smile.

The lights made the audience completely invisible, but Jodie could hear the titters. She winced.

"They're laughing at us," she whispered to Jonah as he slid past.

"Nah. *With* us," he corrected her, as he threw himself into the madness. His devilish glee startled Jodie into a laugh, and she forgot to be scared. He was flittering about like a manic butterfly, leaving the choreography in tatters.

Jonah and the dancers seemed to gain energy as the audience laughed at their corpsing. Maria gave up on the choreography entirely and grinned as she sang. The spotlight found Jodie and stayed there. Jodie had been afraid of being laughed at, and now it was happening. Everyone was staring at her and *laughing*.

Everything shrank to this small patch of stage, this circle of light. Pinned by the light, Jodie felt the laughter rise and crash over the stage.

And . . . it wasn't so bad.

She didn't get washed away. In fact, nothing bad happened at all. The dancers danced, Maria sang, Jonah fumbled his way around the stage, the audience laughed . . . and Jodie was still here, failing to walk earthily and looking completely out of place. In the spotlight.

But so what?

She'd been afraid and for *what*?

As the song built to a crescendo, Jodie threw herself into it. She was nervous as hell *and* terrified *and* out of her depth *and* suddenly enjoying it immensely.

Jonah caught the shift in her mood and grinned. As the chorus soared, Jodie grabbed his hands and they spun under the hot lights, grinning at each other like maniacs. Faster and faster, as Maria's voice spiked through the swell of the chorus, reaching heights that made the hair stand up on the back of Jodie's neck. The other dancers had taken their cue from Jonah and Jodie and were also whirling with joy. Jodie bet the cranky choreographer was plenty cranky now that they'd all thrown his choreography out the window. She laughed, keeping tight hold of Jonah's hands. Who needed to walk earthy when you could *whirl*?

Me siento gaseosa y divertida y bien.

The number came to a panting halt. And then there was thunderous applause. Maria and the dancers pushed Jodie and Jonah forward to take a bow. They were laughing and clapping too. When the audience realized who Jonah was, there was a roar. The applause was deafening. Jodie laughed as Jonah blew kisses, leaving a big red lipstick stain on his palm.

Then he extended his lipstick-kissed hand to beckon Jodie forward. There were whistles and catcalls from the theater.

Jodie drank it in. The whole mad moment.

Bree. It smells of feet. The lights are hot. You can hear the audience breathing. And . . . it does feel amazing. It really does.

After their bows, Jodie and Jonah swirled off stage with the dancers, laughing. Jodie felt triumphant. Powerful. Invincible. She'd done it!

"I've got to change for my next number," Jonah told her. He gave her a short, hard hug. "You were amazing!" He kissed her cheek. "Amazing!"

She laughed as he ripped off his trackpants and hoodie, to reveal his own costume underneath. And then he was gone, and she heard the sound of his powerful voice rising onstage.

Wow. Bree sighed.

Yeah. He was pretty wow.

No, you, dweeb. You were wow.

"Crushed it, Boyd!" Kelly Wong was waiting for her in the corridor offstage. He swept her into a hug and spun her around. "You hit it out of the park!"

Jodie was giddy, full of the biggest adrenaline rush of her life. "I thought I was going to die when they laughed at me!"

"*With* you, not *at* you."

"That's what Jonah said," she admitted breathlessly.

A flash of jealousy crossed Kelly's face, but he covered it with a grin. "Well, it's true."

Jodie kissed him. Dear God, she'd never get used to being able to do that. Or to the idea that Kelly would be jealous of her.

Arm in arm, they tumbled into the dressing room. Where all of Jodie's joy came crashing down around her.

Waiting in the center of the dressing room was a blonde. She was clearly expecting them. She was tall and poised. And not one of the dancers.

Jodie felt the energy in the room change the minute Kelly saw her. The laughter stopped abruptly.

"Jessica," Kelly blurted.

Jodie took in his shock, which was pure and unfeigned. He seemed floored.

"Jessica!" Now he seemed horrified.

Jessica. Jodie felt it sink in. *Jessica.* As in . . . *Jessica.*

It was the blonde from Kelly's Instagram. She was even more perfect in the flesh. Fit, firm, glossy, with a smile so minty that it rivaled Cheryl's.

"Hi, Kelly." And she sure was smiling. Like a model in a toothpaste ad.

"Who's this?" Tish was suspicious. She and Cheryl had tumbled into the room in Jodie and Kelly's wake. They'd watched Jodie's performance on the monitor in the hallway and had been as jubilant as Jodie was. But not now. The room was thick with tension.

Jodie heard Cheryl swear under her breath.

Jodie was fighting dread. *This* was the thing coming to snatch it all away. She knew it was. This was Ashleigh Clark all over again. Only much, much worse, because this wasn't high school anymore.

"Excuse me," Tish said, "who are you exactly?"

"I'm Kelly's wife."

Wife. The word dropped like a nuclear bomb. There was a moment of pure silence. Then a flash of energy.

"What?" Tish turned on Kelly.

Jodie took a step back, away from him.

Wife.

Can we talk?

Oh my *God. Can we talk? That's* what "can we talk" meant.

Wife. He had a *wife.*

"Jodie." Kelly took a step toward Jodie. She stumbled a few steps back, trying to get away from him. "I wanted to tell you," he said miserably.

Jodie felt like she could die right there on the spot.

"Plot twist," Maya whispered to Cheryl, emerging from the shadows, where she'd filmed the whole thing.

"Maya," Cheryl and Tish said simultaneously, "get *fucked.*"

Chapter 35
17. Plant a Tree

He'd humiliated her in front of *everyone*. That fucking video had gone viral. It had even featured on the *Good Morning America* package, no matter how Cheryl wheedled and pleaded and threatened. In that moment in the dressing room, Cheryl's transformation from corporate nightmare to regular person was complete. She was squarely in Jodie's corner.

"No one deserves this shit," she'd muttered as she whisked Jodie away from the scene, wielding her phone like a weapon as she tried to get the pictures down from Instagram.

It didn't work. Everyone Jodie had ever known had witnessed her heartbreak. Her parents. Her grandmother. Her boss. Her *dentist*. Everyone she went to high school with. The list was endless. And then there was the goddamn shot that Maya had snapped, of Jodie's face, riven by horror. By loss. She never wanted to see that photo again as long as she lived.

Jodie's phone vibrated and pinged every couple of seconds with people who *had* seen that photo. People who felt nothing but pity for her. People she knew messaged her directly, people she didn't know posted streams of comments under the images. It was an avalanche of abjection. And it just didn't *stop*.

On Christmas Eve, the checkout assistant at Claude's fancy supermarket actually felt so sorry for her that she gave Jodie a free bunch of Christmas lilies. And then she burst into a tirade about "no-good lying cheating men." Jodie didn't want the flowers, or the sympathy. She glanced back into the aisles, where Claude had disappeared to get whole nutmeg. If Claude didn't get back soon, Jodie was liable to hit the girl over the head with the bunch of trumpet-shaped flowers.

"My ex did the exact same thing. Only there wasn't a wife," the girl confided.

Not *exactly* the same then, was it? Jodie bet the girl hadn't been filmed either, or had her face go viral. She certainly hadn't been accosted by her checkout girl afterwards.

"Her husband was *nasty*," the other checkout girl confided to Jodie. "She's better off without him. And you're better off without that Kelly Wong."

Jodie couldn't hear his name without flinching. Why did everyone have to talk about him all the time?

"I think you should go for that Broadway singer." Great. Now the customer at the other checkout had joined in. "The way he sang to you . . ."

But it wasn't Jonah Lourdes Jodie thought of when she remembered being sung to. It was Kelly Wong, sitting at the piano in the ballroom of the hotel, softly singing *it's very clear* . . .

And it *was* clear. *Now.* She'd been an idiot.

"Nuh-uh. Ryan Lasseter." The checkout girl was clearly not on Team Jonah. "That man is worth *millions*. You'd never need to work again."

"Oh imagine. But he'd probably cheat on you too. He looks the type."

"And a Broadway star *wouldn't*?"

"Pick someone who doesn't cheat," the girl at the other checkout told Jodie, as though she was too dumb to work that one out for herself.

"Tish seemed nice," the other customer suggested.

All these perfect strangers, weighing in on her life!

"Nice, but there wasn't enough chemistry. Don't settle, just because you're on the rebound," the checkout girl told Jodie, with wide-eyed sincerity.

If Hopper hadn't come to her rescue, Jodie might have started screaming. How had she ended up here, with complete strangers discussing her love life, when she didn't even *have* a love life?

"Hey, hey, Skyler, leave her be, huh? She's just here to do her shopping." Hopper had come in through the back entrance, carrying an armful of boxes. He was covered in an icing-sugar dusting of snow.

Jodie didn't miss how Skyler, Skyler's friend, and the other customer sighed moonily at the sight of him. He looked like the hero in a Hallmark movie, in his flannel shirt and beat-up jacket, with his three-day stubble and his cheeks ruddy from the cold.

"We were just offering our support, Hop." Skyler kept scanning the expensive pile of Christmas nonsense Claude had loaded onto the conveyer belt.

Hopper put his boxes down on the bench behind the counter and pulled off his woolen hat. "Merry Christmas, Jodie."

"Yeah." Ugh. Did she have to say it back? Even though she didn't find it happy at all. "I hope *you* have a good holiday, Hopper." There, that was honest, and she didn't have to spit out the word *happy*.

"Me too." He pulled a face. "But you know how it is, families are complicated." Then he lit up like a Christmas tree and Jodie realized that Claude must have reappeared. "Hey, Type A."

"Hopper," Claude said, not giving him so much as the flicker of a short-circuiting Christmas light in return as she dropped her nutmegs on the pile. He didn't seem to care. He sparkled with happiness at seeing her.

Jodie felt the stems of the lilies bending in her grip. She'd been looked at like that. She had a flashback to Kelly standing, dumbstruck, when he saw her in the black dress.

Goddamn him. Why couldn't she get him out of her head?

"I'm just about to whip up some eggnog, if you'd both like to stay and taste test it for me?" Hopper looked so hopeful.

"We have to get all of this back to the house," Claude told him. "The ice cream will melt."

"I can keep your cold stuff in the fridge till you go," he said helpfully. He turned to Jodie instead, with an entreating look. *Help me*, it begged. "C'mon, it's Christmas."

Ugh. Yes. Fine. As jaded as she felt, she couldn't be cruel to Thor. Look at him. Getting Claude to stay for eggnog would clearly make his Christmas.

"OK," she agreed. "Eggnog."

"Great." His wattage got even brighter.

"What are you doing?" Claude sighed as soon as Hopper disappeared into the bar. "You know I have to go visit my mom. I don't have time for this."

Jodie felt a wave of guilt. Claude looked thin and wan. She was limp from long hours of work. Christmas was always an extra busy time of year for her. And now her mom was out of the clinic and in a sober house, so Claude had to deal with her again.

"It'll be good for you. For us," Jodie amended. "It'll be good for *us*. We need some Christmas cheer." She felt abruptly protective of Claude, who seemed brittle and close to breaking. "Besides, it's our new tradition. We had a drink here for Thanksgiving too."

Claude nodded, but she looked more defeated than cheered.

"We'll store your stuff back here and I'll put your cold bags in the fridge and freezer, OK?" Skyler helpfully loaded their bags behind the counter. "Merry Christmas!"

"You too." Jodie couldn't bring herself to say *merry* either.

The bar out front was decorated with holly and white twinkling lights. There were wreaths of brown branches trimmed with white-berried mistletoe and red-berried winterberry decking the foggy windows. The place looked cozy and charming.

"Did you do this?" Jodie asked Claude, as they slid onto the bar stools. There was no sign of Hopper. The bartender smiled at them but clearly knew they were waiting for Hopper's eggnog and so didn't approach them.

Claude didn't meet Jodie's eye. She fiddled with the sugar bowl. "He employed me."

"Did you charge him?"

Claude pursed her lips. "Sort of."

"What does 'sort of' mean?"

Claude lowered her voice. "It means I told him I'd do it if he stopped asking me out. Now, *shhh*. In case he comes back."

"Do you *want* him to stop asking you out?"

"*Shhhhhh*."

"I guess I shouldn't have said yes to eggnog then?"

"Yes, you should." Hopper returned in time to hear Jodie. He was holding a pot of eggnog, which he set down on the hot plate behind the bar. The heavy perfume of nutmeg and bourbon and warm milk and cream bloomed through the bar.

"Wow, that smells good."

"It tastes even better." He ladled out three mugs. He was clearly joining them for the drink. Jodie felt Claude shift awkwardly on the stool next to her.

He wasn't wrong. It was the best eggnog Jodie had ever tasted. And she wasn't usually a fan. "You're as good as Claudia is." Jodie sighed as she cradled the hot drink. "She's the only other person I know who can make it without it being gluggy and gross."

"Is that so?" Thor wrapped his hands around his warm mug and smiled at Claudia. She wasn't looking at him. Which was a shame, because he'd taken off his outdoor gear and was looking pretty great, with his flannel shirtsleeves rolled up to reveal muscular, tattooed forearms. "What do you think of it, Type A?"

"It's perfect," Claude said grudgingly.

He grinned, a lock of wheat-colored hair flopping over his eyes. "I'll make it for you anytime."

She shot him a dark look. He laughed.

"I don't want to hassle you," he said, still grinning, "and I have lots to do. I'll leave you to enjoy the nog. You're welcome to a top up on the house." He winked at Claude. "Merry Christmas, Type A."

"Merry Christmas." Claude watched him go. Jodie could see the naked longing on her face. But only for a moment. Then her usual cool composure was back. "It's the bourbon," she said quietly. "Whatever he used, it's really good. Notes of spice and custard."

He was perfect for her. Who else would care a fig about bourbon notes in a mug of dessert-drink? Jodie remembered the bourbon cream from Thanksgiving. The fact that Claude bought it; the fact that he stocked it. Plus: he looked like *Thor.* So why didn't she say yes when he asked her out? She clearly liked him.

Jodie wasn't about to push it, though. She appreciated the fact that Claude didn't push her over Kelly Wong, so she was happy to return the favor. Ugh. Kelly Wong. Why couldn't she go a minute without thinking about him?

Because she loved him.

Loved. Past tense. She was getting over it fast.

Just not fast enough.

Outside a snowstorm was building. The snowfall was almost horizontal, flicking past the fogging windows with gathering intensity.

"We should get going before it gets too bad," Claude said, pushing her empty mug away. "It's supposed to really blow by tonight."

Tonight. When she'd trim the tree with her family, all of them trying to be shiny and bright for her sake. At least they were more festive than they'd been at Thanksgiving. Mom had her colored lights up and working. She hadn't bothered taking down the white ones—Bree's *coffee lights*—instead she'd just thrown her colored lights on top. You didn't need to turn on the overhead lights or lamps, it was so bright with strings of Christmas twinkles.

Dad had a tree waiting for tonight. Usually the tree was up by early December, but this year they'd waited until Jodie had returned from New York. And then she'd been in a foul mood, and no one had wanted to ruin the tree trimming with her sullenness, so Mom had decided they might as well do it on Christmas Eve and make it part of the festivities.

Festivities. With no Bree and no Kelly. This really shit year just got shittier and shittier.

Jodie and Claude collected their things and trudged through

the snow to Claude's car. Jodie kept her chin tucked so she wasn't whipped in the face by the snow. The wind was wicked. Jodie remembered Kelly saying he missed this when he was in Miami. She wondered if he was spending Christmas with his family in Great Neck, or if they were all in Miami at his mom's. Or maybe he was in Tacoma, where he was based for next season. Was he having a white Christmas too? She had no idea because she'd deleted her Instagram in a fit of rage and humiliation.

Oh, who cared what kind of Christmas he was having. What was *wrong* with her?

She slammed the door as she slumped into the passenger seat. As Claude started the car, the radio leapt on, a bright holiday chatter that did nothing to soothe Jodie. She turned it off. They drove in silence through the curtains of snow, each locked in her own thoughts. Jodie guessed she should be glad she wasn't working at the airport, the way she usually was through Christmas. Cheryl's bargain meant she was still on paid leave from the car-rental stand. Jodie was sure there was some car-rental marketing underway, but she had no intention of going on Insta to see it.

Cheryl had taken control of Bree's account, but Maya still had the unholy power of hashtags. #BucketList #Jodie #IrisAir #100

Jodie didn't want to see it.

"Your mom didn't skimp on the lights this year," Claude observed as she pulled into Jodie's street. The blaze of lights was visible through the storm, the candy colors blinking and twinkling.

"She even decorated that stupid bush." Jodie sighed. The red twig dogwood was laced with lights.

"So, it really isn't a tree?"

"Nope, it's a shrub. I have to do the whole thing over when spring comes."

"Do you get to pick the tree this time?" Claude asked dryly.

For some reason, Jodie thought of the tunnel of ghostly

bridesmaid trees on the High Line. Crepe myrtles. "Mom wants a dogwood." The last thing she needed was more reminders of Kelly Wong.

The front door opened as they climbed from the car. Jodie's mom was there, in her best (worst) holiday sweater, knitted by Aunt Pat. Mom wore it on Christmas Eve so she didn't have to wear it on Christmas Day. They all had one, even Russel Sprout.

"Jodie!" Jodie's mom came dashing down the porch steps, uncaring that she was only in her slippers.

"What?" Jodie felt a rush of fear. What was wrong?

Only Mom was grinning ear to ear. Maybe Iris Air had paid off more of their debts?

Her mom yanked her into a hug, dancing her around on the spot. "This is the one!" Mom squealed in her ear. "I feel it in my bones. *This* is the one!"

Jodie exchanged a bewildered look with Claude.

Her mom was laughing gleefully and spun Jodie around. "I like this one a lot."

"Which one? What are you talking about?"

Of course Mom took her phone out. She held it up for Jodie to see. Jodie groaned. Oh no. *Thor.* Of course there'd been a #JodieSighting at Hopper's. And of course Hopper himself featured, every Hallmark-hero inch of him. In one post, the photographer had caught him cradling the mug of eggnog, gazing warmly at the object of his affection. Which had most definitely not been Jodie. Oh, the poor guy.

Then Jodie saw the hashtag #ScrewYouKellyWong.

"What is it?" Claude shuffled through the snow to peer over Jodie's shoulder. She froze.

Oh, poor Claude too. This was just like with Tish and Cheryl . . . Only this time, Jodie didn't have to play along. She closed the app.

"He's not looking at me, Mom, he's looking at Claude."

"No, he's not." Her mom punched open the app again. "Look!"

There was another post, taken by some sneaky sniper in the grocery aisle. It showed Hopper behind the counter, his jacket and woolen hat still dusted with snow. He was gazing warmly at . . . Jodie. Who was very clearly in frame, holding an enormous bunch of flowers. The picture made it look like *he'd* given her the flowers. Which he hadn't.

"He just wished me a Merry Christmas." Jodie sighed, pushing the phone away. She didn't want to look at it. "The dude only has eyes for Claude. Trust me. Can we get out of the weather now?"

"Well." Mom didn't sound pleased. "But I like him."

"Yeah, he's nice. Claude likes him too."

"I don't!"

"Yeah, you do." Jodie slogged through the snow to dig the shopping out of the trunk. "I just don't have any photos of your face to prove it." God. There was probably a Team Hopper already. Her mom might have already ordered a T-shirt.

"You don't?" Mom brightened up at Claude's declaration. If she hadn't ordered a T-shirt, she was about to.

"No. Jodie's welcome to him."

As *if*.

"Feel free to grab some bags too, Mom," Jodie huffed, as she passed them.

"We like this one!" Grandma Gloria called from the living room as Jodie clomped past on her way to the kitchen.

"I don't," Aunt Pat protested. "I like the other one better."

"What other one?"

"The baseball player."

"The one who cheated on her?"

"He didn't cheat on *her*. He cheated on the other one, the blonde."

Jodie slung the shopping on the counter and grit her teeth to keep from yelling at them.

"Hush up," her dad rumbled. He appeared in the kitchen doorway. "You need a hand?"

"*Now* you ask?" Jodie's mom complained, her wet slippers slapping on the kitchen floor as she joined Jodie at the counter. She dropped the shopping on the floor.

"Is there more?"

"No, that's it." Claude came in and dropped the last load. She was looking pinched. "I'll leave you to unpack, if that's OK. I have to go see my mom."

"But you're coming back to trim the tree and help us cook," Jodie's mom said. It wasn't really a question. "I'm sure there'll be another message from Bree, and you don't want to miss it."

"Don't wait for me," Claude warned. She sounded flat. *Flatter.* She'd been flat all day.

"Of course we'll wait for you." Jodie's mom clucked.

"Alright, bye." Claude ducked out quickly, before she could get caught in a Boyd avalanche.

"This is *the one*, Jodie," her mom said, pulling her phone out again. "I tell you. I feel it in my bones."

Jodie turned her back on her and started unpacking. He was the one; just not her one. He was Claude's, and Jodie didn't need to check the feeling in her bones to know it was true. She paused when she found a carton of pre-made custard in the bags. It wasn't even a fancy brand. Since when didn't Claude make her own custard, from scratch? There were other concerns too. Like no table decorations.

"I mean, look at that *face*." Mom shoved her phone in front of Jodie's face and Thor's blue eyes twinkled out of the screen.

"I don't think you were supposed to bring this in," Jodie's dad rumbled as Jodie batted the phone away to see what he was holding out. It was a big gift sack with the word "Mom" written on the tag in Claude's writing.

"I'll take it to her," Jodie said quickly, snatching it off him and darting away from her mother and the damn phone. She hoped she was in time to catch Claude.

She was. The car was still at the curb, chugging in the cold, its headlights cutting through the shifting veils of snow. Jodie jogged halfway to it before she realized it wasn't moving. Claude was just sitting there, a silhouette in the dark interior, etched in green by the dashboard lights, her hands gripping the wheel. Instead of knocking on the door, Jodie circled the car and opened the passenger door.

Claude jumped in shock and made a startled noise.

"Sorry," Jodie said, leaning in and holding out the sack, "you forgot . . ." She trailed off as she caught sight of Claude's green-lit face. Tracks of mascara ran down her face. She was crying. "Hey." Jodie slid into the seat and closed the door. "What's wrong?"

Claude took a shaky breath and looked away. Her hands still gripped the wheel at ten and two, her knuckles white. "Nothing," she said dully, "I'm fine."

"Clearly." Jodie took in Claude's hollow cheeks. She'd lost a lot of weight. A *lot*. She looked stretched thin as a balloon about to pop. Jodie felt a heaviness settle in her stomach. She'd been so wrapped up in herself and the stupid bucket list and the havoc wreaked on her heart by Kelly Wong that she'd forgotten she wasn't the only one suffering.

"Is it your mom?" Jodie asked.

Claude gave a harsh bark of a laugh. "Always."

"And Bree," Jodie guessed.

Claude's face crumpled up. "I don't know how to do this without her." She made a strangled noise and thumped her head forward against the steering wheel. Her shoulders trembled as she cried.

"Oh, Claude." Jodie reached out and prized her off the wheel. She hugged her, feeling the stick shift gouging her belly. Claude clung to her, crying off every last inch of her makeup. Jodie found her eyes watering in sympathy. Claude had tried to tell her how desperately lonely she was. Why hadn't Jodie listened? Because she'd been too wrapped up in herself.

Look at how she had beaten herself up for not paying more attention to Bree before she'd died. Now here she was making the same mistake with Claude. Claude, who had played fairy godmother and sent her that package from Macy's, clothing her for the ball. Claude, who fussed over their Thanksgiving and their Christmas to make sure the holidays were everything Bree had wanted. Claude, who still went to visit her mom, even after years of abuse and neglect. Who probably had homemade bunting in that stupid sack, who had probably stayed up nights making that bunting for her mom.

But who made bunting for Claude?

"I'm OK now," Claude hiccupped, pulling away from Jodie. She looked a mess, her face splotchy with mascara.

"Sure, except you look like someone tie-dyed your face."

Claude was startled into a laugh. "That bad?" She pulled down her visor and winced at the vision that greeted her in the mirror.

"You could start a trend." Jodie buckled up.

"What are you doing?"

"I'm coming with you."

"You can't."

"Sure, I can. I'll help you hang the bunting." Jodie opened the glove compartment. As she expected, there were tissues and sanitizing wipes in there. She tossed the wipes to Claude.

"How did you know there was bunting?" Claude asked.

"Because you're *Claude*."

"Jodie?" Claude said softly, after she'd cleaned herself up. "Thank you."

"Don't thank me yet. Have you seen what I can do to bunting?"

Claude smiled wanly as she pulled out into the snowstorm. "Yes. Yes, I have."

Jodie switched the radio on, and "Deck the Halls" filled the car. This time it didn't bother her so much.

Chapter 36

There was no message from Bree that night, but it was OK. They had a good night. Maybe the best one in a couple of years. They drank Claude's eggnog (which wasn't as good as Hopper's, but Jodie didn't tell Claude that), trimmed the tree, and snacked as they cooked the feast for the next day. Jodie ate more gingerbread than she decorated and made a mess of the sugar cookies with runny icing. But she felt herself breathing easier for the first time since that horror show in New York. Grandma Gloria's Michael Bublé CD played on repeat and the colored lights twinkled. Outside snow fell in drifts and the wind rattled the windows. The fire crackled and Dad ended the night with a round of hot chocolate, the mouths of the mugs plugged with melting marshmallows.

"Bree's bound to have a message for us tomorrow," Jodie's dad reassured them all, putting his arm around Jodie's mom's shoulder and giving her a squeeze as they sat with their mugs of hot chocolate and watched the tree lights dance. Jodie's parents were more like themselves than before she'd left for New York. Following along with the bucket list on Instagram was weirdly good for them—certainly better than it was for Jodie. Her mom had lost the zombie look she'd had since Bree died, and Jodie's dad actually got off the couch and got involved in the cooking. He even helped Claude with the ham when Jodie refused to do it.

"The message will come tomorrow," Dad repeated, resting his cheek on Jodie's mom's head.

"Of course it will," Aunt Pat said stolidly. "She'd want to be there Christmas morning for the presents, just like always."

Jodie sat cross-legged on the floor by the tree, next to Claude. The lights chased over Claude's face. She was watching the Boyds dreamily. For the first time, Jodie saw her family through Claude's eyes. The Boyds weren't much, just a collection of grieving people in a modest house. Nothing fancy. But they had each other. And that wasn't nothing. Jodie thought back to their evening with Claudia's mom. The sober house had been fragile with hope, white knuckled with willpower. Claude's mom had been twitchy and anxious, talking a mile a minute, but also dull with exhaustion. She'd chain-smoked as she watched Claude and Jodie string up bunting, a constellation of silver and gold stars that caught the fluorescent lights as the stars twirled on their moorings. Claude's mom was whipcord thin and stringy, her eyes so full of ghosts that it was hard to see anything else.

"She won't last." Claude sighed as they left. "She's already talking about checking herself out."

Back home, Jodie felt a hot flame of love for her family, and she was abruptly, intensely grateful for them. She might not have Bree, and she might not have Kelly (stop thinking about him), but she had all these people. And even that stupid dog, who had fallen asleep half buried in Jodie's running shoe.

Merry Christmas, Smurfette.

Merry Christmas, Bree. Jodie looked up at the photo on the mantel. Wish you were here.

"Right, I'm off to bed." Grandma Gloria hauled herself out of the armchair by the fire. "A girl has to get her beauty sleep."

Grandma Gloria and Aunt Pat were staying the night, not wanting to brave the storm, or risk being snowed in and unable to get back for Christmas Day. They were sharing Bree's old room.

"You're staying too, aren't you?" Jodie asked Claude.

Claude looked startled. "I hadn't planned on it. And I don't have anything else to wear tomorrow."

"No need to worry about that," Aunt Pat scoffed, "I've knit-ted you a sweater. You can wear that."

"Lucky you." Jodie laughed, once they'd gone. "Just so you can compliment her properly when you open it, the white lumps are probably meant to be snowflakes and the brown lumps are meant to be reindeer." Jodie pointed to the brown lump on her own sweater. "See the red blotch there? That's Rudolph's nose."

Claude had gone all pink at the thought of the sweater. Jodie didn't know if it was because she was horrified at the thought of wearing it, or pleased that she was getting one, like a real Boyd.

She and Claude stretched out on the floor of the living room and watched the fire burn down to embers. They were lost in their own thoughts.

Jodie's of course were traitorous thoughts that led her back to Kelly Wong. Why couldn't she cut him out like a cancer? Excise him from her mind. She just kept thinking about the High Line, about the piano lessons, about his kindnesses, his tenderness, about his kisses, and his body and his . . .

Stop.

She closed her eyes against the pain of it.

"Jodie?" Claude sounded tentative. "I'll shut up if you want me to . . . but I'd be a terrible . . . friend . . ."

Sister. She'd been about to say sister, Jodie was sure of it. She'd caught herself, but Jodie had noticed the sibilant "s" be-fore she changed it to an "f."

". . . if I didn't ask. What happened?"

Jodie tensed. "With what?"

"With Kelly."

"Nothing happened. He had a wife." She tried to divert Claude. "Jonah Lourdes on the other hand is . . . just lovely." And he was. He'd sent her some very kind and very funny mes-sages since she'd left New York.

Claude didn't take the bait. Jodie could practically hear her rolling her eyes. "Maybe Kelly and his wife are separated?"

Jodie didn't care. He was married and he hadn't told her. And she couldn't get Jessica's face out of her head. The look of joy to see Kelly, the way she'd said his name. The intimacy of it. She loved him. And he must have loved her because he'd *married* her. Surely if they were separated, Jessica wouldn't have looked so damn happy to see him? And Kelly wouldn't have looked so horrified. He would have just said, "Here's my soon-to-be ex-wife," and not been so damned guilty looking. Not guilty *looking*, she amended. *Guilty.*

"Why don't you return some of those messages he leaves and *talk* to him. No one's perfect, Jodie."

Can we talk?

What would he have said if she'd let him have the conversation? Would he have told her?

"Men lie all the time," Jodie said stubbornly. "They tell you about how they're so unhappy in the marriages, blah blah blah, and they're in the midst of a separation, and they never felt about their wives the way they feel about you, and then they sleep with you, and then you find out they have no plans to leave their wives and you're just a bit on the side."

"You know this from experience?" Claude sounded surprised. Shocked even.

"Well, no," Jodie admitted, "but I've seen enough movies."

Claude laughed. "Life's not like the movies, Jodie."

Only some bits *were*, Jodie moaned to herself. Some bits were Christmas lights on Fifth Avenue, and floaty feelings, and a man staring at you dumbstruck, his mouth falling open *just like in the movies*; some bits were slow jazzy piano pieces, and *our love is here to stay* and glinting chandeliers; some bits were silent snowy bridesmaid trees, and a certainty that you were where you were meant to be. Some bits were exactly like they were in the movies. So why not the rest? Why couldn't she have the damned happy ending?

Ugh. Jodie rolled onto her back and pressed the heels of her hands into her eyes. "He was *married*," she wailed.

"Maybe *was* is the operative word," Claude said calmly. She reached up and pulled Jodie's phone off the coffee table. "Listen to your messages."

Jodie kicked her heels against the carpet like a toddler. But Claude's suggestion had filled her with a wild, beating feeling.

Like a whole herd of horses was tearing loose through her chest. She *wanted* to listen to his stupid messages. But she couldn't.

"I deleted them," she told Claude in a small voice.

Claude groaned. "Please tell me you listened to them first."

Jodie's silence was all the answer Claude needed.

"Honestly, Jodie. The man called you . . . how many times?"

"Fifty-seven." Jodie's voice was getting smaller. *Can we talk?*

"What about the text messages?"

"I haven't opened them."

"I guessed. Did you delete them too?" Claude sighed. "Of course you did."

"Well, it worked," Jodie said defensively. "He stopped messaging." And hadn't *that* hurt.

"Please tell me you've stalked him online to find out more about his marriage?"

"Of course not! I don't *care.*"

"Sure you don't."

"I don't care just as much as you don't care about Hopper!"

"Touché."

They both lapsed into silence. And didn't speak of it again.

Chapter 37

In the wee hours of the next morning there was a commotion in the front yard. It was well before daybreak. Jodie's room was at the back of the house, so she had to run downstairs to get a look at what the hell was going on.

It turned out *a lot* was going on.

The storm had blown itself out in the night and the world was an undulating landscape of white. The street was lit up bright as day by enormous flood lights, and there was a backhoe in the front yard of the Boyd's house. By the time they'd all thrown on jackets and stumbled out onto the porch, the thing had already made a huge hole in the front yard, on the opposite side to where the red twig dogwood bristled, its red stalks bravely holding up its cobweb of Christmas lights.

"What the hell is this?" Jodie's dad bellowed, holding his hand over his eyes to see through the glare of the floods. The neighbors were all emerging, blinking like moles.

Then a truck arrived, and Jodie saw all too well what *this* was.

Another goddamn stunt.

The flatbed truck trundled carefully down the street, which hadn't yet been plowed. On the back of it was an enormous Christmas tree, and standing up there on the flatbed next to it, wearing a merry red beanie, was none other than *Sir Ryan*

Lasseter himself. He looked like a jolly elf. Jodie frowned. She'd never worked out if he'd been behind all Maya's meddling or not. This crazy stunt made her think he might have been.

"Jodie!" he cried, taking his beanie off and waving it. As though she couldn't already see him up there. "Merry Christmas!" His spectacles glinted in the floodlights.

Jodie didn't wave back.

"Who the hell is that moron?" Jodie's dad asked.

"Honestly, Joe, haven't you been following on Instagram?" Jodie's mom said, annoyed.

"He can't be thinking to plant that thing in your yard, Denise?" Grandma Gloria said to Jodie's mom. "Doesn't the fool know it's midwinter?"

Jodie bet the tree would "pop" in the snow.

"I wanted to cheer you up!" Ryan called, holding his red beanie aloft. He was having a great time out there.

"Cheer us up?" Jodie's dad growled. "By digging up our lawn?"

"Well, it looks to be a big root ball underneath that spruce," Aunt Pat observed. "It would need a mighty big hole."

"What happens if the tree dies?" Mom asked nervously. It was very close to their house.

"Then you'll all be crushed to death in your sleep as it topples over," Aunt Pat said pragmatically. "A tree that big is hard to transplant at the best of times. In the middle of winter during a freeze, that poor thing is going to shrivel right up and die."

"Enough of this nonsense." Jodie's dad went back inside and pulled his snow boots on. "I'm talking to that lunatic."

"Dad." Jodie sighed. "That lunatic is the guy who's paying off Bree's medical bills."

"What?"

"Well, who the hell else would it be?" Jodie asked. "Who else would have the cash to ship in a live Christmas tree and have a work crew out like this at the crack of dawn Christmas morning?"

"Merry Christmas, Boyds!" His Sir-ship had dismounted the flatbed and came slogging through the thigh-deep snow to the porch. That's when Jodie saw another figure climb down from the cabin of the truck. The vivid red coat made her think of Cheryl. But it wasn't Cheryl, it was Maya. Who of course was taking a record of everything on her phone.

Jodie's stomach curdled at the sight of her. The last time Jodie had seen Maya was that horrid night in the dressing room of the Broadway Theatre. The witch.

"I've brought you a tree!" His Sir-ship announced joyfully as he climbed the steps, which were buried in thick pillows of snow.

"So we see," Jodie's dad said dryly.

"It's our apology gift for Cheryl messing up with the shrub," Maya purred, picking her way through the snow like a cat.

For Cheryl messing up. Wow, what a piece of work.

"I thought a Christmas tree was just what was needed for the occasion!" Ryan said. His cheeks were rosy and his blue eyes twinkling. He looked like he belonged in a Norman Rockwell painting.

Uh-huh, Jodie thought. More like a Christmas tree would play well on social media on Christmas Day. Particularly a Christmas tree this big. He didn't care whether or not they wanted a spruce dwarfing their house, or whether it lived or died. It only had to look good long enough for Maya to take photos of it.

"That's . . . uh . . . very generous of you, Mr. Lasseter." Jodie's mom exchanged a look with Jodie's dad. A whole conversation seemed to pass between them in that single look.

Don't forget the medical bills.

How could I forget?

"Very generous," Jodie's dad mumbled.

"You must be Bree's father." Sir Ryan seized Jodie's dad's hand and shook it, holding it tight between both of his. Everyone else got European kisses. "So wonderful to meet Bree's family. I am truly, deeply sorry for your loss." He made *the face.* "I'm sure you're tired of hearing that from people you've never even met. But Bree was someone who touched a lot of people."

"You knew her?" Jodie's dad was gruff. Jodie could hear the familiar pain in his voice.

Sir Ryan smiled. "I did. She was a force of nature. She still is," he said. "Look at us, all here now, planting a tree because of her. Jodie wouldn't be taking us all on this adventure without her."

"She certainly wouldn't," Maya agreed smoothly. She'd had the grace not to film the moment, at least.

"Oh, and this is my assistant, Maya. You know Maya, don't you, Jodie?"

All too well.

Maya had exchanged her coral-colored lipstick for slick wet scarlet, Jodie noticed. Her lips shone in the light, like they were coated in blood. "Oh yes," Maya said, smiling, "Jodie and I are old friends."

"Right," Sir Ryan said. "Boss us around, Maya. Tell us where you want us. Do you want everyone to go get dressed first?"

"Oh no," Maya protested, "it's piquant to have everyone out in their pajamas."

"Piquant," Jodie echoed. She wasn't falling back into this nonsense again. No one was bossing anyone around. Especially not on Christmas morning. "Ryan," she said, striving for patience, "do you mind if we have a quiet word?"

Ryan cocked his head, curious. "Of course I don't mind."

"Why don't you all go inside," Jodie told her family. "So Ryan and I can talk in private."

"Oh no," Jodie's mom protested, "you should take Sir Ryan inside where it's warm."

"Nonsense," Ryan told her cheerfully. "You're in your pajamas. I'm not going in the warm and leaving you to freeze out here!"

He wasn't a total ass, then.

"He's right. There's no point in you all shivering out here. Especially when it's your house," Jodie said irritably. "Go inside. We won't be long."

"We have more than one room," Jodie's dad said, rolling his eyes. "We can all go inside where it's warm."

"No, we'll be fine out here." Jodie had no intention of being within earshot of any of them. The walls were paper thin in there. And Maya had her phone. Jodie wanted complete privacy.

The double-glazed windows would make sure they didn't hear anything if they were inside. "And take Maya with you, Mom," Jodie instructed. "She's cold too."

"No, she's not," Maya said. "She's in a nice down coat."

Jodie fixed her with a cold stare.

Ryan took note. "Off you go, Maya."

Maya gave Jodie a sour look, but she went. Jodie waited until the door had closed behind them all before she dealt with Sir Ryan Lasseter.

Where did she even begin?

"What kind of stunt is this?" She sighed, opting for bluntness.

"Stunt?" He frowned.

"Yes, Ryan. *Stunt.* You show up Christmas morning, with that"—Jodie gestured at the enormous tree on the flatbed truck—"behemoth. And with your rabid PA in tow to take photos . . . How is it anything other than a stunt? And I for one am *done* with stunts." Jodie crossed her arms. She'd genuinely liked him when they'd playacted in Katz's deli and was disappointed in him now.

Ryan was listening carefully, his eyes serious behind his spectacles. "I see you're not happy with the way things are going . . ."

Happy? "No. No, Ryan, I'm not. I haven't been happy for a while."

"This is the first I'm hearing of this," he said slowly. "Fill me in."

So, she did. And she didn't hold back.

As he listened, he leaned against the porch post. Jodie was aware of her mother and Maya hovering near the window, watching them. She turned her back on them.

"I understand everything you're saying," Ryan said slowly, when she was done. "And it does sound like our communication could have been clearer."

Jodie saw the cool-headed businessman behind the charm. His blue stare was sharp, and he seemed to listen with his whole body.

"This is my *sister*," Jodie reminded him, her voice tight with emotion. "Her last wish wasn't to bring a three-ring circus to town." God, she was sick of saying that. Surely, she shouldn't *need* to.

He nodded and gave her a sad smile. "Yes. Your very savvy sister, who organized all of this before she left you. So, yes, everything you say is true. This is her bucket list, and your journey, but the fact is . . . she sold the rights to it. For money. To us. For *you*."

Jodie frowned.

"I'm not disagreeing with you," he said gently, resting his hand on her arm. "It sounds like you've been intruded upon, and strong-armed, and manipulated. And none of that's OK. But the circus . . ." His gaze moved to the front yard, where workmen were in the process of backing the truck toward the hole. The beeping of the truck as it reversed was like a metronome; Jodie had always found metronomes stressful. "The circus, as you call it, *is* the deal. Bree offered us her followers, and her bucket list, as a platform for our brand."

"It's ghoulish," Jodie blurted.

Sir Ryan squeezed her arm. "It doesn't have to be."

"I feel like a performing seal," she told him.

"It *was* a bit of a deal with the devil . . ." He gave her a crooked smile. "With the devil being me, I suppose . . ." He sighed. "I did offer to just *give* her the money, you know. But she didn't want a bar of it."

Jodie felt like she'd received an electric shock. "What?"

"She didn't want a handout." He took his glasses off and polished them on his sweater. "To be honest, I was always worried that this was a bad look for the brand. No one wants to look like they're cashing in on misfortune, and the last thing I wanted was for Iris Air to be labeled a misery vampire. I liked your sister; I would have been happy to donate the money . . ."

That wouldn't have been Bree's style. Jodie knew how proud she was. How proud they all were. But *this* . . . I mean, *look* at that tree. It belonged in Rockefeller Plaza, not in the Boyd's small front yard. It was ridiculous.

Oh, Bree . . . How she must have agonized over this. Needing the money, but knowing the solution would be a contortion for the family; caught between a rock and a hard place, and knowing she wouldn't be here to make sure things went to plan. Not willing to take a handout, but not wanting to leave Mom and Dad in debt . . .

"Cheryl and Bree assured me it wouldn't be ghoulish," Ryan told Jodie softly. "And Bree point-blank refused to take the money any other way. She said she wasn't a beggar—she was a businesswoman. And she was offering me something valuable."

"Her followers." Jodie sighed.

"No," Ryan said with a twinkle, "*you*."

"Me?"

"This list isn't about Bree, Jodie. It's about *you*. And you, Jodie Boyd, are no clown."

"No, I'm not," Jodie said tartly. "I'm just surrounded by them." Jodie's head was spinning. What did he mean, this list was about her?

"OK. So how do we fix that? Let's get down to brass tacks. We have a contract. There's a job to be done. How do we make this work?" Ryan was direct.

"Let me take my own damn photos? And you keep Maya to yourself?" Jodie said shortly. How was this list about *her*? It didn't make any sense. None of these crazy things would be on her bucket list. If she had one. Which she didn't. "Let me have Cheryl back? We weren't perfect—but we had an understanding."

He smiled. "Done. But Maya isn't all bad; she's a good PA. She's ambitious and prone to overstepping, and she and Cheryl have a rivalry that drives me insane. But she's young and she'll learn. Hopefully from Cheryl, if Maya can drop her insecurity long enough to realize that Cheryl has a lot to teach her, and if Cheryl can realize she doesn't have to do it all alone. But for now, I promise, I will keep Maya out of your way."

"Thank you." Jodie cleared her throat. "I just want you all to stop hijacking the list. I want to do things myself. Like pick a tree."

Ryan gave her a rueful look. "I screwed this up, didn't I? I really did mean well. I thought you'd be having a hard Christmas, this being the first without Bree. Given the mistake with the last tree, I felt I owed you a new one. I thought it would be a nice surprise, and it would make you smile." He was sincere.

"It's over-the-top," Jodie told him. "I mean, look at it."

They watched as the tree was winched into place. There were a lot of ropes involved.

"You have to admit, you did it because it would pop in photos," she said dryly. "And because a circus is good for business."

"Both can be true," he told her with a grin. "Sometimes you can mix business and pleasure. And a kindness can be spectacular."

Jodie found herself smiling back. She couldn't help it. His charm was irresistible. Even when you were frustrated with him.

"You can take photos of the tree, or not, as you wish," he assured her. "Post them online or not, as you wish. But the best marketing advice I can buy will tell you that posting photos of your family, in their pajamas, in front of that—what did you call it?—behemoth, will boost your hit rate. And pay off those medical bills. And that's everything Bree asked for." He smiled again. "It will also be a memory you can look back on one day when you're old and gray. The time that dashing Lasseter chap bought you a tree. Bet no man's ever done that for you before. Most are satisfied with flowers." He winked at her.

Jodie laughed, startled. "Fine. But *I'll* take the photos myself."

"Don't you want to be in them?"

"You ever heard of selfies?" She crossed her arms. "I take the photos. I steer this ship from now on."

"And you take our suggestions under advisement? Because they are sincerely well meant. On my part, anyway. Your sister designed this arrangement; she oversaw the contracts; I'm only trying to jump through the hoops she set up. I *want* you to succeed." His July-blue eyes were kind. "I'll take Maya off the job. Cheryl can advise you, but *only* advise you. You take care of the details. How does that sound?" He offered her his hand to shake. "Deal?"

"Deal."

They shook.

"And maybe you can accept that a little circus magic doesn't have to be all bad?" he asked playfully.

"Don't push your luck."

He grinned, his blue eyes twinkling. "If I didn't push my luck, I wouldn't be where I am today."

"On an icy porch in Wilmington?" Jodie laughed. "Spending your Christmas negotiating deals with a nobody?"

"A nobody?" he protested. "You're not a nobody. You're the world-famous Jodie Boyd. Ringmaster of the greatest show on earth."

"You really don't quit, do you?"

"I will. Once the list is finished. I promise."

As Jodie watched the earth covering the roots of the giant tree, she felt a pang. How could the list ever be finished when there was no one to love?

Sensing her shift to melancholy, Sir Ryan put his arm around her. Jodie leaned into him, taking a deep draught of cold air. She could smell warm leather and rainy woods. It was a good smell. One she'd associate with Christmas for the rest of her life.

Chapter 38

Bree's message came late in the day. They watched it on the iPad, after Sir Ryan had jetted off for his lodge in Vermont, and after they'd cooked, and eaten, and watched the giant spruce in the yard gather snow, looking like something straight from a Christmas card. When the message started to play, the Boyds clustered around the couch. Jodie's mom held the screen in a viselike grip. Just like last time, she started crying as soon as she saw Bree's face.

"Hey, family!" Bree was on oxygen in this video, the clear tubes taped down beside her nose with medical tape. Her face was shiny and there were huge bruise-colored patches around her eyes. She still smiled.

The Boyds didn't.

"Merry Christmas!"

It didn't matter how many twinkling lights there were, the room suddenly felt darker, gloomier. Each and every one of them was transported back to Bree's last days. Jodie felt the same sense of weirdly sluggish terror.

"I hope you enjoyed Christmas. Did you make the ham? The recipe I put in the email looked amazing. I know you couldn't eat it, Jodie, but hopefully the cheesy leeks were good too." Bree could barely lift her head off the pillow. "Did Russel Sprout bury any of the presents this year?"

He had. He'd buried Dad's new universal remote control in a snowdrift.

"I don't know at what point Jodie is in the bucket list when you're watching this—maybe she's only done the first one, or maybe she's smashed most of them—but wherever she is, I have no doubt she's doing great. I know they're not easy." Even deep in their dark sockets, her eyes twinkled. "If they were easy, I would have done them already."

Jodie could hear everyone sniffling. It wasn't as gutting as the Thanksgiving message. Their grief was quieter, still painful, but not as surprising. Somehow it helped, seeing these messages. It was a connection to Bree when other connections had been severed.

"I hope my followers have stayed. Maybe you've even gained a couple."

"A couple?" Claude gave a disparaging laugh. "Try almost a million."

"What?" Jodie was startled. "What did you say?"

"Her account has picked up almost a million more followers. I mean, *you* have. It's you they're watching."

"No way." No. No *way*.

"All that marketing is working." Claude shrugged.

The best marketing advice I can buy, Ryan had said, as he cautioned her to follow it. But then Jodie remembered the waiter and bartender at the champagne bar in New York: *Cady and I miss your sister so much.* Maybe it wasn't all about the marketing.

"Oh my God, you know what this means," Jodie realized, her stomach squeezing tight.

"You're famous?" Aunt Pat said dryly.

"No, what it means for Bree's deal with Ryan. They agreed that if I increased Bree's followers, he'd pay a thousand dollars off the debts of everyone on Bree's ward." Jodie remembered the ward's long corridor, the muffled rooms humming with fluorescent lights and medical machinery; she remembered the wan family members making instant coffee in the shabby lounge, the way people would walk like they were at the end of a marathon, like they didn't have an ounce of energy left to spare. The Boyds weren't the only ones who had suffered seasons of cancer and loss, and they weren't the only ones with debt.

"Go Jodie!" Claudia clapped her hands.

"Go Bree," Jodie corrected.

Claudia rolled her eyes. "Take a compliment, would you? Go both of you."

"Girls, shush, or we'll miss Bree!" Jodie's mom flapped a hand at them.

Almost a *million* more . . . Bree had almost a million to start with . . . adding another million meant . . . Oh God, almost *two million people* had witnessed her abject humiliation.

"I've been thinking about the list a lot, as I get things ready with Cheryl." Bree sighed on the screen.

Again, Jodie was struck by the surrealism of Bree and Cheryl speaking to one another. For Jodie, Cheryl belonged squarely in "life after Bree." It was weird to think she'd existed in "life before Bree" too, talking to Bree, planning, sharing secrets.

"And I've been thinking about the last thing on the list."

Everything went very still. No one looked at Jodie.

Bree stared into the screen, as though she could see Jodie on the other side. "Don't settle, Jodie. You'll know love when it happens. And when it does happen, grab hold of it and never let it go."

Too late.

But could you call it letting go, when you'd never had proper hold of it in the first place?

"I've been thinking about Grandad lately, Grandma Gloria." Bree smiled.

Grandma Gloria covered her mouth with the tissue in her balled-up fist. Her mascara was clumpy from the tears.

"About how even the best love stories have to end." Bree's smile turned melancholy. "But I've also been thinking about how natural death is. How it's just another part of life, another cliff to jump from . . . another trip to take."

A really sucky part of life, and a really sucky trip to take. *And you took it all alone.* The cold horror of grief filled Jodie all over again. The jaw-clenching glacial realization that Bree was gone, body and soul. And all that was left was this talking trace on a screen. Speaking pixels.

"You never really have someone," the speaking pixels said, "not forever. You just get them for a little while, if you're lucky. And you never know how long you have them for."

Bree's words dropped into Jodie's heart like stones dropped into a still pond.

"I don't really believe in tomorrow, let alone in forever." Bree sighed. "This is all a bit rambling . . . it's the medication, I guess . . . but I just wanted to say . . . don't wait, Jodie. When you know, jump. Trust that there's an ocean to catch you. Because if you wait, the tide might recede . . ." Bree blinked, looking a bit fuzzy. "Am I mixing my metaphors? I'm not sure any of this makes sense."

It made total sense. It just didn't help. Because Kelly Wong was married. And Jodie had deleted all his messages. And he'd stopped calling.

"Number one hundred says fall in love . . ." Bree's voice was slurring now. Whatever medication she'd taken was having its full effect. "It doesn't say they have to love you back." Her eyelids were growing heavy. "Because you can't control that bit. And loving is good. Whether you're loved back or not."

As they watched, Bree drifted off into a doze.

"Merry Christmas, folks. Bree loves you." It was Wanda the orderly's voice that came from behind Bree's camera. She must have been filming.

They had another couple of seconds of Bree's sleeping face, and then the camera cut.

Chapter 39

99. Antarctica by Air

The Iris Air lounge at Sydney Airport was like an episode of *The Bachelorette*. Every team was represented. Except for one.

Clustered around the bar in the luxe private club were Tish and Jonah and Sir Ryan himself, and even *Hopper*.

"What's he doing here?" Claude gasped.

"Representing Team Hopper," Jodie said dryly. She had to resist the urge to run, even though she'd agreed to all of this. She understood the logic of it, and she was willing to suffer through it. She liked all of them, so it wasn't really a chore. "You think they'd let a Hallmark-hero get out of this media circus?" Jodie asked Claudia. "I mean, I bet he has his own fan club already."

"Right. Of course." Claude straightened her shoulders. She looked incredible, dressed in all icy white. "Screw them. Let's go pay off those debts." This was yet another reason why bringing Claude along had been a good idea. No one got the better of Claude.

Jodie had refused to go flying over Antarctica unless Claude came with her. Jodie hated flying with a passion and couldn't face the thought of days on long-haul flights without someone to keep her calm. Calm-ish, anyway. Because nothing could really keep Jodie calm on flights, especially during the bumpy bits. And Claude deserved a vacation, even if it was a vacation that consisted of more than twenty hours on a plane to Australia, followed by two days of jet lag, followed by another twelve-hour flight, followed by another twenty hours flying back home. Luckily for Jodie, even that kind of vacation appealed to Claude right now. Especially because Iris Air flew them first-class . . . and because Claude's mother had checked herself out of the sober house. Claude was more than happy to be nine thousand miles away.

Jodie and Claude had crawled out from under their jet lag (which had been spent in the airport hotel, so there weren't even any views of Sydney Harbor to cheer them up) in time to catch the New Year's Eve Antarctic flight. Cheryl was waiting for them in the lobby of the airport lounge, all minty fresh. It was midsummer in Australia and the heat was subtropical in Sydney, but Cheryl was fresh as a daisy in white linen. Everyone was wearing white for this flight; Sir Ryan was throwing an Antarctic-white-themed party for New Year's Eve. On board a plane. Because that was what billionaires did.

Jodie hadn't owned anything white and was going to balk, but Claude had coaxed her into a white tank and pencil skirt. Jodie drew the line at strappy sandals, though, and wore her white canvas sneakers instead.

"Happy New Year!" Cheryl greeted them cheerfully. She looked genuinely pleased to see them as she hugged Jodie and greeted Claude. "How did you survive the flight?"

"It hasn't happened yet." Jodie was dreading it.

"I meant the one out from the States."

"Oh. I've blocked it out."

"Right. Well. Maybe a drink will help? Come on through, there's a free bar. Tish is here too," Cheryl said brightly. "She's already in the lounge. Make sure you congratulate her when you see her."

"On what?"

"She had the good judgment to accept my proposal." Cheryl grinned. "We're getting married."

"Oh my God, congratulations!" Jodie bet Tish was over the moon. "Does this mean Team Tish is done and dusted?"

"Nooooo. Not until this flight lands. You can't tell anyone," Cheryl warned. "Tish wasn't thrilled about not wearing her ring, but we can't let Ryan know yet. As soon as this bucket list is over . . . well, that's a whole other thing."

Jodie pulled a face at Claude, who rubbed her back sympathetically.

"The engagement rate on Bree's Insta is insane," Cheryl told them, as she led them past the front desk and through to the lounge. "After this flight, I think we'll easily top two million followers. You're doing a great job with the posts."

"Everyone wants to know who you'll kiss at midnight, to ring in the New Year," Maya purred, sliding into view. She was like a sniper, hidden where you least expected her. "That's driving the hit rates through the roof. You'll be trending number one by midnight."

"Which midnight?" Jodie needled her. "Midnight in Antarctica is six a.m. in Delaware. I know, I looked it up." What was Maya doing here? Jodie glared at Cheryl.

Cheryl gave a helpless shrug. "She's his PA," she whispered. "She goes where he goes."

"Maya!" Ryan beckoned her away from Jodie. He gave Jodie an apologetic wave.

Jodie frowned. He'd *promised*.

"There's one more person I want you to meet," Cheryl said, wisely pulling Jodie away. Claude followed as Cheryl led them toward a tall, broad-shouldered pilot, who was in full stylish Iris Air uniform. "Jodie, I'd like you to meet Captain Stefan Nowak. He'll be our captain for this flight."

Wow. He looked like an action hero. His jaw looked like it had been chiseled out of polished granite. Jodie couldn't believe this. After promising to stop the stunts, they were adding another man to the cast of *The Bachelorette*.

"Please, call me Stef," he said, holding out a hand for Jodie to shake. His full lips parted in a megawatt smile. "It's my pleasure to fly you for this part of your bucket list."

"Can you stop matchmaking," Jodie hissed at Cheryl as soon as the good captain had excused himself to board the plane.

"This flight is going to be hellish enough for me as it is, without another team to contend with."

"He's your escape," Cheryl said smugly.

"My what?"

"He's your escape. If you need to get away, you can go to the cockpit and hang out with Stef. I've got it sorted. The cockpit is private, the door locks. You can see Antarctica, away from the circus."

Jodie blinked.

"He's not supposed to be a romantic prospect," Cheryl reassured her.

"Oh no?" Jodie scoffed. "He just happens to look like that?"

"Like what?"

"Like . . . *that*. You know, *hot*."

Cheryl laughed. "Yeah, that's just dumb luck. Think of it as a bonus."

"I don't believe you."

"Did I take a photo of you with him?" Cheryl asked.

Jodie frowned. No, she hadn't. Jodie looked around for sniper photographers, but not even Maya was in snapping distance. In fact, Maya was busy over with Ryan, handing out silver party hats.

"No photos because he's not a thing. He's not part of the story at all. He is literally just our pilot, and I've organized with him that you can go to the cockpit whenever you need to escape."

"That's clever," Claude said approvingly. "It means you don't have to hide in the toilet at least, if it all gets too much for you."

Cheryl was proud of herself, Jodie could tell.

"We should get you over to Ryan," Cheryl said, steering Jodie toward the knot of white-clad people by the bar. "He'll want to be a good host and say hello."

"Jodie!" Sir Ryan engulfed her in European kisses. Then he did the same with Claudia.

"What are you doing here?" Jodie heard Claude hiss at Hopper once Sir Ryan had moved on to ordering mimosas for everyone. Mimosas seemed like a risky choice, given everyone was wearing white.

"Jodie told me you were going with her. When they offered me a ticket, I thought why not? The store is closed New Year's anyway."

"Uh-huh, and what about all the days it took to travel here, and the days it will take to travel back? Is the store closed then too?"

"I'm owed vacation."

Jodie took the mimosa from Ryan and downed it. The flight would be hard enough without Claude and Hopper bickering. Why didn't Claude just admit she liked him and enjoy herself?

"Whoa, slow down, cowgirl. You don't want to be sick over Antarctica," Tish warned as Jodie emptied her glass.

"I don't want to be sober either." Then Jodie remembered Cheryl and Tish's engagement. "Hey, congratulations!"

"Thanks." Tish glanced around furtively to make sure no one had heard. "Do you know how shitty it is not to be able to post it on my socials? Or even tell people? I can't even wear my damn ring. And you should *see* the ring. It's *amazing* and I can't wear it!"

"I'm sorry."

"It's not your fault."

"It's my bucket list. And if I hadn't given you all those European kisses in that restaurant . . ."

"Don't you dare take responsibility for this. If anyone should take responsibility for this chaos, it's that toxic narcissist she works for and his cutthroat company. If Cheryl didn't always feel like she was fighting to keep her own job, like she might be replaced by the next glossy model-cum-assistant . . ." Tish trailed off and sighed. "Screw it. Let's both not be sober. More mimosas are needed."

After another mimosa, Jodie and Tish were feeling much zestier. They were also rather tipsy. Cheryl wasn't looking pleased.

"Share yourself around more," she ordered Jodie. "Or people will think Team Tish is winning."

"Maybe Team Tish *should* win."

Cheryl scowled.

Jodie sighed. "Where's your sense of humor gone?"

"Jodie?" Maya interrupted. "Ryan would like to speak to you." She gestured to the cozy cluster of lounges by the window, where Sir Ryan was busy typing on his phone.

Jodie rolled her eyes. "Did he seriously just send someone to speak to me about speaking to me?" she asked once Maya had flitted off again.

"That's what happens when you're rich." Tish laughed. "You get people to do everything for you. She probably chews his food for him too."

"You'd best go talk to him," Claude told Jodie. "He's paying the bills, remember?"

"Or at least getting someone else to pay them." Tish giggled.

"I'm going, I'm going." Jodie was feeling annoyed with His Sir-ship. He'd promised there would be no Maya. What other promises was he breaking? "Hey," she said, dropping into the lounge opposite Ryan. "Maya said you want to talk to me? You know, *Maya*, the one who was supposed to stay away from me."

Ryan looked amused. "I said I'd keep her out of the way of the bucket list, not consign her to another planet."

"*Can* you consign her to another planet? I read you were dabbling in space travel now." Two mimosas had loosened Jodie's tongue.

Ryan laughed. Then he unbuttoned his white linen jacket and leaned forward, resting his elbows on his knees. "I've been doing a lot of thinking since I saw you at Christmas," he said, changing the subject. "About our conversation. About the circus." He waved his hand at the cast of *The Bachelorette*.

Jodie had done a lot of thinking too. And she was only more resolute about finding a way to do this bucket list properly. In a way that honored Bree and didn't just pay the bills. She hadn't found an answer on how to balance her need for privacy with the whole social media thing yet, but she was determined to find one on this flight. Because Bree had always wanted to see Antarctica, and now Jodie was here in her place, and she was going to enjoy it, come hell or highwater.

"Bree and I made a deal," Ryan said. He was thoughtful, his blue eyes piercing as he met her gaze. "But when I said this list was about *you* . . . and then when you said you felt like a performing seal . . ." He cleared his throat. "I realized that you never got a say in any of this. Not really. It was foisted on you."

Jodie was unnerved by his stare. It was like he could see right through her.

"You and your family need this money. And that . . . well, Jodie, that makes me feel frightful." He took his glasses off. Jodie wished he wouldn't. It only made his eyes blaze bluer. And the intensity of his stare made her feel naked. "You are held hostage by this money. And that, *that* has kept me up nights."

Jodie was at a loss for how to respond. What was he talking about? Of course she needed the money. Why else did he think she was doing this?

"Bree wouldn't take my money," he said quietly, "but will you?"

Jodie flinched. *What?*

"We can end this nonsense right now. I'll clear your debts. No more circus."

"No," Jodie blurted, horrified.

"You never asked for this. I can pay off all those medical bills. Right here, right now." He held up his phone. "In less than a minute, you can be free."

"No! It was her last wish!" Jodie felt a surge of anger. And something else . . . Something like grief. She *wanted* to finish this bucket list. Or, at least, as much of it as she could . . . "No," she said firmly. "I have to do this. I just want to do it my way."

Ryan's blue gaze softened, saddened. "I thought you might say that. Please don't let pride stop you. You've more than earned it. You've been amazing through this whole adventure. A trouper."

"It's not pride," Jodie said desperately. How could she make him understand when she barely understood? The feelings were a tangle, with no beginning and no end. "Bree died imagining me doing this," Jodie said, trying to find the words, trying to find the feelings, trying to understand her own mind. "She imagined all of this. She wanted it for me. And I want it for her. And I want it"—Jodie's voice caught—"I want it for me."

The bucket list had been thrust on her like something from a nightmare. It had turned her inside out and upside down, made her do things that scared her beyond belief. But in return it had given her . . . *magic*. More than magic. It had given her purpose. A voice. A sense of herself again.

It was only now, when Ryan was offering an end to it, that Jodie realized that she didn't want it to end. She felt tears welling. Before Bree's bucket list, she'd been down a very dark chasm, and the world had seemed narrow and flat and gray. But item by item, the bucket list had pulled her out of it, had splashed the world with color and light. There had been craziness and music, laughter and vertiginous terror, friendship, and fury, and . . . *love*.

"I need it," Jodie said, her voice swollen with unshed tears.

Ryan put his glasses back on, and then reached out and took her hands in both of his. "OK, Jodie Boyd." He squeezed her hands. "If you're sure that's what you want?"

"It's what I want."

"If you change your mind, the offer stands."

She shook her head vigorously. "I won't change my mind." Jodie took a steadying breath. She hadn't expected any of this. And she certainly hadn't expected to *like* the bucket list. Yet here she was, choosing it, when Ryan was giving her an out. "You know we've picked up a million or so followers?" she told Ryan, changing the topic. She could feel the tears recede. She wasn't going to cry. "You said if I could increase followers, you'd pay a thousand dollars off the medical debts of everyone on Bree's ward."

Ryan laughed. "You sound like your sister. Straight to the heart of business."

"The sooner the better, that's all," Jodie told him. It felt good to be compared to Bree. "It will mean everything to those people."

"Why don't we do it as soon as we get back to the States?" He smiled his charming, crooked smile. "But for now, how about we go see some icebergs?"

Yes. That was exactly what Jodie wanted.

Exactly.

Chapter 40

The airline attendants had seating plans. They wanted to put Jodie right in the middle of the plane, surrounded by team captains.

"Oh no," she told the attendant firmly, "I'm not doing this whole stupid flight without being able to *see* Antarctica. That's why I'm here."

"We have screens, you won't miss anything," the flight attendant assured her chirpily.

"No more screens, I want to see it for real. I'm taking a window seat." Who cared about the seating plan? This was *her* bucket list. Jodie slid into a row and claimed a window seat. "Claude? You're next to me."

Claude slid into the seat next to Jodie.

"Sing it, sister," Tish chimed, taking the seat next to Claude. "Are there more mimosas?"

Jodie found the seats around her filling up. Jonah Lourdes sat directly behind her, Sir Ryan directly ahead; Hopper was behind Claude. The rest of first-class filled with Iris Air's guests.

"There are a *lot* of good-looking men on this plane," Tish said in a stage whisper to Jodie and Claude. "And a *lot* of expensive shirts."

"As soon as we're in the air and they turn off the seat belt sign, you can mingle," Cheryl told Jodie.

Not likely. Jodie was staying glued to this window. She wanted to see icebergs.

"Don't you want to find someone to kiss?" Tish teased.

"We're just onboarding economy and then we'll be off," Captain Nowak said, standing at the entrance to the service area. He radiated confidence and authority.

"What about him?" Tish stage-whispered. "He's *fine*."

"I met him for like two minutes and he'll be *flying the plane*. I'm not picking someone based on how good they look in a uniform."

"What about you, Type A? Do you like a uniform?" Hopper drawled from the row behind.

Claude didn't deign to answer. Tish did. "Who *doesn't*?"

"I think a woman in uniform is hot," Jonah Lourdes chimed in.

"Jodie wears a uniform." Tish gave an exaggerated wink.

"Yeah, neon-green polyester is superhot." Jodie rolled her eyes.

Jonah laughed.

"We're just waiting on one more person," Maya chirped, sinking into the seat beside Sir Ryan. "His connecting flight just landed; they're whisking him right over, and then we can get this show on the road."

One more person. Jodie met Claude's gaze. Who was left? All the teams were represented except for . . .

Oh no. *No. No no no no no no.* They wouldn't do this to her. But of course they would.

Numbly, Jodie felt Claude take her hand as she watched Kelly Wong step into first class. He had a baseball cap on, and a duffel bag slung over one shoulder. He was rumpled, clearly straight off a long-haul flight. Even tired and rumpled he was gorgeous. She always forgot just how gorgeous he really was. The dent in his lower lip. The breadth of his shoulders. The quick way he had of taking in a room in a single glance.

His gaze found her in her seat, and he paused. His dark eyes widened and his whole face lit up. Then his expression flickered, turbulent with a mix of emotions. She kept her expression blank, even though her heart was pounding. She didn't want to give anyone's camera the satisfaction. Because if there was one thing she'd learned, it was that someone *always* had a camera.

Kelly's face flushed a dark brick-red at Jodie's coldness.

"Sir, you'll need to take your seat," the attendant told him. Jodie didn't miss the flirtatious tone, or the way the teal-suited woman sized him up appreciatively as she led him to his seat. And as Kelly Wong took his place in the back row, Jodie kept her face like a mask, knowing the slightest crack would give her away.

Because under the rage and hurt and shame . . . she'd been glad to see him.

"You weren't wrong when you said she was afraid of flying," Tish said loudly, covering for her. "I've never seen someone go that shade of gray."

She wasn't wrong, either. Jodie *was* afraid of flying and she *did* go gray as they took off. It turned out Sydney was prone to thunderstorms in summer. The plane juddered and shook as they bumped their way upward in a steep climb. Jodie closed her eyes but that felt worse. Looking ahead was bad too, as she could see the angle of the plane and the violence of its bucking. She glanced sideways at the window. They were in the thick of the clouds. Seeing the shreds of pewter-gray clouds whip past only reinforced how fast they were going. It didn't help.

"Here, Jodie." Claude passed her a vomit bag. "Maybe you shouldn't have drunk those mimosas."

"Maybe I should have drunk more of them." Jodie flinched as the plane gave a rattle. She groped for Claude's hand. She refused to vomit in front of all these people. And any potential cameras.

"You're OK," Claude soothed.

"I know a fun fact that will help." His Sir-ship's face appeared above the seat in front. "Did you know turbulence won't bring down a plane?"

"Ever? Or it just hasn't *yet*?" Jodie groaned as the whole fuselage shimmied. *Let it end. Please let it end.*

The PA system buzzed and then the captain was speaking. Jodie braced for him to tell them that the plane was going down.

"Good afternoon, everyone, this is Captain Stef Nowak, welcoming you to our special New Year's scenic flight over Antarctica."

"Shouldn't he be flying the plane?" Jodie asked through gritted teeth as the plane gave another buck. The madman kept going on about the day ahead, about the catering and the open bar, and the special guest in first-class . . .

"Oh God," Jodie groaned, "fly the damn plane! No one needs to know!"

"Great," Maya murmured as she lowered her phone and checked the recording. "They *love* your modesty."

"Stop filming me!"

"Yeah, Maya," Tish echoed in a singsong voice, "stop filming her."

And then the plane broke through the clouds and the cabin was filled with brilliant sunshine.

"As soon as we level out," Captain Stef drawled, "we'll turn off the seat belt sign and you'll be free to move about the cabin. The flying time to Antarctica is just under three hours; do keep an eye out for icebergs on the way, they move in herds that can be pretty magnificent to see. Note that the windows on our Dreamliner are sixty-five-percent bigger than a normal craft, to give you a spectacular view of this unique continent today."

Claude squeezed Jodie's hand. "Can you imagine Bree?" she whispered. "How excited she'd be to be flying over Antarctica?" As Claude spoke, the plane leveled out and everything became very smooth.

Jodie closed her eyes in relief. The seat belt sign dinged, and she heard buckles unclipping and soft conversation and laughter. "Champagne time!" she heard Sir Ryan sing, as he got out of his chair and headed out into the cabin to greet the rest of his guests. She took a breath and opened her eyes. Right. That was it for the turbulence, for now. Now there was just the other turbulence to worry about . . .

Kelly Wong was sandwiched right in the middle of the back row of first-class. She couldn't see him from where she was, and she hoped like hell that he couldn't see her. Not when she was clutching a plastic vomit bag and having quiet hysterics.

"Jodie." Cheryl appeared, leaning into the row over Tish.

"Nice view," Tish said, appreciating the eyeful of cleavage her fiancée was offering.

Cheryl ignored her, her gaze fixed on Jodie. "I am *so* sorry. I didn't know he was coming." Cheryl's face was so pale that her lips looked redder than ever. "If I'd known, I would have told you."

"Oh *please*," Maya huffed from the seat in front, "as if he wasn't coming!"

Cheryl fixed Maya with a glittering gaze.

Jodie didn't want any of this. "I'm going to the bathroom." Oh God, there was Kelly. The minute she stood up, she saw him. She also saw him try to catch her eye. No way. She wasn't ready to acknowledge him. Even though they were stuck on a *twelve-hour flight* together.

Jodie felt completely cornered as she locked herself in the cubicle. At least first class had decent-sized bathrooms, she thought as she sat on the closed lid of the toilet and put her head in her hands. What was she going to *do*?

Maybe she could stay locked here in the bathroom all day? It was comfy. It had a window. A sixty-five-percent bigger-than-normal window, according to the captain. She could watch Antarctica from here . . .

Like a coward.

She was tired of being a coward. Besides, *he* was the one who should be hiding, not her. *She* hadn't done anything wrong. He should be running from her, not barging in on her bucket list like this, ruining her trip to Antarctica.

Don't wait, Jodie . . . jump.

Jodie flinched. Panic welled.

Jump.

No. She wasn't ready. The timing was wrong. She'd smash herself to bits.

Jodie checked herself in the mirror, and then straightened her shoulders and lifted her chin. She could face him. He wasn't that scary. He was just a guy.

A guy who happened to be right outside the door when she opened it. Jodie flinched. Which wasn't exactly the plan. She'd wanted to look like an ice queen. Like Claude when she was talking to Hopper. Not like a bunny rabbit faced with a fox.

"Hey." Kelly had taken his baseball cap off and his hair was ruffled. He obviously hadn't got the memo that this was a white-themed party, as he was in jeans and a blue T-shirt. He looked anxious and vulnerable.

"Well, hello." *Well, hello?* Why was she talking like an old schoolmarm? Who *spoke* like that?

Kelly seemed wary, and sad. "I . . ." He bit his lip. "I don't know what to say."

"I didn't listen to any of your messages," Jodie blurted. God, why was she telling him that? "Or read any of them." What the hell had happened to the ice queen? She'd melted like a snow cone in July. She should stop talking now, since she didn't seem to have any control of the words coming out of her mouth.

He looked startled. "None of them? You didn't listen to a single one?"

Don't talk. Don't talk. Don't talk. "No." Goddamn it.

"What about the video I texted you?" Kelly rubbed his hand through his hair. The muscles in his jaw twitched as he clenched and unclenched.

"I deleted everything." Jodie reminded herself to stand tall. Chin up. Ice queen. "Now if you'll excuse me . . ."

"Wait," he said, sounding a touch desperate. "So, you don't know anything about Jess or the divorce?"

Jess. God, the intimacy of it. The casualness.

Wait . . . What divorce?

"You didn't get any of . . ." Kelly closed his eyes and turned his face to the ceiling of the plane. She thought she heard him mutter something under his breath. Something very rude. He took a calming breath and then fixed her with a firm but patient look. "We need to talk."

"I'm busy right now," Jodie said tightly, gesturing at the first-class cabin through the passageway.

"No. No more busy. No more calls from your grandma, no kissing me stupid so I can't remember what I was saying, no running off to rehearsals, no deleting messages. We need to talk. Now." His gaze darted over her shoulder at the bathroom door. "Here," he said, dragging her in and locking the door.

"Let me out." Jodie extricated her arm from his grip. "And stop manhandling me."

Kelly held his hands in the air, in a gesture of peace. "I'm sorry, I shouldn't have done that." He stepped away from the door. "You can go at any time. But I'm asking you to stay and hear me out. Please. I've been trying to talk to you since after that first night in New York . . ."

That first night . . . he meant when they'd kissed. On her bed, to the soundtrack of *West Side Story*. The memory made Jodie feel floaty again. She didn't need that now. She needed a clear head.

"I wanted to tell you before anything happened," he said gently.

"Well, you didn't." He wasn't getting off the hook that easily. "You didn't tell me, and things did happen, and then your *wife* showed up."

"Ex-wife," he insisted.

"You're divorced?"

"Almost."

"Almost. Oh, fuck almost!" Jodie felt a surge of anger. See? It *was* just like the movies, they *did* string you along, keeping their wives and using you for sex. Just like goddamn Cooper and his self-serving hookups. "I have no intention of being your bit on the side!" She snapped open the lock and left him there in the bathroom.

"Can you believe the nerve of him?" she seethed to Claude and Cheryl and Tish, when she found them clumped in a group around the windows over the cabin door.

"Sooooo," Claude said, drawing the word out as she considered the implications once Jodie had unloaded her fury on them. "You're suggesting he's going to all this trouble . . . for a hookup?"

"Yes!"

"Right." Claude and Tish and Cheryl exchanged looks. Claude cleared her throat. "You do remember that he lives on the other side of the country from you, right?"

"Of course I do!" It was 2,806.6 miles away, to be precise. She'd looked it up. When she wasn't thinking about him.

"So he's hardly likely to be getting laid much if you're in Delaware and he's in Washington, is he?" Tish pointed out.

"He's a baseball player," Jodie said through gritted teeth. "He probably has girls all over."

"Right," Tish drawled, "because the Tacoma Whatsits—"

"Rainiers," Jodie supplied.

"—are likely to come to town to play the Wilmington Whosits regularly and he can come by for a hookup?"

"Wilmington doesn't have a AAA team," Jodie muttered.

"Jodie," Cheryl sighed, "can I just put you out of your misery right now, so we can stop talking about baseball?"

The three of them had closed ranks around Jodie, making sure her back was to the cabin and no one could get a shot of her face.

"Kelly Wong got married two years ago to a woman named Jessica Acker," Cheryl recited. "They got married in Vegas, on a whim, when they were on a weekend away before he moved to Arkansas to play for the Travelers."

Ouch. Jodie realized she didn't want *any* of these details. The image of it was vivid. She was picturing a gaudy pink-and-brass Chapel of Love, with a celebrant dressed as Elvis.

"She never moved to Arkansas, Jodie. And when he was moved up to the Rainiers in Washington, she never went there either. They've barely seen each other since the day they got married. And, may I add, they were drunk when they got married."

"How do you know all of this?" Jodie asked, suspicious.

"He told me. When I was vetting him before your piano lessons. And I checked it all out. I wasn't going to set you up with

a maniac. I've been vetting everyone. Unlike some people."
Cheryl sent Maya a dirty look. Maya didn't notice. She was all
the way across the plane, busy sucking up to Ryan.

"He just never got around to filing for the divorce," Tish told
Jodie.

"How do *you* know?"

"We hung out a lot in New York." She shrugged.

"*You* knew?" Tish had known, and Jodie hadn't. Jodie was
shaken. "Did *everyone* know?"

"He should have told you," Claude said gently.

Can we talk? He'd tried. Just maybe not hard enough.

"Cheryl!" Sir Ryan sang from across the room. "Stop mo-
nopolizing Jodie! She's the belle of the ball. Let her circulate."

Jodie didn't want to circulate. She was feeling overloaded.
She glanced around, hoping to triangulate Kelly's location. But
she couldn't see him anywhere.

Cheryl waved and smiled at His Sir-ship. "Don't worry," she
said under her breath to Jodie as she smiled and waved. "Remember the backup plan."

"You have parachutes?"

Cheryl laughed. "Come on. We're going to see the captain.
It'll be quiet. Just you and the crew. No three-ring circus."

That sounded good to Jodie.

"Just going for a photo op with the captain," Cheryl said
brightly as she sailed Jodie past Ryan and Maya. Maya scowled.

"Great idea!" His Sir-ship said, beaming. "Fantastic work."

The corridor was empty. Where had Kelly gone? Was he still
in the bathroom? Jodie glanced at the lock. It wasn't engaged.
Maybe *he'd* found a parachute . . .

Married in Vegas. Pink and brass and Elvis.

Cheryl had the attendant let them into the cockpit. It was
like something out of a *Star Wars* movie. Only more high-tech.
Everywhere she looked Jodie could see screens and buttons and
radars and steering wheel things and so many instruments of
possible death that it made her blood run cold. There were a lot
of systems here. And systems could fail.

"Welcome," the captain said. God, he was ridiculously good-looking.

Too good-looking, as Bree would have said.

"I'll leave you in Stef's capable hands," Cheryl said, slipping out. The attendant remained to take the crew's food orders.

The captain introduced Jodie to his first officer, a practical-looking woman named Vashti. He'd turned around in his seat to talk to Jodie.

"Shouldn't you be flying the plane?" Jodie asked nervously.

Captain Stef laughed. "Vashti's got it under control, don't you, Vash?"

"It's highly automated," his first officer reassured Jodie. Jodie was more reassured by the way she didn't take her eyes off all the blinking things.

"Ever been in a cockpit before?" Captain Stef asked Jodie. He assumed the answer was no before she could speak and went on to explain all the blinking things and compasses and altimeters and all the other possible death traps Jodie didn't want to know about. Jodie thought she caught Vashti roll her eyes. After a while, Jodie realized the captain was trying to flirt with her. He was just really bad at it. Maybe good-looking people didn't need to be good at flirting? Maybe people just fell in their laps?

He seemed to think showing off his plane would be a turn-on. It really wasn't. But Jodie might get to see icebergs through the cockpit window. That was kind of cool.

She stood behind his chair and peered through the window at the frigid ocean below.

"Icebergs!" Jodie felt a shiver of enchantment as she spied them.

"Oh, where?" The flight attendant pulled her phone out. "This is my first time on this flight," she told Jodie as she squeezed in next to her at the window.

"There's more over here too," Vashti told them.

The attendant changed sides, trying to get a good picture.

Jodie watched in awe as the stately blue icebergs migrated like a herd of slow-moving mammoths. They must have been huge; they dwarfed the waves, which were reduced to looking like creases in paper. The crystalline hearts of the icebergs glowed turquoise and aquamarine, and rills of white foamed at their bases as they cut through the water, carving patterns on a cold sea the color of oxidized copper.

"Of course it's summer in the southern hemisphere right now. If we were here in winter, there would be more of them." Captain Stef leaned left so he could speak to her around the chair.

More. Imagine. Jodie tried to picture an ocean full of milky bergs. She felt the magic Bree was chasing when she put Antarctica on her bucket list. "When will we see the shore?" she asked, searching the horizon.

"Another couple of hours. There should be hors d'oeuvres served soon, and the band should start . . ."

"Band?" Jodie was genuinely surprised.

"It's New Year's Eve." Captain Stef laughed. "Of course there's a band. Just a little jazz trio, but it wouldn't be New Year's without a band."

He fell silent and Jodie was able to have a few minutes of iceberg appreciation, before he went and ruined it.

"You ever dated a pilot, Jodie?" Captain Stef asked softly.

Oh God. This dude changed gears at the speed of light. He was giving her a look that was clearly supposed to be seductive. It wasn't.

"I could show you the world," he murmured, trying to hold her gaze.

"Calm down, Aladdin." Jodie straightened up, away from the window. She hoped for his sake the attendant hadn't got any of that on camera. "Thanks for the tour. Loved the icebergs. Better get back before I miss the band." She got out of there before he could say anything else. "Cheryl, where do you find these people?" she demanded, when she ran into her standing guard outside the cockpit.

Cheryl pressed her red lips together, trying not to laugh. She shrugged. "He looked good in a uniform, and he passed the airline's psych test."

"Low bar, Cheryl." Jodie took a minute to collect herself.

Kelly Wong was still out there, unless he'd found a parachute. "They were drunk when they got married?" she blurted.

"Tipsy at least." Cheryl cocked her head. "Haven't you ever done anything impulsive, that you regretted later?"

Yes, she had. Deleting fifty-seven messages without listening to them.

Chapter 41

As the New Year's Eve party unfolded around her in the long summer day of the South Pole, Jodie tried to focus on Bree's original bucket list. *99. Fly over Antarctica.* Who cared that Kelly was slumped against the window in the back row of first class? Who cared that he hadn't approached her again? Who cared that Maya kept trying to take sneaky photos of her? Out there beyond the glass was Antarctica, just as Bree had dreamed about.

Jodie rested her forehead against the window and watched the continent unfold beneath her. There was a tour guide you could listen to on the radio channel, who told you about explorers like Mawson, the race to the pole, the laws about how to approach penguins, and the dire effects of climate change. Which she could see with her own eyes in the expanses of snowless ground, where the permafrost was melting in the unseasonable warmth. Jodie drank it all in.

She ate when Claude passed her food and drank when Tish handed her a glass of champagne, but otherwise she devoted herself to the view below. She kept thinking about her sister and all the videos. About the hours she must have spent setting all of this up. Arranging this flight, filming messages of encouragement. Knowing she was dying. Knowing she would never see the effects of her actions or know if it ever came to fruition. Knowing Jodie would see Antarctica in her place.

God, she missed her sister.

"Nearly there," Cheryl said, as they banked for the last time, turning away from the coast and back toward Australia. She slid into the seat beside Jodie. "That's the bucket list almost done." She peered over Jodie's shoulder, out the window. "I wish Bree could have been here." The note of regret in her voice was keen.

"How did you meet Bree?" Jodie asked abruptly. "How did this all . . ." Jodie shrugged, gesturing to the festivities around them.

Cheryl smiled. It was an expression of happiness *and* pain, all at once. "We met in Mexico. Bree and me and Tish. In fact, I met Tish the same day I met Bree."

Jodie was blindsided. That wasn't at all the answer she was expecting. She wasn't expecting Cheryl to exist that early in the "before Bree's death" timeline.

"You know that photo your mom has on the mantel? The one of Bree about to jump off the La Quebrada cliffs?" Cheryl said. "I took that."

Jodie knew the image by heart. Bree's joy, her arms thrown wide, the glitter of the ocean behind her. The image had all of the visceral beauty of Cheryl's photography.

"All three of us went there to jump." Cheryl smiled, lost in memory. "We met on the bus on the way there. But only Bree jumped. Tish and I chickened out and went and had a beer in the restaurant instead. One thing led to another . . . and here we are." Cheryl's gaze drifted to Tish and the smile twitched. Cheryl was plainly in love.

"I just thought . . . I thought it was a business relationship," Jodie said, feeling unsteady. "I thought you'd met because of the bucket list."

"It was a business relationship. The best kind. The kind with a friend." Cheryl swiped a couple of champagne glasses off a passing tray. "Here's to Bree," she said.

They clinked glasses and drank.

"When you lose someone, you lose everything about them," Jodie said, thinking about all of Bree's memories, all of the untold stories of her life, all the things Jodie would never know about her sister.

"Not everything. Not their love." Cheryl's hand settled on Jodie's arm. She squeezed. "You know what Bree did with this list, Jodie?"

"Paid off our debt."

"Well, yes, but not just that. She got you out of your grief and into the world. She got your parents out of their obsession with her and got them focused on you. She made you cook Thanksgiving and Christmas feasts, and made you go to New York and Antarctica. She got you out of that airport car-rental stand and actually on a plane. That's all proof that love doesn't die." She clinked her glass against Jodie's again. "And in a moment, it will be a whole new year."

"A year Bree never lived in."

"But a year you do." Cheryl craned her neck and looked back at the last row. "A year he does too." Cheryl snagged another passing champagne. "Here, Kelly looks like he needs this." Cheryl gave it to Jodie and then disappeared again.

Jodie sat there holding both glasses, scowling at them. She didn't like being managed.

She stood up. Then sat down again. Part of her wanted to go over there. Part of her wanted to dump both glasses on his head.

It had hurt so much. And it had been so humiliating.

Can we talk?

She scrunched her eyes closed. He'd tried to talk to her. And he'd left fifty-seven messages after she'd run away from New York. That wasn't counting the text messages either. And she hadn't talked to him or listened to him. Or even acknowledged him.

This was what she *did*, she realized. This was her pattern. She ran away from things. She sabotaged them before they could even begin. It was the same reason she wasn't playing baseball. The same reason she'd spent years working at that car-rental stand. She just *ran*.

Vaguely, she realized the jazz trio had slid into playing a familiar song. *It's very clear . . . our love is here to stay . . .* And she had a glass of champagne in each hand. And he was *here*, and so was she. And New Year's was a time for new beginnings. She stood up. She couldn't see him through the press of bodies in the aisles, but she knew he was in the back row. If she could only fight her way there.

Her heart was shuddering like the plane had earlier in the turbulence. For some reason she kept thinking of the New Year's scene in *When Harry Met Sally*, when Harry came barging into the party after running the whole way there. *And it's not because I'm lonely, and it's not because it's New Year's Eve. I came here tonight because when you realize you want to spend the rest of your life with somebody, you want the rest of your life to start as soon as possible.* She was still mad, she reminded herself. But not so mad she didn't want to spend tonight with him. Or maybe the rest of her life . . .

When she reached his aisle, she cleared her throat.

He looked up, bleary-eyed with jet lag.

"Can we talk?" She used his words, unable to keep the chagrin out of her voice. She held out the glass of champagne.

He just looked at it. "I did talk," he said, his red-flecked eyes flicking up to her. "I talked fifty-seven times, and in a litany of text messages. And then I flew for the best part of two days, on *four* separate flights, to make this scenic circus, just so I could talk to you. And you didn't want to. You've never wanted to."

Jodie felt an inch tall.

"You're grieving, I get it," he said. He was holding his jacket tight, like he needed it for protection. Against her. "You're in the middle of this crazy bucket list, and nothing is normal. I get it. I do. But, you know what, Boyd? You're not the only one." His voice cracked.

Jodie felt herself turn rubbery with horror. The look on his face. It wasn't anger. It was something much worse.

"You're not the only one who lost someone, and you're not the only one who's hurting."

Kelly Wong was raw with grief.

"You're not the only one who had to face Christmas without the person you love, who has to get up every day and go through the motions, knowing you'll never get another message, never answer another call, never land at the airport to see them waiting for you at the gate."

Jodie remembered Mr. Wong's long serious face, the way he peered over his spectacles, bewildered by her wrong notes. She remembered the way he smelled of simple soap, and paper, and tea. Those countless cups of tea, which sat all over the room, half-finished. He'd make a fresh cup, and forget about it, absorbed in his lessons.

Kelly Wong had lost his father. And Jodie had known him. Yet she'd gone on, as though his death was nothing much at all.

Jodie had known it must have been hard for him, to sit at his father's piano, to play his father's sheet music, to be dragged into Jodie's public three-ring circus. But knowing and understanding were two very different things.

"Why don't you read the messages and *then* we'll talk." Kelly Wong closed himself tightly, and turned back to the window.

But they both knew she couldn't read his messages. Because she'd deleted them. "Kelly . . ."

"No," he snapped. "I have nothing more to say to you." And then he put his headphones on and dismissed her entirely.

As she stood there, holding the champagne, Jodie felt the world telescoping away from her. She turned and wanted to run but there was nowhere to go. Nowhere. There was nothing but a sea of people.

And then she caught Ryan's eye. He was close enough to have witnessed everything, she realized, feeling sick. And he had, judging by the compassion on his face.

Oh God, she needed to get out of here. Out of *this*.

Bree . . .

"Jodie!" Ryan Lasseter had moved to cut the band off and was beckoning Jodie. The plane fell quiet, and everyone turned to look at her. What the hell was he doing?

Jodie felt like she'd been cast in cement.

"Get up here, Jodie!" Ryan shone in his white linen suit. He held out a hand in invitation.

Jodie felt her feet moving of her own accord. What else could she do? She couldn't stay near Kelly. He didn't deserve it. His grief deserved the dignity of privacy. A dignity she'd been too self-absorbed to grant him before. Sir Ryan took the champagne out of her hand, the glass meant for Kelly. She felt the concrete cracking. No. She wouldn't cry in front of these people and their cameras. She *wouldn't*.

"I have had an exceptional idea for us to ring in the New Year," Ryan announced, putting his arm around Jodie. "As you know, this flight wraps up the penultimate item on the bucket list that we at Iris have been pleased to sponsor. A campaign, I might add, that has been nominated for numerous marketing awards. Three cheers for our team, headed by the wonderful Cheryl Pegler."

Cheryl turned rosy with pleasure as the plane cheered her.

But all Jodie could think about was Mr. Wong, her old piano teacher, and Kelly Wong, his son, who was sitting there in an ocean of grief, listening to all these people cheer.

"And further congratulations are in order," Ryan continued, "as our dear Cheryl has finally snagged the woman of her dreams. Tish, you're a lucky woman. Three cheers again for the lovebirds on their engagement."

Jodie saw Tish spit champagne in shock.

Cheryl's mouth fell open. "You knew?"

Ryan lifted his champagne glass and winked at her. "You can't hide anything in the age of social media," he said cheekily. "Now . . ." He turned back to his audience. Jodie was frozen under the weight of his arm. "As you're all aware, more than a million people are holding out to know *who* the person will be to let Jodie tick number one hundred off the list."

There were cheers and whistles. Jodie felt the blood drain from her face. Somewhere behind that wall of white-clad bodies was Kelly. And Jodie's heart was over there on the floor next to him, in the back row of first class.

Ryan ducked his head, so his lips were next to Jodie's ear. "Trust me," he whispered. "This is for the best."

What was for the best? Jodie turned and met his blue gaze. It was full of compassion.

"This year Iris Air lost a magical brand ambassador in Bree

Boyd," Sir Ryan said. His arm lowered from Jodie's shoulders to her waist. As though he thought he might need to hold her up. "And Jodie lost a sister."

Jodie met Claude's eyes across the plane. Claude's face reflected her own shock. And apprehension.

"When Bree asked us to sponsor Jodie to finish her bucket list, we never could have imagined the past few weeks."

A hush fell over the crowd.

"It's been quite an adventure Jodie has taken us on. And we thank her for it." He gave her a squeeze. "It's been a privilege for us to be allowed into her life, and to be given snapshots into her love for her sister." He cleared his throat. Jodie could feel the strength of him beside her. "Tonight, Jodie has completed the second-to-last item on the bucket list—the list Bree wrote."

There was a smattering of applause.

"There is one more item on the list . . ."

Jodie had no idea where he was going with this, but she didn't think she'd like it. She felt numb. Wrecked. She couldn't even gather the energy to run for the bathroom and hide.

"But it strikes me," Sir Ryan mused, "that number one hundred on the list is none of our damn business."

What?

Jodie looked up at him, shocked.

"Bree wrote the list," Ryan said. "It was *her* string of dreams."

Jodie felt tears rising.

"But Jodie is not Bree. She has her own dreams. And I, for one, cannot wait to see her realize them. But I feel I would be an ass to hold back the money until the day Jodie falls in love, and even more of an ass to make her prove it to us before she should receive payment. That's not how life should work. Not for anyone. Jodie's feelings are hers . . . we have no right to them." He lifted his glass of champagne. "So, as we ring in the New Year, I'd like to announce the bucket list completed!"

The plane erupted into cheers.

Jodie felt like she'd been thrown off her feet by an earthquake. "But it's not," she said, "it's not completed."

As the cheers bled into the New Year countdown, Ryan

pulled Jodie closer. "Bree loved you," he said softly, so only she could hear. "And your family. As far as I'm concerned, she already ticked off the final item on that list. And you have more than shown your love for her. Romantic love isn't the only kind of love worth having."

"But I haven't finished it," she said, starting to cry. "Don't you understand? I have to finish *something*."

"Jodie." He sighed, pressing his forehead to hers. "You can do anything you put your mind to. And one day, you will fall in love, and the list will be complete. But you don't need to prove it to me or anyone. The debts are paid. The rest is up to you."

Chapter 42

17. Plant a Tree

100. Fall in Love

The poor spruce didn't even make it to spring. It was a dead husk within two months. And because of its size, it cost a fortune to remove.

"Maybe we should send Sir Whatshisface the bill?" Aunt Pat suggested. "He was nice. I'm sure he'd pay it. I'm sure he'd *want* to pay for it."

"Let's not." Jodie's dad had been more than happy to see the last of Sir Ryan and Iris Air. "We'll put it on the card and pay it off. If we pull some extra shifts, we'll have it done in no time." Especially because Sir Ryan had kept his word and all Bree's medical debts were no more. Not only Bree's. Sir Ryan had gone above and beyond and paid more than he'd promised. He and Jodie had visited each of the families from Bree's ward, quietly, without a single post on social media. Some families were grieving, others had ongoing treatments, and a couple, miraculously, had their loved ones recovered, healthy and well. But all of them were handed a check big enough to make a significant dent in their debt. Afterwards, Ryan and Jodie had tracked down Wanda, Bree's favorite orderly, and given her an all-expenses-paid first-class trip, courtesy of Iris Air. She was well overdue for a vacation.

Afterwards, Jodie could see the appeal of being rich. It felt good to give people things. Although the way Wanda talked about Claude's bunting of Thanksgiving leaves made her realize that just stringing a few leaves on twine was an option, if you couldn't afford to give someone first-class tickets.

Once the dead Christmas tree was gone, Jodie finally had the tree planting she wanted. They didn't film it or upload it anywhere, although Mom took a photo for the family album. The yard was a mess of mud from the backhoe pushing the dirt back into the huge hole left by the spruce. Jodie had picked out a tree herself. She'd gone to the garden center and wandered around looking for a dogwood to please her mom. But then she'd seen a cluster of twisty trees, black plastic sheeting wrapped around their roots, and she knew immediately that was what she wanted. A bridesmaid tree.

Crepe myrtle. She read the tag. It wasn't a shrub, and it wasn't an evergreen. It had masses of flowers in spring; hot-coal bright leaves in fall; spreading branches to cast shade. Exactly what Bree had asked for. And, every time Jodie looked at it, she would be transported back to a day when she was happy, walking down the High Line with Kelly Wong. Before they'd fucked it all up.

Jodie dug the hole and planted the tree herself. She'd watered it every day since, on her own. As she did, she had long, rambling conversations with Bree. And for the first time since the whole bucket list began, she felt a measure of peace. It was Bree's tree, and it was hers. It was the first thing that was truly part of both of them.

When Cheryl visited, bringing Bree's final messages to everyone instead of posting them online, she stopped to admire the tree. "It'll be OK?" she asked, worried. "It's not too early to plant it?"

"So they said at the garden center. As long as the ground is thawed. And look, it's an early spring." She pointed to Cheryl's red twig dogwood, which was covered in new growth.

Cheryl pulled a face. "Sorry about that one."

"Don't worry about it. Mom loves it. She says it's the exact same color as your lipstick."

Cheryl laughed at that. Then they went inside and began the sad business of formally wrapping up the bucket list.

"It's not over," Grandma Gloria said stubbornly, "not until Jodie does number one hundred. We've done the tree, but there's still the last one to go."

Jodie shrugged. She didn't bother to correct her. Grandma Gloria was wrong, she just didn't know it. *Number one hundred says fall in love . . . it doesn't say they have to love you back.* That's what Bree had said in her message. And Jodie had fallen in love, over and over and over again. With the same man. It just hadn't worked out. And Ryan had known. He'd known and he'd offered her a way out. Privately.

She'd thanked him. They had a quiet beer together after they'd wrapped up all their loose ends.

"Don't mention it," Ryan said, waving away her thanks. "I should never have let it get as far as it did. That last item . . . listening to Maya talk about who you were going to kiss at midnight . . ." He pushed his hair back off his face and groaned. "A performing seal . . ."

It felt good that he saw it. That he understood.

"What are you going to do now?" he'd asked. "Now that you're debt-free and captain of your own fate?"

"I don't know." She'd half laughed, half moaned. "I have no idea."

"I don't believe that," he told her. "You strike me as someone who knows their own mind."

"Not yet. But I hope to." She took a sip of her beer. "One day."

"Well, if you ever need a friend, just give me call." He slid her a business card.

She hadn't called him. But she'd thought about it.

"Bree says to watch these last messages on Valentine's Day," Cheryl told the Boyds as she went through the last of Bree's material with them back in Wilmington. "Also Easter, Mother's Day, Father's Day, your birthdays, and then there's a couple more at the end, one for Thanksgiving and one for Christmas. All the big events for a full calendar year. She filmed them out of order, so you might notice sometimes she looks fine and sometimes she doesn't. They're all labeled." Cheryl handed the portable hard drive over to Jodie's mom. "And if anything happens to that, I have backups, OK? You just call me."

"And none of it's going online?" Jodie asked suspiciously.

"None of it. I've changed all the passwords to Bree's accounts, so it's frozen in perpetuity. Here they are. You'll be the only one with them." She eyed Jodie. "You sure you don't want me to take it down?"

"No," Jodie's mom blurted. "No, leave it. It's all that's left of her."

"Not all, Mom." Jodie gave her a one-armed hug. "We've got photos, and her collection of Homecoming and Prom Queen crowns. And memories." But she shook her head and mouthed *We'll leave it up* at Cheryl. Jodie could put up with the fact that some of her most embarrassing moments were frozen in time on that Instagram account, if it made her mom happy.

"Here, I brought this." Cheryl fished a bottle out of her hand luggage. "I thought we should celebrate the official ending of the bucket list. Everyone's a champagne girl," Cheryl reminded Jodie with a twinkle, handing her the bottle.

"Nah," Jodie said ruefully. "I don't think I am. I've tried it. It's OK. But I'm just as happy with beer."

"Fine, you and your father have beer," Jodie's mom said, fetching the wineglasses. "The rest of us will have a taste."

"She won't drink it, you watch," Jodie warned Cheryl. "She'll have one sip and decide she'd rather have a whiskey sour."

It turned out only Grandma Gloria was a champagne kind of girl. "I'm glad someone likes it," Cheryl said with a wave as she bid them farewell. Jodie walked her out to her cab.

"Don't think you're getting rid of me this easily," Cheryl warned. "You better come to the wedding. La Quebrada cliffs in Mexico this fall."

"I wouldn't miss it for the world." Even if she did have to fly there.

Cheryl laughed. "I think that deserves some European kisses." She gave Jodie three resounding kisses: left cheek, right cheek, left cheek. "I promise we'll have beer at the wedding, you won't have to drink champagne."

"For you I might drink it."

"Send me pictures of the tree when it eventually flowers?"

"You know it." Jodie was going to miss Hurricane Cheryl. She'd got used to some wild weather.

"And don't forget to message me when you fall in love!"

Nah. That wasn't going to happen. Jodie waved Cheryl off, feeling the eerie silence settle, like the morning after a storm.

Chapter 43

Nerves are good, remember? They help you perform. Good luck!

Jodie was too nervous to message Jonah back. She'd do it later.

"Don't forget to tell them how many followers you have. They'll love it." Ryan had forgone a driver and was driving them himself. He'd rented a car from her company at the Sea-Tac terminal. Being Ryan, he was having enormous fun zipping his way through Seattle.

Being Jodie, she was dying of fear. Her hands had frozen into claws around her new leather folder. Which contained her skimpy résumé.

"And don't forget to tell them that you managed a major brand campaign."

"But I didn't!" she protested.

"Sure, you did. You took it over. By the end you were doing everything."

"Throwing a mediocre photo up on Instagram doesn't count as 'everything.'"

"And the hit rates! That was one hundred percent down to your authenticity. You took a contrived campaign and gave it heart and soul—people responded to that."

Jodie put the window down a crack so she could gulp at the fresh air. Seattle in January was cold. Puget Sound was choppy, and thunderclouds tumbled in stacks above the city. It wasn't too different from home. She could do this.

Good luck, peanut.

Dad. It was the third time he'd messaged. He was almost as nervous as she was.

Claude and Tish and Cheryl had bombarded her with messages all morning too.

She couldn't answer any of them.

Mom hadn't messaged, but only because Grandma Gloria had taken her phone away. Jodie bet she'd worn a groove in the carpet from pacing.

"Don't forget to concentrate on your body language," Ryan coached her. "Walk tall, shoulders back, direct gaze, take up space." He zipped into a park by the stadium office. "Say hi to Carolyn for me."

Ryan had wrangled the meeting for her, with the director of marketing for the Seattle Mariners. When she'd finally called Ryan and told him what she was thinking, he'd taken her more seriously than she'd anticipated. She'd just been looking for advice. But Ryan was a doer. And now here she was, on the doorstep of a major league team.

"You're not coming in?" Jodie squeaked. She looked up at T-Mobile Park.

"Nope. You're a big girl. Off you go." He grinned at her. "You'll be great."

This was insane. Jodie was overcome with the craziness of it as she stepped through the door into the front office. The sense of being in a dream only intensified when security ticked her name off a list and buzzed her through, and when she was greeted warmly and led into a meeting room.

She sat there, in her new clothes, and new shoes, holding her new leather folder.

You can do it, Smurfette. I'm with you all the way.

Jodie straightened her shoulders and took up room. And when Carolyn came in, Jodie made sure she gave a firm handshake. Somehow, despite a storm of nerves, she managed to keep her voice calm.

"Have you got any experience with sports marketing?" Carolyn asked her, as she thumbed through Jodie's thin résumé.

Don't forget to tell them you managed a major brand campaign . . . authentically . . . with hit rates through the roof! She remembered Ryan's advice. She just chose not to listen to it.

Instead, she told Carolyn about the bucket list. About Exercise Science at Delaware Tech. About being a girl playing varsity ball. In short, she told Carolyn about herself.

"It went well then?" Ryan hooted, already preparing to celebrate as she skipped out of the building and toward the rental car.

"I did it!" she exploded. "I wanted to be sick, I was so nervous, but I *did it!*"

"Of course you did." Ryan laughed.

Jodie was wriggling like Russel Sprout discovering a new pair of shoes.

"So, when do you start?" Ryan asked. "And where shall we go to celebrate?"

"Oh, I didn't get a job," Jodie said, surprised he'd thought so. "Not yet. But she said she'd think about it and get back to me."

Ryan laughed. "It's not a no then!"

"Even if it is a no this time, it might not be *next* time!"

"Atta girl!"

Chapter 44

Jodie was working extra shifts to pay off the spruce, which was why she was working the car-rental stand on Valentine's Day. The airport was busy in waves, piping sappy love songs over the PA, every store stocked with chocolates and roses and cards. Even the doughnut stall was selling heart-shaped doughnuts.

"Nice shirt," she said to a passerby, who was rocking a "Calm Down, Aladdin" T-shirt. The passerby barely looked at her. The meme and the T-shirt had outlived Jodie's fame, thank God. People knew the phrase but didn't remember who had said it. Which suited Jodie just fine. It probably suited poor old Captain Stef just fine too. Social media had moved on; the circus had found a new town in which to pitch its tents. Life was as it should be. Or it would be as soon as she could find a baseball team that would take her.

Her phone buzzed and she reached for it, grinning in anticipation. It was probably Claude. She must have come home to find the Valentine's bunting that Jodie had strung up all around her apartment. It had taken hours to cut out that many stupid pink and silver hearts, and then hours more to punch holes in them and string them up. It had been worth it, though. Claude's place had been a girly lovey wonderland by the time Jodie had left. And the place had been clean for the first time in ages. Which had actually taken Jodie just about as long as making the bunting had.

But the message wasn't from Claude.

It was from *Kelly Wong*.

Kelly Wong was messaging her. On Valentine's Day.

Jodie's heart was all out of time. It felt like it might actually forget how to beat at all.

I got your messages, Boyd.

He'd gotten her messages. Jodie felt like a fly ball was coming straight at her.

She'd been terrified sending those messages, but she'd done it anyway. She couldn't get the image of him out of her mind, that day on the plane over Antarctica. The look on his face.

She'd hurt him. Badly.

The thing is, she'd written, in one of the long, apologetic messages she'd finally screwed up the courage to send, *my whole life I've been too scared to swing for the ball. And when I finally got a ball in the strike zone, I struck out.* That hadn't been blunt enough. *I screwed up, Kelly. I should have read your messages. And I should have known you were grieving too. I got so wrapped up in myself, I forgot you were suffering.*

That felt clean. It was a scary-good feeling. There was nothing to hide anymore.

All that talk of teams . . . Team Tish, Team Ryan . . . Team You . . . If I'd been properly on Team Kelly I should have read your messages. Hell, I should have been on my own team, you know? But I never was. I have to learn to be on Team Jodie. And Team Jodie would have read your messages. And answered your calls.

She'd sent all those messages into the ether. And waited.

And waited.

And she'd felt his silence keenly.

But now here he was.

You were serious about deleting all my messages, huh?

Of course she'd been serious! Oh my God. What did she write back? What did she *say*? Did she prostrate herself? Say something funny? Type *I LOVE YOU* in all caps? Beg him to forgive her?

Before she could decide, her phone buzzed again. Another message from *Kelly Wong*.

Lucky for you I have everything I sent right here on my phone.

What did that mean?

I'll forward you everything. Once you've read it all, you can decide if you want to talk to me or not. You know how to reach me.

Jodie had to sit down on the stool behind the counter.
Buzz.

p.s. Happy Valentine's Day. Don't go kissing anyone.

Jodie couldn't stop grinning. She felt like someone had sent her a dozen roses. No, better. She felt like *Kelly Wong* had sent her a dozen roses. Every few minutes her phone buzzed, until she had seventy-eight text messages. Had she really deleted so many?

Had he really *sent* so many?

He had. Long, thoughtful explanations. Desperate pleas. Jokes. He'd tried every single way he could to get her to hear him. And she'd deleted each and every one. Including the last one, which simply read:

Everything I feel is here.

It was followed by a short video. It was their duet. A lump rose in Jodie's throat as she watched it. They were in silhouette, the dim jellyfish chandelier chased with reflections from the New York lights; the song was languid and full of longing; Kelly's voice was smooth as butter. But his *face*.

It was the face of a man in love.

"Kelly," Jodie in the video whispered, "I'm going to kiss you now." And then it cut.

Jodie, he'd said, *I'm going to let you.*

The video had never made it to social media, she realized. Kelly had never once exploited her. He didn't offer her up, *them* up, to two million strangers. The moment was theirs alone. And it didn't only show everything *he* felt; it showed everything she felt too.

Chapter 45

"Look at all the roses!" In the Valentine's Day video Bree turned the camera on her hospital room, which was filled to the brim with roses. Mostly red, but some pink. Except for the one blaze of yellow. Jodie had balked and bought her daffodils instead. Bree had spent her last Valentine's Day in the hospital, but it looked like she'd had a good one.

"She was filming these early in the game, wasn't she?" Aunt Pat observed. "And she looks well, doesn't she?"

For the length of the video Bree *was* well again, chattering about love and flowers, telling stories about Valentine's past. Jodie chewed on her nails while she watched it. She couldn't concentrate. Her phone was burning a hole in her pocket. She wanted to keep rereading Kelly's messages. Every time she read them she saw something new.

You used to wear a necklace with a J on it. Really delicate little gold chain. It glinted in the sun when you were on the field. I used to wonder who gave it to you.

Bree had given it to her. When she was fifteen. How did he remember details like that, from so long ago?

I was so in love with you . . .

"I hope you all got flowers this year," Bree said.

Better than flowers. She'd got his thoughts.

"I hope you *gave* flowers too."

Jodie stood stock-still. Yes. It was time. She had to give now. Something better than flowers.

"Not one of her best," Pat said, once the video was done.

"Pat!" Jodie's mom scolded. "It's not a TV show, you don't review it."

"Well, it wasn't."

"It was early in the game," Jodie's dad rumbled. "She was probably just getting the hang of it. She just wanted to make sure we weren't lonely on the holidays."

"Claude." Jodie pulled Claude away from the ridiculous conversation about the video. "I need to talk to you."

"Sure."

"Not here. Grab your coat." Jodie stuck her head in the kitchen, where they'd all retired for coffee and cookies, still arguing over the merits of Bree's video. "Claude and I are popping out." She was out of there before they could ask questions. She whisked Claude along with her.

"Where are we going?" Claude asked.

"Chili's."

Their local Chili's had barely changed since high school. They were lucky to get a table, as it was Valentine's Day. "Can we have a couple of kids' placemats?" Jodie asked as they slid into a booth.

"You want to order something?"

She didn't. But she could hardly be there without ordering something, so she ordered a beer.

"What are we doing here?" Claude asked, but Jodie could tell that she already had an inkling.

"I need to make some decisions about my life." Jodie called the waitress back. "Hey, we need some pens with these placemats."

The waitress rolled her eyes and dropped off a couple of blunt pencils. They'd have to do.

"What kind of decisions?"

"*All of them.* Where am I going to live? Who am I going to love? Where do I want to travel? What do I want to *do*?"

"You might need more placemats." Claude flagged the waitress and ordered a beer too. "I think I'm going to need it."

"Bree managed it on one, so can I." Jodie flipped the placemat over and stared at the blank expanse of white paper.

Claude sighed and flipped her own page over. Jodie bent over and scrawled. It turned out she had a lot of things she wanted to do.

"What have you got?" Claude asked, curious.

"You first."

Claude flushed. Then she turned her placemat around.

1. Go on a date with Hopper
2. Go on a second date with Hopper
3. Keep doing it

Jodie laughed. "That's a *good* list."

"And what about yours, dweeb?"

Jodie turned her own around.

1. Baseball and Kelly Wong

"You're doing it wrong," Claude told her. "Those are two separate things."

"They don't have to be." Jodie grinned. "I'm going to work for a baseball team *and* I'm going to get Kelly Wong. They tie for first."

2. Figure out how to tell the family I'm moving to Seattle (or if the Mariners don't take me, somewhere else).

"You're just moving there? Like that? You don't want to visit first?"

"I have visited."

"One afternoon doesn't count as a visit."

"No," Jodie said firmly. "I don't need to visit. I'm just going to jump."

Chapter 46

Jodie didn't tell him about her new job, or that she was coming. She packed up her stuff and moved all the way across the country, all on her own. She got herself settled into a studio apartment in Fremont; it had a view of treetops and a glimpse of the water, but best of all, it was only a thirty-minute ride on her new bike to her new job at T-Mobile Park.

Jodie was only a junior social media coordinator for now, but she had her eye on bigger things. She'd transferred from her associate's degree at Delaware Tech to a full degree in Kinesiology at Seattle U, which she was doing part-time while she worked. She was psyching herself up to introduce herself to Tammy Stead, the coordinator of sports science at the Mariners, but she was also paying attention to the other roles. It turned out it took a lot of people to get a team on the field. There were opportunities to learn and to figure out where she belonged.

On the first day of spring training Jodie was sent to take photos of the AAA teams for the socials. She went along with Dominic from Player Development and Taylor from Scouting. It was her second week on the job, and she was nervous about being responsible for the multiple social media accounts, the bible of hashtags, and the branding of the teams.

But most of all she was nervous because it was the first time she would see Kelly Wong since the flight over Antarctica.

As she followed Dom and Taylor across the grass to the stands, her heart was in her throat. She ran a hand down the zipper on her jacket, wondering if she'd be brave enough to follow through. She'd bought a Team Kelly T-shirt online. She'd actually bought a whole bunch of them, figuring she might get a lifetime of use out of them if she was lucky. She had to wear a jacket over it on the way to the field, so her coworkers didn't think she was a crazy fangirl. As the three of them settled in the stands, Jodie listened to them discuss the merits of the Rainiers lineup. A lineup that included Kelly Wong.

Jodie felt her heart pounding as he ran out onto the field. God, he looked good. Fit, even though he was coming out of the off-season. And look at the way he moved. He made every pitch look like ballet.

Kelly didn't see her for a few innings. Jodie gnawed on Cracker Jacks nervously, snapping photos for the feed, penciling scores into a makeshift scorecard, and rehearsing speeches in her head. Apologies, mostly. Around the fifth inning, someone pointed out the scout from the Mariners up in the stands. Kelly turned to look. And then he saw her.

He looked like someone had whanged him dead on the helmet with a fly ball.

Once he was off the field, he made a beeline for the stands. Forget Taylor the scout, he couldn't take his eyes off Jodie. He leaned against the railing.

"What are you doing here?" He didn't seem to know how to feel, judging by his expression.

Courage, Sporty Smurf.

"I'm working." She braved a grin and tugged on her Mariner's cap. "I got a job in Seattle."

"A job in Seattle . . ."

Jodie was aware of Dom and Taylor watching them curiously. Oh well. She was used to an audience.

"When you didn't answer the messages . . ." A shadow of pain crossed his face.

"Wong!" The coach didn't look pleased to see Kelly off chatting up a girl in the stands.

"I gotta get back." Kelly backed away. Then he pointed his gloved hand at her. "Don't go anywhere. I'll be back."

"Hey, Kelly!" Jodie called after he'd started jogging back. *Courage.* When he turned around, she unzipped her jacket and held it open. His gaze dropped to her T-shirt. *Team Kelly.* And there was that sideways-comma dimple, flashing like a signal flare.

He laughed and punched the air. "Don't go *anywhere.*" He pointed at her. "I mean it."

"I'll catch you after your shower," she promised. Then she sat back down and enjoyed the rest of training. God, she loved baseball.

After the game he came jogging out of the shower block, grinning from ear to ear. As he approached, Dom and Taylor started laughing.

Because of Kelly's white T-shirt. Emblazoned across the front in wonky black handwritten marker were the words *Team Jodie.*

"You've got to be kidding me," Dom snorted. "Are you two for real?"

Jodie's heart was all scrunched up in her chest. "You ruined your T-shirt," she said stupidly.

"You said you wanted to be on Team Jodie," Kelly told her, grinning. "Well, I figure that's the team for me too."

"You got to get a picture of this for the club's Instagram," Taylor told Jodie. "It's gold."

"No, this is just between us." Jodie shook her head.

"Your call." Taylor shrugged. "But I'm telling you it's gold. We'll leave you love birds alone now; we've got to go talk to the coaches anyway. You need a lift back when we're done, Jodie . . . ?" He raised an eyebrow and glanced at Kelly.

Jodie glanced at Kelly too. "I don't know. Do I?"

"Definitely not," he said firmly. "I'll take you wherever you need to go."

"You pitched a good game out there, Wong," Taylor told him, shaking his hand as they took their leave. "Keep it up."

"I'll try . . ." He stared after them as they ambled off to the dugout. "You know who that was, right?" He sounded tense with excitement.

"Sure, I do. I work with him. Well, not *with* him. But near him." She grinned.

"You're at the Mariners?" He sounded like he couldn't believe it.

That was OK. She couldn't believe it either. "It's a long, very cool story. Maybe I'll tell you over breakfast tomorrow."

"Breakfast?" Kelly's eyebrows shot up.

"If you're lucky." Jodie grinned, and then turned to stare out at the lush lavender evening creeping over the field. The perfume of cut grass and clay hung heavy in the air and everything sparkled with the coming of spring. The bases glowed in the gathering twilight. "There's nowhere more romantic in the whole world than a baseball field." She sighed.

"I love you," Kelly blurted.

She glanced over to find he was looking at her the way she'd been looking at the ballfield. "I know," she told him with a sly smile, "I read your messages." She reached out and rested the tip of her finger in his sideways-comma dimple. She could feel him trembling under her touch. "I love you too," she told him softly. "I was just too stupid to see what was right in front of my face."

"Not stupid . . . I was too scared to tell you."

"You, scared!" Jodie laughed, and then rested her forehead to his. His breath was warm against her lips. "You still scared now?"

"Yes," he breathed. The sparkles in his eyes were spice red. "But brave enough to tell you I love you anyway."

"Kelly?" she whispered, pressing a feather light kiss to his lips. "Can you tell me that every day?"

"For as long as you'll let me."

"Kelly Wong, I'm going to kiss you now."

"Jodie Boyd, I'm going to let you."

And as they kissed, night fell, plum purple and heavy, and a yellow moon rose over the stands, lighting the way to home plate. Jodie felt the shivering promise of a future yet to come, and she fell into it, like falling into water.

Chapter 47
A Regular Monday in March
Bree

Bree wanted everything sorted before they moved her to palliative care. Before she had to pump the morphine button so much that she couldn't hold a thought in her head. On this regular Monday in March, she'd held back on the pain relief to the point that the pain was making her sweat. But it was still easier to think through the pain than it was to think through the opioids. Just.

She needed her wits about her. Until she got her affairs in order, and then she'd be pumping that morphine button like mad. Who knew the pain would be this bad? It was deep in her bones. There wasn't anything that didn't hurt, and it was a hurt you couldn't imagine, let alone explain. It was in the fabric of everything. It made you realize the world you thought you knew had been a dream. An illusion. A membrane on the surface of a deep and roiling ocean.

The hospital bed had been moved next to the window, so she could feel the thin early spring sunshine. Along the sill were old jelly jars and bottles stuffed with flowers her mom and Claude had brought in from the budding world beyond. Forsythia, peach blossom, daffodils, a couple of early cornflowers, a single creamy freesia, and the first azalea from Grandma Gloria's garden.

She couldn't smell any of them. But sometimes as she lay there through endless timeless moments, watching the way the petals were limned with sunshine, a feeling would come over her, a feeling so slow and tidal, so inevitable that it pulled her from the pain, a riptide of rapture. There was something holy in those flowers, and in the sunshine, and in that feeling. The moment flowed; and she was ebbing. And it was OK. The sunshine would fade; the petals would fall; the season of flowers would pass into rain and snow; and she would ebb. None of it diminished the keen beauty of the sunshine filigreeing the veined petal of the freesia, illuminating the hidden golden throat of the daffodil, making the forsythia shiver with light. The moments left their sediment in the tide as they ebbed; as she ebbed; as they all flowed into the inevitable.

Bree unfolded the list. Cheryl had promised her everything was ready. Ryan and Iris Air would do all they could. All that was left was for Bree to sign off on the final list. Bree ran her finger over her own loopy childish handwriting, written as she sat in the booth at Chili's with Claude. She'd been *so* angry after that career fair. It seemed so long ago, so far away. Such a strange thing to be angry about. But how she had raged as they shared a plate of corn chips and salsa and a root beer (which had been all they could afford). *What was it about her that made them assume she would never leave Wilmington?* Bree had raved at Claudia. *That she'd probably never even leave her small patch of the world? That she'd live a life like her parents had: straight into a sensible job after school; marriage; kids; and, if she was lucky, a trip to Orlando or the Rockies now and then during her vacation?* At eighteen, the mere possibility that she'd repeat their lives had filled Bree with horror. "Screw that!" she told Claudia fiercely as she began imagining a future that didn't include much of Wilmington at all. Number one on her list had been "Get out of Wilmington for spring break" (which she had—only to New Jersey, but it was a start), number two had been to get Justin Smith to take her to prom (tick), number three to win Prom Queen (tick), number four to get into her choice of college (tick), and number five to be the first member of her family to graduate college (tick). After that, things got a little more interesting.

Bree took in all the things she'd crossed off her bucket list over the years. She'd hiked the Himalayas; base jumped in Mexico and cave dived in Sardinia; she'd swum with wild pigs in the Bahamas and with whales in Mo'orea; she'd watched the northern lights from Newfoundland and seen a Leonids meteor shower in Peru; she'd managed a green belt in karate and had a capoeira lesson in Brazil; she'd read *Ulysses*, run a marathon, made her own beer, and walked on hot coals. She'd been to the opening ceremony of the summer Olympics and the closing ceremony of the winter Olympics; watched a Formula One race in Monaco; climbed the Eiffel Tower; chased a tornado; milked a cow; and slept in an igloo. She was twenty-six years old, and not likely to see twenty-seven, but she'd lived a bigger life than anyone else she knew. And it had been *fun*. Her only regret was that there couldn't have been more of it.

There were only six things left unfinished on her bucket list. Six things that she would have to leave to someone else.

17. *Plant a tree that will live long after I'm gone. Something shady. That also has blossoms. (I can't quite believe I never got to this one—it seems the easiest.)*

39. *Play poker in Vegas.*

73. *Eat a sandwich at Katz's Delicatessen in New York and simulate the orgasm scene from* When Harry Met Sally. *Make sure to take someone to play Harry.*

74. *Perform a walk-on cameo in a Broadway musical (multitasking while I'm in New York—but probably best to do this on a different day than number 73, as I don't think nerves and pastrami will go well together).*

99. *Fly over Antarctica (that's a thing people do—it's very expensive but Iris Air have agreed to sponsor the trip. It also means I get to add a bonus trip to Sydney, Australia! I should have put that as number one hundred, I guess, but I have another one I want to do last . . .)*

100. *Fall in love.*

Bree took a thick marker and crossed out number thirty-nine. She obliterated it, so there was no trace of the original letters. Then she took a pen and carefully wrote in a new number thirty-nine, just above it, in a very shaky hand. It looked like it had been written by a child. That's what pain would do to you.

There were no guarantees in life. And she wouldn't be here to see if things worked out, but at the very least she'd planted a seed. The rest was up to Jodie.

With trembling hands, Bree took her phone and snapped a picture of the back of the Chili's placemat. Of her bucket list. With unsteady thumbs, she typed Cheryl a message. **Here you go. This is the final list.** She attached the picture. Most of the list was a slash of lines, crossing out the completed items. Except for the six. One of which was brand-new . . .

The replacement for number thirty-nine was the last thing she would ever write on her bucket list, she realized. It struck her like a stone. It was her last wish. And what an odd little wish it was.

39. Find Mr. Wong and finally have those piano lessons Mom and Dad paid for that I never took (long story).

Bree's finger hovered over the send button. Was it enough?

Jodie was stubborn. She might not complete the list. And who was to say she'd bother to track Mr. Wong down? And even if she tracked him down, would Jodie be brave enough to ask after Kelly . . . would she chase that final item on the bucket list?

But Bree couldn't control any of that. All she could do was give her sister a wish. A hope. A chance.

Because Bree knew that Kelly Wong was on Jodie's secret unwritten bucket list.

And Jodie was the last secret item on Bree's.

As she sent the message off into the world, into a future Bree would never see, she hoped her seed would take. That it would grow into something that would long outlive her. That it would blossom for her sister, and give her shade for all her life to come.

Acknowledgments

This book began as the first whispers of coronavirus began to surface; it continued during lockdowns and online working and during months of anxiety and, frankly, existential crisis. You all know what I'm talking about. You're pandemic-survivors too. It has been a time of upheaval: protests and elections, illness and grief, closed borders and isolation, and a few too many extra pounds gained. It seemed apt that this was my Covid book because this is a book about grief. Grief comes to us all, an inevitable price we pay for love. But this is also a book about hope, and resilience, and courage, and the bounties love brings.

I'd like to thank those I love, who give me the strength to get through years like these. And who never fail to amaze me with their capacity for generosity and friendship.

Firstly, thank you to the woman to whom this book is dedicated, my good friend Dr. Tully Barnett. I have had the enormous privilege of working closely with Tully over the past few years, and it has been a highlight of my professional life. I often think that if people would just throw money at her and let her do whatever she wanted with it the world would be a better place. She's wise, kind, curious, rigorous, fair, just, open-minded, strategic, wickedly smart, and just an f'ing excellent human being. Don't ever stop being you, Tully. You're the one who is doing it right.

Thank you to Sean Williams, the Brussels Sprout King, for naming the dog. And for Sean and Alex Vickery-Howe for providing weekly comfort, humor, and essentially therapy, as we recorded our *Word Docs* podcast. Talking writing was helpful as I wrote this book, as it was often a deeply sad one; chatting to you got me out of the quagmire of grief.

Thanks to all the people in the Creative Arts department at Flinders University. I wrote this book while I was on study leave and I am deeply thankful for the gift of time—the one resource a writer truly needs. There are too many people to name, but you know who you are. Academic staff, professional staff, postgrads, honors students, undergrads: it's a weird and challenging time to be living a life of the mind, especially in the humanities and the arts, not to mention the creative arts. Keep up the good fight.

Family . . . ah, there aren't words for what you mean and what you do. My mother went through rounds of cancer treatments and surgeries and other ordeals during the writing of this book—and she did it with her usual acid humor. Love you, Ma. I don't think I've met anyone as strong as you are. Or as funny. And then there's Dad . . . somehow my father managed to build castles, win battles, and save maidens during this insane time of pandemic and crisis. He's a prince, through and through.

Thanks always to Jonny and Kirby and Isla—we spent a year of lockdowns crowded together in a tiny apartment; I thought we'd fight, but we got along better than we ever have. Here's to our Barton year. I loved every minute of writing at the dining table, surrounded by the chaos of our daily life. But thank you most of all for taking my dreams seriously and giving me a push when I need it.

Thank you to Lynn. Because of you, I have danced through some very hard days. And I have laughed instead of cried. Thanks also to the SARA gals, especially Bronwyn Stuart and Anne Oliver, who helped me brainstorm ideas at the very beginning of this project. I have great memories of sitting by a pool in Melbourne with Anne, tossing ideas to Bron as she swam.

I owe a huge thanks to Sarah Younger, who was generous

with her time and advice as I developed the idea that would become Jodie and Bree's story. Her enthusiasm for this book is the reason it exists—thank you, Sarah. And thanks for all the behind-the-scenes unglamorous work that is the secret magic of the book biz. I love working with you, you gorgeous person.

Thank you to Shannon Plackis for falling in love with this story, and for all your work on this book. Thanks also to everyone at Kensington—not just a house, but a home. Thanks for taking me in and for being such wholehearted champions of my work.

And finally, this book came to be after the loss of my best friend from high school, Kate Andrew, who passed away from leukemia a few years ago, far too young. Kate and I sat together in Year 9 Math class and tried to cheat at French tests together (so badly that we always failed the tests). She was a fellow bookworm, and we swapped books constantly. She was the one who got me reading romance; she used to nick her mom's books and bring them to school. She also aided and abetted my love for Robert Smith and the Cure, and I remember to this day the joy I felt when she surprised me on my sixteenth birthday with an epically huge poster of Fat Bob. She wrangled money out of all our friends to buy that poster, which I still have. I hadn't seen her for a long time when she passed away, and her death badly shook me. I'd always assumed we'd catch up again, that we had time; how painfully short a lifetime is. This book came to be after I witnessed the breathless, never-ending grief Kate's parents and sister faced after her death. I think of them often. Death is a part of life, but, man, it's a bitch. Kate knew it, and she made sure they felt her love after she'd left them, arranging for presents for each of their birthdays and for Christmas that first year. And she made sure there were helium balloons at her funeral, so her very young children wouldn't be frightened. Even at the last, her thoughts were for others. That was who she was. Kate—you were a bright and shining person, deeply loved, and now deeply missed.

Visit our website at
KensingtonBooks.com
to sign up for our newsletters, read
more from your favorite authors, see
books by series, view reading group
guides, and more!

BOOK CLUB
BETWEEN THE CHAPTERS

Become a Part of Our
Between the Chapters Book Club
Community and Join the Conversation

Betweenthechapters.net

Submit your book review for a chance to win exclusive
Between the Chapters swag you can't get anywhere else!
https://www.kensingtonbooks.com/pages/review/